THE WOMAN BY THE LAKE

A Misted Pines Novel

Book 3

KRISTEN ASHLEY

ROCK CHICK
PRESS

THE WOMAN BY THE LAKE

A MISTED PINES NOVEL

NEW YORK TIMES BESTSELLING AUTHOR

KRISTEN ASHLEY

ONE

Weaver Cabin

Nadia

The mailbox I was told to look out for, as suspected from the description, was hard to miss.

There were four huge planters surrounding it frothing with peach, pink and orange impatiens. The mailbox itself was a shiny stainless steel with the words WEAVER CABIN painted on the side. It was held aloft by a twisted branch, which, only when I turned in and got close, could I see was actually burnished steel with fake, metal leaves on it.

Last, it was unique and incredibly pretty.

And seeing it made some of the anxiety I had about the decision I'd made start to ebb away.

The lane to the cabin meandered with gentle curves and was edged in small boulders, many of which had bright-green moss growing on them.

The lane was also longer than I expected.

It'd be quite a hike to get my mail in the morning.

1

And it meant my home for the next year was seriously secluded.

Finally, the cabin came into view, and the instant I saw it, the reservations that had recently sprung up about the seclusion of Weaver Cabin vanished.

One story, smallish, with a carport attached that would protect my SUV from the elements on all sides but the front. The roof of the timber house was blue tin, and a porch ran the length of the face of the structure.

On the porch was an arrangement of two rocking chairs—one yellow, one red, both with cute pillows on them—sharing what appeared to be an old whisky barrel as a table, which was topped with an arrangement of fresh wildflowers in a mason jar. At the other side of the veranda, there was a porch swing with a fluffy pad and more sweet pillows.

Yes, a porch swing.

There were lanterns scattered about, along with a plethora of different sized pots and hanging baskets, these filled with more impatiens, plus petunias, begonias, pansies and fuchsias.

It was colorful and charming. A hundred times better than the pictures I saw of it when I was deciding where to go, and those pictures had captivated me, so that seemed impossible.

But there it was, right before me.

Colorful and charming also pertained to the man standing on the porch, not to mention his beat-up, old, faded-white Ford pickup parked off to the side.

He had white hair pulled back, probably in a ponytail, a farmer's cap on his head. Scruffy white beard. Weathered skin. Plaid shirt.

And faded denim overalls.

Overalls!

Yes, that anxiety was fading fast.

I swung around the front, switched off the ignition and exited my vehicle with a small smile on my face.

"You Miz Williams?" he called.

I didn't wince at the name I'd never changed and tried not to use, but it was the name on all legal documents.

Including rental contracts.

"Yes. But I'm Nadia. Are you Dave Weaver?" I called back, moving across the gravel path to the wooden front steps (all lined with pots of flowers, including parts of the gravel).

He held up a hand, palm out, to stop my progress.

I halted.

"I get how it is, gel."

The "g" in "gel" was hard, and I had a feeling he meant the word as "girl."

He kept talking.

"These days, heck, all through history, you gotta be careful. My Brenda was supposed to meet you so you'd feel comfortable during the walk-through. She got to feelin' bad, so, my apologies, but it has to be me."

Before I could fully process what he said, he unexpectedly tossed a set of keys toward me, and fortunately, I moved fast enough and caught them.

He continued speaking.

"I'll keep my distance as I show you around."

Ah.

He meant me being in the middle of nowhere with a strange man.

It was lovely he thought of that, because, considering his Green Acres Santa look, I hadn't.

He swept a hand around to indicate the entirety of the space.

"Brenda told me to put the pillows out so you'll get the full effect. And you can do it if you want, but she said she'd come and water the plants, but she won't come unless you know she's comin'."

Considering I had little else to do, taking care of all these flowers sounded like a good meditative task to have.

A responsibility.

Something that counted on me.

Yes, that seemed a good thing to do.

"If she tells me how much water they need and how frequently they need it, I can take care of it," I told him and shot him another smile. "I'm not known for my gardening chops, but I can learn."

He nodded. "I'll give her that heads up." He hooked his thumbs in the straps of his overalls and carried on, "As a welcome home, we got the essentials in there for you, so you don't have to head back out and grab yourself some groceries. Not like the market is close."

That was nice, though my trunk was filled with about fifteen bags of groceries because I'd had that same thought.

He went on to share, "Coffee. Creamer. Milk. Some bread and cold cuts. Oatmeal. And Brenda added her world-famous taco meat with all the fixin's, so you have some dinner. There's also a bottle of champagne in there for you too."

"Wow," I replied, not hiding my surprise. "That's very generous."

And it was.

Shockingly so, considering how well-kept this adorable cabin was, on top of the fact the rent was very inexpensive. It was, essentially, a one room cabin, but if the pictures were anything to go by, it had kitchen, living and bedroom areas, as well as a reading nook.

I didn't need much, so I hadn't been perusing mansions. Everything I'd looked at was kind of like this, but this cabin was by far the least expensive, and because of that, I worried all the fabulous photos had been taken twenty years prior and the place would be a wreck.

Unless the inside told a different tale, it was not.

"Let's get you in," he said, turning toward the door. He turned back. "We got the boxes you sent. Me and Doc stacked 'em up inside. You got anything in the car I could help you with?"

First…Doc?

Who was Doc?

Second, I had two big suitcases, a carry on, a laptop bag, my purse, and the aforementioned groceries in my car.

"I'm excited to see the inside," I told him.

He studied me, his eyes went to my SUV, which visibly had stuff in it, then he shrugged, opened the screen door, the main door, and walked in.

I followed him.

The minute I stepped over the threshold, I stopped dead.

I noted vaguely he was still giving me a wide berth so I'd feel safe, and was heading all the way across the space.

But this vaguely was *vague*.

Because, if the outside was colorful and charming, the inside was downright quaint.

Lots of windows let in a dappled sunshine, due to the fact the trees grew close to the cabin.

To the left, the living room area, with a denim-covered couch, which at that very moment, I fancied I could hear screaming, *Come and take a nap!*

Accompanying this was a worn-in, but not worn-out, leather club chair. A low coffee table decorated with some coffee table books, which looked to be about flowers and nature, and another jar of fresh-cut wildflowers. Interesting lamps, side tables and a beautiful, braided rug underneath it all finished this cozy space.

Onward from that was an iron bed with a white wedding ring quilt, the rings in the key shades of pink and peach. Bright-white eyelet shams on European pillows over double stacks of pillowcases with pale yellow sheets that had tiny pink polka dots. Full, bolster along the front of the euros in yellow and peach stripes. One of those amazing throws made of huge threads of yarn was tossed diagonally across the bed, and it was pale green.

The elaborate footboard ended with an old trunk, and the nightstands beside the bed were mismatched.

The one I couldn't fully see on the opposite side was distressed white with faded flowers painted on the drawer. The other one I could totally see was a porcelain blue, three-drawer, with ornate flower handles and the middle bulge and bowed feet of French Provincial design. Both nightstands had adorable, shabby chic lamps on top.

At the end of the large, open space, to the left, was a room, the door opened. I could see the sun shining through it and an old-fashioned, white mosaic tile floor. The bathroom.

Across from that, at the back, were two more small rooms, doors closed.

But in the middle, between the bathroom and those rooms, was a short hallway that led to the back door. It had a built-in bench with cubbies underneath, a blue gingham pad on top, and hooks on the wall above it.

To the right, the kitchen area, with pale-green cabinets, butcherblock counter tops, and shelves, on which sat a variety of pastel-colored stoneware and antique-looking glassware. There was a bar/island with three old barstools painted soft yellow, pink and blue, and a farmhouse sink with copper faucets. An interesting, copper light feature with three lights ran along the island. All the appliances looked modern, even new, and were stainless steel.

Next to the kitchen, closer to where I stood, was a six-seater farmhouse table painted in yellow with mismatched chairs. A big vase sprouting with more wildflowers sat on the top.

Rounding this out, directly to my right, the space had built-in shelves, partially filled with books and knickknacks, but with plenty of room to add to the library and the look. In the corner was a gorgeous, cushiony, pink reading chair with a leather ottoman pouf and two side tables, the better to hold beverages and plates of food and rest books, with an overarching lamp that would light your way as you dove into dozens of different worlds.

Even if all of this was amazing, the pièce de résistance of the cabin was an open fireplace in the center of the space, with a stonework, dome chimney that dripped down from the ceiling. It had love seats on either side. One that had a curve and was a dove gray, the other, a traditional shape in a pink and cream plaid.

The floors were wood, with lots of rugs. The walls were timber clapboard. And wispy curtains flanked the windows that had blinds currently raised.

And the twenty boxes I'd sent were all neatly lined up and stacked behind the couch, which had its back to the room so you could watch the flatscreen affixed to the wall.

I loved it. Every inch of it. There was nothing I would change.

In other words, it was perfect.

Perfect for why I was there.

Perfect if what happened hadn't happened.

Perfect in a way I knew I could live the rest of my life there.

"Walk-in closet," Dave Weaver said, slapping his hand on one of the doors beyond the kitchen. He moved to the next one and slapped that door too. "Storage. Also furnace. Water heater. Washer and dryer. If you bring in the outside pillows, you can put them in here and they won't muck up the joint, seein' as my Brenda bought a lotta them. Things get too hot, there's AC units above each door."

He pointed above where I stood, and I twisted to look up to see a slender unit over the door.

I twisted back when Dave kept talking.

"Remotes for the AC are in a drawer in the kitchen. Fireplace is wood burning. There's a wood pile beside the shed outside. Shed has more storage if you need it. There's also some gardening stuff in there."

He moved to the kitchen and put his hands on the counter.

Once there, he continued talking.

"We get storms. They take out the electricity. It doesn't happen all the time, but it happens. Because 'a that, this place has a generator outside. You know how to start up a generator?"

I shook my head.

"You want me to show you?"

"I..." I looked around the cabin, and I did this as I thought about all the stuff in my car, including the fact the closest grocery store was a good twenty-minute drive away, and there was stuff that needed to go in the freezer, which now really needed to be put away.

"I'll call Doc," Dave Weaver said, clearly reading my mind. "I think he's back for a spell. I'll ask him to pop by in a day or two, show you how to start up the generator."

There it was again.

Doc.

"Doc?" I asked, taking a couple more steps in.

"Doc." He jerked his chin to the side. "He lives up the trail a ways. Only other house on this lake. Good man." He pointed to the wall where I saw an actual landline, cordless phone. Next to it was a small blackboard with a list of numbers written neatly on it. "Cell service can be spotty," he shared. "Landline's the way to go out here. I got our house number, Brenda's and my cells on that list.

Also, Doc's landline and cell. You need anything, anything at all, don't hesitate to call me or Brenda. But if you call Doc, he'd get here a lot faster."

"Okay," I said hesitantly.

"Wi-Fi stuff is in the storage closet. Password is on the blackboard."

I nodded.

He moved into the kitchen and his hand disappeared as he indicated something where he was standing. "Microwave is a shelf microwave. Brenda said it messed with her vision to have it visible."

Brenda was correct.

"Right," I replied.

"There's a rope hammock rolled up in the storage room. The hooks for it are on the trees, south side of the pier, close to the water. Enjoy it. All we ask is for you to move it in if there's weather comin'."

A hammock.

Seriously.

This place was *perfect*.

"No problem. I can do that," I assured.

He tipped his head to the side. "You want me to help you carry stuff in now?"

Truth told, I was exhausted.

I'd flown to Seattle yesterday and taken a commuter flight to Misted Pines that morning. From there, I taxied to the car dealership to pick up the SUV I'd purchased from afar, off to the grocery store, then here.

I hadn't run a marathon, but travel took it out of me.

I hated grocery shopping with a passion, and I'd had to do a huge shop to outfit a new house, and now it was late afternoon. I wanted the stuff inside, the groceries put away, my bags unpacked so I knew where my jammies were, not to mention my toothbrush put in its place. After that, I was going to heat up Brenda's world-famous taco meat, eat, drink champagne, and probably pass out.

And Dave Weaver might be in his sixties, but the wrinkles on his face said more like eighties. He was also somewhat rotund. I doubted he was a danger to me, but what I knew was, I could outrun him.

"You've been so kind, what with taco meat and milk and this place being so gorgeous, but yes, I could use the help," I accepted.

"My pleasure," he muttered, coming my way.

We headed out to the car, and within a few minutes I rethought his age, considering he could heft around a lot of luggage and groceries.

It was all inside in record time, and for that, I could have kissed him.

"I'll let you be," he said, going straight to the door after he set the last grocery bags on the kitchen counter. "Again, you need anything, don't hesitate to call. It's urgent or you're worried, get a hold of Doc. He'll sort you out."

I was wandering his way as I replied, "Thank you. So much. For everything."

He touched his forehead with a finger, bid me a, "Hope you're happy here," and he ducked out.

The screen door swooshed closed on a well-oiled mechanism before it snicked shut.

I went to the door, and through the screen watched him walk to his pickup.

I waved from where I stood.

Dave waved back as he drove away.

I then went right to the groceries and put away the stuff that needed fridge and freezer.

That was all I did before I headed to the back hall and out.

Once on the back porch, I again stopped dead.

Wicker chairs to my left that had fluffy pads on them, more pretty toss pillows, an ornate, white wrought iron table between them, and lots more pots brimming with flowers. To my right was a wicker loveseat with a coffee table in front.

And in front of me, the vista was pine trees and a tranquil body of water that could be described as a small lake or a very (*very*) large pond. A short pier sat on the lake, with two bright-red Adirondack chairs on it, which was all that could fit.

Leading off to the right, a stone-edged path led to a small shed, firewood stacked high on one side with a roof over it. Oddly, on the other side, was another stone-edged path, or what looked to have been one at one time.

Unlike everything else about the cabin, quite a number of the stones had been kicked out of place or had fallen away or been rearranged by the movement of critters. The path itself was not clear and graveled but seemed older. The gravel on top not fresh but embedded in the dirt.

And it seemed to lead to nothing.

I could see another trail, closer to the lake, that ran either side of the backyard, indicating there was a well-used walking path around the lake. This one, all dirt but also stone edged, disappearing on both sides into the pines.

I stepped out into what was my new backyard, even if it had no lawn and was mostly just earth, and walked to the edge of the lake.

I looked right.

Winking in the sun, I thought I saw some windows, but they were mostly hidden by trees. If there was a house among those pines, considering where the winks were coming from, it wasn't one story.

What wasn't hidden was the pier at that edge of the north side of the lake (I was on the east, and nothing was anywhere else).

That pier was much larger, had an arm at the end, and what looked like a small outboard fishing boat with a bespoke tarp fitted perfectly on top. The boat sat in the water tied to the pier.

I liked that fitted tarp, it said my neighbor took care of his belongings, and that boded well about this unknown *Doc*.

I felt better having a neighbor.

I needed to be alone.

I needed to sort out my head.

No, I needed to sort out my life.

But this was the literal middle of nowhere, and I felt safer with someone close.

Especially that someone being this Doc person, who clearly had the respect of Dave Weaver, someone I could tell was a nice guy.

I drew in a breath and took in everything around me, including turning to gaze at the back of the cabin.

This view was as adorable as the front.

I heard nothing but the wind rustling the trees, a faraway bird call.

I closed my eyes and felt a gentle breeze touch my skin.

It might have been my state of mind, but that didn't negate the strong, eerie, yet peaceful sense of something saying, *Welcome home.*

Regardless of the eerie part, the anxiety that clogged my decision to move out here for a year drifted away.

Because this was perfect.

Absolutely perfect.

I'd made the right decision.

I could be here…

And I could figure it all out.

I opened my eyes and headed inside to put away the rest of the groceries, unpack, heat up taco meat…

And settle into my new home.

TWO

Doc

____

Nadia

I woke from a dead sleep feeling creeped out and confused.

It was dark. A kind of *dark*-dark I'd never experienced. There was moonlight coming in the windows, but not much, and everything I could see was shrouded in shadows.

For a second, I didn't know where I was.

Then I remembered I'd moved into Weaver Cabin outside Misted Pines, Washington, that very afternoon.

I started to relax, thinking that was why I'd woken. I was in an unfamiliar place with an unfamiliar feel.

And then I heard it.

What woke me.

It sounded like scratching on the window.

Not the brush of pine needles.

Something like…

Fingernails.

Full-body pinpricks of fear and adrenaline assaulted me as I lay perfectly still, listening to that sound.

It kept going.

The last of the sleep left me as I listened, and as such, the sense of vulnerability of being recently unconscious also faded away.

It couldn't be fingernails.

Right?

I was a down-to-my-soul city girl.

My *dedulya* took us to rustic places, but only if there were five-star hotels in the vicinity, or luxurious houses with daily maid service and a personal chef available.

I'd been fishing (once, because I didn't like it).

I'd been hiking (I liked that all right, if there weren't too many bugs, though I much preferred hiking the Rue Saint-Honoré in Paris —what could I say? I was my mother's daughter).

I'd never been camping (and had no desire to do so, note aforementioned bugs, but also, who in their right mind would want to sleep on the ground?).

I didn't mountain bike, canoe, bird, climb, and no way I'd ever hunt.

Truth be told, I had no idea why I'd picked this cabin.

Wait. I did.

I needed something completely different. A shake-up of my life. I needed to be away from the people and places I knew in order to figure out who I was, now that the only thing I was sure about was, who I thought I was, wasn't me.

What I did know: I might be in the middle of nowhere, but I wasn't in a horror movie.

Whatever that noise was had an explanation. Someone who was used to the outdoors, nature, etcetera, would know exactly what it was.

But that someone wasn't me…yet.

And I wasn't going to climb out of bed and figure it out. I could investigate tomorrow.

The scratching continued, and it was creepy as all hell.

Honestly, it didn't sound natural.

But it had to be.

I reached to the nightstand, grabbed my ear buds, put them in, took my phone from charge and cued up a sleep story.

With the narrator murmuring into my ears, I couldn't hear the scratching anymore.

Even so, it took me forever to fall back to sleep.

THE NEXT MORNING, I was stiff and grouchy from lack of sleep, and it being fitful when I got back to it.

Even though it was early May, there was a chill on the morning, so I'd put my pink cashmere robe on over my sleep shorts and cami, pulled on some socks, and I was sitting cross-legged on the wicker loveseat on the back porch, cradling my coffee and scowling at the lake.

What I wasn't doing was figuring out how to hack through the mental detritus that covered the entrance to the path I needed to take to learning who I was, now that I knew who I thought I was, was a total lie.

I was also realizing I lived in a one-room cabin—as adorable as it was—that had some books, a bunch of boxes I needed to unpack, which would probably take me an hour, and a TV that was supposed to be connected to Wi-Fi so I could load my apps on it, which might take fifteen minutes.

This meant I had a little over an hour of things to do, I was in a crappy mood, not only that day, but the entire year yawned before me, and I had no idea how to crack the seal on figuring myself out, but also, I didn't have any motivation to do so.

It was on this cranky thought, I heard noise, then caught movement out of the sides of my eyes.

It was the same side of the house the scratching came from last night (though, last night, it sounded like it was at the window by the reading nook, which was closer to the front of the house, and this new sound came from closer to the lake).

Therefore, I tensed, and those pinpricks of fear came back, attacking my skin.

Then *he* came into view.

With grave emphasis on *he*.

Sweat slicked body, covered only by a pair of cutoff jean shorts, and running shoes on his feet (*sans* socks—I mean, who ran in jean shorts and shoes with no socks?).

His dark hair was too long. Not *long*-long, like lumbersexual long, but the wet curls not only hugged the sides of his face, but also all around his neck. His all-over-tanned body was fit and buff—ankles to neck lean, defined muscle. He sported chest hair, fuller between his bulging pecs, a smattering from collarbone down to everywhere, a dense line leading down the center of his six-pack and into his shorts.

And he had a masculine face hewn by a loving hand. Strong nose. Hollowed cheeks. Prominent brow. Square jaw covered in dark scruff.

Gazing at him, I felt a stirring, the power of which I hadn't felt in seven years.

In fact, considering it had been seven years, that stirring felt more powerful than any I'd ever had before in my life.

His head turned to me as he ran into the clearing. He stopped, put his hands on his hips, that gorgeous chest rising and falling with his quickened breaths. He started walking toward me, and he smiled.

A slash of perfect, white teeth made a normally extraordinary visage deliciously *criminal*.

"Hey," he called.

The sound of his deep voice shook me out of my stupor, and I replied, "You're in my yard."

He stopped walking and his head swiveled slightly on his neck, shifting a bit to the side, his ear dipping toward his perfectly muscled shoulder.

"Sorry?" he asked.

"You're in my yard," I repeated.

He looked down at his beat-up running shoes, then again to me.

"Yeah," he confirmed. "Run through it every morning a few times when I'm home."

The *when I'm home* bit was intriguing.

I refused to be intrigued.

"Well, I live here now and"—I swung my coffee cup out—"as

you can see, I'll be taking my coffee on the back veranda in the mornings. So from here on in, if you'd refrain."

His lips were quirking as he asked, "The veranda?"

I swung my coffee cup again. "The back porch."

"I know what a veranda is," he shared. "Just don't know anyone who'd call it that when it's attached to a shack in the woods."

I was offended, not only on my behalf, since I now lived there, but on Dave and Brenda's. They clearly put a lot of work into this place and kept it in tip-top shape.

"This isn't a *shack*," I refuted with some heat. "It's a *cabin*."

"Same thing."

"Hardly."

He pointed toward the south but didn't take his eyes off me when he proclaimed, "It takes me five seconds to run through your *yard*."

His inflection on *yard* was not at all missed.

Sure, it wasn't a *yard*, per se, but instead, a big patch of dirt with a healthy scattering of trees that ended in a lake.

It was still my *yard*.

"I'm Doc," he introduced himself, taking another step forward, clearly not of Dave's bent to keep his distance so I, a woman alone in the wilderness, would feel safe. He was now only maybe ten feet away.

And I knew with no doubt I couldn't outrun him, and I definitely couldn't overpower him.

That muscle.

Lord.

And this was Doc, my helpful neighbor who was going to teach me how to use the generator.

Fabulous.

"The next part is you telling me who you are," he prompted when I made no reply.

"I'm a woman who functions a lot better after she's enjoyed two *solitary* cups of coffee." I lifted my cup. "This is cup number one, and I'm not halfway done."

This amused him, greatly, and I knew that because the smile he gave me was bigger, wider and whiter than the last one.

That stirring came back.

Terrific.

"I'll be quiet when I do it," he assured. "And I won't bother you."

"You won't run through my yard," I returned.

"You won't even know I've come and gone," he told me.

I had a feeling every heterosexual woman in a hundred-mile radius knew when he'd come and gone, certainly if he ran in cutoff shorts through her yard, so I wasn't buying it.

"I won't because you won't be running through my yard," I retorted.

"It isn't a big deal," he said, and he still sounded amused, not like he was getting annoyed, which made this whole conversation worse than if he'd stop being *a man*, listen to me and do as I requested without an irritating conversation.

"Is there a reason I'm repeating myself?" I demanded.

He dropped his head and lifted his hand to me. A hand, not incidentally, that was big, had long fingers, looked strong, and I could see even at this distance, was calloused from work. But he didn't do this to hide him losing his temper.

It was to hide his laughter, something he failed at doing, since those powerful shoulders were shaking with it.

Who was this guy?

No.

Nope.

I didn't want to know.

I arranged my face in another scowl, which only made him bite back a bark of laughter when he lifted his head and saw it.

Obviously, this made my scowl scowlier.

"You don't want me running through your yard, you got it," he acquiesced (finally!). "I won't run through your yard."

I nearly said *thank you*, but decided against it, because I shouldn't have to thank him for not doing something he shouldn't be doing in the first place.

I didn't run.

But I did know, if you did, you ran on roads.

You ran on sidewalks.

You ran on public trails.

You didn't run through people's yards.

When no one lived there, okay (sort of).

But I lived there now, so…not okay (definitely).

Therefore, I just stared at him.

He didn't hide his hilarity (though it wasn't vocal) when he said, "Nice to meet you Solitary Coffee Lady."

I did nothing but raise my brows.

His hilarity became audible with his chuckle, which was as rough and attractive as the rest of him.

He then turned, *ran through my yard*, and disappeared in the pines.

Ugh.

Whatever.

I sipped my coffee.

Stared at the lake.

Put that conversation behind me.

And felt the crushing weight of a year in the pines with nothing real to do, except the impossible, settle on top of me.

The sun was shining, glinting off the peaceful waters of a lake that was a good twenty yards away.

And still, I felt like I was drowning.

THREE

My Pocket

Nadia

I turned to my back in bed, stretched my body ramrod straight, and snapped to the dark ceiling, "Oh my *God*. I'm going to kill him!"

I'd heard the party spark up at a little after nine.

This was a surprise because it was a weeknight, and according to me, who hit the sheets anywhere between nine and eleven every night (and okay, that tended to lean toward the nine o'clock hour), it was too late to start up a party.

Sadly, the music that filtered through the trees between his place and mine only got louder and moved from seventies rock (which I could tolerate) to metal (which I could not), with a penchant toward Rage Against the Machine, Korn, Tool and Slipknot (yes, I knew the bands, because Trevor was a metalhead).

With this came loud voices, including intermittent shouting, laughter, and even loud conversations that carried across the water to my lovely abode.

They sounded like they were having fun, *raucous* fun that included people jumping into the water and frolicking there for a goodly period of time (which was *insane*, I'd stuck my toe in, and it was *freezing*).

Fortunately, that stopped, but the rest of it carried on.

And on.

And on.

I couldn't sleep with noise outside white noise (say, a fan or traffic), unless it was the drone of a narrator telling a sleep story, which I had also tried in order to get some sleep, but the noise even filtered through *that*.

Definitely not music, laughter and voices.

Which meant, right then, it was after three in the morning, and I'd not yet been able to fall asleep.

It had been two weeks since I'd moved in, and I hadn't seen (nor heard) Doc in all that time after our first, unsuccessful meeting.

It was Dave who showed me how to use the generator, coming over with Brenda after she called to set an appointment to walk me through keeping her flowers watered and healthy.

At that time, I learned Brenda was a woman much like her husband. That being of indeterminate age (I'd peg her at anywhere between mid-fifties and mid-seventies). She had a mad cap of thin, wispy hair that was dyed an unbecoming, unnatural blonde (not being offensive, there was no other way to say it). She wore glasses, no makeup, was pleasingly plump, sported oversize shorts that went to her knees and an equally oversized T-shirt that had a trio of graphic kittens on it sniffing flowers.

She also had a kind smile that lit her eyes behind her glasses and a patient demeanor.

However, she refused to tell me her taco meat secret, something I had a desperate need to know, because when I'd opened the container, it looked just like seasoned ground beef, but when I ate it, it was flavorful and so tender, it was a minor miracle.

Though, she did say she'd bring more by when she made another batch, which I thought was really sweet.

Other than Dave and Brenda, and the people I ignored the two times I'd gone into town to hit the dread grocery store, I hadn't seen a single soul.

I'd unpacked all my boxes.

I'd programmed the TV with all my streaming services.

I'd kept the plants watered and healthy.

I'd binged more television than I allowed myself to keep track of.

I'd read five books.

I'd shopped online, because, although Brenda had outfitted the cabin splendidly, she didn't have cloth napkins, the placemats on offer weren't as cute as the ones I'd found when I'd discovered the napkins, and her pretty, antique wineglasses and tumblers didn't hold near enough liquid (and she didn't have martini glasses at all). She also hadn't provided plastic ones for outside should I, say, want a glass of wine while sitting on the pier (which I did). Nor did she provide a marble wine cooler should I, say, drink a whole bottle of wine while sitting and reading on the porch (which I also did).

And other stuff.

I'd also semi-kinda met my postman, who drove packages all the way up the lane to my front door.

What I did not do was journal my innermost thoughts and fears and feelings about all that had happened four months ago (not to mention, seven years prior) in any of the five matching, silk-covered, cherry blossom embossed journals I'd sent to the cabin in my boxes.

I didn't meditate in an effort to achieve a higher consciousness.

I didn't do any research to see if Misted Pines offered a thoughtful and supportive counselor I could make a standing appointment with to go and hash out all that was clogging my brain and make a plan on how to open the drain and let it slip away.

No, I did none of that.

It seemed the only thing I learned about myself was that I became so unmotivated as to be nearly incapacitated by days of having nothing to do and no one I was responsible for.

Namely, around twenty-five munchkins, who filled my days with alternating bouts of extreme pride and sheer frustration who counted on me.

Sure, I texted my friends, sent emails and had a couple of phone conversations, but I was social media-ing it through all of that, even if I wasn't doing it on social media.

That being faking it.

The cabin and the lake made it easy. A picturesque cottage in the pines on a lake with me smiling through a selfie, looking honey-tanned and healthy, because me and my wineglass would head to the pier at around two each day. Along with the fact there were a lot of pots of plants to water, and they were all outside (a tan was all about faking the healthy bit).

All my friends took one look at these photos and told me to invite them out *ASAP*.

I didn't invite a single one of them.

I was wallowing and drinking too much. And it got worse, because every day, I'd wake up, determined that would be the day when I'd grab my imaginary staff and head down the path to battle my demons and figure it all out, and then I'd go to bed, beating myself up because that was not the day I'd done *anything*.

Now...this.

Mr. Cutoff Shorts who forgot how to get to his barber just as he'd forgotten he had a neighbor who didn't listen to metal (I was a Swiftie, and damn proud of it, not that he knew that, still). And I might no longer have a job, but I liked my sleep, and I didn't find Limp Bizkit good at lullabies.

The only fortunate thing was the scratching from that first night hadn't come back. I'd checked out that window and the area around it. It had a tree close, and maybe I was wrong about it being pine needles, because they didn't touch the window, but there was no other clue as to what it might have been.

In my ruminations, I hadn't realized the noise was lessening, so when the music cut out entirely, I turned and looked at my cute, blue Echo Dot (something else the mailman brought to me).

It was 3:57 in the morning.

Immediately, I grabbed my phone and snapped a photo of the time.

I did this because I was good with a grudge, even better with revenge fantasies.

And worse than that for Mr. Cutoffs, I was third generation American, but Russian flowed unhindered through my veins. Mom taught me some, *Dedulya* taught me even more. And *his papachka* was hardcore, from the motherland, so the man who taught my *dedulya* was the real deal.

Thus, I lay in bed, bided my time, and at exactly a quarter to six, I threw the covers back and got up.

I washed my face, brushed my teeth, flossed, and then headed to the walk-in closet.

I pulled off my sleep shorts, pulled on a pair of faded jeans, left the skintight shelf-bra cami I'd slept in, but shrugged on a light cardigan.

I then shoved my feet in the pink velvet Birkenstock slides with the gold buckles I bought before I moved, because I thought Birkenstocks said, "Washington State," but if I was going to do them, they were going to be velvet with a gold buckle.

So far, I hadn't worn them.

Today was the damned day.

I then took my phone and marched out the back door to the trail that led to my neighbor's house.

When I suddenly emerged into a clearing after what could only have been a five-minute walk (if that), I was stunned immobile for a number of reasons.

First, his house was extraordinary.

A mish-mosh of stories with a timbered roof and siding painted an attractive midnight blue with polished wood accents around the windows.

There was no rhyme or reason to it. I couldn't place it in an architectural era either. I wasn't even sure how it was standing, with this bit sticking out and that bit rising high and windows everywhere.

Yet, it wasn't fanciful.

It seemed solid, sturdy, like it sprouted out of the earth because it was meant to be placed right there, and when humans eradicated our own species through our pride and avarice, taking many other species with us, this house would remain.

Forever and ever.

Topping that, it gave me another eerie feeling, the first I'd felt since I'd arrived at that lake, but this one was further complicated by being both peaceful and exciting.

I didn't understand that sensation and was in no mood to try.

The other thing that threw me was, off to the side, there was an attractive area with a built-in grill, handsome seating made of logs, a table and chairs for eating outside, and not far from that was a fire pit with logs around it to sit or lounge against, covered in heavy, colorful wool blankets that were so big, they also draped across the ground.

This wasn't what threw me.

What threw me was the sheer number of spent cans and bottles everywhere. Three opened coolers that still had drinks floating in the now melted ice. Ashtrays here and there filled with cigarette butts and the blunt ends of spent joints. There was a lone football resting in the dirt not far from the area, and I noted two Frisbees also left where they'd fallen when the people using them lost interest.

Several massive Bluetooth speakers were scattered around, and it didn't take a techie to know they were synced. My sleepless night told me that.

And there were three bras drunkenly hanging from a pine tree, and what looked like a pair of panties tangled with a pair of boxers sat on one of the wool blankets by the firepit.

At least the massive garbage bin that had been rolled out had its lid firmly in place, or every critter near would be running amok. In fact, I didn't know how the lingering scent of hops and cooked meat didn't call to them.

I didn't need this visual representation of what had gone down at my neighbor's place, I'd heard it, but it looked worse than what I'd heard.

By far.

Distractedly noting the massive, shiny, black truck parked off to the side, I marched up to the small square deck that butted the front door. The deck had no railing and was not meant to hang out on.

Partly because it wasn't big enough, mostly because the attractive outdoor area had been built, maybe ten feet away, so you wouldn't sit on a front porch when you could sit in that side area and see the lake through the trees.

The front door was open, the storm door had its screens in, and it was closed.

But through it, I could see into a sunken living room.

Precisely, I could see Doc, flat on his back, no shirt, jeans covering his lower half, bare feet, one leg on the couch, one foot on the floor, passed out.

And on top of him, in nothing but a bra, straddling him, also passed out, was a brunette.

I'd never met her and still, I felt I knew her intimately.

Gross.

I hammered on the door.

Both of them jumped immediately, and I couldn't stop my lips curving up.

Yes.

It was cold in Russia, and that chill ran through my veins.

I kept hammering on the door.

She lilted to sitting astride him, her neck bent like she didn't have the strength to raise her head, hair covering her face.

He put his hands to her hips, his long fingers curling into her flesh, (this causing me to feel something I resolutely ignored) and turned his head to me.

When he saw me, his handsome, sleepy face morphed to granite.

I thinned my lips on principle.

He lifted the woman off him as he curled up, then set her on the couch as he got out of it.

He then prowled to me, crafting a new miracle, considering his ultra-faded jeans had a button fly, and as far as I could tell, only one button was done up, so how they remained on his slim (but power-ful) hips was unfathomable.

They also provided the solution to the mystery of what that dart of thick hair down the center of his abs pointed to, and it was a bigger patch of dark hair. Not to mention, I had an inkling whose boxers and panties were left on that wool blanket. Either that, or the man preferred commando.

He got to the door, and I had to jump back when he pushed it open hostilely.

"What the fuck time is it?" he asked me, also hostile (obviously), one arm held out to keep the door open.

Perfect introduction.

I engaged my camera, pulled up the picture I'd taken earlier and shoved it in his face.

"That was the time your party ended," I declared.

His eyes, which, this close, I could see were a silvery gray, and I could also see they were ringed with a very thick fringe of dark lashes, glanced at my phone before they came back to me.

"Get your fuckin' phone out of my face."

I dropped my phone and kept at him.

"Please allow me to explain what it appears you do not know, that being what appropriate neighborly conduct is."

"I'm not sure you know a lot about that," he retorted.

"Oh really?" I asked fake-sweetly. "Well, I know you don't run through your neighbors' yards."

"We live in a fuckin' forest. We don't have *yards*," he cut in.

I went on like he didn't speak. "And you don't have wild parties with loud music and loud people on a weekday, or any day, where it goes nearly until dawn. Weekdays, you pipe down at nine. Weekends, midnight."

"Is that a rule?" he asked snidely.

"Yes," I answered loftily.

"Woman, I moved out here to live like I wanna live without some uptight bitch wakin' me up in the wee hours of the fuckin' morning and getting up in my shit."

"Then you should have picked a lake that didn't have another house on it." I jabbed a finger at his house to indicate the lake beyond it. "*That* lake"—I leaned into him—"*has another house on it.*" I leaned back and jerked a thumb to myself. "*Mine.* So if you'd behave appropriately from here on out, it'd be appreciated."

"Kiss my ass," he returned.

Oh no he didn't.

"You can do that, or you can speak to the local police about whatever fine they levy for excessive noise," I threatened.

"We don't have noise ordinances out here, princess."

"Law enforcement is tasked with keeping the peace, and what was going on last night was far from peaceful."

"If you had a problem with it, why didn't you walk your sweet ass over here last night and ask nice instead of pulling this shit?"

I felt my eyes get round in affront, and I was feeling so affronted, I missed how his attention laser focused on my reaction.

I also missed the change in his demeanor at what he saw.

"Excuse me, Mr. Hell's Angel," I snapped. "Crawl forward from where it appears you live in the roaring, anything-goes, good-times seventies to today and tell me, what woman in her right mind would walk alone into a rowdy party in the middle of nowhere to ask a man to keep it down? In short, are you *insane?* And that doesn't even account for the fact *I shouldn't have to.*"

"I'm not in an MC."

My head jerked at this confusing announcement.

"What?" I asked.

"I got a bike, but I'm not in an MC."

"A what?"

"An MC." When I was obviously looking as confused as I actually still was, he educated me. "A motorcycle club."

"Oh," I mumbled then shook my hair to get myself mentally back on track.

But this time, I didn't miss how his gaze went right to my hair.

I put that in my pocket to forget about and wash until it was nothing but fluff and carried on.

"My point still stands."

"You called me Mr. Hell's Angel."

I twisted at the waist and looked pointedly at the mess in his party area.

When I went back to him, he'd leaned out to have his own look, and a smile was flirting with his full lips.

This guy!

"I'm not asking for a lot," I pointed out.

His attention returned to me. "Really? Because last night was a good fuckin' time, and it woulda sucked for a lot of people, including me, if I had to kick my friends out at midnight because my neighbor has a stick up her ass."

"I don't have a stick up my ass," I said hotly.

His brows rose.

"I don't!" I declared.

"Babe?" a woman's voice drifted from the interior of the house. "Get rid of her. She's a drag."

I put that in my pocket too. Not only what she said, but her entire existence, though, primarily where she woke up that morning.

"You done?" he asked me.

I was not.

"Listen, it's very simple. At around midnight, just ask everyone to keep it down, turn the music down and switch it over to Fleetwood Mac or the Eagles or something."

"No, woman, you listen," he retorted. "People who live like us do it because we don't want anyone telling us how to live. If you picked the wrong place to land, that's on you. Don't hang your shit on me."

After delivering that, he did a full body scan of me that was *entirely* inappropriate considering not only our conversation, but that he had a woman inside he'd clearly had relations with not too long ago (as in, perhaps only hours had elapsed). It lingered on my hips, on my bust area and then on my hair before he locked eyes with me, muttered a cutting, "Nice Birks. Fuck, velvet."

And then I had to jump out of the way when he stopped holding the storm door open and it whizzed closed.

If that wasn't enough, he shut the inner door right in my face.

Well!

"What a dick," I whispered to the door.

On that, I marched down the stairs and to the trail, my eyes to my Birkenstocks, my blood pressure out the roof.

And as I flicked my slides off into a cubby in my back hall, I thought, *Fuck him. Those shoes are adorable.*

I then went into my equally adorable kitchen and made coffee.

FOUR

Fuck Him

Riggs

Riggs pushed out of Aromacobana with a much-needed paper cup of coffee in his hand and nearly ran into Harry Moran, the county sheriff and one of Riggs's friends since they were kids.

"Yo, brother, sorry," he said. "Got a little loose last night, not firing on all cylinders yet."

Harry's lips quirked, and he replied, "Not a problem. Been a while. Back from a job?"

Riggs jerked up his chin. "Finished yesterday. Had the boys over, celebrated last night."

Harry faked looking hurt. "You didn't call me."

"Not your scene," Riggs muttered, wishing it was.

Harry needed to loosen the fuck up, and that wasn't about his job in law enforcement. It was about him holding onto something Riggs knew it would be tough as hell to let go, but you had to do it to move on and have a life.

His friend was breathing.

But he had no life.

As usual, Harry glossed over that and asked, "You in town for a while?"

Riggs nodded. "'Bout a month."

"We'll set something up, go fishing."

Riggs nodded again.

Harry headed toward the door to the coffeehouse, Riggs got out of his way so he could do it, but as he moved, a thought occurred to him.

So, as Harry opened his mouth to say something to end their brief conversation, Riggs said, "Some chick moved into Weaver Cabin."

The night before, he'd had his fair share and then some, smoked some weed, got ridden hard, so he came harder, and then he'd been woken up a couple hours after he passed out to a beautiful, but bitchy, woman up in his shit.

He wasn't as sharp as he normally would be.

Even so, he didn't miss how Harry's body jolted, then stiffened, and how his movements seemed wooden when he turned back to Riggs.

"Yeah, I heard," Harry replied.

Riggs was referring to his friend's reaction, not his words, when he asked, "She trouble?"

"Not that I know," Harry answered.

"You had a weird reaction when I mentioned her, man. You know her?"

Harry shook his head and asked, "You meet her?"

"Yeah, twice. The first time, she told me not to run through her yard during my morning runs, and the last time was a coupla hours ago when she got in my face about the party last night. So, warning. She said if it happens again, she's calling the cops. It's gonna happen again, and this woman, how she is, I know she'll call the cops."

"Your job done, do you have some time to talk right now?"

It was Riggs who stiffened at this invite.

Therefore, he pushed, "I'll ask again, Harry, is this bitch trouble?"

"You had breakfast?" Harry pushed back.

"No," Riggs told him.

"On me," Harry said, then, without Riggs agreeing, he took off toward the Double D diner.

It was Princess Solitary Coffee's big rack, sweet ass and head of thick, long, blonde hair that made Riggs follow his friend.

Oh yeah.

And those bright-blue eyes.

Fuck him, but all of that was so good, even though she'd demonstrated she could be a serious pain in his ass, he was curious.

They hit the Double D, were seated, and Heidi, the waitress, gave his Aromacobana cup a look, but he ordered another mug because he knew after last night, he was going to need it. He also ordered a full stack of pancakes with a side of bacon, because it was arguable, but he might need that more.

Harry went the granola, fruit and yogurt route.

In normal circumstances, Riggs would give the man shit for his healthy habits.

Not liking Harry's vibe, he reined it in.

After Heidi wrote down their orders and took off, Riggs dove right in.

"What gives?"

"Gonna ask you to keep it down for a while, Riggs," Harry said.

Riggs sat back and stretched both arms out to rest them on the booth behind him.

With Harry being good at his job, he didn't miss the body language.

"I know you don't like I asked that," Harry noted.

He was going to say more, but someone called, "Hey, Harry. Hey, Doc."

Riggs looked over his shoulder to see Declan, a kid he'd known since he was in diapers, which he was now not, being married and all, carrying a big white paper bag toward the door.

"Yo, Deck," Harry called.

Riggs just lifted his chin.

Declan left.

Riggs looked back to Harry.

"No," Riggs confirmed, low and slow. "I don't like you asked that. So now I'd like to know why you'd ask that shit."

"Normally…*damn.*" Harry pulled a hand through his hair, looked away, none of this making Riggs feel any better, then he returned to Riggs. "This is not mine to give you, but she's your neighbor, and, brother, I didn't know you were back in town, but even so, I knew when I found out you were…" He dragged his hand through his hair again before he finished, "I've been wrestling with coming to you or not about this so you could keep an eye on her."

Instantly, Riggs took his arms from the booth and leaned into them on the table. "What the fuck are you talking about?"

"Your neighbor is Nadia Antonov," Harry announced, like that'd explain everything.

"Am I supposed to know who that is?" Riggs shared it didn't explain everything.

"Antonov, Riggs. As in the vodka."

Riggs whistled low before he whispered, "Holy fuck."

"Yeah. The shit that's been going down around Misted Pines the last few years, word came to me someone was renting Weaver Cabin, that was news in itself."

Yeah, it was.

Riggs had lived in Misted Pines his entire life, but he bought his house on that lake three years prior, and he did it thinking no one would rent Weaver Cabin, and if they did, they wouldn't stay long, which had been the way of it for fifteen years.

He didn't believe any of the rumors. They were all bullshit. One of the reasons he had no reservations about buying his house on that lake.

But the fact remained, no one stayed long at Weaver Cabin, or his house, even before the Weavers took it over and fixed it up, but also after.

Which gave Riggs the lake, free and clear of the kind of hassle he'd experienced that morning.

Until, well…that morning.

"So, these days, I'm being extra cautious. Rus and I looked into her because I didn't want more trouble in this town," Harry explained, and Riggs was down with that too. Misted Pines had seen more of its fair share of trouble the last couple of years, and everyone, including Riggs, was sick of it. Harry, in his job, more than most. "We didn't have far to look. Her shit is swung way the fuck out there."

"And that shit is?" Riggs asked.

"So you haven't heard?"

"Heard what?"

"It hit the national news."

"Again, *heard what?*" Riggs pressed.

Harry seemed surprised, but knowing when Riggs was on a job, which he had been, nearly back-to-back for six months now, he worked, and then he worked more, and when he couldn't do it well, he slept. After that, he worked more.

He didn't tap into the local gossip line.

He didn't even watch the news.

And when he wasn't working, he did what he worked to do: enjoy his life.

Every second of it.

So he didn't bother with catching up on current events when he wasn't working either.

"You know anything about the Antonovs?" Harry queried.

"I know I like their vodka. And I know it's top shelf. Other than that…" He shrugged.

"Right, well, quick history lesson. Big daddy Antonov got on Stalin's hit list. He was a capitalist through and through. As such, no surprise, he wasn't a big fan of communism. He also wasn't a big fan of keeping his mouth shut about his feelings. There's a lot of lore about how he escaped the gulag, and the USSR as a whole, but there's no denying, the man was tough as nails and a hardass on top of it. He brought his vodka recipe to America and set about living his American dream. Single-minded in that effort. Word is, the dude was cutthroat and bottom line terrifying. But he built his liquor empire, and that empire is expansive, going well beyond vodka, and when he died, he passed it on to his only child, a son, Fyodor."

"Yeah?" Riggs prompted when Harry stopped talking.

"Fyodor was a chip off the old block. But there were two big, royal-type weddings of that era. Grace Kelly to Prince Rainier, and Fyodor Antonov to Vilma Rayburn."

Finally, something familiar.

Riggs had heard that last name. "The actress?"

Harry nodded. "Bombshell. Gorgeous. Destined to be another Marilyn Monroe, until she met Fyodor and left Hollywood behind for true love."

"And money," Riggs cut in.

"I don't know," Harry said thoughtfully. "She gave Antonov a daughter, then, pregnant with his son, irony hits and she and the unborn baby were killed by a drunk driver who reportedly got sloshed on Antonov vodka. Fyodor never married again. Everyone says he was heartbroken. She was the love of his life. He never got over losing her. But when he lost her, he turned all his affection to his daughter, Alyona, and when she came, his granddaughter."

"Nadia," Riggs filled in, now understanding what put the princess in his princess.

The woman actually *was* a princess.

A vodka one, but it was the same thing.

"So I got some rich bitch living close to me," Riggs noted.

"No, you have a second-grade teacher whose mother was murdered by her father four months ago living next to you."

Riggs sat back again.

This time, though, he did it like he'd been pushed.

Even after he was back, he felt something pressing hard at his chest.

"Against her father's wishes, Alyona fell in love with a man named Peter Rogers," Harry went on. "She had no idea, but her father did, that this guy was a piece of shit. She went all in with her rebellion, married the guy. They had a kid, Nadia, but Alyona starts cottoning on and wastes no time shaking him loose. Divorce papers say emotional and physical abuse. She gets that finalized, but he keeps coming back, threatening to take his infant daughter. Alyona wants him gone. Fyodor wants him gone. But Rogers isn't about to give up the high life or the direct line he has to their bank accounts. The thing he didn't factor in is that Fyodor is old school and he's gonna put up with shit for half a second, but he's gonna put up with his daughter taking shit for less than that. Somehow, they get rid of him."

"But he comes back," Riggs surmised.

Harry nodded. "Yeah, after he became a black widower. He was a conman, Riggs, and that graduated to him becoming a murderer. He'd find some small-time heiress, charm her, marry her, then somehow, she ends up dead, he ends up with her money, then he vanishes. Took the cops decades, but after the last one he killed, they strung together his aliases and how he'd change his appearance. They were onto him. Froze the assets he inherited so he couldn't get to them and evaporate. He needed money and he needed another disappearing act. He knew how to do the last and where to get the first. Easier for him, he thought, since Fyodor was dead. So he went after Alyona."

Harry stopped talking when Heidi came and put their plates on the table.

Riggs sucked back some of his Aromacobana coffee in order to get rid of the sudden shitty taste in his mouth, but also to give her time to leave the table, and when she was gone, he noted, "This isn't a fun story, Harry."

"It doesn't get better," Harry warned.

Riggs sighed, set his coffee aside and picked up his fork, trying not to think about how huge of a dick he was to Nadia that morning.

Granted, the woman bore down on his place raring for a confrontation, and the way she did put him in the mood to give it to her.

He'd still been a huge dick.

"Apple doesn't fall far from the tree," Harry went on, picking up his spoon and mixing his healthy breakfast. "Not sure how Rogers didn't figure that out, but even with Fyodor gone, Alyona was no pushover. She wanted to be a lawyer. She became a prosecutor. Fyodor had sold the family business because she had no interest in it, but this meant she was loaded. Rogers showed, probably demanded money, murder scene says she was not about to give it to him or take his shit. He was in a bind, desperate, the cops on his ass. It was messy, Riggs. Brutal and messy. He took some licks, but in the end, he beat her to death."

"Fucking hell," Riggs muttered, setting his fork aside.

He was no longer hungry, and he no longer wanted to hear this story.

He looked out the window.

Brutal and messy.

And he'd called the woman's daughter a bitch at least once that morning.

Fuck.

"I don't know what they told Nadia about her dad," Harry kept at him. "But police reports note that she had no idea who her father was. No idea, until he came back and killed her mother."

At that, Riggs looked direct at Harry and demanded, "So you want me to look after her?"

And to that, Harry asked the obvious question.

"Who better?"

"Brother—" Riggs began.

"Nadia was married," Harry stated.

"She's not wearing a ring," Riggs forced out.

"Yeah, because she met and fell in love with a firefighter. They got engaged, and a couple months into the engagement, he finds out he's got terminal cancer."

Goddammit.

Riggs tipped his head back and hissed, "Jesus Christ," to the ceiling, wondering why he followed Harry to the Double D.

And no, that weight in his chest hadn't lessened.

It just kept getting heavier.

"Word is, he tried to break it off," Harry told him. "Nadia refused. Fast-tracked everything. Married him. Big, lavish wedding. Fyodor sent them on a two-month-long honeymoon where they did everything on his bucket list. They got home, five months later, he's dead."

"When did this happen?" Riggs asked, all four of the words tight.

Harry lifted one shoulder and said, "Think around seven years ago."

"So, dead granddad. Dead mom. Dead husband. Incarcerated, murdering, conman, asshole, piece of shit dad."

Harry swallowed the bite he took, and how he could eat and tell this story was one of the reasons he was sheriff.

Then he shook his head. "The dad got pinned in at a motel and committed suicide by cop. Came out gun blazing, took six bullets, died at the scene."

"Even better, he's a criminally selfish, murdering, piece of shit conman who went out making men have to live the rest of their lives with taking his, even if he was waste of humanity."

"I'm not sure they're losing much sleep over that guy," Harry replied.

"Doesn't negate the fact they gotta live with pulling that trigger."

Harry nodded.

"I was a dick to her when she got in my shit this morning," he told Harry.

"I can imagine," Harry murmured.

"She's an uppity pain in the ass," Riggs defended himself.

"Her mother was beat to death by her father four months ago. A father she didn't know existed, but now she knows he not only killed her mom in a vicious attack, he also killed four other women. I think she deserves some grace."

"I don't disagree, but I didn't know that."

Harry pointed at him with his spoon. "Now, you know." After saying that, he dug into his yogurt again.

"And you know what this story is gonna bring up in me," Riggs said low.

Harry didn't break eye contact when he replied, "I know."

"You're a motherfucker," Riggs muttered and nabbed his fork.

"I've seen pictures of her," Harry said.

"Fuck off," Riggs returned before shoving pancakes in his mouth.

"She and her mom both took after the bombshell in the family line," Harry noted.

Riggs did nothing but swallow his pancakes and grunt.

But his friend was right.

He couldn't put his finger on it until now, but even in a tight cami, faded jeans, ridiculous Birks, a sloppy sweater with sexy-as-all-fuck, messy, bedhead hair, Nadia Antonov looked like an old-time Hollywood goddess.

And what cut it?

Her damned attitude made him fight his dick getting hard.

His father had used his charm and good looks in much the same way Nadia's had.

There was a time Riggs considered taking a blade to his face because the attention could get annoying, and sometimes it was downright oppressive.

But Nadia Antonov…

The woman wasn't about to drop to her knees and suck his dick if he just snapped his fingers.

Which of course made him want to feel his cock in her mouth all the more.

Fuck him.

"To circle back, live as large as you want, my brother, just keep it down so your neighbor can get a good night's sleep," Harry finished.

He had no choice but to do that.

And more.

No choice but look after the woman.

Yeah.

Fuck.

Him.

Hard.

FIVE

The Hole

Riggs

Before opening time, Riggs pushed through the door of The Black Hole, one of the many bars in Misted Pines, or in The Hole's case, on the outskirts of it, but not one of the better ones.

He did this in search of his bud, Bubbles.

The place was dark, only the lights over the bar illuminated, but it was clear the staff at closing the night before hadn't bothered with clean up before they took off. There were empties everywhere, and as usual, the soles of his boots stuck to the floor with every step he took.

He headed to the door at the back, lifted a hand and rapped his knuckles on it, shouting, "Yo, Bubbles, it's Doc. You in there?"

Riggs had known Bubbles since high school, so he was prepared for the door to crash open with more enthusiasm than was needed.

And Bubbles stood there, balding, stout, not short but also not tall, looking like Riggs felt before he'd caffeinated and carbed up.

However rough Bubbles felt, very little broke Bubbles's good ole boy.

Bubbles wasn't called Bubbles for nothing.

"Yo, buddy!" he cried like Riggs was a football field away. "You're back in town."

"Yeah. Got back from a job yesterday."

Bubbles pulled a bogus frown. "Didn't see you here last night."

"Had a thing at my place."

The frown that bought wasn't bogus. "Didn't get the text."

Riggs shook his head. "Brother, Lucille told me if I invited you over one more time and you skipped looking after The Hole to get drunk at my pad, she'd kick your ass out."

"Well, Lucille is history, so no worries about that anymore," Bubbles returned, the expression on his face defiant, but hearing the words, Riggs saw the sadness it was hiding.

This was news, and not good news. They'd been together awhile, and Lucille was a kind woman. She cared for Bubbles, and Bubbles felt the same. She also had the patience of a saint, and the same capacity to forgive, something important for the woman in Bubbles's life. Riggs had thought this time for Bubbles, it was going to stick.

Though, truth told, it wasn't surprising news.

Even so, Riggs had been out of town for less than two weeks.

But when Bubbles was ready to make a trainwreck of his life, he didn't fuck around.

Riggs heaved a sigh.

"Where are you crashing?" he asked.

Bubbles suddenly couldn't meet his eyes.

That meant he was crashing on his mother's couch.

A forty-year-old man who was crashing on his mother's couch… again. All because he found it impossible to keep his shit tight.

At least he hadn't asked to crash at Riggs's, which would put Riggs in the position of telling him *fuck no*. Riggs had learned that lesson the hard way years ago when a "couple of nights" turned into three months, and by the time the man left, Riggs's cupboards were bare, there wasn't a drop of booze left in the place, he'd had to buy a new couch, and he'd nearly lost a good friend.

As messy as his bud was, he loved him, because Bubbles was impossible not to love.

That said, right now, Riggs didn't have the time or patience for this shit.

"Listen, need a bottle. A good one. I pissed off my neighbor, and I need to make amends."

Bubbles eyes got huge. "So, rumor is true? Someone's living at Weaver Cabin?"

"Yeah," Riggs confirmed.

"Holy shit!" Bubbles yelled.

"It's a rental house on a lake, Bubs, and it's good Dave and Brenda finally have someone in it."

It was like he didn't speak when Bubbles said, "I gotta start a pool about how long they're gonna last."

Even if the rumors were true (which they were not), Riggs almost wanted to see someone try to fuck with Nadia Antonov, even the type of "someone" they claimed messed with the people who stayed in that cabin.

The woman could deep-freeze Putin himself.

Hell, she could deep-freeze Stalin, and since that was her bloodline, Riggs had no questions about how her great-granddad bested an infamous despot.

But now knowing the shit she was wading through, he hoped like fuck she was left alone.

"Bubs, the bottle," Riggs reminded him.

He watched his friend's body jolt, then he nodded too fast and too much before he pushed through Riggs and led him to his storeroom.

Anyone else, Riggs would wonder if he was on something.

Bubbles had always had more energy than he could expend, case in point, how he was walking to the storeroom right now, freaking fast and every other step wasn't a step, but a half a skip.

Riggs followed a lot slower.

They hit the storeroom and Bubbles flipped the light switch, saying, "Couple of year ago, went with Candy…" He stopped and stared into space, "Or was it Barbie?" He shook his head and ignored the shelves haphazardly stacked with cases of beer, bottles of booze and rolls of inexpensive toilet paper and headed to a locked cabinet that held the back stock for his top shelf. "Doesn't matter, was in Sonoma, and, man, I musta entered a fugue state when I tasted it. But this shit was so good, I couldn't help myself."

He'd pulled out his keys and was opening the cabinet.

He was also still talking.

"Should have my head examined. A good shot of whisky, they're all over it. The occasional snifter of Hennessey, sure. But that stuff doesn't go bad. Someone orders a glass of this for twenty-five bucks in my joint, they won't be buyin' another one, and that bottle'll stay open since no one who comes here has the cabbage to drop on a twenty-five-dollar glass of wine unless they're celebrating a wedding, or a divorce. So I'd have to pour the rest of it down the drain."

"Or you could drink it before it went bad," Riggs suggested.

Bubbles looked at him, his face a picture of utter confusion, before it brightened, and he replied, "Fuck, shoulda thought of that."

Christ, how this guy kept The Hole running, Riggs had no clue. He was funny, and affable, but he was a funny, affable and loveable doofus.

Bubbles reached into the locker and grabbed an expensive-looking bottle of wine, one of about twelve identical ones piled in there.

Riggs narrowed his eyes on the bottles as Bubbles jerked the one he'd nabbed his way.

Riggs didn't take the bottle.

He asked, "When were you in Sonoma?"

"A couple years ago," Bubbles murmured.

And damn, that was one of his many tells, considering the man rarely murmured.

"Anyway," Bubbles went on. "Wine doesn't go bad that quick, unless it's opened. It's good. Real good." He shook the bottle at Riggs. "Here. Take it. Great apology."

Slowly, Riggs took it, saying, "You're not handing me a bottle of hot wine, are you?"

"'Course not." He was again murmuring.

Shit.

"Bubs—"

"Seriously, Doc. Your neighbor will be impressed."

"Not if I'm giving her a bottle of stolen wine. We got a deal. You do you, but I want no part of it when it's like that." He pushed the bottle Bubbles's way. "No shade. You know that. But I can go to a liquor store."

Bubbles held up both hands. "Doc. No. This is really good wine. And it isn't like that."

He wasn't murmuring anymore, but he also wasn't looking Riggs in the eye, which was often another tell.

Though, Bubbles sometimes simply didn't look you in the eye.

But when Bubbles caught his gaze and gave him a goofy smile, Riggs relaxed and stopped extending the bottle.

Bubbles reached in, grabbed another one and held it to Riggs. "You take both of those, then we're square."

"We're already square."

Bubbles shook his head. "You did me a solid. Now I'm doing the same."

He wasn't talking about overstaying his welcome and eating and drinking Riggs out of house and home.

He was talking about something else.

"I told you when I did it, I wasn't keeping a marker." Riggs set the bottle on the shelf and pulled out his wallet.

"Not gonna take your money, Doc," Bubbles declared.

"Twenty-five dollars a glass?" Riggs asked.

"Bud, seriously." Bubbles was getting agitated.

Riggs had no problem looking his friend in the eye, which was what he did.

"Lucille kick you out because you didn't pay your half of the rent, or because you did that *and* borrowed money off her to make payroll again?"

Bubbles's lower lip stuck out a beat before he stated, "Hassle don't come with paying my marker."

"I don't hold a marker on you," Riggs muttered, opening his wallet and counting four hundred-dollar bills, and two fifties.

He offered them to Bubbles.

Bubbles didn't take them.

"You know I'm not gonna walk out of here with that wine without paying for it," Riggs told him. "Take the money."

Riggs knew Bubbles would take it before he took it, just as he knew he wouldn't enter that income as a line item in his books against the expense of the wine, and not only because that wine might not have been from a visit to Sonoma, but there was a possibility it was bought out of the trunk of a car after some asshole stole it from another bar or someplace else.

Instead, the man would blow it at a poker game or a steak dinner at The Lodge.

Riggs just had to hope Bubbles wouldn't do him dirty that way.

A thought that prompted him to demand, "And don't start a pool about Weaver Cabin."

Bubbles was shoving the money in his back pocket when he asked, "Why?"

He wasn't about to mention Nadia Antonov. Not to Bubbles. The Vodka Princess's mere existence would set Bubbles to running his mouth. But if his friend caught sight of her or saw a picture of her, and he knew a piece that hot was living that close to Riggs, that shit would go viral.

"I didn't move up there to have aggravation, Bubs. If that cabin gets attention, it's gonna affect me one way or another. When I'm home, I wanna do what I wanna do. Not have folks sniffing around my lake or people harassing me about shit when I'm in town. It's all bullshit, you know it, everyone knows it."

"I don't know it."

Right, he forgot for a second.

His friend was a good guy, he'd give you the shirt off his back, and he was a good time.

But he was a doofus.

"Even if you don't, put a lid on it. You think you owe me a marker, you do that, consider us square."

That got to him.

Bubbles smiled so big, you could see the missing tooth deep in the left side of his mouth that he tried hard to hide.

Jesus, this guy.

Riggs grabbed the bottle from the shelf, the other that Bubbles still held, said, "Thanks, man. Later."

And then he was out of there.

He had someone else to visit that day, and he hoped that went a lot better than his breakfast with Harry and this deal with Bubbles.

He also had to get home and clean up his yard.

After that, he had to figure out how to smooth things over with Nadia Antonov.

He was only looking forward to one of those things.

So that was what he was going to do next.

SIX

The Only Ones That Matter

Riggs

Early evening, Riggs caught sight of her while standing at his kitchen sink.

She was sitting on her pier, staring at the lake.

She was in the distance, but he could see she didn't move much, except she was drinking something.

She wasn't reading or talking on the phone.

Just staring at the lake.

And Riggs knew exactly what that was about. He felt it flow straight through his soul.

Goddamn.

Fuck him and fuck Harry Moran.

He'd enjoyed his last visit in town, grabbed some groceries, came back to his place and picked up the mess around his house.

Once he'd hit the shower, ran a comb through his hair and dressed, he went back to the window to see she wasn't on the pier.

Probably inside, making dinner.

It was time to head out.

He nabbed one of the bottles and made his way to the trail.

47

The lanterns on her back porch were lit, along with the line of lights Brenda had asked him to tack up around the edges of the porch roof. They were Christmas lights covered in alternating pink, blue, green and yellow plastic flowers. Dave had hated them. Riggs wasn't a fan either. Brenda was gleeful the minute she saw them up.

Now, he got it.

That tableau suited Nadia.

More to the point, it was peaceful and pretty, and it suited what Riggs felt Nadia needed.

He walked up the steps to the back porch and frowned at the screen door.

He'd had several conversations with Dave about that old wooden door with the big screen in it. The cabin needed a secure storm door, and not only because they got storms. It was safer. Anybody could jump right through that screen without much effort. A storm door would pose a problem to someone who wanted to get in that the person inside wanted to keep out.

Dave and Brenda had dumped a load into that cabin (mostly Brenda), and Riggs could understand why Dave tried to find things to save money on.

Nadia there now, Riggs reckoned they could have done without the flower lights and the fucking pillows everywhere and bought decent security doors.

He knocked on the wood, and his frown intensified because even the sound of his knuckles striking made it sound rickety.

She appeared at the top of the hall. Her mass of hair pulled in a high ponytail. No makeup, wearing a dark-green sundress with tiny pink flowers on it that hit above her knees, the thick straps tied in bows on top of her shoulders. Her feet were bare. Her skin glowed with a light tan.

In other words, she was just as fuckable as the last two times he saw her when her hair was a mess from sleep, she was wearing slouchy clothes and her blue eyes were shooting icicles at him.

Except more.

The thing was, she was wearing an apron with big, bright flowers over the dress.

Never in his life had he seen anyone wear an actual apron, not to mention one that looked thrown forward in time from the fifties.

Even so, it didn't surprise him in the least that she did—his prim and proper princess telling him the weekday rules were to quiet down at nine, and weekends at midnight.

Though, it did make him want to bust out laughing.

Fortunately, he didn't do that, and when her gorgeous face went cold at the sight of him, he lifted up the bottle of wine and said, "Peace offering."

She hesitated a moment before she moved down the hall and stood opposite him without making that first move to open the screen door between them.

She also didn't say anything, though she took a good look at the wine.

So he spoke. "I was a dick. You were right. I'm not used to having anyone living close, and I didn't factor that into my plans for last night. I get that you wouldn't feel safe coming over and asking us to keep it down. I also get you shouldn't have to. In future, I'll have a mind."

She didn't say anything or move, which sucked, but considering the little he knew of her, it also wasn't surprising.

So he bent, put the bottle on the porch to the side of the door and straightened.

"Don't know wine, and you should know, I have it only on dubious authority that's a good bottle. Still, hope you enjoy."

She tipped her head slightly to the side, but that was it.

He made to turn.

But then he didn't turn.

The woman wore an apron, for Christ's sake.

He drew in a big breath and said, "My father was a piece of shit."

Her body moved like she'd sustained a blow, and he got that too.

But he went on.

"Abusive to my mom. Abusive to me and my sister. Stepped out on Mom all the time. Didn't even try to hide it. Mom got shot of him, but he'd still come around and give her grief, give it to all of us, even after she got a restraining order. He did time in county jail, a lot. In prison, twice. If he had money, you could bet the way he came by it wasn't legal. But he didn't often have money, which was usually why he stopped by to give Mom grief. The man never worked an honest job, not a day of his life. He fucked over any friend he made, any woman who gave her heart or body to him. He hated the cops, for obvious reasons. And he was on the run from them, high speed chase, when he went over a cliff."

She gasped.

Riggs kept going.

"His car exploded on impact and set off a wildfire. Took out fifty acres and three houses before they contained it. And I'll tell you, the man was very dead, but still, I know down deep in my gut, he'd be pleased as fuck his last act on this earth was to burn down all the worldly possessions of three families. He'd love that to the marrow of his bones. That was just how big of a piece of shit he was."

She stood, still as a statue, but he wasn't feeling a chill from her anymore.

Not even close.

Her face was pale, and those blue eyes were big, her lips were parted, and he could see her tits rise and fall fast, taking the apron with them.

"So, I get it," he concluded. "I didn't do any of that shit, and I had to live it down. He died ten years ago, and sometimes, I *still* have to live it down. It sucks. Huge. But you learn, the people you know, who know you, are the only ones that matter."

She remained silent.

He'd said his piece.

He tipped his chin toward the bottle and bid, "Hope you like it, Nadia."

That was when he turned to leave.

He'd only taken a step when he heard the screen door open.

He turned back and she was reaching for the bottle.

After she grabbed it, she was still bent in half when her head went back.

She swung the bottom of the bottle side to side, and asked softly, "Have you had dinner?"

He felt one side of his lips draw up and ignored what her invitation caused in his groin before he answered, "No."

She straightened fully. "It's nothing fancy. Just spaghetti."

"I like spaghetti."

She nodded and let the door go as she turned to move inside.

Riggs caught it before it closed.

He followed her in, and for the first time, he understood Brenda's vision.

Lights were lit, not all of them, just enough to chase the shadows away and make the space inviting. Though, the kitchen was fully lit, and he smelled the garlic before he hit it, the kind of smell he knew, it wasn't just spaghetti, but garlic bread.

His stomach suddenly reminded him he hadn't eaten since breakfast.

He and Dave had told Brenda repeatedly that she was alienating at least half of the rental market with the girlie way she decorated.

But now, he saw it, and thought maybe Brenda was a weird kind of genius.

Because straight up, he wouldn't mind hanging a good long while in this space with Nadia.

She'd made it her own, he could see, with more books in the bookshelves and framed photos scattered around. There was a candle lit on a nightstand, and a bunch of them around the fireplace. The door to the walk-in wasn't fully closed, and it was a big closet, but from what he could tell from the glimpse he got, she'd filled that fucker up in a way he was guessing that most of the boxes he helped Dave lug for her were clothes and shoes.

She also had a digital photo frame on the far end of the back kitchen counter that scrolled through pictures.

Happier times for Nadia, and it looked like she had a lot of friends.

Those happier times included the picture that came up when he stopped at the island.

Nadia with an attractive older woman who looked a lot like her, a much older man, and a good-looking blond guy in a tux.

Nadia was wearing a wedding dress.

She looked amazing, happy, and only someone like Riggs would notice the pain shadowing her eyes.

"That's my mom, my grandfather and Trevor," she stated, taking his attention to her, and catching her watching him staring at her frame. "My husband. He died."

This was succinct, matter of fact, and it was seven years ago, so he could see that. He could also see she said it in a way that meant she didn't want to talk about it.

He should have told her that he knew, but he didn't want her to know people were talking about her.

She'd know, obviously, especially considering how he earned his invitation to dinner.

But she didn't need to know how much he knew, nor did she need that shit in her kitchen.

"Sorry," he murmured.

"I am too."

Time for another topic.

"Anything I can do?" he offered.

She put a wine key by the bottle of wine on the counter, along with a big-bowled, sparkling clean wineglass.

A vodka princess who kept her wineglasses sparkling clean and did that herself.

A piece of wisdom he liked to know about her, at the same time he wished he didn't.

"You can open the wine so it can breathe," she replied.

She took her glass, which was used but empty, to the sink and rinsed it out.

"Place looks nice," he noted.

"Have you been in here before?"

"Sure, I renovated it."

This made her stop drying her wineglass and stare at him.

"I own a contracting business. We do mostly renos and refurbs all through central Washington," he shared. "So I'm journeyman electrician, plumber, welder and a licensed contractor."

She kept staring.

He pulled out the cork.

"That seems a lot of education for a man your age," she remarked.

He unscrewed the cork, set it and the wine key on the counter, leaned into a hand and raised his brows. "How old do you think I am?"

"I don't know, thirty-three, thirty-four."

He chuckled. "Now you're just being nice."

"Actually, I'm not."

Well, shit.

"I'm thirty-eight."

Her astonishment was unhidden.

But she said, "That's still young for that amount of training. It's my understanding it takes years for each of those trades."

"It does," he confirmed. "And it helps that I started early, seeing as I skipped third and sixth grades. With my dad being my dad, it wasn't easy entering high school at twelve. But even without my dad, it wouldn't have been easy."

"Wow," she said quietly. "Not easy, but it's impressive."

He wasn't so sure about that.

"It's why I'm called Doc," he told her. "My teachers started to talk to Mom about moving me up in second grade. She said I had to be a genius and began calling me that as a joke. It stuck, and everyone started calling me that. Even my teachers. The name I was born with was Jonathan Andrew Riggs, Jr. But my dad was such a dick, when I was twenty-four, I went in front of a judge and changed it to Andrew Doc Riggs, and obviously dropped the junior. Andrew was my granddad's name. Mom's dad. He was the shit. The judge knew my dad. Didn't ask a single question. Slammed down his gavel, though I figure he didn't need to do that, he just did it for the fun of it, also since he knew when my dad found out I'd changed my name he'd pitch a fit, and he granted the change. Dad was pissed as all hell. It was a brilliant 'fuck you' I was glad I could deliver before he went up in a ball of flame."

Her lips tipped up and her eyes lit, and he liked both.

"Sure way to piss me off," he carried on, probably due to that light in her eyes and curl in her lips, "is call me John. Dad went by that, so did I when I was younger."

"So now it's Doc," she noted.

"That or Riggs, whichever works for you."

She nodded, ducked her head in a shy way, and turned to the stove where she dumped an entire box of spaghetti in boiling water.

She picked up a wooden spoon and stirred the long lengths of pasta, saying to the pot, "And you know who I am."

"Yeah, Nadia," he said gently. "Went into town today, heard word. I know that sucks, but in a twisted way, you should be glad. Means I'm gonna stop being a dick to you."

Her ponytail had fallen down to hide part of her profile, so she peeked around it to look at him and give him a tentative smile.

And damn.

He liked that too.

She pulled it together, put the wooden spoon down, picked up another one and started to stir the sauce, commenting, "You do apologies really well."

Now he was uncomfortable.

So much so, he had to clear his throat before he said, "It's not the same, but there are similarities to our stories, and misery loves company."

She turned fully to him and said outright, "Your openness means a lot, Riggs."

So she picked Riggs.

Not many people did, but that's how he thought of himself, more than Doc.

And there was something about the fact she called him what he thought he was that started getting under his skin.

Though, if he was completely honest with himself, she'd done that when she told him not to run through her yard.

"I was talking about the wine," she continued. "A five-hundred-dollar bottle of wine is a pretty classy apology. I'm not sure how dubious your authority actually is. They know good wine."

And now it was Riggs who was staring.

"What?" she asked, putting down the spoon and going to the fridge.

"Got that bottle from a bud of mine. Keeping the honesty going, it cost a whack, but not that big of a whack. And after we're done with it, I'm going to have to take the bottle home with me because, I'm not certain, but better safe than sorry, so I'm gonna have to get rid of the evidence."

She laughed as soft and sweet as she spoke when she wasn't pissed off.

No surprise, he liked that too.

"He knows right from wrong," Riggs went on. "He just chooses to ignore one side of that on occasion."

The laugh she gave him after he said that was bigger, but it wasn't louder.

"How long we gotta let this shit breathe?" he asked.

She was pulling out a bowl to toss the bag of Caesar salad mix she'd taken from the fridge.

She set the bowl on the counter and went to the bottle. She checked the label closely and said, "Half an hour."

"So you know wine," he noted.

A slight shrug.

She knew wine.

"Would you put together the salad while I set the island?" she requested.

"You got it," he agreed.

He hadn't done anything truly domestic with a woman for years.

But as he tossed that salad, and she put out placemats, cloth napkins, cutlery and pasta bowls, that thought didn't enter his mind.

It wasn't until a lot later he realized how easy he fell into it.

And how bad that was.

SEVEN

Flower Lights

Riggs

It was after dinner.

She made good spaghetti, spiced up the sauce just right, not too hot, not bland by a long shot.

It was excellent.

Riggs had steered the conversation out of the heavy.

He told her about his team, how he took jobs, and they worked them, twelve-hour days, six days a week, until they were done. Then they'd come home for a break that was never less than a week, though the longer the job or string of them, the longer the break before they headed out again.

He also told her his last job started the day after he met her on his run and ended the day before.

She'd asked how long he was in town now, and he'd loved and hated how the little wrinkles around the edges of her lips formed when she was trying not to smile when he told her a month.

On her side, she'd told him shit he knew, but he didn't tell her he knew.

That her husband died of cancer after a short marriage (she didn't dive deep into that, this time, because he guided her out of it). That she was thirty-three years old. And that she'd taken a year's sabbatical from her teaching job to come to Misted Pines to "get away from it all."

He talked more than she did, mostly in an effort to put her at ease.

In fact, he talked more that night than he ever did, with any woman, or man.

Now, they were out on the back porch in her loveseat with the last of the wine, sitting close, both their feet up on the coffee table, and Riggs was studying that view. Her legs shorter than his, and they had a shine to them, showing she'd shaved and recently. Her toes were painted a creamy, pale yellow that he found somehow more feminine and sexier than red. This juxtaposed against his faded jeans and scuffed, brown, lace-up boots.

Straight up, it was a fucking turn on, one of the biggest ones he'd ever experienced, seeing their legs like that, entirely indicative of all that was him, all that was her, and hinting at what it would feel like if his legs were tangled with hers, or hers were wrapped around his ass.

It didn't help he could feel the soft flesh of her hip against his and smell the flowery, powdery, supremely female scent of her perfume.

But that wasn't where this could go.

He'd fucked his way through half the attractive women in this county, so it wasn't like he was above shitting where he lived.

But she was there to escape something brutal and tragic, and she didn't need her neighbor making moves on her.

It was more than that, though.

There was something about her that told him he couldn't take it there. She'd let down her shield that night, the ice queen was gone, and the sometimes shy, all the time sweet, definitely vulnerable woman who had pain shadowing her eyes, was not someone he was the man to wade into.

He was a good-time guy.

He could take her for a ride on his bike so she could feel the wind in her hair. He could cook her an excellent brat, not on his grill, in a skillet filled with brown ale. He could get her drunk and make her laugh hard, then later, make her come harder.

But he'd learned along the way he wasn't the other kind of man for a woman.

You wanted to get loose or get high or get off, Riggs was the guy for you.

You wanted more, he wanted no part of it.

She moved her foot and the side of it skimmed the leg of his jeans.

He didn't feel it, but he *felt* it.

Jesus, he had to get out of there.

"So, um…I take it your other neighbors were less, we'll say, dedicated to their sleep than me."

He turned his attention from their legs to her face at this comment.

"Sorry?"

"Whoever rented this cabin before me," she explained.

"No one's been in this cabin before you. At least not while I've been in my house."

She was fucking with his head so much, the words were out before he realized he shouldn't have said them.

But it hit him when her expression turned instantly confused, as it would. "How long have you lived in your house?"

Fuck.

"Three years."

Her chin shot into her neck. "No one's been in this cabin for that long? How long did it take to renovate?"

Fuck.

"Six weeks."

"But…I mean, when did you renovate it?"

Fuck!

"Before I moved into my house. Renovating here, I saw my place was on the market. I bought it while I was doing up this pad."

Sluggishly, her head turned to look at the back door, and he knew why, because he'd done the work, and he prided himself on doing solid work. The best. One of the reasons why he was so busy, because that was his reputation.

Brenda's décor might alienate half the population, but it was still nice, and the reno was fantastic, and because it was hard to rent—or hard to keep rented—the rental fees were rock bottom. The same could be said for his house, though he didn't tell her that. But he'd gotten it for a song.

Which would of course make Nadia confused.

When she came back around, she put her wineglass to her lips, but she didn't take a sip.

She spoke into it while staring at the moonlight on the lake. "I haven't spent much time in town, but it looks like a cute place. My understanding is, it's pretty touristy. I don't get it."

Riggs shifted uneasily.

Her gaze went from the lake to him, and she surmised, "There's a reason."

"Nadia—"

Her brows drew down and pinched at the bridge of her nose, "Please tell me you didn't run off all of Dave and Brenda's tenants so you could throw wild parties."

He busted out laughing.

"I'll take that as a no," she said through his laughter.

"I like my lake, Nadia, but I like Dave and Brenda too, and I'm not *that* much of a dick."

"Well, I should say at this juncture, even though it behooves me to do so…"

Fuck.

She said *behooves*.

He fought busting out laughing again.

She kept speaking.

"But perhaps I was in a wee bit of a bad mood when I forbade you to run through my yard. And Dave left me your phone number. I could have called and told you how I felt about your party and not, erm…woken you post-*in flagrante delicto*."

And now she was saying *in flagrante delicto*.

This woman.

"We were post-coital, not post-*in flagrante delicto*," he disputed. "Courtney's not taken."

Her eyes moved over his face in a way he both liked and made him feel awkward.

"Your correction is noted, though it's more fun to say *in flagrante delicto*. And just to say, not a lot of people know the distinction between those two," she said, her voice softer than its normal soft.

"You forget, I'm a genius," he joked. "And I might like a good time, or to mellow out with some good weed, and I work with my hands, but I also know how to read."

She shifted and said swiftly, "I didn't mean to offen—"

"You didn't, Nadia. I'm teasing you."

"Okay," she whispered.

"And your non-apology apology is accepted," he continued teasing.

She rolled her eyes, looked away, and finally took a sip of her wine.

He smiled into his glass before he took one from his.

"You can run through my yard," she told the lake.

"Obliged," he replied.

"And if you give me a heads-up you're going to have people over and want to let loose, maybe I can, I don't know, check into a spa somewhere."

"Or you could come and join us," he offered a different option.

She made a face at him.

He wanted to find it funny, but *that* offended him.

"I hope you get from tonight I'm good people, and so are my friends."

"You listen to Tool."

Oh yeah.

He was offended.

"I don't," he shot back. "I lost control of the playlist somewhere along the way."

"Well, that's a relief," she mumbled, attention back to the lake.

"They're not my favorite, but what's wrong with Tool?"

She turned back to him. "I listen to Taylor Swift. And Lizzo. And Sara Bareilles. Pink. Florence and the Machine. Miley Cyrus. Lady Gaga. Adele."

He held his hand in front of her face. "Stop."

She smiled. "I think you're understanding me."

Yeah, he was, and it was good to know she wasn't dogging him, she just wasn't a good-time girl.

At least, not the kind he was used to.

"I think if I let you take over the playlist, my friends would drown us both in the lake."

At that, he got her sweet laughter.

But then she pulled both shoulders forward and said, "I've never been much of a partier. But if you are, I don't want to be a wet blanket. Obviously, I don't want to be checking into spas once a week, something it seems won't happen if you work out of town a lot. But on an occasion, I can figure something out."

"Or seriously, you can join us."

"Well, for now," she looked again to the lake, "I need to do... other things."

He agreed.

He just didn't think those other things should be diving deeper into her head. He knew what a shitshow that could be. He'd lived it a long, fucking time.

And she needed that wisdom.

"I figured out a while ago that the best way to fuck him was to get as much out of life as I can, be as happy as I can, do the things I enjoy as much as I can, without my dad casting a pall over it, which is what the asshole would want." He bumped her thigh with his. "Just to say, you should think on that."

She was watching him closely when she replied, "It's good advice, Riggs, so I will."

"Right," he replied, turning his own attention to the lake because that look on her face made him want to kiss her, and that was not where this was going.

"And what I have to just say is you're not getting out of explaining why no one has been in this cabin for three years."

It wasn't three.

For all intents and purposes, it was fifteen.

And the same thing could be said for his house, but he wasn't going to tell her that either.

"Riggs?" she called.

Goddamn it.

"It's bullshit," he said.

"What's bullshit?" she asked.

He sucked in breath through his nose and looked back to her.

"Do you know who Roosevelt Whitaker is?"

Her brows knit. "Why is that name familiar?"

"Because he's half of the identical twin brother team of thriller writers known as Roosevelt Lincoln. The second half was Lincoln Whitaker."

"Yes." She nodded. "I've heard of them."

"You would. They were John Grisham, Dan Brown, Tom Clancy big. Seriously successful. Three movies were made of the first three books in their flagship series before shit went south."

Her interest was piqued, and she showed that to him with more than her question of, "What was the shit that went south?"

"Roosevelt lived here, year-round," he said, swinging out his glass of wine to indicate the cabin.

"Really?" she asked, her surprise as evident as her interest.

"Yup."

"It's amazing, but it doesn't seem very 'abode of a big-time author.'"

"True. But he was known as kind of a recluse. Lincoln Whitaker was the opposite. Friendly guy. Social. Everyone knew him even if he lived in Seattle. He'd come out here six months of the year to research and write with his brother. Eventually, he got married to a woman named Sarah, and they had kids. They bought a patch of land from Roosevelt and built my house."

"Ah," she murmured.

"Roosevelt owned the lake and all the land around it," Riggs explained. "Now I own the lake and all the land around it, except the three acres that go with this house."

"Ah," she repeated, but she did it with those wrinkles forming at the corners of her lips.

He ignored how cute that was and got back to the story.

"Sarah would come out with the kids. She'd also leave the kids with her parents and come out alone. She loved it here. Apparently, Lincoln swung both ways. He dug the outdoors, but he also was a city guy. So they kept houses both places. Word was, though, Sarah wanted to move out to Misted Pines full time."

"Right," she said when he paused.

Now, the hard part.

"So, one day, when Sarah was in Misted Pines, Lincoln was out fishing. He got a headache, came home, and found his wife gone. There was no note, and he got worried, because apparently, she didn't take off without telling him she was going or leaving a note. Since Sarah and Roosevelt were close, and Roosevelt lived here, before he started to panic, Lincoln came to see if she was here."

"Oh boy," she whispered, eyes glued to him like he was telling a ghost story, and she liked fake stories about things that went bump in the night, and she kept them glued to him as she took a sip of her wine.

"Yeah," he agreed. "When Lincoln hits this place, the door is open, which isn't unusual, and he checks it out. But she's not here either. Neither is Roosevelt. But he hears music coming from the stables."

That threw her. "The stables?"

He indicated the dark forest at the south side of her property. "There were stables there then. Roosevelt had horses. Three, precisely. His, Lincoln's and Sarah's."

"Mm," she hummed, her eyes dancing, because she'd figured out where this was going.

Though, she couldn't know how it would end.

"I think you've guessed that Lincoln went to the stables, and what he found, and that, honey, was Sarah and Roosevelt *in flagrante delicto* in the hayloft."

At that, she actually giggled.

It was girlie and hot as all fuck.

Riggs pushed the sight and sound of it into the back of his mind and moved forward with the story.

"What no one could guess was that Lincoln would walk back to his house, get his shotgun, return, shoot them both dead, let the horses loose, run the hose out to the stables and drench the earth and trees all around so a fire wouldn't spread, before he set that fire, burning the stables to the ground."

"Holy cow," she breathed.

"Yeah. It was also him who called the fire department and the cops. He was sitting on this porch when they showed, and he immediately turned himself in for double homicide to the first uniform he clapped eyes on."

"Whoa."

"Mm-hmm," Riggs agreed. "He served seven years in prison, got out, spent a couple days with his kids, then drank a whole bottle of arsenic, I guess as any good thriller writer would, leaving his and his brother's estate in disarray. This caused a bitter family feud that rages to this day between his kids, his extended family, his in-laws, and anyone else who wants to cast their hat into that ring. One of the reasons why no more films were made. No one can agree who owns the rights to the books. The brothers had only sold the first three books to be made into films, Lincoln had other things occupying his mind while he was in prison, so that franchise died when Sarah and Roosevelt did."

When Riggs stopped talking, Nadia pointed out the obvious, "That's a lot."

"Yup," Riggs agreed.

"And it explains the path to nowhere in my yard."

Christ, he loved that she called it her "yard."

It was, but it also wasn't.

"Yup," he repeated.

"It's a terrible story, but it was a long time ago, and the bad stuff didn't happen in the cabin, so I'm not sure I get why no one has rented this place because of it."

That part, he wasn't going to tell her, and he hoped the people of Misted Pines were kind enough to let that nonsense lie when it came to Nadia.

"Shit like that can cast a pall over a place."

"I guess so," she mumbled, but he could tell she wasn't buying it.

That, and considering he'd sucked back the dregs of his wine, gave him indication it was time to go.

He gave her that same indication by standing and teasing, "I think it's about that hour the princess needs to be alone, or her car will turn into a mouse or some shit like that."

It was a blow to watch her get up slowly, not hiding she was disappointed he was leaving.

He put his glass down on the coffee table.

She put hers down too and moved so he could get out.

But he stopped in front of her and warned, "Don't let that story give you shitty dreams."

"I think we both know humanity can get up to some messy stuff, Riggs," she replied.

He did, and it fucked with him to know she did too.

"Yeah," he muttered.

"I'm glad you brought your peace offering," she said.

Damn.

Sweet, but no longer shy, though still vulnerable.

Because of all that, Riggs couldn't stop himself from lifting his hand and wrapping his fingers around the soft skin of her neck. He could feel her pulse against his palm—delicate, alive, defenseless.

Damn.

He shouldn't do what he did next, and he knew that more when she tipped her head and closed her eyes as he bent his.

But he did it, touching his cheek to hers and rubbing his stubble there, because, bottom line, he was an animal, a male one, so it was instinct, and for the life of him, he couldn't stop himself from marking his territory.

When he pulled away, dropped his hand, and she opened her eyes, she didn't hide her disappointment that was all she was going to get either.

"Sleep well, Nadia. Thanks for dinner."

"You too, Riggs. Thanks for the wine."

He jutted out his chin and didn't delay.

He stepped off her porch and walked into the night.

Even so, the vision of Nadia standing in her sundress, illuminated by flower lights and lanterns, was burned in his brain in a way he knew he'd never forget it for the rest of his life.

EIGHT

Happy Place

Nadia

On my way into Misted Pines the next morning, the screen on my dashboard changed to indicate I had a text.

I glanced at it and saw it was from my best friend, Maribeth.

That was when I frowned.

Maribeth had been my bestie since we met in seventh grade.

Now, she was the closest thing to family I had left.

So, of course, she was the one who was most worried about me after all that happened with my mother, and my until-recently-unknown father. This after I still really hadn't gotten over losing Trevor and the way that happened.

She was also the one who was being the pushiest about getting an invite out to Misted Pines…ASAP.

This had exacerbated in the last couple of days, with her sending now five texts, all of them saying a version of, *Nothing's wrong. But call me. We need to talk.*

I hadn't ignored them (or, not all of them), but I'd let them sit and then given some excuse about being busy (when I was not).

I just didn't want to talk, because I was painfully aware I was

67

not doing what I'd sworn to her I was going to do when I moved all the way across the country and out from under her watchful eye.

Heal.

In other words, if anyone could see through my faking-it selfie malarky, it was Maribeth.

And I was deducing she wasn't falling for it.

Though, now, I did have something to do.

Because Riggs's wild party and subsequent peace offering had broken my rut.

And that morning, I'd jumped out of bed, determined to keep it that way.

Not to mention, what he'd said about living the best life you could being the best revenge stuck with me.

It was wise.

Although I wasn't ready to take it there, at the very least, I could stop moping around, drinking too much wine, eating too much food and watching too much television.

I might not start exploring my mental state, but I was going to start by exploring my environs.

I also had plans. Plans to pack a bag sometime soon, maybe around the time Riggs left town again (but after the way he'd firmly put us in the Friend Zone last night, for my mental health, I wasn't thinking about why that hurt so much, and instead was telling myself I felt safer when he was around). I was going to take a commuter flight back to Seattle and spend a few days there.

I'd only ever spent a night in Seattle, that being before I came to Misted Pines. Since I was this close, it would be a shame I didn't take the opportunity to look around.

I'd also cracked open my computer and looked up local spas, and apparently, there was an award-winning one in a place called the Pinetop Lodge.

So I was also going to set up a spa day.

With all of this on my horizon, I felt invigorated. Even though this wasn't about sorting out my head, it made me feel lighter than I'd felt in over four months.

I hit town, which I'd only driven through to get to the market, not paying much mind to it.

This time, I paid mind.

And I saw what I'd distractedly seen in the pictures from the minimal research I'd done about the place and while driving through it.

Taking it in, honestly, it looked like an army of Hollywood set designers had swarmed the place and built an image of smalltown Americana.

There were some discrepancies, of course, since it wasn't a movie location.

The huge mural on the side of what appeared to be the local coffeehouse, called Aromacobana, an obvious indictment about climate change, being one. Another was the local cinema that had one of those old-fashioned lit overhangs above it. But there wasn't a new release on that sign. It sported a double bill of "Walking Tall," with the letters JDB next to it, and "Walking Tall," with the letters DJ beside that.

But underneath those, it said, ONLY MRDRS IN THE BLDG FEST with next weekend's dates.

So, bizarrely, they were going to do an *Only Murders in the Building* festival next weekend.

Fantastic show.

But yes.

For a smalltown cinema, a newish TV show fest was kind of strange.

It was lunchtime, and in my car crawl through the town, I realized I was hungry when I saw what looked like a fifties diner that hadn't changed since that time. It was called the Double D.

I decided my next adventure was to stop and sample a local restaurant.

It was on the other side of the street, so to experience more of the town, I took a left turn, drove around a block, which was all modest, well-kept houses, then back to the main drag to find an open parking space among the ones that were angled toward the sidewalk.

It was only then, a creeping sense hit me, and it got worse as I located a spot a couple of doors beyond the Double D, got out and started to walk back to the diner.

I couldn't put my finger on it.

But maybe it was the near perfection of the place.

There was a flower shop, with stands of bright flowers out front, and a market with fruit and veggies on display. The sidewalks were clean and uncracked. The windows of the shops and restaurants were sparkling.

Main Street America in Misted Pines was maybe five or six blocks long, and the town itself wasn't that big, but it was bustling, and from what I could tell, you could spend hours there buying not only flowers and the orangest oranges I'd ever seen, but also attractive hiking gear, homemade candles and greeting cards, and everything you might need to decorate your home in *America!* for Memorial Day and the Fourth of July, because they had a dedicated holiday shop.

However, this place was very rural. I couldn't imagine how these shops could not only stay in business, but apparently thrive.

I read in my research that Misted Pines was a tourist destination due to the many outdoor activities on hand, so that could explain the bustle.

But there was a vibe.

No.

An *undercurrent* that was exhilarating, at the same time oddly disturbing.

It wasn't that eerie feeling I'd felt a couple of times at the lake. Although that was indisputably eerie, it also felt warm, welcoming.

No, this was bizarrely sinister. Telling you not all was as it seemed in Misted Pines.

This was my thought when I was about to hit the door to the Double D, and I saw her with several bags dangling from her fingers, walking my way.

I didn't know who she was, I only saw she was very pretty.

That was, I didn't know who she was until she smirked at me.

I'd never seen her face, but she'd obviously seen mine, not to mention, I'd seen that healthy brunette hair, and that smirk said, "You want him, but I've had him."

She was the woman who'd passed out on top of Riggs post-coital.

Courtney.

I felt the nasty sting of jealousy it wasn't mine to feel, but I simply dipped my chin to her and pushed through the door of the diner.

Once inside, I saw it was busy, perhaps not a surprise, because it was Saturday.

What was a surprise was that it was, indeed, a meticulously cared for diner straight out of the fifties, and this was to such an extent, I felt I'd stepped into that era.

I took a stool at the horseshoe shaped counter that dominated the middle of the space.

I'd barely sat down and grabbed a plastic-coated menu from its silver holder in front of me, when a woman in a knee-length diner dress, complete with little apron and cap, was in front of me.

And I was definitely feeling the strangeness when I saw her nametag said DOT.

Nothing wrong with the name, it was just that she looked younger than me, and it wasn't exactly modern.

I must have been staring at it, because she didn't greet me.

She said, "My real name is Maggie. But tips are better from the tourists if I go the extra mile."

This explanation caused a wave of relief to hit me, and I smiled at her.

"Get you something to drink while you look at the menu?" she asked.

"Do you have Perrier or San Pelligrino or something like that?" I asked in return.

She just stared at me.

I decided that was a no.

"Tea?" I requested.

"Iced and sweet?"

"Um, no, like chamomile or mint."

She stared at me again.

"Just water," I said.

She nodded, turned, filled a milky-turquoise plastic tumbler with water, which sloshed with the ice from the pitcher, and set it in front of me.

She then took off.

I looked at the menu and decided what I wanted immediately, so I put it back.

Dot/Maggie returned and raised one brow along with the pad in her hand with her pencil on it.

"Can I have a patty melt, without the onion, and instead of the fries, maybe a side salad?"

She sounded part offended, part astonished when she queried, "A patty melt without onions?"

I shrugged. "Onions aren't my favorite."

"I don't recommend our salad," she went on.

"Cottage cheese?" I tried.

She stared at me some more, mumbled, "I'll see what we got," then took off again.

Barely surviving that, I was rethinking my foray into Misted Pines, because it didn't seem big-city girls were super welcome, as I reached for my water and took a sip.

I nearly did a spit take when a woman hopped onto the stool beside me, and she did this by putting both her hands to it, swinging her legs out to the sides as she hefted herself over it, and landing on her behind on the seat.

I stared at her in shock because, not only was this a strange thing to do, she wasn't young, though she wasn't exactly old, but she was quite a bit older than me.

That wasn't the half of it, though.

She was wearing a white T-shirt with a red Santa face emblazoned on the front and the words SMELLS LIKE CHRISTMAS SPIRIT surrounding it. Dangling from her ears were lines of little gold, red and green bells, and on her head was a slouchy red beanie with an edge of white fur.

All of this, and it was mid-May.

"Hey," she greeted, sticking a hand toward me aggressively for a shake. "I'm Kimmy."

"Uh…hey," I replied, hesitantly taking her hand because I didn't want to seem rude.

She shook, and her grip had about ten pounds more power than it needed before she let me go and asked, "You the woman renting Dave and Brenda's place?"

That was quite a guess.

Unless, from what I'd learned from Riggs's visit, word was getting around about me.

Seemed I was going to learn quickly about life in a small town.

I didn't want to confirm I was, because I didn't know this person, however I had another year to get through in Misted Pines, and she might find out eventually.

So I was forced to say, "Yes."

To this, she whistled…*loud*. Loud enough, people turned to look.

I fidgeted uneasily on my stool.

"So, have you seen him?" she asked.

I figured she was asking about Riggs, since any red-blooded woman would want to know that. But since I wasn't sure, I asked, "Seen who?"

"The ghost of Roosevelt Whitaker."

I felt my throat close.

Kimmy's sure didn't.

"I think all the others got it wrong. It isn't ole Rosie who's haunting the joint," she declared. "I mean, the man was messing around with his brother's wife. His *twin* brother's wife. He knew he was doing his brother dirty. I figure he went into that forever good-night and stayed there because he knew he did wrong. I knew 'em, and seemed to me, those two men were *tight*. But a woman can hold a mean grudge."

"Um…"

"Everyone says she married the wrong brother, including me. Plain as day. Thick as thieves, Sarah and Roosevelt were. How Lincoln didn't see it, no one knows. Damn fool, if you ask me. Still, they shoulda come clean rather than carry on behind his back."

"Uh…"

"But that doesn't negate the fact she was his *wife* and the *mother of his children*, and he blew a huge hole in her chest instead of just blowing his stack. They say she was happy there. Happiest times she had was when she was at that cabin with her true love, even if the old ball and chain was around. So I say, she doesn't want anyone else there. She wants it all to herself. That's why she chases everyone off."

Chases everyone off.

And now I knew why no one had been at the cutest cabin west of the Mississippi (and possibly east of it) for three years.

"Kimmy," Dot greeted as she set a turquoise tumbler of some brown colored pop in front of her. "What's it gonna be today?"

"Reuban, Mags, thanks," Kimmy said, picking up the tumbler and sucking back a quarter of it in one draw.

I was uncertain she should have any more caffeine.

Dot/Maggie strolled away, and Kimmy turned back to me.

"Stick it out, girl. Things were looking dire, so Dave wanted to Airbnb the joint, but Lord knows, with all the hassle MP has been through the last few years, we don't need more strangers traipsing through here." She jerked a thumb at herself. "I'm not complaining, though I'd want other circumstances that brought it on. Fresh blood for my shop. I own the holiday store," she explained.

"You don't say," I mumbled.

She went directly into her spiel. "Yeah. Got one section, all Christmas all the time. But the rest of the store, I switch it out. Spring. Summer. Winter. Fall. Halloween. Thanksgiving. Easter. St. Patrick's Day. Fourth of July. The whole shebang."

"I saw that when I walked by your shop," I told her.

"You should come in," she invited. "Everyone could use an American flag, year-round, and I got every size you could need."

Actually, a flag would look good at the front of the cabin.

"I'll think on that."

"Anyway," she said over me finishing the word "that." "Brenda declared she put too much work in the place to have people going in and out, breaking her glasses, staining her toss pillows, not giving two bits because it's a vacation rental. She wanted a long-timer. So you gotta dig in. Ole Rosie, or Sarah, whichever one it is, never hurt anyone. They just moved some rocks around or scratched the windows…"

Scratched the windows?

My heartrate spiked.

Kimmy jabbed a finger at me. "…and that right there is why I think it's Sarah. Somehow, her spirit can't get inside. The stables are gone, which…*obviously*…was their happy place. That cabin was her other happy place. So that's my theory."

She then sucked back more pop.

I sipped my water to alleviate my suddenly dry mouth.

"So, one of them visit?" she pushed me.

"No," I lied, but I did it hoping I wasn't lying.

She seemed disappointed.

She explained this—*insanely*—by sharing, "Got no more serial killers hitting MP, never thought I'd say this, but things are kinda getting boring. But what I know is, business sure is dropping off."

"Serial killers?" I croaked.

She narrowed her eyes on me. "Yeah. Don't you know?"

"Um…"

"Damn, woman, how'd it escape you?"

I was wondering that myself, and I didn't even know what she was talking about. I just knew it was more of, from my brief experience, her general *not good*.

That said, I was an Antonov. My great-grandfather garnered media attention because of his backstory, and his ever-increasing wealth and tenacious pursuit of more. My grandmother and grandfather did the same, also because of their wealth, but Grandma was already famous before she even met my *dedulya*. Their tragic story was dredged up constantly over the years simply because it was tragic, and people loved a good tragedy.

Trevor and I had earned our own mentions, and they weren't minor, ditto the tragedy.

Then, obviously, there was the most recent calamity that had befallen the Antonov line.

I'd been trained by my mother and grandfather since I was young to ignore the media as much as I could, and truth told, more recently, I did it because they seemed dedicated less to the act of informing the public and more to dividing it.

I scanned the *Chicago Tribune*'s daily e-newsletter to keep on top of current events, rarely clicking on any stories, and definitely not clicking on anything about serial killers.

I liked a good story, but I got mine from books.

Morbid, real-life stories weren't my thing.

Sure, one could say I was fascinated when Riggs told me about the sordid tale of the Whitakers last night, but I was living in their cabin.

And he was Riggs. He had an amazing voice that was deep and managed the miracle of being smooth and rough at the same time. So I could listen with fascination to anything he said, even if he was reciting his grocery list.

But...serial killers?

Plural?

Kimmy shimmied on her seat, settling in, and stated, "First, there was Ray Andrews. He wasn't a serial killer so much as a psychopath. Or a sociopath. I get those two mixed up. Anyway, he just wanted Cade Bohannan's attention. And he sure got it, along with a life sentence. Just wished he didn't kill those two girls before he got it. I mean, little Alice was only eight years old."

Eight years old?

Lord.

Unfortunately, Kimmy kept talking.

"Then there were those two numnuts, Ezra and Carrie, who murdered poor Brittanie out at the Good Times Motel. It's The Blue Mountain now. It's cute. So cute, I'd consider a stay-cay there. It needed fixing up, and Britt dying flushed out the Crystal Killer. Both good things, but again, I wouldn't want Brittanie dying in such an ugly way for us to get a nicer motel in town. Though, her sacrifice probably saved a lot of other girls, 'cause Richard Sandusky wasn't going to stop."

I'd heard of Richard Sandusky aka the Crystal Killer. I'd also heard he'd been caught. I even knew it happened in Washington State.

I hadn't heard it had anything to do with Misted Pines.

Boy, I hadn't done enough research before I'd moved.

And Riggs sure left a lot out when he was telling his story last night.

A lot.

"But that was a while ago," Kimmy continued. "And don't get me wrong. I don't want more of our girls getting dead. But you can't deny, it made things interesting and brought in the lookie-loos. Now, even the coven has stopped getting new members."

Dot/Maggie was now putting my plate in front of me.

I stared at her, probably like prey stuck in a predator's mouth.

I knew this was true when her eyes went from me, to Kimmy, back to me. She gave a short shake of her head, which wasn't much movement, but it spoke volumes, and those volumes said not to put much stock in what Kimmy said.

But still.

Dot/Maggie moved away, and now that I was in for a penny against my will, I might as well go for the pound.

So I asked, "Coven?"

She was finishing the last of her drink, but she barely swallowed when she said, "Yeah. The women wronged. I don't recommend watching the videos," she advised. "I'll just say, they got a knack for revenge that's original, if entirely pornographic."

Eek!

She went on, "But that whole thing going viral brought in like-minded ladies, and they all took over a subdivision. They don't cause any problems, though. Least, not after they expelled Ellen from their numbers after the crap she pulled at the town meeting."

I reached for one half of my sliced patty melt, noting that Dot/Maggie had managed to dredge up a small bowl of cut cantaloupe and honeydew, the first I liked okay, the second I didn't, but A for effort.

And I did this having hit my limit.

Yes, I needed to do the work I clearly didn't do in learning more about where I'd decided to land to sort my head out.

And yes, there were some words I needed to have with Riggs, because we'd spent hours together last night in what more and more seemed to turn into an impromptu date, but in the end he made it clear it absolutely wasn't (which hurt enormously, and thus was incredibly disappointing, at the same time I was glad he obviously wasn't attracted to me, because even though it sounded like he was out of town a lot, I had enough going on, I didn't need an entanglement with my neighbor that might turn awkward).

And he hadn't shared any of this.

And he should have, mostly because I'd asked.

Therefore, I urged Kimmy, "Tell me about your shop. Do you carry those beanies there?"

She straightened and declared, "Sure do. After lunch, we'll walk over, and I'll show you."

I did not want to own a fur-trimmed beanie that looked like a riff on a Santa hat.

I did want her to stop talking about dead girls, serial killers, revenge porn and ghosts that might or might not haunt the cabin I was living in.

So as she launched into the vision behind her patriotic summer campaign, I listened and adjusted my plans for that day.

Those being, after buying a Santa beanie I'd never wear, I was going to sit in my car, get on my phone and learn about Misted Pines.

Belatedly.

But necessarily.

And then I was going to go have a chat with Doc Riggs.

NINE

Bermuda Triangle

Nadia

Ibraked beside Riggs's big, shiny, fancy truck in his driveway on a dramatic skid of gravel.

I did this because I'd just finished buying a Santa beanie, an American Flag, and the apparatus to fly it from a post on my front porch.

And I'd also spent the last hour and a half reading about Ray Andrews, Richard Sandusky, Ezra Corbin, Carrie Molnar, the Misted Pines "Coven" and their reason for forming.

Not to mention not one, not two, but *three* articles in the local paper that told tales of the Haunting of Whitaker Lake, which shared the heretofore unknown knowledge that it hadn't been only three years since someone lived in my cabin.

It had been fifteen.

In fact, the judge-appointed, but bitterly disputed trust that was managing the Whitaker brothers' estates had made the decision to sell off the lake and its properties because they'd been sitting mostly derelict. This was because no one would stay in either of them, including Riggs's house, for more than a few weeks. This due to the unexplained, but highly creepy stuff that happened there.

As such, I jumped out of my car, raring for another go-round with Riggs, because, yes, perhaps I should have looked into things more before I leaped.

But first, who knew you had to research a small town for their serial killer history, and second, research the cabin you were considering renting for news of recent hauntings.

He also should have told me.

I was marching toward his house when Riggs all but burst out of the front door in a full-on jog, coming at me.

This surprising circumstance, of course, made me halt.

"Jesus, Nadia," he said when he got to me and grabbed my upper arms. "You okay?"

He knew my state of mind, for sure, considering his history, and his knowledge of mine. And it was sweet, his obvious concern at me skidding to a dramatic stop in his driveway.

He also knew my cabin was possibly *haunted*.

So there was that.

"No, Riggs, I'm not okay!" I yelled. "I just got back from lunch at the local diner where I got an earful from a shopkeeper who told me my cabin was haunted! Why didn't you—?"

I wasn't able to finish that because Riggs looked over my head, gritted out, "Kimmy," let my arms go but grabbed my hand and dragged me toward the front door, doing this yanking his phone out of his back pocket.

I was so astonished by this reaction, I didn't think to say anything until we were inside. And then I couldn't say anything because he was hauling me down into his living room, then up, up and *up* into his kitchen.

Jeez. If this place was wild from the outside, it was wilder inside.

One could say it wasn't too much of a shocker Lincoln Whitaker blew his brother and wife away, if the chaotic design of his house reflected his mental state.

And then I couldn't say anything because I was confronted with an eight or nine-year-old mini-Riggs sitting at the counter in the kitchen eating a peanut butter and jelly sandwich.

His mouth full of sandwich, his silvery-blue eyes looked to me, his dad's hand in mine, then back to me.

I stopped still.

Riggs let my hand go.

"Ledger, this is our new neighbor, Nadia. Nadia, this is my boy, Ledger," Riggs introduced, then said, "Yeah, it's me, Kimmy. What the fuck?"

I looked to him to see he had his phone to his ear.

New priority task at hand, I returned my attention to his son and greeted, "Hey, Ledger."

He swallowed and said, "Hey."

We both turned to Riggs when he started growling.

"No, you didn't *need* to tell her," Riggs said, paused, then, "And no, I wasn't going to say anything because it's all bullshit. Why people are still talking about that crap, I do not know."

"Let me guess," Ledger began. "Kimmy told you the lake is haunted."

Seemed Kimmy might have a bit of a reputation.

"Yes," I replied.

He did a kid shrug, took a bite, chewed a couple of times, but with mouth still full, he said, "This place was supposed to be haunted too, but Dad's been here years, and nothing."

Well, I'd been at my place for weeks, and the first night, someone was scratching at the windows.

I didn't tell Ledger that.

I said, "Good to know."

We both looked back to Riggs when he irately announced, "I don't care about Hoover or Kennedy or the fuckin' Bermuda Triangle, and hear me, Kimmy, neither does Nadia. Lay *the fuck* off."

With that, he took his phone from his ear, hit it with his thumb and tossed it with a clatter to the counter.

"Jesus. Kimmy," he muttered, still irritable, if his tone and the laser beams he was trying to shoot out of his eyes to annihilate his phone, and Kimmy through it, were anything to go by.

"Can I talk to you?" I asked, and shifted my attention back to Ledger, "No offense, but I need a few words with your dad alone."

"Bet," he replied.

Cool is as cool was, the father and son version.

I went to Riggs and grabbed his hand, intent to walk him out the front door, but he had other ideas.

He twisted his hand from mine, curled an arm around my waist, and part guided, part shuffled me around the corner of the kitchen counter that had a clear view of the lake through windows across a landing big enough to waltz in. From there, he pulled me into a shadowy recess that I saw led to a winding staircase made into a wide column paneled with dark wood.

Whoa.

It was weird and gorgeous all at once.

We climbed one floor to another landing, hooked a left rather than going down a long hall that led to some rooms, and almost immediately entered another wood-paneled alcove winding staircase, and we went up that.

We came out directly into a bedroom made almost entirely of windows. It had a king-size bed covered in cobalt-blue sheets with a matching comforter (unmade and no toss pillows or euros to be found). The room also had a tan leather club chair that sported an exploding duffle bag and a variety of button downs, T-shirts and jeans of various fading thrown over it, to the point that I knew the chair was tan leather only by a bit of the arm showing through.

There were attractive nightstands with equally attractive lamps on top, both all but covered with books, coins, crushed receipts, and dual smatterings of new and opened condom packets (of course).

There was further a gorgeous low bureau that was so long and fit so well against the half wall below the windows, that it looked made for the space.

And there was a stone fireplace cutting through the windows, above which was a flat screen TV.

I had no idea why I was, but I was in Riggs's bedroom.

I felt a shiver much like the one I'd felt when he'd rubbed his whiskers on my cheek the night before, just as pleasant and promising, but not as strong.

I turned to him.

"Uh…" I didn't quite begin, so stunned was I at my current location.

"Kimmy's a nut. She knows who killed Kennedy, she thinks, and she'll tell anyone in her vicinity. Not anyone who *asks*, mind. Anyone in her vicinity. She also knows where Hoffa is buried, and who put him there. And she's got some wild-ass theory about the link between Roswell and the Bermuda Triangle that you don't want to hear. In short, Nadia, she's good people, a good mom, a good grandma, but she's still halfway around the bend, and she gets off on taking people there with her."

"The first night at the cabin, there was scratching at the window."

I watched in fascinated horror as Riggs's long body went completely still.

I didn't have time for him to go still, mostly because it *freaked me out*.

"Why didn't you tell me any of this last night?" I asked.

He came unstuck and answered, "Because I don't believe the stories, seeing as there's no such thing as ghosts. And no, before you ask, I wasn't ever going to tell you, not only because I think it's shit, because I know it is. The whole lake was supposed to be haunted, but I've lived here for a while, and nothing. Are you sure you heard scratching on your window?"

"I don't know," I admitted. "It might have been a tree. But I checked, and that doesn't seem possible. But I've lived my whole life in lakefront properties, that lake being Lake Michigan, and those properties being in Chicago proper. Thus, I don't know nature living."

He put his hands to my arms again, but this time to rub them soothingly.

And one could say, Riggs's sweet touch could sooth.

It also did other things. I just ignored those things.

"I'll have a look," he promised. "But it was probably nothing, Nadia, because, again, ghosts don't exist. Kimmy's harmless and mostly hilarious, unless you're not in the state of mind to hear her stories. And the reason I didn't tell you and didn't want you to know, full stop, is that I figured you aren't in the right frame of mind."

He wasn't wrong about that.

And it was kind, how he didn't share because he was looking out for me.

I didn't tell him how I'd foolishly moved to what appeared to be a serial killer and scorned woman mecca before I knew it was either.

Instead, I shifted our conversation to something else that was pressing.

"Ledger?"

He smiled. It was bold and white and proud and *gorgeous*.

"Yeah," he said, dropping his hands from my arms and taking a step back. "I didn't get around to that last night either. But I bought two of those bottles from my bud, so I meant to, eventually."

"He's a mini Riggs."

The smile got bolder and prouder. "He is."

"How old is he?"

"Nine."

"Ledger is a cool name," I told him.

"Agreed," he replied, but said no more, and I didn't get the chance to ask him why we were chatting in his bedroom and not out by my car, because we were joined by the person we were talking about.

He was holding out his dad's phone. "Dad, your phone was ringing. The screen said it's Lucille."

"Thanks, buddy," Riggs murmured, and with a dip of his chin to me, he stepped to a window moving his thumbs over the screen, and then he put it to his ear and his eyes to the view.

Ledger looked to me. "You fish?"

I shook my head. "No."

"Kayak?"

More shaking of my head. "No."

"Run trails?"

"Only when chased by a ghost."

The kid cracked a smile.

We both whirled to Riggs with the way he whispered, "*Fuck*."

"Is everything okay?" I asked a question I knew was stupid considering the look on his face.

"I need to ask a favor," he replied urgently.

The urgency got me, and I said softly, "Anything."

"I'm gonna call Ledger's gramme and ask her to come look after him. But she probably won't be able to get here for at least half an hour. I know you two just met." He glanced at Ledger. "Sorry, buddy." He came back to me. "But can you look after him until she gets here? I gotta get to the hospital."

"Why?" Ledger asked, a little-kid thread of alarm snaking through that syllable, and my heart lurched at hearing it.

"Something's happened to Uncle Bubs," Riggs told him.

Ledger went pale, so obviously "Uncle Bubs" meant something to him, and he definitely meant something to Riggs.

Riggs approached his son and wrapped his fingers around his boy's shoulder. "I don't know what's happening. But I gotta go. I'll let you know what I know as soon as I find out."

"'Kay, Dad."

Riggs looked to me.

"We're good. Go," I urged.

At that, Riggs shocked the breath out of me when he came right to me, wrapped his hand around the back of my head and bent to kiss my forehead.

As fast as that happened, he did the same to Ledger.

Then he vanished into the murky alcove staircase.

I looked to his son who was staring after his dad.

Then I went to his son and touched his shoulder.

He looked up at me.

"Finish your sandwich?"

He nodded.

"Wanna see a haunted cabin?"

He smiled, not entirely committed to it, but it was there.

"Sure," he replied.

"Righty ho, let's go so we can be back before your grandmother gets here."

He nodded and led the way.

I followed.

TEN

Keep Going

Nadia

It was late-ish, and I was in the reading nook with a cup of tea and a book I wasn't reading because I was thinking about Abigail Riggs, Ledger's grandmother and Rigg's mom.

She was not what I expected, not any of the things that could be.

She wasn't broken down by having an abusive husband who didn't leave her alone even after she left their marriage. She wasn't a hardened, bitter woman who endured the same. She also wasn't a no-nonsense, outdoorsy type who looked like she could chop her own wood and definitely tended her own garden and canned her own tomatoes.

No, she was trim, though not slim, and wore nice jeans and a stark-white blouse that had some embroidery in it and looked part-prairie, part-southwest. Her jeans had a cool, thin, tooled belt with a lovely silver buckle threaded through the loops.

And silver, for Abigail, was a theme, since she had a lot of it around her neck, her wrists, on her fingers and at her ears.

She was also very pretty, with great skin that did not say she had a thirty-eight-year-old son and nine-year-old grandson.

And she was a redhead. It wasn't flaming and brazen, or strawberry and demure, but auburn and probably dyed, but it didn't look it, and I suspected it had been her natural color before time took it away.

She was also quiet, and looked at me in a thoughtful and kind way that told me on his drive to the hospital, Riggs had shared a few things, and although he and I being in the Friend Zone was one of them (because she didn't look me over), I knew other things were shared besides.

She was grateful I'd stepped up for Ledger, and before she took Ledger with her, she asked if I might want to get a coffee with her someday soon.

I agreed.

We exchanged numbers.

And that was that.

It made me wonder what Riggs's sister was like, because with a dad like he described, and the good-time, rough and ready, big-truck driving, part-time biker guy vibe Riggs gave off, Abigail Riggs was a surprise, so I wondered if the sister was the same.

This was on my mind when I heard it.

A noise coming from outside like two stones being cracked together.

I sat motionless, my eyes aimed at the hall to the back door. A door I could not see from where I sat.

I'd lit the fairy lights and the lanterns out there (when I'd found the AC remotes, I discovered the lanterns had remotes too). Same with the front lanterns, which were now also lit. I lit them all every night, because they were pretty, but also because they cut away the dark that pressed at the windows when night fell, something I wasn't yet used to.

The sound came again. It was louder, though didn't seem closer.

What it did seem like, was it was coming from the south side, or the trail that led to stables that had been burned to the ground fifteen years ago.

Okay, ghosts did not exist.

But I'd seen a variety of wildlife, in fact, a lot of it. Rabbits, squirrels, deer, even what I suspected was an elk. They were all over the place, and clearly not used to, nor overly fussed by, me taking over Weaver Cabin, because they didn't shy away when I wasn't outside, and even when I was out on the pier.

A deer, or an elk, could easily dislodge a stone with one of their hooves.

Couldn't they?

The sound came again, three times, in quick succession, and those noises sounded like they were getting closer.

For the second time that day, my heart rate spiked, and my mouth went dry while that prickling sensation covered my skin before I heard a strange, whispering noise I couldn't place at all, and it faded into the distance.

And as I sat there for an unknown amount of time listening hard, I jumped nearly out of my skin when a sharp rap sounded on the screen door.

I set the book aside, got up and moved just enough so I could look down the hall.

I saw Riggs standing at the back door.

When he spied me, he held up a bottle of wine identical to the one he'd had last night, and called, "This time, a thank you gift."

I moved that way, pulled the hook lock out of its holder and pushed the door open slightly.

Riggs pulled it open the rest of the way, and my invitation to come inside was me walking to the kitchen.

He followed and put the wine down on the kitchen counter while I examined his face.

I didn't have to examine very long before I said quietly, "It's not good."

"No," he confirmed. "It's not good. My friend, Bubbles, was beat to shit. So bad, he took so many blows to the head, they had to induce a coma in an effort to control the brain swelling."

"Oh, Riggs," I whispered.

He nudged the wine and said, "He's the one who sold me this.

He owns The Hole. Or that's what locals call it. Officially, it's The Black Hole, a bar just out of town. One of his staff came in this morning, found him unconscious in the storeroom. He went in and out of consciousness until they induced, but he was so messed up, they couldn't get much out of him. They don't know what happened, when it happened, why it happened or who did it. But with Bubbles, the list of culprits could be a mile long."

"Do you want me to open the wine?" I offered.

"You got anything stiffer?" he asked.

"I could make you a gin martini."

"Done."

I set about doing that while asking, "Where's Ledger?"

"He's staying with Mom tonight."

"Right," I said, putting down the martini shaker and gin and heading to the fridge.

"His zygomatic bone was shattered, three ribs fractured, one punctured a lung," Riggs went on with the litany of trauma his friend endured. "He took some hefty shots to his kidneys and is generally bruised and battered everywhere. He also has a broken wrist, but the way that's fractured, they think it happened when he fell on it."

"Oh my God, I'm so sorry," I said as I grabbed a martini glass.

"Hup."

At this strange noise from him, I looked over my shoulder to see Riggs shaking his head.

For a second, I was confused.

Then I realized hyper masculine, good-time, rough and ready, big-truck driving, part-time biker guys didn't drink out of martini glasses.

I put it down and showed him a pink glass that could be used as an old-fashioned, but it had a bulbous bee formed from the glass sticking out the side.

"This is your other choice," I told him.

He shook his head again and said, "Martini."

As I suspected.

I grabbed it and went back to the counter asking, "Olive or lemon twist?"

"Honey," was his only reply.

Okay, hyper masculine, good-time, rough and ready, big-truck driving, part-time biker guys also didn't do "sissy" things like olives and twists.

"Gotcha," I mumbled and set about making the drink.

When I poured it through the strainer (thank you, Misted Pines postman and Williams Sonoma online store) and handed it to him, I watched in stunned silence as he downed it in one.

He then handed the glass to back to me.

"Again?" I asked with no small amount of surprise.

"Yup," he answered.

I used the same ice and set him up again.

That time, he just took a sip.

When he was done, he set the glass to the counter, his fingers still to the stem, and said, "Fuck, Nadia, should have known Bubbles being a mostly fuckup would catch up with him."

"I don't know what to say," I admitted.

"Nothing to say," he replied.

"You wanna hang for a while?" I offered.

"Am I gonna drink alone?" he asked.

"I'll be there with you, but I'm not imbibing tonight. Until our spat and your peace offering, I was wallowing, and a lot of that was accompanied by a bottle of wine, so I need a break."

"Hear you." He cocked his head. "Outside?"

I nodded mine.

He nabbed his glass and led, I followed, and we resumed the positions we had last night, with our feet up on the coffee table.

I liked sitting there with him, but it wasn't as nice as last night, when there seemed a promise that it would go somewhere different, a promise I knew now wasn't going to lead to fruition.

It still felt good.

He took another sip of his martini, and I watched, noting that the glass truly wasn't him at all, but it was still appealing, watching him drink from it.

Who was I kidding?

Nearly everything about Riggs was appealing. Yes, Lord help me, even when he was being a dick.

He turned his head, caught my eyes and stated, "Angelica."

"What?"

"Ledger's mom."

It seemed he didn't want to talk about this Bubbles person anymore, and I understood why.

Anyway, I was interested in Angelica because I was interested in Riggs.

Dang.

"Right. Angelica. Talk to me," I prompted.

I felt relief when his lips twitched with genuine amusement at my words, then he looked to the lake and said, "Actually met her at The Hole. One-night stand that came back about six weeks later telling me she was pregnant, and she wanted to keep it. Apparently, the condom broke."

The way he said the last four words held more meaning, so I murmured, "Oh boy."

He looked to me. "Yeah. I was flipped out. I had no intention of becoming a dad, definitely not a baby daddy. I was twenty-nine years old and not a domesticated guy."

"*Quelle surprise*," I teased.

That got me a genuine smile before he continued, "Also wasn't sure, with Angelica being Angelica, and that's not throwing shade, you'll get me as the story goes along, that it was mine. But I helped out through the pregnancy, and I got a DNA test as soon as I could after Ledger was born, but I didn't really need it. He looked just like me when I was a baby."

"As he does now," I remarked.

"Yeah," he agreed, and his attention went back to the lake. He let out a big breath and carried on, "But DNA came back as expected, and Angelica took advantage of me falling instantly in love with my kid and talked me into giving it a go. She pushed for marriage. She said it was for Ledger's sake, but with her, I wasn't going to make anything legal unless I knew we could hack it."

Smart decision.

"Me being me," he carried on, "and her being her, we couldn't hack it. Us being a thing ended about five months into Ledger's life, and those were not good months. I moved into the extra bedroom and didn't move out until he was four years old, mostly for selfish reasons. I didn't want to miss anything. It also didn't totally suck, because she's Angelica, but she's a good mom, and those years were a lot easier on both of us because we had each other's backs. So it wasn't great, but it worked in a way for both of us. More importantly, it worked for Ledger."

"I can see that," I noted.

He hesitated a moment before he asked, "Want kids?"

"I used to."

Another hesitation before he suggested, "How 'bout we hit that when you're not taking a break from alcohol."

"Good call," I replied.

"So," he thankfully took us off that subject and went back to our other one, "I moved out, and that's when the fun began."

"I'm sensing facetiousness," I remarked.

"You sense correctly," he affirmed.

"Oh boy," I repeated.

He did a short head shake with another lip twitch and kept talking.

"It worked for Angelica when I was around, because Angelica could have a part-time job, and even though she loved our boy and looked after him, without me in her bed, she had needs she needed to see to. I got it. Same went for me. The thing was, once I was gone, I was all in to take care of my boy. I made more than her and I wasn't about to see him suffer when he was with her. But I wasn't about to make it so she could work sixteen hours a week, take care of our kid some of the time, then pawn him off on her mom and sister, my mom and sister, or some babysitter, and party the rest of the time on my dime."

"As you shouldn't," I stated firmly.

He gave me a small grateful smile at my support and shared, "Fortunately, a judge saw it the same way. She could earn. We never married. We weren't a couple but for a few months, and we were only for Ledger. She was given a choice. Appropriate child support payments with her contributing financially to the rearing of our son, or she could give up custody and I'd take the full financial burden of raising our boy. She didn't like that last choice, so she took the first one."

Another hesitation, before he went back to it.

"Then another condom broke."

I had begun staring idly at our feet on the coffee table while listening to him, but that brought my gaze to his face.

"No." I drew that word out.

"Yeah," he replied. "Another guy who isn't rolling in it, but he makes real good money. Know the guy, not well, but he's been around, and I've seen him and met him in that time. Though, he was not happy with the surprise of impending fatherhood, and not in a flipped-out way. He straight up wanted nothing to do with it."

"Shit," I whispered while he took another sip of his martini.

"Yeah," he repeated. "He told her to get rid of it. She didn't. He didn't support her while she was pregnant and demanded an immediate DNA test when the baby was born. Kid was his, only then did he kick in. Unless you're a total asshole, you can't have a kid and not fall for that kid, and he's not a total asshole, so he fell for the kid. She tried the same thing to get him to help her live free and breezy, including pushing marriage. He had less patience with it than I did, and I had zero patience."

I pressed my lips tightly together.

"Yeah," he said once again. "Things were rough for Angelica for a while, and I can't say I'm thrilled that Ledger has a little brother, who he adores, but he's only around every other week. Nor am I thrilled that Angelica and her second baby daddy get into it a lot, and sometimes, Ledger sees or hears that shit. But I can't deny, she really does love her kids, and this guy, his name is Storm, truly isn't an asshole, and he likes Ledge. So, after Ledge told me what shit was going down, I had a word with Storm to share I wasn't a fan of him hanging his shit with Angelica on my son, and he promised to pick his times so Ledger and his little brother Viggo didn't see it."

"First," I stated, and tried not to sound judgy, but failed. "*Storm?*"

Riggs grinned. "It's a nickname. Like Doc was before I changed it. His real name is James. Lots of talk around how he got his nickname. Some say it's because he can be broody. Others, mostly women, say it's about the color of his eyes, which to me are gray, like mine."

Riggs's were not stormy. Not at all.

Enough about Storm.

"Have things evened out?" I asked.

He nodded and took another sip.

"Do you think she got pregnant on purpose?"

His expression turned thoughtful, and he said, "With Storm, no clue. With me, I come prepared." He gave me a wolfish grin. "And I'm active."

I did an eye roll and replied, "I noticed."

"So I'm sure to keep that covered and it's never happened before or since," he carried on. "Not sure, with how it went down between us, how she'd have managed it. Though, the coincidence of it happening twice gives a man pause."

It gave a woman pause too, that woman being me.

"Do you think she's going to do it again?" I asked.

This time, he shook his head. "I think Angelica learned her lesson when she didn't have someone around to help with diapers and grocery shopping and baths and midnight feedings, and she also had a six-year-old to look after. But who knows? She's also still at The Hole, The Halfway Inn and The Squirrel's Nest a lot. So maybe not."

"How do you manage with being away so much?" I asked, then quickly added. "It's not my business, so—"

Riggs cut me off. "Nadia, we're becoming friends, am I right?"

He was right, and I was glad to have a friend close, especially one like Riggs, who would rush out of his house because he was worried I was showing there upset about something.

But there was another part of me that felt something else.

I tamped that down and answered, "You're very right."

"So, you can ask. And the answer is, once I started taking jobs out of town, I paid her more. Not enough she can cut back hours or some stupid shit like that, but enough to make absolutely certain Ledger doesn't do without when I'm gone. And we have a deal. I see him as much as I can see him, and that means, for the most part, he comes and stays with me when I'm home. Also, on my Sunday's off, no matter where I am, I drive back to MP, even if I can only spend an hour or two with him. That way, he knows his old man will bust his hump to have time with him, so he knows, every week, his dad is thinking about him through that week. And when I get back, he's mine."

"That's very sweet."

"That's being a dad."

That hit me, *hard*, and I could see from the gentle look on his face he felt it for me, and considering his history, *with* me, and this was why he instantly went on.

"Fortunately, I left when he was four, too early for him to remember his mom and dad living together, which was why I picked that age to leave. But it was also when he was starting to put things together, so his whole life is being shuttled back and forth. It's what he knows. It's *all* he knows."

"Does that bother you?"

"Knowing him now, it's impossible to believe I had these thoughts, but it can't be denied, I did. I didn't want a kid. Which means I didn't want him. That's history, and maybe one day when he's a grown man he'll consider it, put it together, but put himself in my shoes and know where my head was at. By then, I hope like fuck I put in the work that'll show I couldn't imagine life without him, and I love him to my soul, so he'll get it, and it won't wound him. All that said, warning, I'm gonna get crass."

I nodded for him to go on.

He went on.

"His mother is a knockout, not as gorgeous as you, but she's a fine-looking woman, but she was only a decent lay. I had no intention of going back for more, because what I got wasn't all that good. So I definitely had no intention of having a relationship with her.

This means it is what it is. Life is like that. Shit happens, you deal the best you can trying not to harm anyone in the process, and no matter what it throws at you, you keep going."

"You keep going," I whispered, focusing on that rather than his *not as gorgeous as you* comment.

And it was a good thing to focus on.

More wisdom from Doc Riggs.

"Yeah," he whispered back.

"You've got a great kid," I told him.

"I know. What did you two do?"

"I showed him the cabin."

He threw back more martini before he said, "He's been here before."

"I know. That's how I know he's a great kid. He humored me even though we both knew he'd been here before."

Riggs grinned.

I enjoyed it in the way I could, and tucked the way I couldn't somewhere I hoped it never escaped, because I knew, the more I got to know this man, the more power it would have to hurt me.

"I also like your mom," I shared.

"She's awesome," he muttered.

"Is your sister like her, or you?"

Another cock of his head, this one curious, when he asked, "What am I like?"

"A really great guy, but one who doesn't wear crisply ironed, blemish-less white, cotton prairie shirts, but instead, lives in a house that it's good no one in it is living with a disability, and it's as weird as it is frightening and fantastic."

He let out a bark of laughter.

There it was.

His friend had been assaulted by an unknown attacker, and it only took two martinis, some history sharing and me to crack a lame joke to get him to laugh.

Good.

"My sister, Kate, is like Kate," he answered after he stopped laughing. "She's the branch manager of a bank in Seattle. She moved about a year and a half ago when her partner got a promotion and had to head that way."

"Right."

"We miss her. Them. Her man is a good man, and they've been together since high school. She isn't far, but it also isn't easy to fit the trip into life."

"I bet."

His gaze became searching. "You okay about the bullshit Kimmy landed on you?"

"I heard some stones cracking together, maybe a couple of minutes before you showed."

His brows drew together ominously. "Where? Out here?"

I pointed in the direction of where the stables used to be.

Then I had to shift my legs unexpectedly because he instantly got up, putting down his glass and pulling out his phone to engage the flashlight.

I got up as he jogged down the steps, and with the light aimed to the ground, he moved in the direction of the derelict trail that used to lead to the stables.

"You come this way at all?" he asked, having stopped with his light still to the ground.

I went from house to pier and back. I hadn't explored. Something else I intended to do, and soon. I hadn't even put out the hammock.

"No," I called back. "Are there footprints?"

"No."

Well, that was a relief.

He kept looking around, and he did this awhile, veering from the path, from what I could tell, and also going farther than I thought was needed.

Only after he looked around the space where I thought the stables had been—not that I'd investigated, just that the trees there weren't as tall, so they had to be younger—did he come back.

I'd gone to the top of the steps, and I didn't move out of his way, even when he was only one step down from me.

And I didn't because I wasn't certain about the expression on his face.

"Well?" I prompted when he didn't say anything.

"Looks like some stones have been freshly dislodged."

"But no footprints?"

He shook his head.

That meant animals probably did it.

That expression, however, was still on his face.

"What?" I asked.

"It's not a thing," he didn't quite answer.

"What's not a thing?"

"It's dark. I'll come out tomorrow when it's daylight and look again."

Oh no.

"*What*, Riggs?"

He took a second, and I was about to ask again, when he pushed out, "There aren't any animal tracks either."

I stared at him.

No animal tracks either.

So who—or *what*—dislodged those stones?

I knew one answer.

And that answer was *great*.

Just great.

ELEVEN

Our Patch

Nadia

I woke to the sound of two things.

One was thunder rumbling in the distance.

The other was scratching at the reading nook window.

My nose was cold, the covers up to my neck because it got super chilly at night, so much so, I considered turning on the furnace, and I was a girl who not only grew up in Chicago, but also liked being cold at night so I could cozy into covers to sleep.

And slept I did, mostly well, except the first night and Riggs's party night.

But that night, the thunder rolling woke me because my sleep had been fitful after Riggs's declaration about the animal tracks.

Even if he'd forced his way up the last step to get into my space, and he'd wrapped both his hands warm and firm around my neck, not to mention dropped his head so far his forehead was nearly touching mine (and I could see the impossibility of counting his eyelashes, they were so profuse), he gave me a litany of plausible explanations.

Even with all of that, I wasn't having it.

He was right. He could see better in the daylight.

But he hadn't heard the sound.

It wasn't stones *rolling*. Or *dislodging*.

It was stones *cracking together*.

And in the end, that noise was headed my way.

Now this.

I lay there, wondering if I should call Riggs, or the police, or get up and turn on all the lights before I packed my bags and the boxes I'd kept for my stuff's return journey to Chicago, and get the hell out of there.

I did this along with listening to that infernal scratching.

And the thunder rumbled again.

The scratching stopped.

I lay tense.

The scratching came back.

I went back to my terrified indecision.

Eventually, the heavens opened, and I heard the rain hit the roof.

More thunder came, much closer, and along with it, a flash of lightning, but the scratching stopped entirely.

Holy cow.

That was when I knew.

I didn't believe in ghosts.

But if I did, one thing I suspected, they weren't all that fussed with a thunderstorm.

But a human being?

Whole other story.

This meant someone was messing with me.

Some *asshole* was messing with me.

That was when I lay in bed, fuming.

But that night I learned one thing about nature living.

As mad as you were, it was impossible to be in the forest with rain hitting a tin roof and not fall fast asleep.

I learned this because this was exactly what I did.

.   .   .

IT WAS STILL cold and drizzling the next morning when I sat cross legged in my love seat on the back porch wearing heavy socks, pajama bottoms, another tight cami, my cashmere robe, and one of those cute headbands snow bunnies wore to show off their hair while still keeping their ears warm.

I'd seen it in a window in town and couldn't resist, so I bought it the day before, between Kimmy's holiday store and going back to my car and reading disturbing stories about Misted Pines.

I had both hands wrapped around my coffee cup, which I had held to my face as I glared at the soothing sight of light rain hitting a tranquil lake.

I was not surprised this time when I heard noise coming from the north, and I wasn't surprised because, after teeth brushing, face cleaning and moisturizing, even though it was early, I'd texted Riggs that the scratching came back last night but went away when it started raining.

Only then did I make coffee.

And there he came, wearing a dark canvas jacket, slicked with wet, the hood up, his hands in the pockets, jeans on his legs, and on his feet, his ever-present brown boots.

He left the trail and came to a stop opposite where I was, but he didn't alight the porch.

He looked at me.

"Which number is that?" he asked, tipping his head to my coffee cup and taking in my glare with barely concealed humor.

"One," I grunted.

"How far into it are you?" he asked.

"A sip."

"Drink up, honey," he urged, then he took off down the side of my house.

I did as told as he did whatever he was doing at the side of the house. And I kept doing it as I watched him pass in front of me to go to the stable trail.

I continued sipping even as I turned my head and watched him tramp around in the drizzle.

He came back, but this time ascended the steps, shrugged off his jacket to afford me the pleasure of seeing him in a fabulous fisherman's sweater, and he tossed it on one of the wicker chairs.

After he did that, without invitation, he went inside my house.

I was getting to like him a whole lot, but I liked him more when he made sure to wipe his boots thoroughly on the outdoor mat before he went in, because the cabin wasn't all that big, but it was a whole lot of floor to mop.

He came back with a mug of coffee, and I only scooched enough he could squeeze his ass in the seat beside me. This meant he had to lift my knee, but when he was settled in, he dropped it and it rested on his thigh.

His thigh felt warm regardless of the chill, and hard, and I liked it too much, but I was so angry, I was too mad to move.

He took a sip and said to the lake, "If there were tracks, rain washed them away."

"Figures," I grumbled and took my own sip.

"Kids get up to stupid shit," he noted.

"My exact thinking," I replied, and it was, because if Riggs had learned about me, and Kimmy had guessed I was at this cabin, then that meant it was official.

Word had gotten around.

I was now glaring at the lake again, but I knew he'd turned to look at me when he asked, "How pissed are you?"

I turned to look at him. "On a scale of someone running through my yard being a one, and someone keeping me up all night with metal music and lake frolicking a ten, I'm at about a two-hundred-and-seventeen."

He grinned at me, then took another sip.

"This isn't funny, Riggs."

"Nope," he agreed. "And I'm gonna talk to Dave about installing some cameras so we can catch these fuckers, and they better hope I'm in the mood to turn over whatever video we get to Harry instead of acting on my own, because I reckon I'll be more in the mood to knock some goddamn heads together."

At that, I grunted unintelligibly, but even so, it was in accord.

But something he said struck me, so I asked, "Harry?"

"Moran. The county sheriff and a good friend of mine."

Excellent.

It was good to know people in high places.

"Gotta head out soon to get my kid. Rain lets up, me and Ledge are going fishing today. Wanna come with?" he offered.

"Now offer me the alternate option of having my nails pulled out at the roots so I can enjoy your shock and amazement at which one I pick."

He chuckled, looked to the lake and took another sip before asking, "Not a fisherwoman?"

"Any time I even consider how meat in whatever form comes to me, I consider vegetarianism. I've even tried to go that route. Twice. The smell of bacon always foils me. I gave up and just ignore that a creature gave its life to nurture mine."

"I'm taking that as a no."

"Good take."

"Ledge sucks hard at fishing, and so he won't feel like a loser, I go that route. So I'll be frying up some brats tonight. Wanna come for dinner?"

That was an invitation I could accept, so I did.

"Sure, I'd love that."

"I'll call Dave sometime during the day and install those cameras as soon as I can source them."

"Awesome."

"Honey?"

I turned to him.

He pointed at the lake. "That's our lake." He aimed his finger down. "This is our home. No one fucks with us on our patch. You with me?"

I was suddenly lamenting him not being a dick. No one wanted to live close to a dick. But I was finding it was worse living next to a really great guy who was beautiful, could be protective, and tramped over to your cabin to wander around in the drizzle, looking for the footprints of some probably high school punks who were playing a prank.

With all that, and what he just said, and the power behind the words when he said them, which told me he meant them, I knew my *dedulya*, who had liked Trevor, would love this guy.

"I'm with you."

"People around here, we take our privacy seriously," he informed me. "So much, recently, the town council hiked up fines and even added jail time for trespassers. It's minimal, but it's still a strong deterrent. I don't have fences up, but got signs all over the property, and you can't miss them. We catch someone doing this shit, they're gonna pay, honey. Literally."

He watched me nod before he threw back more coffee, came in, slid his rough, yet sweet whiskers along my cheek in what he clearly had no idea was a cruel tease, pulled away and urged, "Keep the faith."

"Right."

He put his coffee mug down, got up, went to his wet jacket, shrugged it on, and with a chin lift to me, he tramped into the woods.

THE RAIN DIDN'T LET up all day.

Sometimes it came harder than others, but even if it was just a trickle, it came.

I felt bad the Riggs boys weren't going to get to go fishing.

But I felt kind of excited that afternoon that I could don the cute, pink slicker I'd bought before I came there, the hiking boots I already had, but had used minimally, and I headed out.

I looked where Riggs looked earlier, at the side of the cabin, on the stable trail and around the stable area, but I saw what he probably saw.

A bunch of earth that was smooth, wet through, and I knew that because, in some parts the water on top of it gently washed down toward the lake.

I then took the trail that Roosevelt probably cut, but it was Riggs running it that kept it clear, and for the first time, began to make my way around the lake.

The trail didn't stay clear the deeper I got into the forest. It was there, but the stone edge ran out about a hundred yards deep, and sometimes I went off it altogether because it disappeared, but I'd eventually find a swatch of it again.

It took a while for me to see them. In fact, I was nearly to the north end of the lake by the time I did (and I noted, to my surprise, the lake was bigger than I expected, curling around the trees and opening wide, which made me pause to reflect, if Riggs owned this whole lake, and a good fifty yards up it, if the signs I spied were anything to go by, he owned a ton of land).

I trudged through the trees to the signs, the back of which I saw were painted a bright, *Don't Miss This!* orange.

When I made it to them, nailed to the tree, I saw they weren't rinky-dink plastic signs bought at a hardware store, but steel ones that were full-on orange at the front, with black words.

And there were three tacked one on top of the other.

PRIVATE PROPERTY
TRESPASSERS WILL BE PROSECUTED
NO HUNTING

The warning wasn't vague.

As I returned to move along the trail, I didn't miss the others. They weren't copious, but they were hard to avoid. If you were traversing the area, you'd definitely run into a set of them, eventually.

I finally made it all around the lake and saw Riggs's crazy house from a different point of view.

I could see how the living room was built into the earth, as was the arm of the house that spread down the other side, with the lower floor (that being the kitchen level) naturally being shorter because the lay of the land made it that way.

As such, I could further see the kitchen rising above it before that level fed into the slope.

I could also see it looked like there was a circular room that jutted out, and from what I could tell, was a dining room off the kitchen.

Above it was another floor that meandered deep into the trees, the option we didn't take when Riggs was leading me to privacy the day before.

And topping it all was Riggs's bedroom, which was a lot bigger than what I experienced, because it undoubtedly had a bathroom and closet I wasn't invited to peruse.

The winding staircases were visible outside, looking like truncated turrets built into the structure.

I also saw how it was all stabilized with beams built into the ground and buried posts that were hidden with trees, shrubbery and paint purposefully chosen to meld with the earth around it.

It was totally nutty, and totally Riggs. Imposing and inviting. Earthy and otherworldly. Understandable and contradictory.

And it gave me pause for more reflection, making me wonder what hand Lincoln Whitaker had in designing it. And if he had a heavy hand, just what it said (because it was big, I hadn't taken much in, but I also hadn't missed the sheer size of his kitchen, living room and bedroom) about Lincoln and what the cabin said about Roosevelt.

Last, what it all said about Sarah.

Sure, a man would want room for his family, but Lincoln's family didn't actually live there.

Roosevelt, year-round, lived in only the space he needed.

As wild as that house was, it was interesting, and I liked it.

I also liked my cabin.

Did Sarah somehow love both men?

Or did she yearn for a simple, uncomplicated man, and the life he led, in a one-room cabin twenty minutes from anywhere?

I would never know.

And something else I was learning about being an outdoorsy girl, when it was cold, you didn't stop moving.

It was faster to walk through the Riggs space to get to my place.

But I figured they were home, and I didn't want to disturb them, so I turned back and retraced my steps.

Halfway home, my phone vibrated in my back pocket.

I pulled it out of my jeans and saw a text from Riggs.

Brats. 5:00.

See you then, I returned, and I did it smiling, because I had plans that night, and that made me happy. Because those plans were with Riggs and Ledger, and that made me happier. And because a great idea struck me, and I was excited about it.

Then I shoved my phone back in my pocket, and with deter-mined strides, trekked through the drizzle the rest of the way home.

TWELVE

Beer Theme

Riggs

Riggs was learning that vodka princesses could be shy, were sweet, and definitely funny.

And annoyingly late.

Sure, Nadia had texted to share how sorry she was that she couldn't get there until 5:30.

But she wasn't there at 5:30.

He heard her pull up in her car at 5:45.

And by that time, he and his boy were hungry.

So he wasn't in a great mood when the doorbell rang, and he knew by the look on Ledger's face, his son wasn't either.

Riggs left the brats, which were done, and had been for ten minutes, in the skillet and headed to the door.

He opened it, and he wasn't pissed anymore.

Not even a little.

Because Nadia stood there, her hair done up in a bunch of big curls that looked great, and for the first time that he'd seen, she had makeup on. It was subtle but seriously fucking gorgeous. He could also see the soft green turtleneck coming out of her traditional trench coat that gave her an elegant outdoors vibe he liked too much.

But there was more.

She was holding a cake plate by its stem in her fist, on which were thick layers of some dark chocolate cake that looked moist as fuck, this topped with swirls of creamy frosting.

In her other hand dangled a plastic grocery bag he could tell held a gallon tub of ice cream in it, and outside, a six-pack of bottles of beer.

"I'm sorry. So sorry. I got a wild hair," she said swiftly. "This stout cake is *insane*. Perfect for *après* brats. I took a walk around the lake, and you texted me with the time, and I got the idea, but I didn't have the ingredients, so I had to run to town. I also didn't have a springform cake pan, or a cake plate, so it was more running around than I thought it would be. I forgot to factor in cooling time so I could frost it, and as such, it all went haywire."

He felt Ledger behind him, so he took the cake plate from her and handed it off to his boy, who also was no longer pissed, considering he was staring at the cake with big eyes like he wanted to shove his entire face in it (you could say Angelica wasn't a baker, or a cook).

It was no longer raining, but it was still cold, so Riggs then reached out and pulled Nadia in before he took the beer and ice cream from her.

He'd closed the door by the time she launched in again.

"It's incredibly rude to be so late. *God*, I'm so sorry. But I thought you guys would really like the cake, and once I started, I couldn't stop. And I didn't want to say anything, or it would spoil the surprise."

"Honey?"

She nodded.

"Shut up. I was pissed. I'm not now because I like cake, and Ledge likes it more. So lose the coat and come in so we can eat."

She smiled brightly at him in an easy, open and relaxed way he'd never seen from her, and for a second, he was stunned inert by it.

Her shrugging off her coat and hooking it on the hooks by the door, exposing her sweater was slouchy and bunched at her waist. But on the bottom, she was wearing skinny jeans that did incredible things to an already great ass, showcased her long legs and ended in spike heeled booties that made the crotch of his jeans suddenly uncomfortable, and that didn't help matters.

She didn't seem to notice as she pulled the beer and bag out of his hand and muttered, "I'm gonna get this in the fridge."

She sashayed off, that ass swaying, which made shit even worse.

It took some effort, but Riggs got a handle on it and followed her.

He hit the kitchen as she was asking Ledger, "Did you get to fish today?"

"No. Dad and I kicked back with some beer and binged *The Witcher*."

Her eyes sped to Riggs.

"*Root* beer," he amended for his son.

"Ah," she said, turning her gaze to Ledger and giving him a wink.

After she did that, she opened the freezer and shoved the ice cream inside.

Ledger watched her do this while Riggs watched Ledger.

Then his son looked at him and his grin was enormous.

Apparently, it didn't take much with his kid, except a leggy blonde with a great ass and a fantastic head of hair, not that any of that would do much for him. But even at Ledger's age, she wasn't hard to look at. For Ledge, she was also a woman who could bake and brought ice cream along with beer, not to mention, took his dad's back when shit went south without a moment's hesitation.

She turned, clapped her hands together, and said, "What can I do to help?"

"Get yourself a plate since we're ready to roll," Riggs replied, then to his son, he said, "Ledge, show her the way."

Ledger jumped off the stool he'd assumed and rounded the counter to go to the stack of plates Riggs had set out. His boy took one and handed another one to Nadia.

They all loaded up with brats in buns with whatever fixings they wanted, store bought macaroni salad, air fried curly fries, and Ledge and Nadia sat at the bar while Riggs dragged a stool around it to sit in front of them so they weren't in a line, and they could talk while they ate. The lower cupboards were there, so he didn't have anywhere to put his legs. But he had a direct line on watching Nadia, so he had zero fucks to give he had to eat twisted to his food.

Nadia started it by asking Ledger, "So you're a *Witcher* fan?"

But it was Riggs who answered. "He likes anything with lots of sword fights and gore."

"This is not my preferred viewing fodder," she admitted to Ledger.

"Why am I not surprised?" his boy quipped.

She grinned at him, took a huge bite of brat, then Riggs felt something he'd never felt before when he watched her eyes roll back into her head.

Mouth still full of brat, she asked, "What miracle is this?"

"Slow skillet cooking in ale," he told her.

She munched in between exclaiming, "Oh my *God. So good.*" She swallowed and declared, "Better even than Brenda's taco meat, and that was crazy good. But she refused to tell me her secret."

"She cooks that shit slow too, reducing it in extra water and extra seasoning from a packet," Riggs told her the secret. "Normally, it'd take about ten minutes to brown some meat and add the seasoning. Brenda simmers hers for around forty-five."

"That's it?" Nadia asked.

Riggs shrugged.

"I'm trying that," she declared before another big bite.

"Ask us over when you do," Ledger put in, then took his own bite.

"Will do," she muttered then stated, "Beer theme tonight, brats in ale, stout chocolate cake."

Fuck.

He forgot to offer her a drink.

"You want a beer?" Riggs offered. "Also got some wine if you want me to open a bottle."

"You don't drink wine with brats, Riggs," she chided.

You did not, and he dug it that she knew that.

He smiled at her and hauled his ass to the fridge.

He got her one, him a fresh one, popped the caps and brought them back.

"You walked around the lake today?" Ledger asked her.

"Yes," she answered, sucking back some beer.

"In the rain?" Ledger pushed.

"I have a new slicker I wanted to try out. It's pink," she told him.

"Why am I not surprised about that either?" Ledger asked, grinning at her.

"I'm a girl," she pointed out.

"Yeah, I noticed," Ledge mumbled this to his plate.

Riggs regarded his son closely.

Well, shit.

Was his boy crushing?

He tried to remember when he realized girls were girls and what he felt about that.

And yeah.

It was around that age.

"I learned last night, rain on a roof lulls you to sleep, even if you're wide awake when it starts," she announced, taking Riggs out of his thoughts. "And I learned today that, when it's cold and you take a hike, you don't stop until you're out of the cold. So…look at me. I'm becoming a nature girl."

Not even close.

And he wanted her comfortable in her surroundings, but he still hoped that shit never fully took.

"Good for you, honey," Riggs murmured while smiling at her.

She smiled back, again it was untroubled and cheery, and again he was transfixed by it.

She put her brat down to fork into her macaroni salad when he heard her phone vibrate.

She pulled it out, looked at it, frowned, then shoved it back while he could still hear it vibrating, meaning it wasn't a text, but a call.

"You can deal with it, whatever it is. We don't stand on ceremony at the Riggs house," he told her.

"It's a friend from home. I'll call her tomorrow."

Her phone went again, and the blithe look went out of her face as a worried one set in.

"Take it, Nadia," he urged gently.

"I'm so sorry," she muttered, slid off her seat and pulled her phone out.

She moved down into the living room as she took the call.

"Hey, Maribeth. I'm at my neighbor's for dinner so I'll have to —" She stopped, bent her head, listened, then said, "Listen, I know. I found out—"

She was interrupted again.

She listened some more, then said, "Maribeth, slow down and let me say something." A pause and then, "I *know*. Sure, I just found out, but—"

Another interruption and then she looked their way, gave the one-minute finger and walked out the front door.

Riggs and his son exchanged a glance, then Riggs took another bite, chewed it, swallowed it, decided that was enough time to give her, so he put down his own brat and followed her.

He was through the storm door, eyes on her standing on his front deck, when she turned and slammed right into him.

"Gah! Sorry!" she cried, as he wrapped his fingers around her upper arms to steady her.

It was then he noted she was off her phone.

"Everything okay?"

"That was my friend, Maribeth," she explained. "We've been besties since middle school. And she wasn't buying my fake, *having the time of my life in the Pacific Northwest* communications. So she looked into things and learned about Ray Andrews and Richard Sandusky."

"Ah," he murmured, thinking that would do it for any friend, best or not.

Having no reason to keep his hands on her anymore, he let her go and took a step away.

"So she's a little freaked, and I've been semi-kinda ghosting her, which made her more freaked."

"That tracks," he noted.

"And, well, she was done with being freaked and about to buy a ticket out here to hunt me down to make sure I was okay. I talked her down from that. Though, she's planning to come out soon."

"That'll be good, right?" he asked.

"Yeah, I just…" she let that trail.

"You just what?"

"Well, first, I have some probably punk kids who are playing tricks on me. Second, I live in a famous haunted cabin. But most of all, she didn't want me to come out here because being out here was being out from under her watchful eye. However, I told her I needed space to get my head together about all that went down, and I haven't really set to work on that," she admitted.

"This is your best girl?" he asked.

She nodded.

"So she'll get it, yeah?"

Her white teeth came out to bite the side of her lower lip, and he could feel that bite all over his flesh, so he stopped looking at her mouth and switched to her eyes.

They were so stunning, it wasn't a whole lot safer, but it was safer.

"Yeah," she finally said.

"So, you okay now?"

She nodded.

"Right, then let's go in and finish dinner so we can eat cake."

That made her smile, and it might not have been as carefree as the earlier ones, but it wasn't weighed down like all the ones he'd had before.

So he'd take it.

THIRTEEN

Doesn't Add Up

Riggs

Riggs sat in his couch, sipping a beer and watching Nadia and Ledger on their knees on the floor on opposite sides of the coffee table.

They were playing some card game Nadia taught his boy where you tossed cards one on top of the other and smacked any duplicates. If your hand got there first, you got the whole pile. But if one or the other threw down a jack, then you laid down a line of three cards, and the winner of the entire pile was the highest end card.

Ledger was competitive, and to an untrained eye, Nadia was too.

But Riggs was good at ferreting out a tell, so he caught her occasional brief hesitations that allowed Ledger to clap his hand on the cards before she got there.

This meant the three decks Riggs had dug out so they could play were mostly in his son's hand.

They both laid down the final turn of four cards, which was all Nadia had left, before Ledger threw up his hands and shouted, "I win! *Again!*"

Nadia collapsed onto a hip and reached for her beer, muttering a fake gripe of, "Lightning Quick Ledger, fastest hand in the West," before she threw back a drag.

"You said it," Ledger crowed, shuffling the cards in his hands and asking, "Go again?"

"Buddy," Riggs said low.

It was late. He had school in the morning.

His kid looked at him and his shoulders slumped.

He hated seeing that just as much as he hated stopping the fun, for both of them.

And he didn't have time to deeply contemplate that Angelica wasn't the card-game-playing-with-her-son type of mom. She was the park-your-kid-in-front-of-the-television—either with a show on, or a game controller in their hand—so-she-could-do-her-own-thing type of mom.

Angelica loved her son, kept him fed and clothed, made sure he got his schoolwork done and didn't miss a parent-teacher conference or a football or baseball game.

But that night, Nadia's teacher came out, and Riggs knew it wasn't fair to compare, because it was only one night, she didn't have a job, loads of laundry to do or any shit like that, but she was all about conversation and engagement and keeping his son's mind active at the same time subtly challenging it.

She'd be an excellent mother.

And that was something Riggs just wasn't going to contemplate, deeply or otherwise.

"If you're jazzed, you can read for a while," he told his son quietly.

Nadia took her feet and made it easy, saying, "Great night, Ledger. I had fun, even though you trounced me three times. But thanks for having me over, and I demand a rematch on taco night."

"Thanks for the cake," Ledge replied on a victorious grin. "It was awesome. And you're on because you're easy to beat."

She did a fake eye roll before she said, "My pleasure."

Ledger moved to the stairs and Riggs called, "Be up in a sec, buddy."

"'Kay, Dad."

He looked to Nadia when she hooked a thumb to the door and asked, "Should I go? Or I can tackle the dishes while you guys sort that out."

"You touch the dishes, I spank your ass."

Her head jerked, and that look he sometimes caught in her eye, this one saying she wouldn't mind that, he also wasn't going to contemplate.

"And don't go, unless you want to." He indicated her nearly full beer with his head as he pushed out of the couch. "At least until you finish that."

As answer, she lifted it and took a sip.

He felt one side of his mouth go up, then he followed his kid.

He found Ledger in his bathroom, brushing his teeth.

Riggs stretched out on his son's bed, hands clasped behind his head, until Ledger came in wearing his sleep shorts and a tee.

Riggs rolled off and Ledger crawled in.

His boy had pulled the covers over himself before he said, "Just so you know, I approve. She's pretty, makes good cake and lets me win card games."

So Ledge had noticed the tell too.

Not a surprise, his kid was sharp.

That said.

"Nothing to approve of, buddy. We're just getting to know our new neighbor."

Ledge gave him the side eye, mumbling, "Right."

Damn.

Ledger had read this wrong.

"Seriously, Ledge. She's in MP working through some stuff. Then she's gonna go back to Chicago. But everyone needs friends no matter where they are, or how long they're there, so we're gonna be that for her."

Ledger took this in and replied, "You should go for it anyway, because she's pretty, makes good cake and lets me win at card games."

"It doesn't work that way, Ledge."

Ledger gave him a look Riggs had never seen, before he said, "Well, maybe you should work it to make it that way so she'll stay, seeing as her cake was that good."

This suggestion made him uneasy.

"Is there another conversation we should be having, kid?" Riggs asked.

"No. It's just that you're a good guy. And you should be happy like Aunt Kate is happy."

"I *am* happy," Riggs asserted.

"Not like Aunt Kate is happy."

He wasn't going to explain how he took care of that particular happy in his way to his nine-year-old son.

Instead, he said, "How about you let me do my job as your dad and look after you, rather than the other way around."

"Just sayin', while she's here, make sure she makes us Brenda's tacos."

Riggs shot him a smile. "I can do that."

Ledger reached for the book on his nightstand.

Riggs took his cue, mussed his son's hair then strode out.

When he hit the bottom of the stairs, he heard, "I'm in here," coming from the dining room.

So he rounded the stairwell and saw Nadia standing at the dining room window, looking out.

The rain was gone, but the clouds remained, and dusk was settling in.

She had her arms crossed on her chest, beer bottle still in hand, and he should keep his distance.

But he didn't.

He was a demonstrative, affectionate kind of guy with people he cared about, primarily women, though that wasn't why he walked to her, got behind her and rounded her chest with his arms.

It was because she undoubtedly needed a hug.

And because he couldn't stop himself.

She didn't get stiff or pull away.

She settled into his chest.

"He good?" she asked.

"Yeah. He likes you."

"Good," she murmured. Then, "I hesitate to ask, but have you heard anything about your friend?"

He had.

"Swelling going down, but other than that, no change. They still have him induced and the prognosis is still guarded."

She twisted her neck to catch his eye and whispered, "Sorry, Riggs."

He gave her a squeeze.

She looked back to the lake, and so did he.

"I wasn't snooping," she told him. "But I saw your house from the opposite side of the lake during my walk, particularly this room, and I was curious. It's amazing. The view from here is spectacular. And I don't know where you found that table, but it's perfection."

"I made it."

Her head twisted again, this time faster. "You made it? You made that table?"

"Yeah. Got a workshop west of the house. During down time, I make furniture, refurb it, and create other pieces on commission. Like, I made the mailbox structure for your cabin."

He watched her eyes grow wide.

"Wow, I'm impressed. That piece is magnificent."

He gave her another squeeze, a smile with it this time, and muttered, "Thanks."

"I'm seeing now, but barely, how you can afford your own lake," she teased. "Seems to me you work all the time, even when you're not working."

"Got the ghost of Roosevelt Whitaker to thank for that," he explained. "All that mess, people freaked about it, the trustees couldn't keep the houses leased, and in the case of this house, the vandals from fucking with it."

"Vandals?" she asked, openly shocked.

He lifted his chin. "Yup. Graffiti. Broken windows. Once, they tore up the pier, and I know that because the trustees hired me to fix it. Heard word they even threw rocks to break the windows when they had renters inside in the early days. It was a situation."

"But nothing while you've been here?" she pressed.

He shook his head. "Nothing." He smiled. "Not even a…*boo*," and he gave her an abrupt squeeze on the last word.

Her body mildly jumped, then she shot him a fake glare.

To that, he grinned.

Her gaze dropped to his mouth, he felt it there, but after that, he lost her.

"That's good," she murmured, her thoughts seeming to fade to something else.

"Then again, I'm not a guy to fuck with," he told her.

She came back to him, smiled in return, and remarked, "I've noticed that."

"Yeah," he replied, then got back to what he was saying. "Trustees also couldn't give them away, but no one was buying. They tried several times to put all this property on the market. They'd get offers, but nothing near what it was worth, so they couldn't take them. Even tried once to parcel off the land so people could build."

She gasped in horror, and he chuckled.

"I know. But that didn't work either. Years went by, the stink from the mess Lincoln made didn't lessen, they were still paying property taxes out of the estate, not to mention all the legal action eating into it, something had to give. Dave and Brenda got your cabin for a song. I heard that, had a good look at this place, the resources and know-how to fix it up, bid seriously low thinking they'd tell me to go fuck myself. They took my first offer."

"Boon for you," she noted.

"Everyone in town thought I'd lost my mind. But now I got a legacy to give my son, so I'm laughing."

"Right," she whispered.

He gave her another squeeze and really should have walked away, moved it to the living room.

But he didn't.

He looked back to the lake and felt it when she did too.

"You know what I've noticed?" she asked the view.

"What?"

"Well, two things. The only outdoor space is your pier, and that area set off to the side, which is surrounded by trees, your house and the driveway. That space just barely has a view to the lake, though nothing else, but your trees, house and driveway."

"Yeah?" he said leadingly because he didn't know where she was going with this.

"This house, this location, no balconies, no decks, no porches?"

"Yeah?" he repeated in the same tone since he still didn't know where she was going with this.

"Which leads me to the second thing. Your place has a lot of windows, but from what I can tell, you can't see the cabin from any of them."

He looked in that direction, and he saw her pier in the moonlight, but she was right.

He couldn't see the cabin. It was tucked too far back in the trees. And even from the back bedroom on the next level, you probably couldn't see it.

He'd just noticed it, but he didn't miss noticing how he really didn't like it, since now, Nadia lived there.

"Do you know how much of a hand Lincoln had in designing this house?" she asked.

"Word is, he worked closely with the architect to create it."

"Well, that tells me, even if he wasn't about to go there in his head, he knew something was up with his brother and his wife. I don't have a sibling, but if I built close to one, especially if I was emotionally close to them, I'd want to be able to see their space."

He would too.

"Methinks Lincoln wasn't as surprised as it seems he was with what he found in those stables," she remarked. "You said he served seven years? That's not much for two murders."

"He confessed and was sentenced for manslaughter."

"Thriller writer would probably know what premeditated murder would buy him," she noted. "And the man didn't shoot them then call the police to turn himself in. He made sure he didn't start a wildfire before he set the stables alight. I mean, how much work would it be to drench the land and trees around an entire building?"

Jesus.

"A lot," he grunted.

"Mm," she hummed before she allowed, "I could see being in emotional overload after you shot your twin brother and wife to death, so you went through the emotions, doing strange stuff while not thinking clearly. But how long would that actually last? And seven years is a long time, and it isn't like he's thrown into a room and not allowed to speak to anybody during that time. How could he not sort his affairs so his children and family were taken care of when he took his own life? *Especially* if he was going to take his own life, you'd think he'd make those plans. Furthermore, how easy is it to get your hands on a bottle of arsenic? I can't imagine that's something you can stroll into the local CVS and source."

"Nope," he agreed.

"Not to mention," she kept at it, "Roosevelt obviously couldn't know he was soon to die, but if you have a lot of money, you make arrangements. How is his estate tied up with Lincoln's?"

"I don't know, and when I bought this place, I didn't ask. But you're correct. All this shit is fishy."

"No one ever asked these questions before?"

"I didn't, because other people's mess isn't something I give a shit about."

Though, he was starting to give a shit about it now.

She settled even deeper into his chest as she took a drag from her beer and then murmured, "Well, I think this house tells a tale about Lincoln Whitaker. Just as the cabin tells one about Roosevelt. One was complicated. Brilliant, but complicated. The other enjoyed the simple life. It isn't surprising, they might have been twins, but they were two different men. Still, something doesn't add up here."

She was correct about that too.

He'd had plans for the next day of taking his kid to school and spending the rest of the day getting Nadia's cameras set up, the American flag she told him she bought, and if there was any time left, working in his workshop.

But he slotted a visit to Harry on his schedule.

After doing that, he gave Nadia another squeeze and asked, "Feel like more cake?"

She twisted her neck again to look at him. "Seriously? I don't think I'll be able to eat for a week."

"Well, I feel like more cake."

Her sunny smile came back, stating plain she dug that he liked her cake, and while she was still blasting it at him, he let her go, but took her hand and led her to the kitchen where she watched as he cut himself another wodge of her amazing cake.

And she kept watching as he downed it.

FOURTEEN

Case File

Riggs

Late the next morning, Riggs pushed through the door at the sheriff's department a couple minutes after Harry told him he'd be free to have a chat.

He gave a few nods to the deputies milling around.

But since all of them knew him because he'd done work on their houses, or their parents' houses, or they'd gone to school with him, partied with him, drank at a bar with him, or they just lived in the same small town, no one stopped him as he made his way back to Harry's office.

The door was open, and his friend's eyes came to him from where he sat behind his desk, but Riggs still knocked on the doorframe, since Cade Bohannan and Rus Lazarus were sitting in the two chairs in front of Harry's desk.

Bohannan was an MP native and retired FBI profiler who now did consultant work and taught courses.

Lazurus was Fret County Sheriff's new detective. Also former FBI, he'd come to town the year before to track the Crystal Killer.

While doing that, he'd fallen for a local, Cin Bonner, and now he was shacked up with her.

Riggs had known Cade his whole life, though Cade had spent a lot of his living elsewhere when he was with the FBI. But Riggs had always liked the man. He couldn't say they were close buds, but there was mutual respect. On Riggs's part, this was mostly because Cade had always treated him like Doc Riggs, not John Riggs's son, and that meant something to Riggs, especially from a world-renown criminal profiler.

On the other hand, he'd only known Rus for a few months, and he called the man his friend. They'd shared beers while watching a game at Harry's more than once. He was a good man, smart, funny, and making him better, he was a good friend to Harry. He had Harry's back at work and, Riggs sensed, emotionally.

After Harry lost what he lost, he didn't let many people in.

But he'd let in Rus.

"Am I interrupting something?" Riggs asked.

"We're finishing up," Harry said. "Grab a chair and join us, unless what you have to talk to me about is private."

Riggs came in, nabbed a chair from the small conference table in the corner and turned it around toward Harry's desk before he sat in it.

"No. Actually it'd be good to have you all here when we talk about this," he shared.

The other men glanced at each other, and Riggs didn't make them wait.

"Nadia, my neighbor," he said the last just in case Cade didn't know of her, "has had someone fucking with her."

"Jesus Christ," Harry muttered in a harassed way.

"Yeah. Scratching her windows in the middle of the night and banging together some rocks by where Whitaker's stables used to stand," Riggs explained. "I grabbed some surveillance stuff, heading back to install it after this. But thought you should have that heads up."

Knowing him better than the other two in the room, it was Harry who demanded, "You get some video, you phone me."

"I'll try to stay in that frame of mind, and whoever's doing this might not know what she's going through right now. Even so, that shit is whacked. She's not happy about it, and it's arguable, but I'd argue I'm even less so."

Harry didn't take his eyes off Riggs, and Riggs got that, because, again, the man knew him well, so he knew Riggs would put himself in front of a bullet for his son, mother, sister or a good friend, but this protective streak with Nadia was telling.

Cade and Rus just exchanged a glance.

"How do you know it's not Whitaker's ghost?" Cade joked.

Riggs looked his way. "Rain washed away any tracks, but Nadia told me the scratching stopped when the storm came, and my guess is the same as hers. If there was such a thing, ghosts wouldn't feel rain, so they wouldn't give any fucks about it."

"Excellent observation," Rus muttered.

"Also gotta ask about the Whitaker investigation," Riggs aimed that directly at Harry.

His friend's brows went up. "Why?"

"Because Leland Dern was sheriff when that shit went down, and we all know Dern was a waste of space," Riggs noted.

"The man confessed," Harry pointed out.

"Yeah, after he hosed down the stables. This being after he blew holes in his wife and brother. Think that did the job, so why'd the guy burn down the stables?"

Harry again didn't take his eyes off Riggs, and again, Cade and Rus exchanged a glance.

"Rus up to speed about all that shit?" Riggs asked Harry.

But it was Rus who answered.

"Yeah, Nadia Antonov moving to that cabin, Harry filled me in."

"Being a big FBI guy, how do you feel about that scene?" he asked Rus.

"Can't say I pulled the case file, Doc," Rus replied. "Only know what Harry told me, and seeing as a man confessed and turned himself in at the scene, it sounded pretty open and shut."

"Maybe you should open that file," Riggs remarked.

"Again, I'll ask why," Harry put in. "Everyone involved in that mess is dead."

"Nadia was at my place last night…"

All the men exchanged glances at that.

Shit.

"…she's my neighbor, and Ledger is home, so we were getting to know our new neighbor," he felt forced to explain.

"I thought you two were butting heads," Harry noted, both observationally and probingly.

"We worked shit out," Riggs replied impatiently.

"Right," Harry muttered.

Moving the fuck on.

"And she made the observation that you can't see Roosevelt's cabin from any of the windows in my house. A house Lincoln helped design. A house that has a fuckuva lot of windows. And straight up, this morning, I went into every room that faced the lake, and she's right. Even in the farthest room on the third level, that part of the house is built into a hill, angled away from the cabin, so the windows are positioned toward the other side of the lake. You can't see anything but Roosevelt's pier."

The mood coming from Bohannan had them all looking at him.

"What?" Harry pressed.

"Gotta say, that's another excellent observation," Cade said. "Got all my kids living close on our land, though not that close, and I can see all their houses from mine, to the point I had some trees removed around Jace's place so it wasn't so secluded. Not that me and Larue spy or anything, but you just keep an eye. And Larue and I both felt off about Jace's place, until those trees were removed. Further, it isn't like my boy can't take care of himself, it's just a family thing."

"That's pretty thin to pull a file on a closed case," Harry noted.

"Not if you're a profiler and you got some guy going overkill on murdering his wife and identical twin brother," Cade returned. "With this new information, gotta admit, it's hinky, Harry. The wife is already a thing. Though, last I read, eighty percent of female homicides are done by their partner or an ex, so it's a thing to men like us who would never do it. But an identical twin?" Cade shook his head. "They got a bond. I've got a pair of my own, and I've read a lot about it. Think it'd take a lot for a man to pull that trigger. And even more to burn his body to ash. From what I understand, and seen with my own eyes with my sons, that would be akin to destroying himself."

"Which would explain why he entered a fugue state after shooting them and while hosing down the area around the stables and setting them on fire," Harry threw out.

"Maybe. It's not like wildfires are common here, though," Cade retorted. "It's too wet. That's going the extra mile, and it takes some synapses firing to think, fire, trees, I just killed my wife and brother, but I don't want to be responsible for burning down a few acres of forest. If synapses are firing, you aren't in a fugue state."

"And again, the man who did it is dead after doing time for the crime. It's not like I can recharge him," Harry pointed out. "I couldn't even do that if he was still alive."

Riggs knew Harry was thinking about his department and the resources at hand, and not being a lazy ass. That wasn't Harry's style.

Still, he was beginning to piss Riggs off.

"Though, you could charge someone if they're still around, and this guy didn't do the crime," Rus piped up.

Now Harry was interested, and Riggs knew when he demanded of Rus, "Talk me through that."

"Wasn't here, but say this guy didn't actually do it. Why would a man confess to a crime he didn't commit, and set a fire that would destroy all evidence?"

"Taking the fall for someone else," Harry answered.

"Someone he loves a whole fucking lot," Rus replied. "This guy have kids?"

"He did. If I remember right, they were in Seattle," Harry told him.

"How old were they?" Rus asked.

"No clue. I wasn't in the department when that happened," Harry shared.

"The old sheriff do due diligence?" Rus pushed.

"Again, I wasn't on the force then, but I could guess, and my guess would be a good one that would be a big fat no," Harry answered.

"So maybe it was someone else," Cade put in. "Someone else who's still around."

"Shit," Harry muttered.

"So maybe we pull the case file?" Rus suggested. "Just to have a look for curiosity's sake."

Harry nodded.

"Why are you opening this can of worms, Doc?" Cade asked Riggs.

Riggs looked to him.

"There's this shit, and there's also the mess of both Whitaker brothers' estates," Riggs said. "There's also Lincoln doing seven years' time, only to get out and *then* kill himself. Why would he wait to do that? Why would he do it at all? Why are the estates such a mess? And we all know there's no such thing as ghosts, but not everyone who's ever tried to stay on that land got creeped into believing a ghost story. Shit's been going down. Real shit. The kind that runs people off. This tells me, fifteen years, someone has worked hard to keep people away from that cabin, my house, and the whole lake."

"You have any incidents occur while you've been there?" Rus asked.

Riggs turned to him. "One, no. Two, I'm known as a man you don't mess with. Three, I'm known as a man who doesn't believe that ghost story shit. And four, I'm out of that house more than I'm in it."

"So, someone could need the place clear because they're looking for something they haven't been able to find, or they know something is there they don't want someone to find," Harry deduced. "Someone who might have killed two people and got away with it."

"That was what I thought," Riggs said.

"You remember any of this?" Harry asked Cade as Riggs felt his phone vibrate against his ass with a call.

He pulled it out as Cade answered, "Heard about it, but I didn't live here then."

"You got time to go over that file with me and Rus?" Harry asked Cade as Riggs checked his phone and saw it was Nadia.

Immediately, and without a word, he got up, walked across the room and took the call.

"Hey. What's up?" he asked.

His stomach dropped when he heard the panic in her voice as she said, "I'm in my car at your house, but you're not here."

"Why are you at my house?" he asked, and he felt the room go wired at the vein of urgency that snaked through his words.

"Because I went into town to experience that Aromacobana place, got back, and someone had broken into the cabin."

He put his hand over the phone and announced, "Someone has broken into Nadia's place."

He didn't wait to watch Harry, Rus and Bohannan finish bolting from their chairs.

He was hoofing it to his truck.

"On my way," he told her.

"Thanks, Riggs," she whispered, still sounding freaked.

"Be there soon, honey."

"Okay."

He disengaged, angled into his truck, and hauled ass to his house.

FIFTEEN

Desi and Lucy

Riggs

This time, it was Riggs skidding to a halt in the gravel of his drive next to Nadia's green Range Rover.

And he felt two things as he knifed out of his truck, his eyes glued to her as she jumped from her SUV still in an obvious panic.

The first was a weight crush his chest.

The second was his head fixing to explode.

He rounded the hood of his truck with long strides but only got halfway across before she crashed into him.

She threw her arms around him and held tight.

He wrapped his around her but used one hand to stroke her hair while he murmured, "It's okay, honey. You're all right."

She tipped her head back, her face pale under her honey tan. "Aromacobana' s coffee is really good, and I treated myself to a salted caramel cookie, and it was delicious."

"Good to hear, though I know that already. Just not real sure why you're sharing it with me right now," he noted cautiously.

She pulled from his arms, fisted a hand and smacked it into her other palm before she shouted, "Because I like it here at the same time someone is *fucking with me!*"

He wasn't sure he'd ever heard her say any form of the word fuck.

Yeah, his head felt ready to explode.

"I was with Harry when you phoned," he told her. "He hit me up on the way here and told me they were en route to the cabin. He's gonna call when they know it's clear, and we'll head over there together."

"You were with the sheriff when I called?"

"I was giving him a heads up about someone fucking with you." Since he'd learned from the last time about keeping shit from her, he continued when he didn't want to. "And I was asking about the Whitaker brothers."

He was instantly glad he shared since her expression lost some of its fright and her eyes lit with interest.

"You talked to him about that?"

"Yup."

"What'd he say?"

"First, you wanna come inside and have a shot of tequila then tell me what you saw when you got to your place?" he offered.

"Sure, *sans* the tequila. It's barely eleven, Riggs."

"Right," he muttered, throwing an arm around her shoulders and guiding her inside.

He took her right to kitchen, sat her ass on the stool, rounded the counter and leaned into his forearms across from her.

"Want coffee or something else?" he offered.

"I'm good."

"Okay, then, tell me. Did you see someone?"

"No, I came in the front and saw the back door open. There was a slash in the screen door. I didn't leave the back door open, and I made sure the lock was hooked on the screen door when I left. Obviously, I can't do that on the front door."

It was good he got contractor rates on all sorts of shit, because not only was she going to get surveillance cameras on every side of her house and pointed toward where the stables used to be, she was getting security doors.

"And you locked the back door?"

She nodded. "I got home and headed that way, and I was feeling creeped out, Riggs. You know, like, it was weird, and I couldn't put my finger on it."

He felt his muscles get solid all over when he asked, "Again, did you see someone?"

"No. I've been thinking about it, and it was just a feeling. Like, I *felt* someone had been there who shouldn't have been. I didn't get very far before I saw that there was some damage around the doorframe. Like someone pried it open or kicked it in."

And they could do that because they slashed her screen and unhooked the lock so they could get to the door.

"That's when I ran to my car and came to your house," she finished.

"What was the inside like?"

"That's what's weird, because, except for the back door, everything seemed like it was as I left it."

Yeah.

That was weird.

"Did you notice anything taken?"

She shook her head. "That said, I didn't get a good look."

"Sure you don't want a shot of tequila?"

She nodded her head.

"Anyone do any shit to you last night? Scratching. That rock bullshit?"

"I didn't hear anything," she replied as his phone vibrated in his pocket.

He pulled it out and looked at it.

"Harry," he told her.

More nodding from Nadia as he took the call.

"Yo, Harry."

"We're here. It's clear. Called the team in to see if we can get prints or anything. But the place looks perfect, except someone fucked up the back door in a big way in order to get in."

"Yeah?" he prompted, without saying the words that would push Harry to give more because he didn't want to tweak Nadia…or tweak her further.

But Harry got him, and he gave more.

"Whoever wanted in, really wanted in, Riggs. And from what I'm seeing, they didn't know how much time they had, so they made a mess of it. But this doesn't jibe, since it doesn't look like they ransacked the place. The state of the doorframe and the house contradict each other. 'Fraid I'm gonna need you to ask Nadia to come back and look around so we know what we're dealing with."

"I'll talk to Nadia. It'll be me bringing her back."

"See you soon."

"Yeah."

They disconnected and Riggs said to Nadia, "They're there, and it's all clear, but they need you to come and have a look because they can't tell if anything's missing. You okay to do that, or do you want me to call Harry and tell him you need some time?"

She shook her head. "I'm okay to do it."

"While we're there, want you to pack a bag."

She was moving off her stool, but at what he said, she stopped.

"For what?" she asked.

"You're staying with Ledge and me tonight. Tomorrow, I'm gonna fix your door, put security storm doors in and install the cameras. Depending on the damage to the frame, all that might take me more than a day. So pack for two nights, it shouldn't take more than that."

"I can check into a hotel."

"Yeah. You can. And if that's the way you wanna go, it's your call. But I'd feel better, and if Ledge hears word of this, and just sayin', in a small town, word travels fast, so he'd feel better if we had eyes on you."

"That really isn't—"

"I got a guest room, so it isn't like you'd be sleeping on the couch. It has its own bathroom. It's like a hotel, but the room service is shitty."

The corners of her lips did that wrinkle thing before she said, "I don't know. In all honesty, the macaroni salad was uninspired, but still yummy, and the brats were fantastic."

"What I meant to say was, I cooked last night, you're on that detail tonight. I'll deal with dessert." He got a full smile at that, and only when he did, did he say, "Let's go."

He did the arm around the shoulders gig again and took her right to the passenger side door of his truck.

Then, he was stunned it happened considering the mood he was in, but he had to fight laughing since she had so much trouble climbing up, he had to put his hands to her waist and practically lift her into her seat.

By the time he got in beside her, closed his door and was engaging the ignition, she joked, "I feel like I just climbed Mount Everest."

Vodka princesses clearly didn't ride around in fully-loaded, jacked up Rams.

He put the truck in reverse, saying, "I was there, and it was more like I hefted you to the peak."

"Whatever," she mumbled.

He headed down his drive.

"Should I call Dave and Brenda?" she asked.

"Maybe not now. Talk to the police. We'll call them later."

"Well, if word gets around fast—"

"Honey, I know them. They're gonna be more worried about you than their doorframe. Trust me. Take this one step at a time."

"Okay. I trust you."

His head didn't feel like it was going to explode anymore, but that weight hadn't left his chest. Though, her saying that helped alleviate some of it.

Her cabin was maybe a one-minute drive from his place, once you navigated the lanes, which, both his and hers, added another couple minutes.

So they were at her place in no time, and there were three Fret County Sheriff's vehicles in it, lights still flashing, though one of them just arrived, because the deputies were grabbing gear to prepare to see if there were any forensics to be collected.

When he switched off his truck, he turned to her. "Wait there. I'll lift you down."

"I can climb out, Riggs."

He raised his brows.

"I'll wait," she mumbled.

He ducked his head to hide his smile and got out.

"Hey, Doc," Wade Dickerson, one of the newly arrived deputies called.

"Yo, Wade," he called back as he rounded his vehicle.

She had her door open and her belt off, and he didn't bother spotting her as she gave it a go. He just grabbed her waist, hauled her out and put her to her feet.

"Well, that was expedient," she said.

"We'll practice it," he teased.

"You carting me around?"

"No. You getting in and out of my truck."

She did an eye roll.

He grabbed her hand and pulled her toward the cabin.

"Footies." Sean Stole, another deputy, met them at the door and handed them both two slips of blue fabric with elasticated edges.

Damn, they were taking this seriously.

Maybe their discussion about the Whitakers tweaked Harry.

Or maybe Harry liked someone fucking with Nadia about as much as Riggs did.

"Hold on to me to steady yourself as you put them on," he ordered Nadia.

She did as told and pulled the footies over a pair of strappy flat sandals.

He followed suit, balancing on each leg.

"You're so macho, I think they have to alter the definition of macho to describe you," she said like it was a complaint.

"What?" he asked.

"You couldn't hold on to me when you put on your footies like I did with you?"

"I got good balance."

"So do I."

"My house wasn't just broken into so I got my head together."

"You skidded to a halt in your driveway not fifteen minutes ago."

"Because I was intent to get to you because you sounded panicked due to your house being broken into."

"Another indication of your machismo. I need to inform Webster so they can be thorough in their redefinition."

"See you got two different reactions to possible peril. Being a pain in the ass or being a smartass," he returned.

Her mouth dropped open.

Harry broke into their conversation by saying, "Desi, Lucy, you two wanna come inside and have a look around?"

Nadia swung a scowl Harry's way.

Riggs hooked a thumb at her. "That's the pain in the ass version."

She latched onto his thumb and hissed, "Stop it, Riggs."

He grinned at her.

Harry took her attention.

"Mizz Williams, I'm Sheriff Harry Moran."

"Hi. Nadia. I'm Nadia," she replied, letting Riggs go and sticking out her hand to Harry.

Harry took it, squeezed briefly then let it go and stepped aside so they could go in.

"Have a look around," Harry instructed. "As thorough as possible, but please don't touch anything. If you think you need to touch, let us know and we'll get you some gloves. If you see anything amiss, no matter what it is, bring it to our attention."

She nodded, glanced at Riggs, then started moving around the space.

Riggs crossed his arms on his chest and watched her. Harry settled in beside him and did the same.

She was taking this seriously, and he noted, after a cursory walk-through, she went right to the closet, where the door wasn't open, but it was ajar.

Sean was close, and she asked him to open it for her, which he did.

She went in with Sean and came out to call, "They didn't take my jewelry."

"Please keep looking, Nadia," Harry returned.

She nodded and looked.

After a while, and that buzzing in his head coming back when he saw how pale she became when she got a closer look at the back door, she stopped on the outside beside the kitchen island. Once there, she put her hands to her hips.

Harry and Riggs approached.

When they got close, Nadia shared, "I don't see anything missing. I don't even see anything that's been touched, outside the obvious, the back door."

"You're sure?" Harry pressed.

She nodded while doing a sweep with her eyes.

It was when she looked over her shoulder toward the kitchen that he noticed her body jerk.

"What?" Riggs asked.

Her head whipped around to him, and her eyes were big.

"What, honey?" he pushed.

"Riggs, that wine from your friend is gone."

Riggs stood completely still.

Except his lips.

Those he used to growl, "Motherfucking Bubbles."

SIXTEEN

It Takes One to Know One

Riggs

Riggs'd had a shitty afternoon.

Part of it was, he was, right then, standing outside Bubbles's hospital room with Harry after hearing the doctor say that they'd brought Bubbles out of the coma, but he hadn't regained consciousness yet.

Before that, he'd gone with Harry to The Hole to have a look in the storeroom, and he was able to report that the other bottles of wine he'd seen in the locked cabinet were gone. Though he couldn't say exactly the number that had been there, or report if anything else was missing, because he hadn't paid that close of attention.

He'd also given Harry Bubbles's story about tasting it in Sonoma a couple of years ago and buying a case. However, he didn't share his suspicions that his friend had been lying about where he got that wine. Mostly because he didn't have to, Harry figured that out on his own.

And he felt like a dick, and a snitch (but not too much of one since Nadia had been dragged into this crap), when he shared that Bubbles had mentioned women named Candy and Barbie. Two women Riggs didn't know, nor did Harry, and between the two of them, Riggs reckoned they knew five sixths of the population of Misted Pines, though a bit less of the entirety of Fret County.

He'd gone to the hospital with Harry to interrogate Bubbles if he'd regained consciousness, not only because he wanted to hear what that fucker had to say, but also because he could tell Harry if the man was lying.

Unfortunately, they didn't get to do that part.

In the midst of this, Harry reported to Riggs that Rus and Karen Wilkins, another FC deputy, had been looking around outside Nadia's cabin while they were inside, and apparently whoever this was didn't take the time to cover their tracks like the "ghosts" did.

Therefore, with all the rain from the day before making the dirt wet, they had tons of tracks leading from the road to and all around the cabin, including Nadia's back door, and back to the road, where they also found tire tracks that suggested a truck or an SUV had pulled off to the side and parked.

They were canvassing the people who lived on the road to see if they'd noted a vehicle parked there, and Harry had asked Riggs to call Nadia to ask the same.

She hadn't.

The canvass wasn't done. With Bubbles's security system at the bar being out of action, so no camera footage, and nothing pinging so far with prints and blood and other samples they collected from the bar, except Bubbles's own blood and prints, and prints of staff (although they'd identified some blood from another source, they just had yet to identify that source), until Bubbles woke up, they had nothing.

Except now they had the fact that someone really wanted to get that wine back.

If it cost five hundred bucks a pop, times twelve (if there had been a case of it), Riggs could almost see that.

But to expend that effort for one of twelve bottles, when they'd already recovered ten, it was clear something else was up.

Harry felt the same. And since it was Riggs who bought two

bottles, and whoever was behind it knew Nadia was going to get one of them (something only Bubbles could tell them, which gave indication of what he gave up during his beating), and they only recovered one, this meant his house could be on their radar. Therefore, Harry had parked a deputy in his driveway after Riggs left Nadia there.

His mom was picking Ledger up from school and taking him home, which was where Riggs wanted to be, because he'd had a bottled smoothie for breakfast, no lunch, he was fucking hungry, and he wanted to see his kid…and Nadia.

Harry got close and Riggs shook off his thoughts to focus on him.

"I'm gonna tell you something that's only for you to know. My team knows, but if you get a shot to have a chat with Bubbles, with or without me, I want you to bear it in mind."

"So I can tell you what he says," Riggs filled in what he left out.

"You don't want this shit sorted?"

"I know he's a fuckup, but Bubbles is a friend," Riggs replied.

"A friend, who Nadia is lucky she didn't come home earlier and catch this—"

"I wasn't finished," Riggs gritted, ticked that Harry interrupted him, and not about to think of Nadia coming home when whoever broke in was there.

Harry jerked up his chin.

"He's obviously gotten mixed up in some serious shit, Harry," Riggs reminded him. "And I'm pissed as all hell at him right now, but I haven't forgotten he got the shit knocked out of him a couple of days ago, so bad they had to induce a coma."

"And you're worried about him."

"Well…yeah," Riggs said sarcastically.

"So me finding the person who did it to him would be good."

"Yeah again. And no shade on the job you do, but first, you gotta take your time with it and be thorough. Second, you got rules you gotta adhere to, which is why your job takes so much time. Third, like I told you, Nadia and me already drank the other bottle, and they might have gone through her recycling and seen it, or they might still be searching for it. So last, I got my kid and Nadia at my house, and Nadia is already more mixed up in this shit than I want her to be. I want it nowhere near my son. In short, I want this done, and done fast, without anyone else I care about getting beat to hell or freaked the fuck out."

"I hear you, so can I say what I have to say?" Harry asked quietly.

This time, Riggs jerked up his chin.

"There's been a string of robberies through Chelan and Fret counties," Harry told him. "And one of them, the victim reported a case of wine, valued at five thousand dollars, was stolen."

Riggs blew out a breath.

And then he asked, "You got more?"

"Only that this is very organized. And we've had eyes on Bubbles for a while, because this isn't the first time he's fenced stolen goods for one of his less law-abiding buds."

Yeah.

Damn.

Bubbles was a fucking doofus.

"However," Harry carried on, "you don't beat the shit out of your fence unless he's done you dirty. So there's a lot of scenarios that could be at play here. Either he was supposed to hold onto that wine for some reason, and they were pissed he sold a couple of bottles to you. Or he wasn't supposed to have that wine, maybe he stole it from the people who stole it, or he was holding it for people who went up against the big man, and now all their asses are swung out there. Or there's something more here I'm not seeing, because it makes a big statement to beat the crap out of a guy to grab some wine and then go out of your way to break into someone's house to regain possession of a single bottle of it."

"Right."

"We need Bubbles to talk because the unknown has a way of escalating, Riggs. And a man beaten nearly to death is already farther than I want this to escalate. That means he'll have security, so he'll be good. It also means we'll get the word out we recovered that last bottle, and it was not only spent, but it's now in the possession of law enforcement."

"Obliged."

"But when you talk to him, if I'm there, or I'm not, I need you to get him talking about whatever he's messed up in before things escalate. I want a pin in this, Riggs, and I need your help to do that."

"I can't shake him conscious, Harry. My hands are as tied as yours. But if what you're not saying is that you think I'll back some fool play of Bubbles's, or close ranks to protect a gang of thugs who violate people's homes because I don't want people to think I'm a rat, then you can fuck off."

"You're not your dad, Riggs. I know that. Everyone does."

"Then I'm not sure what your fuckin' problem is."

"My problem is," he stabbed a finger toward Bubbles's room. "I got a man beat to shit. I got some idiots messing with one of my citizens, trying to convince her she's being haunted. That citizen also happens to be worth half a billion dollars. And that fact is really not hard to come by. And I got an organized and efficient crew of burglars, who so far have hit over eleven homes and businesses and stolen over a million dollars' worth of property and might cotton on I got a vodka heiress on my patch. And topping that, I might be reopening a fifteen-year-old murder that has kept Misted Pines in its thrall since it happened, and I already know what I'm gonna see when I open that file. Confession or not, it'll be shoddy police work that's gonna remind my county that the man who had my office before me was a piece of shit. And if it's found out the Whitaker murders weren't investigated correctly and the wrong man went away for that crime, people are gonna wonder what other files need to be reopened. Which will mean I'll be the ringleader of a shitshow. I've already had that job once when I took over for him, and I don't want it back. This all on the heels of six murders that caught national attention. So right now, I got some footprints, tire prints, and an unconscious man going for me. Which isn't fucking much. So, when it comes to you, all I'm doing is asking a friend to help."

"I hear you, Harry," Riggs said low. "And not once have I said I wasn't gonna take your back. But just to note, that vodka princess has come to mean something to me, so this is your job, and I get your job means a lot to you, but this is also pretty fuckin' personal to me too."

"Right, since we're being honest with each other, I'll repeat, you're not your dad."

"I know that," Riggs ground out.

"Good. So that means you'll stop fuckin' around with a woman who clearly does it for you. It hasn't been long since you've known her, but I have never in my life seen you the way I saw you with Nadia today. Not the way you hauled ass out of my station to get to her, not the way you bickered with her at her front door. Fuck, man, you shot out of your chair simply because you got a call from her."

Riggs had no response to that, but even if he did, he wouldn't have been able to say it because Harry kept at him.

"You're not gonna beat her, Riggs, because you're not that man. You're not gonna steal from her, because she's got a lot, but you aren't hurting, though mostly *because you're not that man*. And you're not gonna put her in danger by doing asshole shit with asshole people."

Riggs cut in at that, at the same time burying the rest, "Right, and buying that bottle from Bubbles didn't put her in it?"

"That's on Bubbles, it's not on you. You know you got a woman who knows expensive things on your hands, and you wanted a decent apology. If I had a friend who owned a bar, I'd go to him and swing a deal on a bottle of wine that'd cost me a shit ton more if I went to the liquor store. It makes sense. It's Bubbles that put you both in it, not you. Though, I'll note, you missed my whole fuckin' point."

"Right, we'll talk about me getting serious with Nadia after we talk about you getting your head out of your ass and realizing you're pissing your life away. I loved her, fuck knows you loved her, but your woman died a long time ago, Harry. You'll never get over it, but she'd be pissed as all fuck at you that you stopped living when she did, even if you didn't quit breathing."

Harry's face was stone when he said, "I think we're done here."

"I coulda guessed you'd shut down the minute you heard that honesty."

"I hate to take us back to the playground, brother, but it takes one to know one."

They scowled at each other.

Riggs was angry, hungry, and he wanted to be with his son and Nadia, so he ended it.

"I get a shot at Bubbles, I'll do all I can," he bit off.

"Appreciate it," Harry bit back.

Riggs walked by him to get the fuck out of there.

"Riggs!" Harry called.

Goddammit.

He turned back.

"You shrug off the baggage he landed on you, I'll consider finding my way to do the same," Harry said.

Goddammit.

"She lives in Chicago, man."

"Rus lived in Virginia, now he's here. Delphine lived in Cali, now she's here. Stop putting up walls."

"She's not my type. We're total opposites. She can barely climb up in my truck."

"And Delphine is an award-winning author, and famous actress, and she's with a retired FBI profiler. And Rus is former FBI, living with a woman who runs a burlesque club. Got more?"

He didn't, damn it.

"Fuck off," Riggs bid, earning a dirty look from a passing nurse.

Harry cracked a smile.

Goddamn.

He flipped his friend the bird.

Then he got the fuck out of there.

SEVENTEEN

Pick A Lane

Riggs

Riggs's mood had significantly deteriorated by the time he pulled into the lane to his house.

This was because the hospital was a good twenty minutes out of town, but since he was responsible for dessert that night, he'd had to swing by the grocery store to get it.

He should have grabbed something from the deli to eat, but he didn't want to spoil his appetite for whatever Nadia had planned for dinner. He'd had her spaghetti, and her cake, so he knew whatever it would be, it was going to be good.

So he had a shit day to contend with, and now he was even hungrier, because it took him more time than he would have liked to get home.

His mood didn't get better when his house came into view.

This was because there was a Fret County Sheriff's cruiser there, and standing outside it, leaning against the fender, was Raul Hernandez.

Riggs didn't know the kid well, he just knew he was one of the newer deputies, and young, so inexperienced.

Riggs could see that call from Harry, since he needed his more senior deputies to be dealing with investigating a break-in when a rash of burglaries were happening, but he still didn't like it.

The other part was that his driveway was clogged with vehicles: Nadia's Range Rover, his mother's Lexus, and Dave and Brenda's truck.

He parked off to the side, grabbed the grocery bag, got out, shot a chin lift to Hernandez, and saw his day looking up, minimally, when Dave and Brenda exited his house as he got close to it.

He liked them both, but for once, he was in no mood to play host.

Dave looked pissed and worried. Brenda just looked worried.

They came right to him.

And Dave, being how Dave was, didn't fuck around.

"Gail says you're gonna take care of the cabin."

"Yeah," Riggs confirmed.

"Send me the invoices," Dave ordered.

"You got it."

"We came to see if Nadia was okay and offered her the option of staying with us until you got things sorted," Dave declared.

Riggs's neck got tight.

"She said she already unpacked her toothbrush, whatever that means. I just know it means she's staying here," Dave muttered.

Riggs fought a smile.

"We're gonna get out of your hair. She's got dinner ready," Dave stated, not a talker, but when he did, he was a straight shooter.

And…

Thank fuck.

Dinner was ready.

"You spilled my secret," Brenda added on an accusation aimed at Riggs.

Riggs looked at her, and he saw she now also looked pissed.

"Sorry, Bren," he murmured, not actually sorry because tacos always sounded fantastic, but right then, they sounded miraculous.

She blew out an annoyed breath.

Dave clapped him on the shoulder and Brenda shot him a glare, before that melted, and she gave him a finger wave. They then headed to their truck.

Riggs headed in.

He smelled the tacos the instant he stepped inside, his stomach made itself known again, and he looked right.

His son was sitting at the kitchen bar, Nadia leaned into her forearms opposite him, and his mother was at the end of the bar, by the open landing that led to the stairs, and beyond, the dining room. She had a glass of white wine held up in her hand.

It was then Riggs saw what Nadia was talking about when it came to his mom.

She was wearing dark jeans, a crisp blouse, a lot of silver, her hair was perfect, as was her makeup. She had her back ramrod straight, her legs crossed, one arm along her midriff, resting her other elbow on her hand to hold up her wine.

And she had an air of matriarch about her, surveying the scene, keeping an eye, even if all she surveyed was not technically hers, she was making it clear she claimed it on principle.

He was in a faded tee he got at a Springsteen concert years ago, a jean shirt over it, the jeans covering his legs had a split in one knee, and there was mud on his boots.

Abigail Riggs looked like she belonged in that fancy kitchen he'd renovated so everything was top of the line.

He looked like he was coming in for a glass of water after doing her yard work.

This thought making his mouth twitch, he went to his mom first, kissed her cheek, then to his son, where he mussed his hair while Ledge tried to duck it without really wanting to duck it.

And finally, he rounded the bar, dropped the grocery bag on it, put his hand on Nadia's back and started rubbing, at the same time he smiled at her since she'd twisted her head to look up at him and was doing the same.

"Where we at?" he asked.

"Nadia is helping your son with his *vocabulary* homework," his mother drawled.

He cut his eyes to his mom, then to his boy, catching his guilty look, then to Nadia, who was still beaming.

She was in her zone, happy to be doing teacher shit.

He looked to his kid.

"Ledge," he warned.

"Dad, she likes doing it," Ledger defended himself.

He had no choice but to let his hand fall away when Nadia straightened, asking, "What?"

"He's in fourth grade, but he tests in reading at a seventh-grade level," Riggs explained. "When they get into vocab, it takes him about a minute to finish the work. Sorry, honey, but he doesn't need your help."

Her jaw dropped and her eyes moved to Ledger.

"You were having fun!" he cried.

"Rascal," Nadia replied through a smile.

Riggs pulled the clear plastic container of grocery bakery cookies out of the bag.

"Dad, totally lame," Ledger decreed, eyeing the cookies. "I'm having leftover cake for dessert."

"I don't know," Nadia said, also eyeing the container. "I'm going to soften some ice cream and make myself an ice cream cookie sandwich."

"I change my mind," Ledge stated immediately, "I'm having that."

Christ, they were killing him with all this talk about food.

"Are we going to eat soon?" Riggs asked, his attention having moved to the meat simmering on the stove. "I haven't had anything since this morning."

Nadia instantly jumped to it, exclaiming, "Oh my God! I'll get on shredding the lettuce."

"We're eating like civilized people," his mother announced. "In the dining room."

So his mom was staying for dinner.

His lips started twitching again.

"Help me set the table?" Nadia asked Ledger.

"Sure," he answered, starting to put his work away.

"Where are your placemats?" Nadia asked Riggs.

"Honey," he replied.

No lip wrinkle that time.

Her eyes actually fucking twinkled at the way he admitted he was not a man who owned placemats.

"Time for more online shopping," she muttered to herself before she asked the room at large, "What am I working with? Is this a family that does premade tacos, and they handle the fixin's? Or do you go from the base up?"

"Base up," all three of the Riggs in attendance said at the same time.

Nadia laughed then started ordering Ledger around. "You and I will get the table set and then you can take in all the stuff while I deal with the lettuce and start warming the tortillas."

"You got it," Ledger agreed.

They hustled off with plates and cutlery and paper napkins while his mother strolled Riggs's way, likely on a trajectory to the fridge to top up her wine.

But she stopped at him.

Close.

And spoke.

Quietly.

"Your son is knocking himself out to make your neighbor fall in love with him. Actually, the both of you."

That didn't make a weight settle on Riggs's chest.

It made it feel tight.

"She and I had a quiet moment, however, and after some subtle probing, she shared what it was clear she thought I already knew. That you two were firmly in what she calls the *friend zone*," his mom kept on. "It's my impression, you're the one who put her there."

Fuck.

"Mom—"

"From what *I* see, my son is delivering a dizzying array of mixed messages. Pick a lane, Doc," she ordered. "But a warning. This time, you can't whiz by all the others on a joy ride. This time, you go as slow as it takes and get where you're going in one piece, keeping your passenger safe alongside you."

She didn't let him respond, not that he could, due to all his attention shifting to the tight knot that had formed in his chest.

She headed to the fridge just as Nadia and Ledger came back, Nadia babbling, "The cheese is ready to roll. You can take that in, sweetheart. I'll drain the corn and dish out the beans closer to. We don't want them to get cold." This she said to Ledge, but to him and his mom, she commanded. "Hit a chair. We got you."

Riggs hit the fridge first, asking Nadia, "Wine or beer tonight?"

She shifted her chin toward a half-full wineglass on the counter then started hacking at a head of lettuce.

So he took the wine from his mother and topped her up.

Then he took his beer, Nadia's wine, and hit a chair in the dining room.

He put Nadia's wineglass at the seat beside him.

RIGGS CAME DOWN from making sure his boy was settled in for the night to see Nadia on his couch, her stocking feet on the edge of his coffee table, her laptop on her thighs, her head turned to watch over her shoulder as he approached.

His mom was gone.

Hernandez was still out there.

And later, Nadia was going to be in a bed that was as far away from his as his house could put her, and still, that was way too close for his peace of mind.

"He good?" she asked.

"Yeah," he answered.

"Good. Come here, I want to show you something."

He descended the steps into the living room and sat beside her.

Nadia instantly scooched closer and then listed into his side.

It felt good. It felt comfortable. It felt right.

But damn.

He'd been fucking with her head, he knew it, but even if he

knew he shouldn't do it, he couldn't stop himself, and now he knew he'd fucked up.

Even having that thought, he shifted to pull his arm from between them so he could drape it across the back of the couch, but mostly because that was close to her shoulders.

He could tell himself that made him even more comfortable, and that would be true.

But it wasn't the only reason he did it.

Nor the primary one.

"So last night, when I got home, I emailed a friend of mine who practices estate law in Chicago," she stated. "And she sent me some super interesting stuff."

She was scrolling through a document that looked legal on her laptop.

"I haven't had a lot of time to read through it," she carried on. "But Susan started with a cursory search as a favor, but then she got engrossed, because she told me she's never seen a case this bizarre. So she wrote a whole brief to me detailing what she's found so far, along with sending a ton of stuff."

"What are you talking about?" Riggs asked.

She was clicking into another document, but she stopped doing that to tip her head back to catch his eyes. "Lincoln, Sarah and Roosevelt Whitaker."

Well, goddamn.

"She found something already?" he asked.

"She found a lot of things, Riggs," she answered. "All through filed court documents. First, she was intrigued, because she said the courts can go slow, but eight years of contention is unusual."

"No shit," Riggs remarked.

"I know, right? So she started at the beginning, and get this, they had joint accounts."

"Who?"

She pressed into him and made her eyes big. "All accounts and all of *them*. Lincoln, Sarah *and* Roosevelt."

"All three of them shared joint accounts?"

She nodded.

"Fucking hell," he muttered.

"*I know*," Nadia replied. "And Lincoln and Roosevelt had set up a trust for their royalties, and this trust had three trustees, Lincoln, Sarah and Roosevelt. But upon one or the other brother's death, Sarah was the managing trustee. Now, no surprise, there were stipulations, and if something happened to Lincoln, Sarah got it all. She's his wife, and he would assume she'd use what she inherited to take care of herself, and their kids. But, *surprise*, if something happened to Roosevelt, again, *Sarah got it all*. Though, that said, she kinda already had it all, considering she was named as managing trustee in the trust."

"Right," Riggs said when she stopped talking.

She started again. "Onward from that, if something happened to Sarah, both Lincoln and Roosevelt got it all. Down the middle, equitable split."

"I guess, considering they made their money writing those books together, that's not a surprise," he noted.

"No. But the trust was adjusted twice since it was formed. Not when the kids were born, but instead, five years before the murders, this in order to umbrella all the possessions, monies, investments, contracts, future earnings and properties of the two brothers. The second was a year and a half before the murders, and this was to release the properties from the trust, because, *get this*, Lincoln and Roosevelt worked through a title company to have everything, the cabin, this house, the lake, and Sarah and Lincoln's place in Seattle transferred to Sarah's name."

"What the fuck?" he asked.

"Right?" she asked back. "And it gets weirder, because, even after Sarah was dead, for some reason, Lincoln did bupkus to change this trust, though he *did* take possession of the properties, and everything else, since he inherited them from Sarah. Now, the dissension begins not simply because the managing trustee was dead, the other trustees were dead, and no other trustee was listed, nor inheritor named, and there was a whole lot of dough up for grabs. Not because Lincoln murdered their daughter. But because Sarah's parents never liked Lincoln *or* Roosevelt. And I say that, but from what Susan could tell from filings, it was more like hate. They *hated* the brothers. Didn't want their daughter to marry Lincoln or have anything to do with either. Since she essentially posthumously inherited everything, they're not youngsters, they're both still alive, and they think they should have it all."

"Not their grandkids?"

"I'm getting to that."

He grinned at her and shut up.

"Due to their attitude to the Whitaker boys, and Sarah's, shall we say, connection to both, there was no small amount of estrangement before the incident occurred. It's reported through the documents, none of the family, including the kids, had seen their maternal grandparents for a good decade. And before that, things were already ugly. So the twins' parents, also both still alive, don't think they should have anything. And considering they believe Sarah was the root of both their boys' downfall, they don't think Sarah, or her descendants, should have it either."

Jesus Christ.

"They want to cut out their grandkids too?"

"I know," she repeated. "Seriously, it's dysfunction to the highest degree. And that doesn't take into account Sarah's sister, Mary, who is also a claimant, who also wants it all, cutting out everyone, her sister's children, her parents, definitely the in-laws. The whole lot of them. She, too, is estranged from her own parents. But she says she and Sarah were close, and Sarah's will gave Lincoln and Roosevelt everything, Lincoln actually getting it, because he was the only one left alive. But the sister says, when the two of them were out of the picture, Sarah would want her to have it all."

"Over her sister's children," he remarked, but it was a question.

A quick nod from Nadia and, "That's what she claims. But this is where it gets even more interesting, Riggs, because, according to quite a bit of evidence they were able to produce, which Susan said is expansive and difficult to refute, particularly the publishing contracts, this being that, although Lincoln and Roosevelt came up with the idea for their flagship series together, and their folks admit that the first three books the brothers wrote as a team, after that,

Lincoln essentially tapped out. So there were twenty-nine books published, twenty-one in their flagship series, five in a new series they'd launched, and three standalones. And of those, they contend Roosevelt, and Roosevelt alone, wrote twenty-six of them."

"So Roosevelt was carrying Lincoln?"

She nodded. "Yes, supporting Lincoln, not to mention providing for his wife, his family and his living large with two properties in two locations, both of which were rather impressive. Because this house is very nice, but he also had waterfront property in Seattle that was worth some big bucks."

"Jesus," Riggs muttered.

"This means, if the Whitaker parents can sway a judge, Sarah's parents, and her sister, at least, have no claim to anything that came from what those twenty-six books produced, which, obviously, is quite a bit of the whole banana."

The whole banana.

Christ, she was cute.

"Yeah, it is," he agreed.

"And just to say, several of the parties, namely the Whitakers, noted that the brothers were fighting about the movies. Lincoln wanted to sell more rights. Roosevelt did not. He apparently didn't like the notoriety it was causing him. And if it's true that Lincoln didn't have a hand in writing any of the books after the first three, which were the only rights sold, it could be that Lincoln didn't have a leg to stand on in pushing his brother to sell more. The elder Whitakers contend things were coming to a head between the brothers, and Roosevelt wasn't changing the pen name they'd come up with, because by then, it was branded. But Roosevelt had shared with them, if Lincoln didn't back down, he was going to let it be known his brother was no longer creatively contributing, and the intimation was that things might get financially dicey for Lincoln if his brother cut him off."

"Motive for murder," Riggs noted.

"I'll say, premeditated at that," she replied. "And I'm not done."

"Jesus, does this shit end?"

"Susan said she's only skimming and hasn't had near enough time to do a deep dive, so I guess the answer to that is no."

"Great. Give the rest to me," he invited.

She cozied up to him and went back to it.

"Now, Lincoln and Sarah had three kids, two boys and a girl, with the girl in the middle. And not only are they up against both sets of grandparents and their aunt, they're combatants against each other, with the oldest boy on his own, and the younger two ganging up against him. There is no love lost between any of the interested parties. The only ones sticking together are the two kids, and each set of grandparents."

"What are the kids claiming?" he asked.

"The oldest wants an equitable distribution of the estate among him and his siblings. The younger two want the oldest disinherited, because, they claim, that's what their parents would have wanted. Apparently, the oldest didn't see eye to eye with either Lincoln or Sarah. In fact, he was closer to Roosevelt than any of them, including his siblings. Apparently, he spent all the time he could at the cabin with his uncle. He was in Misted Pines nearly as much as his mother was."

If memory served, that was true.

Though, Riggs didn't really know any of them. He'd seen Lincoln, Sarah, and Roosevelt in town, but it was mostly Lincoln or Sarah. He couldn't recall seeing any of the kids, but one boy, a few years younger than Riggs, he'd seen a couple of times with Roosevelt.

And Roosevelt stuck close to his patch. Rumor had it, and from what Riggs had noticed himself, he barely left it, and to do mundane things like keeping his larder full, it was known he had an assistant take care of it so he could stay on his patch.

"Do you know how old the kids were when their parents died?" he asked.

"Um…" She looked back at the laptop and started scrolling and clicking. "No," she mumbled. Then, "No, wait, here. The oldest was seventeen. The younger two were fifteen and fourteen, respectively."

"So the oldest was old enough to drive to Misted Pines the night his family imploded."

That got him her attention again.

"Wait…*no*," she breathed "Do you think…? Holy cow, yeah. That makes sense. The oldest finds out his mom is cheating on his dad with his beloved uncle, he loses it. The dad walks in on the situation and moves heaven and earth to cover for his boy, including sacrificing himself."

"It's a scenario," Riggs allowed. "Though, it doesn't fit with Lincoln purposefully setting it up so all hell would break lose when he offed himself. If you go that extra mile to protect your kid, you'll engage an attorney to make sure all of them are covered when you're gone."

"Yeah," she whispered, looking again to the laptop.

"It's a stretch, got no clue and never will, where my head would be at after I murdered two people I loved, so he could have just been fucked up. But this all could also be Lincoln's last fuck you. Revenge. Because it doesn't seem like anyone, including the kids, are real great people."

"Yeah," she repeated to the laptop where she was now closing all the documents.

"And it'd be masterful, considering what I bought this property for, because it's probably around the same amount Roosevelt bought it for decades ago. So they took a massive loss on that investment by being a pack of hyenas."

"Yeah," she said again.

"It could just be they're all greedy fucks who are so intent to suck off the teat of two men's hard work, they'll grasp at anything to get the golden milk, so dedicated to the task, they aren't realizing they're sucking that teat dry."

She slapped the laptop closed and shot him a smile. "A colorful metaphor, but also very likely."

"How old are the parents?" he asked.

"I don't know that either, but considering the ages of the three principles, my guess is that they're all in their seventies by now, at least."

"That's dedication," he stated.

"I'll say."

He then did something else he shouldn't do.

He caught a lock of her hair and started twisting it in his fingers.

It was softer than he would have guessed.

Shit.

He did this before he asked, "You doing okay after today?"

"I am. Of course, preliminarily, it was a shock. Now I'm just annoyed. We can just say it takes more than that to bring an Antonov down."

He had no doubt.

"And Ledger was around, so you didn't give the full brief of your afternoon," she continued. "What's up with that?"

"I don't know, and Bubbles isn't conscious yet. The only thing I can tell you is something you already know. It has something to do with the wine. Harry is as baffled as me. It sucks, but we gotta wait until Bubbles wakes up. He's the only one who might have answers."

It wasn't the entire truth, but close enough to it, and seeing as Harry had trusted him with what he'd shared, he wasn't going to break that trust, even for Nadia.

"I think they got what they were looking for, so I don't think they'll be back," he told her. "But I'm still doing that work on the cabin, and I want you to put my number and the sheriff's office number in your favorites so you can get to us fast if something tweaks you."

"I can do that," she agreed.

"And I'm just gonna put it out there that immersing yourself in a fifteen-year-old double homicide is a lot easier than facing the tragedy that's happened to your own family. But I'll remind you, you got a resource and a sounding board close at hand who gets you, so think about taking advantage of that."

When he stopped talking, she did a face-plant in his shoulder.

Oh yeah.

She was avoiding it.

He was forced to let her hair go with her movement, but he cupped the back of her head when she landed.

He also bent his neck so his face was in her hair.

It smelled phenomenal.

"Sorry, honey," he murmured there. "Although, I'll share I don't think you need to do a deep descent and get mired in that shit, because bottom line, it's someone else's shit, not yours to take on. But since the fallout for you is extreme, I also don't think it's healthy to flat-out avoid it. Obviously, this is all about me. I don't want Maribeth showing and finding out I've fallen down on the job."

She laughed softly and lifted her head.

And fuck him, he kept his hand where it was.

"I'll start dealing," she promised.

"I wasn't pushing you, just reminding you. And while I'm doing that, from what I can tell, my mom likes you. And she might have some insights too."

"Does she know about what happened?"

He shook his head. "Not that I know. I can ask, and I can tell her so you don't have to, if that's what you want."

She seemed surprised. "So you didn't tell her?"

"I told her you're my neighbor, you're a good sort, you're dealing with some deep shit because your dad was an asshole, and considering the last part, that was all she needed."

"Right," she whispered.

"We need to unwind. You don't watch *Witcher*, so what do you wanna watch?"

"There's an *Only Murders in the Building* fest in town this weekend. Have you seen that?"

"Honey, I have no fucking idea why, but they've had that festival since that show started. I made the mistake of being in town when it was on last year, and I ran into Kimmy wearing a fake fur with a fake bird stuck to the shoulder and weird glasses with her telling me all weekend, if I saw her, I had to refer to her as 'Bunny.' Then she shoved a tray full of bowls of dip in my face. I haven't seen the show, but I'm already traumatized by it."

She started laughing even as she said, "You have to see it. It's hilarious."

"Whatever you want," he murmured.

She grinned at him, then she leaned forward to put her laptop on the coffee table and grab the remote.

The instant she sat back, he commandeered the remote, because there weren't many rules at his house, but the man having the remote in his hand was one of them.

It was a brand-new rule he'd made just then, but he was sticking by it.

She settled back into him, grumbling, "Macho man."

"Whatever," he replied, and he switched on the TV.

He could see how it would have been easier for her to have the remote, since she had to tell him what service the show was on and guide him to finding it.

But he didn't give a fuck.

And she didn't either, seeing how she curled up into the couch as well as into his side when he lifted his feet to the coffee table and stretched out his legs.

He didn't want to like it.

But he saw from the get-go, she was right.

The show was damned funny.

EIGHTEEN

Puppy

Riggs

They tried to be quiet.

They failed.

Still, his sleep had been such shit, he let them have at it the next morning, Nadia making breakfast for his kid, his kid eating it, until, from where he was stretched out on his couch in the living room, his gun on the coffee table, he heard Nadia say quietly, "Go brush your teeth, sweetheart. We'll let your dad sleep. I'll run you to school."

Riggs heard his son's sneakers clambering up the stairs and sat up.

He looked over the back of the couch at her and caught her staring murder at him.

Seemed she hadn't had cup two of coffee.

He pushed up, the throw falling off his body, and he let it remain where it fell, still in his jeans and Springsteen tee from last night, socks on his feet.

He went direct to the coffee pot, managing to do that without being mortally wounded by the daggers she was shooting out her eyes, and he made himself a mug.

He turned, leaned his hips against the counter, and before he took a sip, he took his life in his hands and asked, "Is it the caffeine level or did I somehow do something in my sleep to piss you off?"

She stopped rinsing plates in the sink, turned off the faucet, and got dead in his face.

Fuck, it killed him not being able to kiss her, even as pissed as she was right then, and he could see she was seriously fucking pissed.

Her eyes slid up to the ceiling, as if trying to sense where Ledger was in getting his shit sorted, then back to him.

She launched in. "First, a nine-year-old and a gun on the coffee table do not mix, Andrew Doc Riggs."

"My gun is always locked, except last night. Even if it wasn't, he knows I'll lose my mind if he even touched it. And I was right there, and I've been awake since you two came downstairs."

Nadia didn't miss a beat.

"This brings me to my second, which has two parts, since obviously you didn't sleep great last night if you had to fake sleep for the last half an hour instead of getting up and joining us for breakfast, and I'm guessing that doesn't have to do with the fact you slept on the couch."

It'd be good if sometimes, like this time, she wasn't as sharp.

"So that leads me to part two," she went on, "you on the couch at all. Were you keeping something from me last night when you told me all was good with what was going on and the bad guys got what they wanted when they got that wine?"

"I haven't even had a sip of coffee yet," he growled back. "So I don't know how many parts my comeback has, but I love my boy, I give more than a passing shit about you, and someone wrecked your door, not to mention, wrecked Bubbles's skull. So I didn't lie. As far as we can tell, it's about the wine. But that doesn't mean I'm taking any chances."

"So you're not keeping anything from me to protect me like you protected me from ghost stories?"

"I am."

Her eyes got huge.

"But it's not a lot, and I'm doing it because this county's sheriff, and my good friend, told me in confidence, and in no uncertain terms I couldn't share it, even with you. But if I was worried, or hell, Harry was, we'd be moving more than a few nights' worth from your closet to the one in my guest room."

She backed off.

But since they were on this subject.

"I know you're worth a lot of money, Nadia," he stated. "And that's not difficult intel to come by. So I'm gonna say straight out, it worries me, you alone in that cabin."

"How do you suggest I live my life, Riggs?" she asked. "Have a security guard follow me around. Get dogs? Build a twenty-foot wall around me?"

An idea sprang to mind.

"I'm getting you a dog."

She blinked.

"Are you two done fighting?" Ledger called, the echo of it telling him it was from the stairs.

She started it, so Riggs cocked his head before he righted it and took a sip of his coffee.

She'd lost the attitude (and it was around the time he'd said he gave more than a passing shit about her, but he wasn't going there— he had to think on it, but he'd do it later, when she wasn't right in front of him after cooking his kid breakfast).

Now that attitude came back.

"We're fine!" she yelled.

Ledger showed.

She looked to him. "And we weren't fighting. We were discussing."

"Guns are stupid, and they're used to kill kids in schools. Dad has one because we live in the middle of nowhere and there are bears. But he doesn't like them either. Harry made him get it. Because crazy stuff happens in MP a lot."

"You can say that again," she muttered under her breath.

At that, Riggs hid his smile behind another sip of coffee.

"And you were fighting," Ledger contradicted. "You shouldn't lie to kids. It teaches us to lie."

"I'm understanding now why Jenny fell in love with Forrest," Nadia griped.

Riggs choked on his coffee.

"What does that mean?" Ledger asked.

"Nothing," she said. "Got everything?"

He went to get his book bag.

She turned to Riggs. "You. Call the school and add me to the drop-off, pick-up list." She turned to Ledger. "You. Out into the Range Rover."

Ledger saluted. "Aye, aye, captain."

"Someone kill me," she mumbled, snatching her purse off the kitchen bar.

Ledger was out the door, and she was nearly the same, when Riggs called, "Honey?"

Hand on the door, she looked his way.

He had a lot of things to say.

The one he picked was maybe not on top of the list, still, it was important.

"Thanks for taking my kid to school."

"Stop being sweet after you've annoyed me."

"I gotta swing however I swing," he replied.

"Ugh," she grumbled.

Then she was out the door.

HALF AN HOUR LATER, after a quick shower and change, he called Nadia from his truck on the way to the hospital.

Harry had phoned, and Bubbles was awake.

"If you're going to be sweet, I'm not listening," she said as greeting.

Which meant he was grinning at his windshield.

"Bear down, this might be considered sweet."

"What?" she asked, not sounding annoyed, or curious, just normal.

"The cruiser was gone when I left. Probably took off when you and Ledger did. I'm headed to the hospital. Bubbles is awake. I told Harry I wanted a deputy to return, and he's gonna see what he can do. But if you don't see a cruiser in the drive when you get home, head back to town and grab a coffee then find me some placemats."

"Fine."

"And figure out what else you're gonna need to bring over. You're spending an extra night at mine."

"Why?" that sounded suspicious.

"Because I called the school and put you on the list. And when I get back, I'm not gonna work on your house. We're headed into the mountains. I called a friend and found our luck has changed. He's got an adolescent cane corso ready to place that hasn't already been claimed. Though, he says you'll need to go out every day for the next week to work with him, and he'll need to come out to the cabin every day for another week to keep that training going."

"I…sorry, I'm not following."

"He breeds and trains Malinois and cane corsos for police and guard work. He doesn't have a Malinois ready to be placed. But I'm down with that. I'd prefer a cane corso. The Malinois can be vicious as fuck, and they don't like any strangers. The cane corso is more loving and accepting, but they're huge, more visually intimidating, and its bite force can fuck someone up."

"Riggs—"

"You get a dog, Nadia, or we talk to Dave about an extensive security system being put in, including perimeter sensors and motion detectors. And we also talk about buying you a gun, and getting you trained in using it."

"I'm not buying a gun."

"Then you're getting a dog."

"Maybe we can have a chat—"

He cut her off. "Don't make me do it."

"Do what?"

"Ask you what your grandfather would say about you alone in that cabin."

Silence.

He gave her some time.

Then he stopped doing that.

"Nadia?"

"I'll get a dog," she said softly.

"You pissed at me?"

"It wasn't low, though I want to think it was. You're right. My *dedulya* would not be happy, nor would he think it's smart, me at that cabin with only you close, and not that close. Especially with all that's happening. Mom would be pretty ticked too."

"You got security at your place in Chicago?"

"I live in a high rise, and yes, it has very good security because *Dedulya* bought it for me."

"Right."

"So I guess I'm getting a puppy," she mumbled.

"Honey, this is no puppy."

"It'll be a puppy to me."

He'd give her that.

"Letting you go. No girlie placemats," he warned.

"As if," she replied.

He was grinning at his windshield again.

"Later," he said.

"Bye, Riggs," she replied.

He disconnected and drove the rest of the way to the hospital.

NINETEEN

Winning

Riggs

Harry was outside Bubbles's door when Riggs got there.

"Yo, brother," Riggs greeted, and they clasped hands and bumped forearms.

All forgiven, because if you had a brain in your head, you didn't hold onto a beef with a good friend if it started with the best of intentions.

"How we gonna play this?" Riggs asked when they broke.

"Doctor says he woke up last night. He was groggy, but lucid. Report is, he's more lucid today. They're gonna run some tests, but from the ones they can do without shit that's plugged into a wall and costs your insurance company five grand, if you're lucky enough to have insurance, they say he's doing good."

"Thank fuck for that," Riggs muttered.

"Yeah," Harry agreed. "They also gave me the all-clear to talk to him. Which is why I called you. So I'm thinking, you go in alone. You can tell him I'm here. You can tell him what he says you're gonna tell me. Or you can not mention me at all. I'm not gonna coach you or call the shots. I want to know why he was assaulted, and I want to know what he knows, and right now, I don't care how I come about that information."

"He could tell me, and not want to go on the record later," Riggs noted.

Harry shook his head. "I don't give a fuck, Riggs. I gotta know which way to steer this investigation."

"Right then, I got an appointment with a man about a dog, so this needs to get done."

"A dog?"

"Hutch has a cane corso ready, and in a week, it's going home with Nadia," Riggs told him.

Harry did a slow smile. "They always said you were a genius."

"They didn't lie," Riggs joked, flicked up his chin, then moved the five steps that took him to Bubbles's door and through it.

Bubbles's attention came right to him, his body jumped in bed like he wanted to jump out of it, then he winced. After that, he smiled huge and winced again.

Riggs understood the wincing, his friend was fucked right the hell up, bruised, battered, swollen, near on unrecognizable. Even without the bandaging around his left eye.

Christ.

He came to a stop by the side of the bed, but closer to the foot, planted his feet and crossed his arms.

"Hey, bro!" Bubbles slurred.

"I'll start by saying, I'm glad you weren't beat to death. I'll move on to share the news that someone did a number on my neighbor's back door in order to take one thing. That bottle of wine you sold me to give to her."

Bubbles's lips turned down at the sides and his eyes moved over Riggs's shoulder.

"Eyes to me, Bubbles." When he got them, though it took a while, he asked, "What the fuck?"

"I owed you a marker," he said, still slurring, and Riggs figured it was partly drugs and partly that his mouth was fucked up from getting his face bashed in.

"Bubbles—"

"I tried to tell them that. They didn't give two shits."

His said "shits" like "shitsh," which normally Riggs would razz him about.

Riggs was in no mood to razz Bubbles.

"Let's start at the beginning," Riggs suggested.

"I'm just gonna say, I did go to Sonoma."

"You just didn't buy that wine there," Riggs surmised.

"Trust me, all I said is all you want me to say."

"Because whoever you got that wine from is worse than the normal dipshits you deal with."

"Doc—"

"She wasn't home. If she was home, I might be moved to add to the pain whatever they've jacked you up with is keeping at bay right now."

Bubbles threw up both his hands, including the casted one.

And winced.

Then he said, "I fucked up. Okay. Big news. Bubbles fucks up."

"There's a way to stop doing that. It starts and ends with not fucking up."

Bubbles's eyes turned to slits, and Riggs had to admit, it threw him. He'd never seen Bubbles look that way.

"Not everyone has an IQ of two thousand."

Riggs didn't think it would be cool at this juncture to share such a number didn't exist.

Instead, he noted tightly, "I don't hold myself above you, and you know that, so don't give me that shit."

"Tall. Good-looking. Smartest guy in every room. You ate more pussy in high school than I have my whole life."

"How is you selling me what was apparently a very important bottle of wine you never should have sold me, that clearly wasn't yours to sell, suddenly about me?"

It was like he didn't speak.

"Knock some bitch up, get a great kid outta it," Bubbles complained.

"She and me aren't tight, but I'm not down with you calling my son's mother a bitch."

Bubbles flicked out a hand, winced again, then said, "There it is. True blue Doc Riggs. Wake up, eat a bitch out so she comes so hard she's walking on air all day. Even knowing she'll be one and done, she'll brag she got tagged by Doc Riggs. Then spend the day making art that sells for a whack, running electrical wire while your clients slobber all over you that *you* picked *them* to receive the great work of Riggs Contracting. And then maybe saving a kid from drowning. Go to bed after banging another bitch, whose only hope and dream is you'll let her stay the night so you'll go down on her in the morning. Must be tough bein' you."

Riggs was so blown away by the garbage coming out of his friend's mouth, he had nothing to say.

Bubbles did, though.

"Got my face literally fuckin' caved in, they gotta put me in a coma, I get out of it, you stroll in and give me shit about a bottle of fuckin' *wine*? You asked what the fuck, that's my question too, man."

"I came on strong because, with the state of you, and this being about those bottles, I had to sleep on the couch with my gun on my coffee table, my kid in his bed upstairs, and my neighbor in the guest room because her home is no longer secure."

"Poor you. I been in a coma for two days."

"What I'm trying to impress on you is that *you* put yourself in a coma, Bubs. And you had a place in my heart, so I also had to deal with that. And just to say, the five hours I spent in this hospital with your mom and Lucille after it went down was not a good time for any of us. I also gotta deal with the understanding a friend of mine put me, my kid and my neighbor out there for fuck knows who to target."

"They got their wine back. They won't give a shit about you."

"She and I drank a bottle."

"*She*," he hissed.

"Yeah, *she*. So if this wine is so fuckin' important, they're one short in a way they're not getting that back."

"Seems you gone blind, seeing as you could just look at me and see, you mighta shelled out a few hundred bucks, but *I* paid for that precious, fucking bottle."

"What I see is you got a comment about my earlier remark, and it's that you don't know how not to fuck up."

"I got my own problems, Doc. You said we're square I didn't do a pool on your neighbor. I didn't do a pool. We're square."

"I'm not as smart as you think I am, Bubs, because I didn't get it until now. How you hung on to that when I told you what I did for you was because I was your friend, and it ended there. But you kept up with that marker bullshit, and I didn't see it. But I see it now. You don't understand what being a friend means."

He watched Bubbles wince again, but this was more like a flinch, and it came from a different kind of pain.

But Riggs was beyond caring.

"Not sure this will get through the drugs and you processing what happened to you, or your thick fuckin' skull," Riggs continued. "So it might be a waste of breath, but when I walked into this room, I gave a shit about you, and after listening to you spout your damage, I've got about a half an inch of that shit left. So I'll use the rest of it by sharing, a friend doesn't hold markers when he's doing something for a buddy in need. He also doesn't sell him a bottle of wine that's gonna swing his bud's ass out there. He sure as shit doesn't lay his damage on him. You got a problem being this version of Bubbles Novak, don't foist that on me. Seek change. Now I'll leave you with this. I hope you get better. I really fuckin' do. Like I said, I've been worried about you, and seeing you, I can see you went through hell. But lose my number, man. We're done."

"Doc—" Bubbles called.

But Riggs was out of there.

Harry was studying his boots, but when Riggs came out of the room, his head came up, and he looked expectantly at Riggs.

Then his eyes narrowed a nanosecond before his expression turned concerned.

"Jesus, what went on in there?" Harry asked when Riggs stopped at him.

"I probably should have eased into it, but Bubbles would have known something was up if I was all about apologizing I didn't bring him a get well card. But we can just say, I got a crystal-clear understanding of what Bubbles thinks about me, and it's too much, and not in a good way."

"What does that mean?"

"It sounds arrogant, but he's jealous as fuck."

Harry swayed back, and said quietly, "Can't be the first time you faced that, Doc."

"Not that ugly, and not from someone I'd call a friend."

"He's not in a good place right now," Harry noted.

"With what came out of his mouth, I don't care if that fucker was on his death bed."

Harry gave him a long, hard look before he said, "Shit, brother, I shouldn't have sent you in there."

"You didn't know."

"It was a bad call."

"Harry, you didn't know. One thing I learned the hard way, and it wasn't an epiphany, my old man spent about twenty-three years teaching me this lesson, people do what they do. We wanna make it about us. With my dad, I actually *wanted* it to be about me, because, even if it was in a jacked way, something with him would be about me. But it's never about you. Especially if it's filth they got that they want to get rid of. That's not about you at all. You can take that on, but that's them winning."

Riggs let out a long breath.

And then he finished it.

"This is saying, I didn't get dick. He admitted he didn't get that wine in Sonoma and said that's all I'd wanna know about it. He also referred to whoever did that to him as 'they.' I don't know if he was being cagey and that 'they' was singular. But the state of him, we both can guess there was more than one of them. So your hunch that this is something else, and it's big, I reckon is right. But that's all I got for you, brother."

"It shits me you came all the way out here to do me a favor, and you're leaving with the look you got on your face right now."

Riggs shook his head. "Let that go too. I wish I'd learned this when I was a freshman in high school, and I first met Bubbles. At the very least, it would have saved Nadia her back door and a lot of anxiety. But I know now. And that's also winning."

"You're about as fucked up as you are adjusted, and that fucked-up part is only what we talked about last night."

"Takes one to know one," Riggs retorted.

Harry grinned at him.

Riggs cuffed him on the arm.

Then he walked out of the hospital and put that scene and his friendship with Bubbles where it belonged.

In his overflowing shitcan of memories.

TWENTY

High Time

Riggs

In a rare moment of coincidental synchronization that, if Riggs had the headspace to give to it, he really should give it that headspace, he rolled up behind Nadia's Range Rover a little over a mile from his lane.

He found she went a studious six miles over the speed limit on a low traffic, rural road, which had him laughing his balls off.

Something that he also should have given headspace to, considering, after what went down with Bubbles, he'd been in no mood to laugh.

They slid in beside each other outside his house, and he tooted his horn.

He knew she got him instantly when she gave him a jaunty thumbs up, turned, grabbed some stuff, then jumped out of her car carrying a big, brown paper bag with handles, a little, white paper bag he knew held treats from Aromacobana, her purse over her shoulder, and a white paper coffee cup with drawing on it.

She opened the door and leaned in, ordering, "Here, take this."

He took her coffee and put it in the holder.

"And this," she went on.

He took the bakery bag and put it between the seats.

She tossed the other bag in the footwell, nabbed the hand hold, put her foot on the rim of the door, then heaved herself up.

And fell to her back foot.

She tried again.

And fell back.

A third time she remained suspended in air for a second.

And fell back.

"Jesus," he said through laughter. "I don't have a problem getting in."

"You're six inches taller than me," she snapped.

"Ledger doesn't either."

"Huh," she forced out, then gave it her all and landed in the seat. She turned to him. "There!" she cried triumphantly.

He grinned at her. "Well done, princess."

She slammed her door, grabbed the bag in the footwell, and demanded, "Look!"

She then pulled out some circular placemats that looked like crushed leather and were forest green.

"Aren't they perfect?" she asked.

"They actually are."

She shoved them back in the bag, noting, "You sound surprised."

He put the truck in reverse. "I didn't know they made placemats for people with dicks. And belt up."

She reached for her seatbelt and educated, "They make everything for everybody."

"Good to know," he muttered and headed down the lane.

"I didn't think we'd meet up like that, or I would have gotten you a coffee."

"I'm good, honey. But thanks."

"Though, I got treats for the road."

"Saw that."

"How's your friend?"

"Not my friend anymore."

For the second time that day, he was met with silence from her, and having her actually with him, he could feel how profound it was this time.

It was her turn to break it.

"What does that mean?" she asked softly.

"I'm thinking he's freaked about what happened to him. Definitely they got him on drugs for pain. But still, seems he's feeling some, and not just the kind that comes from the body. Even so, he let loose in the kind of way there's no coming back."

"Oh, Riggs," she said gently. "What did he say?"

"You don't want to know."

"Actually, if it's upsetting you, I do."

"Right then. He's pissed I ate more pussy in high school than he's had in his whole life. And it seems that's a thing for him, because he went on to share how he thought I spent my days, starting them eating more pussy and leaving a woman satisfied even if I didn't give her anything more than that. He made some comment about how much I make on my commissions, my contract work, that I'd then save a kid from drowning, and end the day banging another woman before I went to bed. He also referred to Angelica as a bitch."

"Are your commissions unusually pricey?" she asked cautiously.

"I get what people will pay me for them, and I don't aim low."

"So the answer to that is yes."

"I'll say, when the math is done, I make about five times an hour more working on a commission than I do working a job. And I don't bid low on jobs either."

"Wow."

"Yeah."

"Definitely understanding why you own a lake."

"Honey," he warned low.

"I know. I'm sorry. I'm being flippant because, if I'm not, I'm going to get really, double, super, extra pissed off."

He glanced from the road to her. "What?"

"I don't know this person, but he sounds like his blood turned green somewhere along the way, and that green can be acid."

"That's about the gist of it," he concurred.

"So, honestly, Riggs, what the fuck?" she asked.

There was her saying fuck again.

"Nadia—"

"No, Riggs." Her voice was rising. "What *the fuck*?"

"Honey, calm down."

"I'm not going to calm down," she shot back. "You've been worried about this guy. He sells you a bad bottle of wine, the kind of bad you have to sleep on your couch with a gun next to you, and you go visit him, and he's mean to you?"

Mean?

All kinds of cute.

"He isn't worth it," he told her.

"Is he your friend?"

"He was. And I'm gonna tell you a story, and it's not gonna make me sound good, but it's going to explain that I should have been smart about Bubbles a long time ago."

"Okay," she said sharply, not worried about the story he was going to tell.

She was still pissed.

Oh yeah.

He had to find time to give the situation with Nadia some headspace.

"I met Bubbles in high school. He's an odd kind of guy. A ball of energy. Always moving. Not sure how he can be like that and still be pudgy, but he is, and that's not shade on people who carry weight. He's just got that much energy. He always had thin hair, and now he doesn't have much of it, and he wanted to be everyone's friend. So kids, being assholes, took advantage of that. He was bullied, but he didn't know it because he just wanted everyone to like him, so he took it. Though, maybe he did know it."

"I'm thinking, he did," she confirmed.

His mouth went up on one side, fortunately it was the side opposite her, just in case his humor might piss her off more, and he kept talking.

"That shit was shit. I intervened because I was feeling some of that, being twelve years old and a freshman in high school. Both of us in the same boat, we became friends. I learned pretty quickly that he'd do just about anything for anyone if they'd just like him, and it made him kind of a doofus, but also, bottom line, he'd do just about anything for anyone. And 'anything' comes in a lot of varieties. When my dad died, he slept on my couch for two weeks, and he had a live-in girlfriend then. Not to mention, I didn't need moral support, but he did it anyway. When I found out Angelica was pregnant, he came over with a bottle of Jack, and we got drunk. That's one kind of Bubbles's anything."

"I'm not feeling like I want to kick him in the shin anymore, that is, when he's up and walking again."

"Right," Riggs murmured, tamping down his humor so he could get into his next.

Because it was going to be a lot harder.

"Other shit he did was just stupid. He got himself in a situation where he owed a favor to someone who wanted him to do something, and this someone was really not cool, so even though what he wanted Bubs to do seemed innocuous, it probably wasn't. But Bubs had to get out from under this guy. Bubbles was freaked. I was freaked for him. And he asked me to go with him. He was making a delivery, and we were right, it wasn't innocuous. The situation was dangerous, and it could have gone really fucking bad. Fortunately, they wanted what we were delivering more than they gave any fucks about us, so we laid it on them and got the fuck out of there. I don't know what it was. It could have been ransom or drugs or illegal firearms. I just know it wasn't Girl Scout cookies. It felt dirty, and it was the only time I felt like I was inching closer to being like my dad."

"Riggs," she whispered.

She got that feeling all right.

"Bubbles knew what that would do to me, so I know he didn't stop doing stupid shit for and with bad people, he just never dragged me into it again."

"Until the wine."

"Of a sort," he allowed. "But he felt he owed me a marker, and in his head, that's part of how he paid me back."

"He did owe you a marker, but selling you that wine was no payback."

More training from her *dedulya*, no doubt.

"I didn't hold a marker, honey, and I told him that a million times. But Bubs didn't get it. He didn't get friends have each other's backs. I should have seen that, but I didn't. Until today."

"Just to say, now I want to kick him in the shin again because he used your friendship to drag you into doing something that made you feel dirty."

"It was my choice."

"You were looking out for a friend."

"It was still my choice."

"We're just going to have to agree to disagree, Riggs, because bottom line, you're right. It was your choice. But we do things for people we care about. Especially if you're a good person. And he played on that. I don't know how much of a doofus he is. On the one hand, he sold you a bottle of wine that got him a stay in a hospital, and that's pretty damned stupid. On the other, he played the only thing he could play when he was dealing with a highly intelligent man, his emotions and the feelings he felt for him. Which is pretty ingenious, and downright nasty. So, fuck Bubbles whoever-he-is."

Totally needed to give Nadia some serious headspace.

"Warning, the Russian is coming out in you, princess," he teased.

"Warning right back, Riggs, it's always close to the surface."

"No shit? It got in my face this morning about the gun."

"I've never been to Russia," she announced. "My grandfather used to spit after he said the word. Mom told me great-granddad would do the same. But she said he missed it even so. The pain was like a toothache he had every day of his life. I think that kind of love flows through bloodlines."

"I know his story, just so you know."

"It isn't a secret. It's actually famous."

"Yeah. And if I had to leave the country I love in order to be free to be me, I would feel the same."

"Agreed."

"What does *dedulya* mean? Grandpa?"

"It's kind of an endearment for grandpa. *Dedushka* is grandfather. Mom called her grandfather *deda*. He was still alive when I was born, though I don't remember but snatches of him. To distinguish the two, I was taught *dedulya*."

"Right."

"How far is this place where we're going?"

"About forty-five minutes."

"We should stop and get you coffee," she said as she reached for hers.

"Like I said, I'm good."

"Okay."

He drove for a while.

When she put the coffee back in the holder, he called, "Nadia?"

"Mm?"

"Thanks for being pissed on my behalf."

"You're welcome," she said softly.

He reached out and squeezed her knee.

Instead of leaving it there, like he wanted, he put his hand back to the wheel.

Absolutely.

It was time to find the headspace to figure out where he was with Nadia, and then set about discovering where she was.

It was time days ago.

So it was high time now.

FORTY-FIVE MINUTES LATER, he stood back and witnessed a mother and child reunion.

That being a big, blue cane corso loping right to Nadia, who had crouched to make herself less threatening without Hutch telling her to do so, and the dog slobbering all over Nadia's face after barely a sniff.

Whereupon Nadia threw her arms around the terrifying-looking animal's neck and cried out a joyful, "Puppy!"

"Jesus Christ," Hutch muttered, standing at his side. "I've never seen anything like that. And I been doing this awhile."

Hutch was a former SEAL who'd been breeding and training police and guard dogs for at least seven years.

"She's Russian by heritage," Riggs told him.

"That explains it," Hutch replied.

Nadia turned to Hutch and called, "What's her name?"

"Gia," Hutch called back.

She returned to Gia and cooed, "Oh my God. Gia. Who's a darling girl? Who's a pretty girl? Who's the *prettiest girl in the world?* Gia is!" while the ninety pounds of packed muscle that made up Gia pranced around her like she was, well…fuck.

A puppy.

"She's gonna undo six months of training in two minutes." Hutch was back to muttering.

"Welcome to my world," Riggs muttered in return.

But in his case, he reckoned, it was more like thirty-eight years.

TWENTY-ONE

That Did It

Riggs

"You gotta go low, hit it on the back flat, like this," Ledger said, then let fly, and the stone he was holding skipped seven times across the lake before it sank.

Riggs watched as Nadia bit the tip of her tongue, tried to mimic Ledger's stance, then let fly.

Her stone immediately kerplunked.

"I'm failing my latest nature girl test," she said to the lake.

And *damn*, she was.

That was about her fifteenth stone. And Ledge was giving her the best ones.

"They don't have stone skipping in the Olympics, so it's okay," Ledger placated her.

She turned to his son, "I'm much better at looking cute in a pink slicker and tramping through the rain."

Ledger burst out laughing.

Riggs smiled.

"They don't have that in the Olympics either, but they should," she went on.

Ledger kept laughing.

Riggs kept smiling.

Then he turned to the drive when he heard a car pulling in.

And he stopped smiling.

"You two, stay here," he ordered as Lucille parked then got out.

"Who's that?" he heard Nadia ask Ledge.

"Lucille. Bubbles's girlfriend," Ledger answered.

"Stay here," Nadia said urgently.

Shit.

Riggs stopped, and she nearly ran into him because she was racing up the pier.

"Stay here," he repeated when she made it to him.

"No," she replied.

"Nadia."

"No."

"Please."

"Absolutely not."

They went into staredown.

"Heya! Doc?" Lucille called.

"Fuck," he grunted, turned to his son, pointed at him and said, "Don't move."

Nadia dogging his steps, he strode up the slope to where Lucille was standing.

Her eyes were pinging back and forth between him and Nadia, and they didn't stop, even when Riggs and Nadia stopped in front of her.

She finally looked to Riggs, thankfully, before she gave herself a stroke.

"I was worried I'd interrupt dinner," she said.

"We ate earlier. What's up?"

She looked pointedly at Nadia.

"Nadia, this is Lucille. Lucille, this is Nadia, my neighbor," he introduced.

"*Ahhhhhhhhhh…*" Lucille let out, low and slow. "Your *neighbor*."

He felt Nadia stiffen at his side.

"That's what I said," Riggs replied.

"Does Bubbles know all about *your neighbor*?" Lucille asked.

"Not to be rude, we just met, but why are you saying it that way?" Nadia asked.

"Darlin', you looked in a mirror lately?" Lucille asked.

"Yes," Nadia answered shortly.

"Just sayin', if Bubs knew you were Doc's *neighbor*, he would have made a different decision about the wine," Lucille replied.

"So now it's my faul—" Nadia started heatedly.

"Honey," Riggs whispered.

Nadia clamped her mouth shut.

Lucille's eyes nearly bugged out of her head.

Fuck him.

"Lucille, not that I don't wanna see you, but we were in the middle of something," Riggs told her.

The woman looked beyond him toward the pier. "What were you in the middle of?"

"Ledger was teaching me to skip rocks," Nadia answered.

Lucille's head tilted to the side sharply before she smiled genuinely and said, "Well, that's real important, so I won't keep you long, just gotta have a word with Doc."

"Then have your word," Nadia invited.

"I was hoping it might be private."

"Your boyfriend was already mean to him today, and we were having a nice night, so I hope you don't mind if I stick around to see that nothing ruins it," Nadia returned.

After listening to this, Lucille's eyes swiveled to Riggs, and she declared, "You totally should have told Bubbles about this chick."

Riggs looked to the sky and sighed.

Lucille's tone was different, and it brought his attention back to her when she said, "He went too far today, Doc. He knows it. He feels like a total asshole. He's been kicking himself all day."

He waited for Nadia to field that, partly out of curiosity at what she'd say, mostly because what he had to say, he didn't want to say to Lucille. She was a nice woman.

She did field it, just not the way he expected.

She wrapped both her hands around his biceps and leaned her tits into him.

Lucille didn't miss it, and honest to fuck, he could swear he saw tears in her eyes.

"Lucille, how about you leave what happened between Bubs and me between Bubs and me?" he suggested.

"He's not feeling good. He's hopped up on pain meds—" she began with the excuses.

"That's not leaving it between Bubs and me," Riggs warned her. "And I gotta say, I'm confused. He told me you two were over."

"I kinda forgave him after he got the shit knocked out of him," Lucille shared.

That would do it.

At least it would with those two.

Her expression turned pleading. "He's in a bad way, Doc. You're his only real friend. He knows it. He's going through some stuff. He piled on you. He shouldn't have. He—"

Lucille cut herself off as they all looked to the drive to see another car pulling in.

God fucking damn it.

He looked down at Nadia who was peering questioningly up at him.

"Angelica," he said.

"What's *she* doing here?" Lucille asked.

"She's my kid's mom," Riggs shared something she already knew.

Riggs didn't have a good feeling when Lucille whirled, appearing suddenly panicked, and sounding it when she said a quick, "Doc."

Ledger joined them, with a little huff from his run, announcing excitedly, "Mom's here!"

Angelica was striding toward them, and yeah.

Riggs had a type.

Leggy. Great rack. Easy.

But brunette.

Until recently.

Riggs was learning a lot that day.

"Hey, Mom," Ledger called.

"Hey, kid," Angelica called back.

When she arrived at them, she gave Lucille a once-over and dismissed her.

Then she gave Nadia a much longer one, and Nadia let him go and moved a step away.

Only then did Angelica look to Riggs. "This the bitch you put on Ledger's pick-up list?"

At that, it was Riggs who stiffened.

"Mom!" Ledger yelled.

"Maybe you should go inside," Angelica ordered her son through a suggestion.

"No!" Ledger shouted, and Riggs's eyes sliced to him. "Not if you're gonna—"

"Son, what did your mother say?" he asked quietly.

Ledger looked up to him. "But...*Dad*!"

"We have a deal, right? You mind your mom and me. Yeah? Even if you don't agree, later, we'll talk it out. But when it happens, what happens?"

"I mind," he said to his sneakers.

"Please, kid. Go inside. We'll talk later," Riggs finished it.

Pink hit Ledger's cheeks, he glanced at Nadia, glowered at his mom, and after kicking the dirt, he bolted toward the house.

"I see how it is. Like father like son, both hankering after the hot neighbor," Angelica sneered.

"Gross!" Lucille snapped. "He's just a boy."

"A growing boy," Angelica shot back. "They learn what girls are, you know. Seein' as you're fuckin' the biggest boy in all of MP, you *should* know."

Lucille reared back.

"Angelica," Riggs growled.

"I think I'm going to go in the house too," Nadia said softly.

Angelica's eyes cut to her, but Lucille had spoken over her, saying, "You know what's good for you, you watch your mouth, Angelica."

"Please," Angelica drawled to Lucille. Then she aimed her next at Riggs. "You think to give me a heads-up you add someone to my son's pick-up list?"

"No, since he's my son too, and Ledger knows her, Mom knows her, she's a teacher for fuck's sake, and I trust her, so that should be good enough for you," Riggs replied.

"Newsflash"—Angelica threw her arms out—"*it isn't*. You can't put all your fuck buddies on our son's pick-up list, Doc. They don't have enough paper in that whole school to keep that shit on file."

Lucille gasped.

Nadia took another step away from him.

And he felt that.

Deeply.

And what he felt was not all about the fact that he'd never, not once, put anyone on Ledger's list except his mother and sister.

That was only part of it.

The rest was about Nadia moving away from him.

So that did it.

He didn't need to give any headspace to his situation with Nadia.

He knew.

But as for the matter at hand…

"I think Lucille is right and you need to watch your mouth, Angelica," he gritted. "You also need to calm down. We can discuss this when you're in a different mood."

"You got it good, Doc," Angelica shot back. "I don't complain because I gotta take care of our kid most of the time because you're not around. Or keep him when you throw one of your rowdy parties. And I give him back to you whenever you're ready to remember you're a dad."

Riggs held completely still.

But she wasn't done.

"I could take this to a judge, and he can give him to me full and you can have your coupla hours every Sunday and no say in who's on the pick-up list, you push me," she threatened.

Riggs felt the buzzing in his head again.

But what would come next wouldn't make his head explode.

It would rock his world.

Because Lucille was done too. "Yeah, then I can get sworn in and tell the judge how you fixed it with Bubbles to get hold of Doc's wallet so he could punch holes in Doc's rubbers the night you conned him in your bed. See how a judge feels about that, hunh?" Lucille sniped. "Same with Stormy. Bet Stormy would love to know *all about* that. He was *all the way* down for you to have his kid and take his money. Or wait, no. Seems my memory is faulty."

Riggs didn't have it in him to search for Angelica's tell.

Though, he already knew it.

But seeing as the color drained from her face, he didn't need to search for dick.

Angelica tried for the save.

"That's a flat-out lie," she said to Lucille, but her voice was trembling.

And there was one of her tells.

Lucille opened her mouth, but suddenly, Nadia was standing between him and them.

"Both of you need to go," she demanded. "Now."

Lucille seemed to cotton on to what she said in the heat of the moment, and her gaze swung to Riggs. "He was in a bind. She paid him."

"Shut up, you dumb bitch!" Angelica shouted.

"*You shut up*, you greedy *cunt*!" Lucille shouted back.

"Both of you, be quiet," Nadia said, not in a schoolteacher voice, in a voice he didn't know she had in her.

A voice that made both the women turn and stare at her.

And if he had his shit together, he'd see they were scared shitless of her.

"There's a child in the house, and it's like you don't know he's a person with feelings, but Riggs is standing *right here*. You've done your damage. *Go…now*."

Lucille started to leave with a haggard, apologetic look aimed at Riggs.

But Angelica stood her ground and turned her attention right to him. "We need to talk."

Abruptly, he couldn't see her because Nadia was in her face.

Nadia didn't say a word, but Angelica said, "Okay, I see you. Back down, woman."

"Go," Nadia whispered aggressively.

Angelica glared at her.

Then she looked to Riggs.

After that, she turned and jogged to her car.

Lucille was already pulling out.

And Nadia was in his space.

"What do you need? Do you need to walk? Talk? Go for a run? Should I bring a bottle of something out to the pier?"

"Keep an eye on my boy," he forced out.

"Okay, baby," she whispered.

Riggs turned on his boot in the opposite direction to his driveway and walked into the woods.

TWENTY-TWO

Let It Ride

Nadia

I was sitting on a stool at the kitchen bar when Riggs came through the door.

I didn't move but watched as he locked the storm door, closed the main one, locked it, then turned to me.

"Ledger?" he asked.

"He's up in bed," I told him. "I've checked three times. He was edgy, trying to read, but the last time I went up, he was out. I took the book out of his hand and turned out the light. I hope that was right."

"It was right," he replied and walked to the kitchen.

I spun on the stool to follow his progress.

He went to the fridge and got a beer. He opened it. He took a long pull from it.

Then he came to the bar on the other side of me, not catching my eyes, which I found alarming, and put the beer on the counter without uncurling his fingers from around it.

He pulled his phone out and ran his thumb over the screen.

Then he put it to his ear.

"Yeah, it's me." Pause, then, "I know it's late. Shut up and listen." Another pause, then, "If you ever, *ever*, Angelica, threaten me again with taking my boy away from me, you won't see him again. Listen closely because I. Am not. *Fucking with you.* You might not see Viggo either. That's Storm's call. But he's gonna know the shit you pulled on him because I'm gonna pay him a visit." Pause then, "Woman, you don't start to play this right after getting it so fucking wrong, and find you fucked with the wrong men, that is not on me. Consequences."

He then disconnected, tossed the phone on the bar and put the beer to his lips.

He drank a good third of it before he put it to the counter again.

Finally, he looked at me.

"You didn't have to wait up."

"Yes, I did."

"It's late."

"Really, Riggs?" I asked gently.

He dipped his chin, then let the beer go, and I rotated on my stool again, further this time, as he rounded the bar twice, once on each end, and disappeared into the stairwell.

I sat there for a long time not knowing what to do.

So long, I thought he probably went to bed.

Maybe he was embarrassed. By what I saw. By my being there when he learned it. By me hearing him talk to his son's mother that way (in a way she deserved, but he didn't give me the opportunity to share my opinion).

Maybe he was still feeling so much, he needed to keep processing it (though, he'd been out in the woods for four hours, but what he just learned after what had happened earlier that day was *a lot*, truthfully, just learning the most recent stuff would be *a lot*).

So I got up and went to the bank of switches that operated Riggs's plethora of outside lights and flipped all five of them (he'd been out there, it got late, I was worried, it was dark as all hell, so I needed to light his way home).

I was down in the living room, turning off the lamps when he came back.

"He's out," he confirmed.

Right.

Of course.

He was checking on his son.

And, I noted, taking off his damp boots.

He went right to his beer.

I turned out the last lamp down in the living room, then climbed the steps back to the kitchen.

I didn't take a stool.

I stopped at the end of the bar, close to him, and asked quietly, "Do you want to talk about it?"

"Not sure guys categorize this shit like women do. But I took time to think about it, and I wouldn't say Bubbles was my best bud. That'd go to Harry, in town. But actually, Murphy, who I met in third grade, and we were tight from the minute we met. I was his best man at his wedding. He was in the hospital the entire time I was in with Angelica when she had Ledger. He moved to Oakland a few years ago. It sucks he's gone. Still, I'd put Rus before Bubbles, even if I've only known Rus a few months, because Rus is a solid guy, and he would never put me in a position where I had to go against everything I never wanted to be to take his back. And Bubbles is a mess."

I wasn't entirely sure why he was telling me this, outside the obvious of Bubbles being foremost in his mind for a variety of reasons that day, but still, I said, "Okay."

"He threw Ledger in my face today. Bubbles did."

I pressed my lips together.

"Said I knocked someone up, got a great kid out of it. I thought he was just talking about what he thought was my good luck, when he thinks his is bad, because he has to think that way or he'd have to admit he's a mess. But now I'm not sure. Now I think he got some sick thrill outta putting me where I was back then with Angelica. Which was not a good place."

"I don't know him, so I can't say," I replied carefully when he stopped talking.

He took a pull from his beer, then said, "Well I do know him, and I heard his shit today, so I *can* say. I think he wanted to watch me stumble. I think he was hoping I would fall. I think he's so twisted with jealousy, he wanted to take a piece out of me. And then he brings over a bottle of Jack, like he's my good friend, looking out for me."

I couldn't imagine someone I considered a friend doing something like that to me.

"That *is* really messed up," I agreed.

"Yeah, so when he said that shit today, it was about him being pissed that I got Ledge out of it. I got the best thing life ever gave me, and that wasn't his intention."

It did sound like his ex-friend Bubbles did that.

"Damn, Riggs, I don't know what to say."

"Nothing to say." He took another drink from his beer. "He's a piece of shit. And that's what dogs me in my life. I get wound up with pieces of shit."

"You were just being a good friend. You're a nice guy, Riggs."

"Yeah."

He didn't sound like he thought that was a good thing.

"I have to ask, it seems pretty clear it's true, but considering you're you and I can't imagine it's easy to pull one over on you, did Bubbles actually get your wallet?"

"Thought it was weird but had my mind on other things seeing as Angelica was all over me, though I remember clear that night, one of Bubbles's waitresses handed me back my wallet that I 'lost.' Never done that shit before, or since, and when I checked, nothing was taken from it. What I know is, Bubbles could pickpocket a pickpocket."

Damn.

"So, while you were out, all you thought about was Bubbles?" I probed as kindly as I could.

"Nope," he said, popping the *p*, which would be the only mildly cute thing I'd ever seen Riggs do, if he didn't do it because he was hurt and angry. "I gave lots of thought to what a piece of shit my baby momma is too."

I reached out and covered his hand on the counter with mine.

"But I can excise Bubbles," he said. "Her, I gotta deal with for the rest of my life."

"Do you think she listened to you? What you said on the phone, I mean."

"Oh yeah. She listened to me. She's shitting her pants, she's so freaked."

"It's not mine to say, you didn't ask, but so you know, I believe she should be. I've been teaching for ten years. I've known hundreds of parents, and you're a good dad, Riggs." I wrapped my fingers around his hand and squeezed. "A *really* good dad. I've known fathers who live in the same house as their kids all the time, and they're less engaged than you are with Ledger."

Some of the tension seemed to ebb from his broad shoulders before he said, "Honey, I know. I don't question that."

"I'm glad."

"And don't worry about Angelica. I've never seen her like that, at least not since things smoothed out, but it wasn't about me. It was about Ledger. She's a female Bubbles in a way. She's more scared of you than she is of me because she knows her strengths, and her weaknesses. She loves her kids, but she's competitive, and again, she knows her weaknesses."

"Ledger seemed pretty excited to see her."

"He loves his mom. But Angelica had a problem with Kate. Mom, she doesn't see as competition. She can't steal one of Mom's boyfriends or whatever it is that makes her feel like she's come out on top. But she hated Kate. Tried to make a move on Kate's man kind of hate. It pissed him off and made him sick to his stomach, and he told Kate immediately. That was fun times."

Yuck.

"God, Riggs, this is awful."

He drank the rest of his beer, then looked right at me. "I think you get I like to have a good time."

"Yes," I said, because I sure got that.

"I've never put anyone on Ledger's pick-up list, but Mom, Kate, and now, you."

"Okay."

"I've had women. A lot of them."

"Okay," I repeated.

"But I've never done that."

I squeezed his hand. "I know. We're friends, right? Like you said. But I get it, even though she didn't give you the chance to explain it. You had to do it because things have been a bit topsy-turvy lately."

"Topsy-turvy," he whispered, staring at my mouth.

And he kept staring at my mouth.

Um…

He was staring at my mouth.

And since he was, I couldn't stop my eyes from dropping to stare at his.

He had a beautiful mouth.

Was this…?

Were we…?

He turned his hand so we were palm to palm and curled his fingers around mine.

We were.

Weren't we?

I thought of the way he held me while we were in his dining room, looking at the lake.

The way he twirled my hair in his fingers last night.

The semi-argument we had on the ride home from Hutch's about who was going to pay for Gia (she cost thousands of dollars, and I was loaded! and we left that on what I considered a temporary stalemate, but I believed Riggs thought he won).

None of that said we were just friends.

We weren't just friends.

I moved around the bar, got close, and when he turned his head and looked down at me, all that had happened with him, all he'd done for me, all he was becoming to me, and just how beautiful he was, washed over me.

I rocked up to my toes, pressed into him…and kissed him.

His mouth was hard, and soft, and very closed.

And he didn't move.

Oh shit.

I popped back, letting his hand go, and saying fast, "God, I'm sorry. That was wrong. I shouldn't have violated your person like that. I read the situation...I was thinking..." I shook my head. "That was just all wrong. You're in no state, I didn't mean to take advantage. We're friends and—"

"Nadia."

My name in his mouth whipped at me like a lash.

My body jolted at his tone, my stomach sank, my heart pulsed, and I whispered, "What?"

"It's time to go to bed."

I nodded frantically. "Right, right, you're right."

"I'm gonna follow you up the stairs..."

I went still.

"...and it's your decision which way you turn at the top of them."

I quit breathing.

"But so you go in knowing what you're getting into, you turn left, honey, it's on."

"It's...on?" I pushed out.

"That's all you're gonna get, princess. You spin the wheel with me, you let it ride."

I feared hyperventilation.

"Go to bed," he ordered.

I felt my pussy contract.

"Now, honey," he demanded.

I hustled around the counter.

I swallowed back a scream when the kitchen light went out, and I was plunged into darkness in the stairwell.

I put my hand to the wall and slowly wound my way up, the grooves in the wood paneling ebbing and flowing under my hand, a caress I felt through my fingers slink over my whole body, like Riggs, through his house, was touching me.

I knew when he entered the stairs, and I knew he was climbing when I got to the top.

But I stopped.

He stopped behind me, one step down. I couldn't feel him, but I could feel his heat.

It felt amazing.

And his breath on my neck.

That felt even better.

Then I sensed him get closer, my hair was swept away, the bristles of the whiskers on his chin grazing my skin, and his breath was *on my neck*.

I shivered.

"Not fair," I whispered.

"Who said I play fair?" he whispered against my skin.

The wheel was turning.

I was either in for a fun ride that I'd eventually get thrown off.

Or the ride of my life.

With Riggs, the first was probably a better bet than the last.

I thought of the way he held me while we were in his dining room, looking at the lake.

The way he twirled my hair in his fingers last night.

The semi-argument about Gia we had on the drive home from Hutch's.

I'd played it safe and fallen in love with a wonderful man who was dying.

I'd lived a good life from my birth of abundance and privilege with good people who utterly adored me and showed it, but there were only two of them, and they were both dead.

Now, I was on my own.

I didn't have *Dedulya* to turn to for advice.

I didn't have Mom to talk things through with me.

The rest of my life, it was all me.

Just me.

Fuck it.

I turned left.

Riggs fingers closed on my hips instantly. He crowded me and shuffled me the short way down the dark hall to his stairs.

I felt a thrill whoosh through my belly like I was on the downs-lope of a roller coaster.

It was spectacular.

Come what may, feeling that, I knew one thing.

I'd made the right choice.

I stumbled when we made it to his stairwell because I couldn't see.

He knew his house, so he lifted me up, guided the way, and halfway up, he turned us, so he was up, I was down. His mouth landed on mine, his tongue spiked inside. I moaned at the feel of it, getting it after I'd longed for it what seemed like ages, experienced the heady taste of beer and Riggs, and it was good he dragged me the rest of the way up, because my legs had stopped functioning.

He let me go at the top, and I opened my eyes to being able to see due to the moonlight flooding his room, and then my arms were up, and I was blind again because my sweater was being pulled over my head.

My hair tumbled down while I watched Riggs's sweater go off.

The moonlight shaded the muscles of his chest, arms and shoul-ders. My legs trembled. His hands went back to my hips, and he hustled me to bed.

I fell back, he fell on top of me, and he was right.

It was on.

There was a lot of kissing—*a lot*—but I had that body to explore, the one I'd wanted my hands on since the first time I saw him run into my yard, slick with sweat.

And I explored it.

That was, I did until he undid the button of my jeans, slid the zip down, and dove right inside.

He didn't mess around.

He glided a finger over my clit, through my wet, and buried it inside me.

My head shot back.

Riggs put his lips to my throat and growled as his finger stroked aggressively.

I didn't hesitate.

This was my ride, and I rode it.

His lips went up the side of my neck, he nipped my earlobe and whispered, "Yeah, honey."

"Riggs," I panted.

"I hear you," he murmured, and his finger went away, as did his entire hand, so, clearly, he didn't hear me correctly.

Then my jeans and panties were whisked away with a fierce tug, and okay, maybe he did hear me.

I went after the buttons on his jeans as he reached for a condom.

I got the last button undone and yanked them over his hips, Riggs helping by bucking them up powerfully.

Just that nearly sent me over the edge.

Lord, have mercy.

His cock sprang out, and from what I could tell in the dark, I liked it, *very much*, and he immediately rolled a condom on one-handed and expertly.

Not expert enough. I nearly slapped his hand away so I could do it.

But finally, it was done, and he reached for me, but he didn't have to reach.

I threw a leg over, grabbed hold of him, guided him where he needed to be, and bore down.

"Shit, Nadia," he groaned.

Taking all that was him, I moaned.

Sensory proof, he had a great cock.

I bounced. And bounced. And *bounced*.

He clasped his hands behind his head, I saw the white flash of his teeth through the moonlit shadows, and he teased, "Tell me if you need me."

But his deep voice was sexy thick.

I dropped my torso to his and hissed in his face, "Stop it, Riggs."

I then gasped in delight as he spun us so I was on my back, he was on top, managing to do this without his cock losing purchase inside me.

Wow.

He fisted a hand in my hair, tossed one of my legs around his ass, hauled the other one bent and up, tucking it tight to his side, and he put his lips to mine.

"Let's get busy," he growled.

"Oh yes," I breathed.

He slanted his head and kissed me.

And then we got very, very, *very*, amazingly, magnificently, gloriously, ridiculously, dizzyingly, earth-shatteringly *busy*.

TWENTY-THREE

Easing Into It

Nadia

The first slap I endured was the cold hitting my body when the covers were pulled off me.

This woke me.

It was followed immediately by the second slap, which was a sharp, delicious smack to my butt cheek.

This made me groan.

Then I felt the bed depress at my hip as well as on my opposite side before Riggs said in my ear, "Wake up, honey, you got shit to do today."

I forced my eyes open only to experience full-on daylight, and I turned my head to look up at him from where I lay in his bed, naked and on my stomach.

He was leaned into me wearing a faded red, long-sleeved thermal that he'd either purchased when he was fifteen, or it was designed to mold to his upper body like I'd often molded myself to it last night.

His hair was wet and slicked back with a comb.

And every inch I could see was yummy, and I now knew in reality, that was an indisputable fact.

"You've…showered?" I mumbled.

"Got my kid up, fed, to school, came back and took a run, and now I'm hauling your lazy ass out of bed."

This was impossible.

I didn't know when I finally passed out last night, seeing as I lost track of time due to his body being a wonderland (I know it was cliché, but the description was apropos), his entire bed an amusement park, and his giving me an extravagant amount of the best orgasms I'd had *in my life*.

But I was pretty sure when I'd passed out, first, it was very late (or very early in the morning), and second, I'd done it while I was mid-kissing Riggs.

How was he up and…

Moving?

I was faintly sore all over (in a nice way) and one part of me was gently throbbing (in a fabulous way), and I wasn't sure I could move.

I tested this and reached for the covers, pulled them around my body and up over my chest as I expended the supreme effort of pushing up to a forearm in bed.

"Are you for real?" I asked.

His expression went guarded. "What's that mean?"

"You've done all that and showered after last night. It's like you're a machine."

His face cleared, and he smiled at me.

"Did I pass out mid-kissing you?" I queried.

The smile he was aiming at me turned wolfish, and he answered, "Yeah. But you can make up for that shit tonight."

I had to wait until tonight?

Whoops.

I was wrong. His smile had turned a touch roguish.

At him reading my mind, now his wide grin was absolutely *wolfish*.

I witnessed that and had woefully too short a period of time to process it, much less memorize it, before I let out a muted scream when he dragged me out of bed, with me still clutching the sheet to my chest, and he planted me in his lap.

Once there, he circled me with his arms and asked, "You sore?"

Oh God, was this embarrassing?

Why was this embarrassing? He'd been there the whole time. In fact, the sore part was all his fault.

I didn't know why it was, but the answer was, yes. It was embarrassing.

I shoved my face in the side of his neck.

He tangled his fingers in my hair and slid them through, going back and doing the same as he said, "Not a surprise, honey. You can take a seriously solid fucking."

I shivered in his arms at the memory.

"And a lot of it," he went on.

I shivered again.

Those arms got tight, and a rumble rolled up his chest and through his lips.

He had memories too, and he liked them.

I shivered more.

"Look at me," he ordered.

I tipped my head back and caught his eyes.

"That means we wait for tonight," he decreed.

"Okay," I whispered.

He came in for a lip touch, then moved back. "I gotta get to your house and get on that door. We boarded it up, but it's far from secure. You need to get your ass in gear because you're meeting Brenda out at Mix's. It's two towns over and an hour away. She wants your input in picking storm doors. Then you gotta head up to Hutch's for training with Gia."

"Mix's?"

"It's a posh home supply store. We got nothing like what they stock around MP, and Brenda isn't one to cut corners or have anything fuck with her 'vision.'"

I'd already figured this out about Brenda.

"Ah."

"So you need to get moving."

My eyes fell to his mouth, and I mumbled, "Right."

I lost sight of his mouth when he was using it to plunder mine.

So I didn't have to wait until tonight.

Awesome.

The kiss started hot and heavy, so it just got hotter and heavier, until he broke it by standing and putting me on my feet.

For a second, I was dazed.

And unhappy.

Then I wrapped the sheet I'd somehow managed to keep with me more firmly around me.

"Get to it, princess," he commanded.

I rolled my eyes, sighed and took off toward the guest room. I could bring the sheet back when I was done.

"Nadia?" he called when I was halfway to the stairwell, juggling the sheet while gathering my clothes.

I looked back to him.

"Honey, I've seen, touched, tasted and fucked every inch of you," he said gently. "And Ledger's not here, you can lose the sheet."

I thought about Angelica's slim hips even after birthing two babies, her flat stomach (same about the babies), and all-around slender frame (except her breasts, which, it might be mean, but it could be true, kinda looked fake).

I did not have slim hips or a flat belly.

Again, he was in my head when, still gentle, he shared, "She had more weight on her back then. I'm not that guy. I like soft, and I think you know by now, I get off when I got something to hold onto."

Was this man for real?

He was, because I tried not to see (but I saw…so much), though it couldn't be missed, Courtney was curvy.

Even so.

"I'm not a dude, Riggs. I can't traipse around nude after one time."

The wolfish grin came back. "I was pretty into what we were doing, so my counting might be inaccurate. Still, think it was more than one time."

Good Lord.

He was such *a man*.

I did another eye roll, grabbed my sweater, and strutted out of his room.

I took the sheet.

EARLY THAT AFTERNOON, I rolled to a stop in my Range Rover in front of the cabin, doing this next to Riggs's truck.

I really loved Riggs's house.

But being there right then with the sun shining and another warm spell hitting the area (I'd learned at dinner last night that things didn't really warm up until June, and the weather we were getting when I arrived was what they called a "heat wave," even if it was only in the mid-seventies), I realized I missed my cabin.

I got out, noting I needed to water the plants, and the front door was open. From there I could see through the screen all the way to the back and beyond, where Riggs was working on the back door that was resting on two sawhorses.

I went in, dropped my purse on the kitchen island, and walked along the back porch under Riggs's watchful eye.

I came to a stop at the top of the steps.

"The storm doors will be delivered tomorrow, delivery window ten to noon. And I think Hutch is mad at me because Gia was more interested in playing with me, I was more interested in playing with Gia, so we got distracted a lot."

I got another smile from Riggs.

He wasn't a man to dole them out frugally. Still, I hadn't seen much of him that day, but that was all he seemed capable of doing.

I felt that.

After last night, and this morning, I was in the same place.

I just loved seeing that he was too.

But I had to be careful in hoping too much.

I'd done a lot of driving that day, and since I trained my thoughts while doing it, it occurred to me that maybe Riggs did want to put us in the Friend Zone because we were neighbors, but things blossomed from there. Or maybe he wanted to take it slow, due to what had happened to me, then, to what was happening to me in MP.

He'd certainly made it clear last night, us being in the Non-Friend Zone was what he wanted, and it was my choice if we were going to take it there.

But the truth was, since his peace offering, he'd shared thoroughly and often he was into me. I'd just thought he was an affectionate guy.

I sensed he was.

Though, he was also very obviously into me.

That said, I hadn't known him long, but what I did know was that I had to keep in mind this was probably firmly casual…and ride it out.

I knew that because that was what he told me.

And I was in to ride it out.

But I sure was going to enjoy him seeming so happy while we did it.

"Don't worry about it," he replied. "Hutch told me she'll be a great pet, and if the need arises, her training will kick in. *Your* training will be being able to call her down before she tears a man's leg off."

Yikes!

"I should probably focus," I allowed.

He was still smiling. "Probably."

"You want a drink?"

"Could use some water."

"Perrier?"

He stared at me.

That had me smiling.

"I'll do filtered," I said, and moved back into the cabin.

I was starting to handle that when he came in, and then I was scrambling back into the counter when he was on me.

Slightly sweaty, dirty from work and smelling of the outdoors, he was all over me, and I didn't mind, because he was Riggs, and he was good at being all over me.

It also meant I got to be all over him.

Eventually, we came up for air, but he didn't move away.

"Called Stormy this morning," he announced.

"Oh boy," I breathed (what could I say? again, he was all over me).

"Asked if I could have some time to talk privately about something heavy. Seeing as I asked that, he made time right away. He owns the tire shop on the east side of town. Asked me to his office. I went. Gave him the news about Angelica and Bubbles, and we can just say, it rocked my world, but it was worse telling him. Not only giving a man that information, but also seeing my reaction through him. Though, when I learned, I wasn't holding a coffee cup I threw so hard it shattered against the wall and drenched everything around it because it was full."

I winced. "Were you around it?"

"No."

"So I can deduce he's ticked."

"You can deduce that, yeah."

"Is this going to come back on you with Angelica?"

"Gave her the heads up it would happen, if she was smart, she would have done it before me."

"I sense Angelica's intelligence is more the devious sort," I remarked.

"You'd sense right," he agreed. "Still, thought about it before I did it, including that. Wondered if it was better if I didn't know, and I could give him that. Then I thought, I'm glad I know. I gotta understand what I've got on my hands with her. What she's capable of. Also, if the tables were turned, how I'd feel if he found out, and didn't tell me. Bottom line, he shares a kid with her too. So he had to know."

"This is true."

"And don't worry. She doesn't have a leg to stand on to make any trouble for him or me. What she does have is a history. A history of jacking both of us around. And it isn't illegal to trick a man into getting you pregnant, we had a hand in that, we made choices, and condoms do actually break. But that shit is shady. Fortunately, she's not a woman who takes her shit out on her kids. Not sure what she could do to us, since the only thing either of us got with her that matters is our kids."

"Well, silver lining for you both, it's clear your swimmers are powerful if one go gets a woman pregnant."

"Her campaign with Storm was more persistent. Not sure which time it happened, but he told me he was with her three times. And yeah, the first night, his wallet had gone missing. And yeah, it did this at The Hole. The other two, she had the chance to see to things herself."

"So it's just your swimmers that are super powerful."

He shot me another smile and squeezed my behind besides.

Totally riding this out.

"Have you heard from her?" I asked.

"No," he answered.

"Good," I muttered. Then I shared something with him that had also occurred to me in all my driving. "So, I had occasion to casually chat with Brenda about the Whitaker family situation, and she shared with me that Roosevelt had an assistant. And she still lives in town."

"Honey," he said in a tone I wasn't sure about.

"What?"

He hooked an arm around my waist, shifted us down the counter, then I tensed as he reached out and touched my digital photo screen.

He scrolled forward until he hit the photo of me and Trevor on a cliff in Cornwall, a pirate's cove and the stormy sea behind us, wind ruffling our hair, smiles on our faces.

"Now," he said quietly, "we can scheme a way to go interrogate Roosevelt's assistant without letting her know we're interrogating her, when neither of us know the woman, or you can tell me about your husband."

"Riggs," I whispered.

"You're not ready, okay. Your call. But you bury shit, it always finds a way to bite you in the ass."

"He died a long time ago."

"So I'm starting with the history stuff so we can lead into the more recent shit."

Fun times ahead, I saw.

Ugh.

"He had cancer when we met," I blurted.

He blinked rapidly several times before he asked, "I'm sorry?"

"He had cancer when we met," I repeated. "But he didn't tell me. He'd tried some holistic stuff, which didn't work. And when he started Western medicine, he hid it from me."

"Jesus," he bit out.

"He genuinely believed he could beat it when he asked me to marry him. The doctors weren't so sure, but they were trying to be optimistic. He was young. Healthy. If there was a candidate who could, he could. But it spread, fast and aggressively, and eventually he couldn't hide it anymore."

"He should have told you," he gritted.

"I know," I replied running my hands up and down his arms because he was visibly angry. "And I get your reaction. I had that too. In waves, when I found out he was sick, when he admitted to me how long he'd been sick. I even felt that after he was gone. But for the life of me, I can't fault a twenty-eight-year-old man for being determined to live his life, and survive, and maybe going into denial about the possibility, that turned into a probability, that ended in a definite that he wasn't going to."

He seemed to be looking at me, though he really wasn't, when he asked, "Did you love him?"

I knew my smile was sad. "Yes. I loved him a whole lot."

"And you wanted kids."

"We both did."

"So he took that from you. The you wanting kids part."

"No, my sperm donor father did."

"Honey—"

I lifted my hands to his neck and held tight. "Riggs, I loved Trevor, and I lost him. It was not all good times, but we knew those times would be short, so we packed a lot into them. I'm glad I met him. I'm glad I married him. I'm blessed to have the time I had with him. I love that I got to be the woman who he loved who would be by his side through all of that. He had great parents, and we're still in touch, but I'm the promise of the life he should have had, so we're no longer close. But I also got them through him. And maybe I wallowed in all of that after he was gone. I don't think anyone would blame me. He might not have played it all perfectly, but what he did was understandable. He's not baggage, even though I will admit, I carried him like that for a long time. Now I see he's a part of my life, memories of loving someone and being loved by someone, and a lot of laughter. That's what I carry with me from Trevor now, and it isn't heavy."

"All right," he muttered.

"Okay," I whispered.

He touched his mouth to mine.

When he moved away, I got up on my toes and touched mine to his.

"Now, can we talk about Roosevelt's assistant?" I requested.

He burst out laughing, gave me a squeeze, then said, "No. I'm gonna fix your door. And if I have time, install a couple of cameras. You're gonna get me some water then make me some lunch. I haven't had any yet, and I'm fucking starving."

"You forget to eat a lot."

"I live. I eat when it fits in. I work when I have to. I fuck when I'm lucky enough to coax a gorgeous blonde into my bed."

"It took a lot of coaxing," I joked. "I'm still not sure how you tricked me into it."

"I'll remind you tonight."

As delightful as that promise was, I frowned as another thought I'd chewed on during my driving hit me. "We need to consider Ledger."

"Yeah. And your shit stays in the closet in the guest room, but you bring your toothbrush and shower stuff up to mine. He won't know."

I didn't know about that.

"Is it smart, hiding it from him?"

"I walked around a long time last night, and Bubbles and

Angelica weren't the only ones on my mind. I think you get it, but so you got it clear, this, where we're at right now, isn't about ending a good time by giving to, and getting from a fine piece of ass. I don't know what it is, but it's not that. Not even close."

God, that was good to know.

He kept going.

"But while we ease into whatever it's gonna be, we gotta ease Ledger into it with us. He and I had a chat this morning, and he made some good points. His mother was being a bitch, and he's getting older. He felt he had call to have a say about her being a bitch to a woman who's coming to mean something to him. I embarrassed him in front of Lucille, but mostly you, and he was understandably pissed at me about it. I still think he's too young to be talking back to his mom, especially if that blends with talking back to his gramme, me, or now, you. But I gotta say, shit he said struck, and I need to get into a zone that he's now starting to pick up some threads of the man he's going to weave himself into, and I gotta be careful not to stand in the way of that."

"I will, at this juncture, remind you of my assertion that you're a really good dad, Riggs."

That got me yet another smile, before he kept talking.

"But he's not old enough to get how things have changed with us in that way. He already told me he approved of you, thinking that's where we were that first night you had dinner with us."

"Wow, that's sweet," I said happily.

"Yeah," he replied, again smiling. "I told him we weren't that. I'm not gonna sit too long on telling him we actually are that, but right now, my sense is, it's too soon. Having you suddenly waking up in my bed in a way he knows that's happening, especially when you'll be back at the cabin when Gia comes to you. It might get confusing."

I cut in. "I thought I was coming back tomorrow."

He gave me another squeeze and stated firmly, "When Gia comes to you."

Oh well.

Whatever.

"Okay, when Gia comes to me."

"He's not grown up enough to understand all the intricacies. Sometimes, Nadia in his dad's bed, up and eating breakfast with him, sometimes Nadia is not. Where he stands with that. Him having me only part time, and suddenly having to share me. And in case I'm wrong, Angelica being under fire, and she acts on that shit with her kids, I gotta keep my finger on his pulse."

"I don't disagree with any of this."

"Even so, I got you close, you sure as fuck aren't sleeping in the guest room."

"I don't disagree with that either."

"So we're good."

"We are very good."

"Right," he murmured, then he was all over me again.

We didn't come up for air until he heard my stomach grumble.

I hadn't had lunch either.

"I gotta get back to work," he said.

"Turkey and Swiss sandwich?" I asked.

"Works for me."

He dove in and kissed my neck, then rubbed his stubble on me.

Gooseflesh covered my skin.

Riggs got back to work.

I brought him a glass of water.

Then I got to work on lunch.

After we ate, I went to work on watering the flowers.

And we continued easing into it.

TWENTY-FOUR

We'll See

Nadia

I was setting the dining room table at Riggs's house.

Abigail had broken the seal on it, and I'd kept that open considering the view, the fact I loved Riggs's gorgeous, round table with its intricately carved pedestal and beautifully veined marble top, and that, even though it was huge and seated twelve, we could sit on a curve and see each other in order to talk.

But mostly, so Riggs could sit with his legs under it and eat comfortably.

It was Friday evening and the last three days had been blissfully uneventful.

First, no "hauntings."

Second, no break-ins.

Riggs had fixed the cabin's back door, installed the storm doors and the cameras (and mounted my new flag, which I was right, it looked great out front), and I had a program on my laptop where I could see what was happening on all sides of my house and into the area by where the stables used to be. These feeds were sent immediately to a cloud so we could review them if needed.

Or provide them as evidence.

Riggs then got stuck into a commission he was supposed to be doing during his down time. Sometimes, I hung with him while he did that, due to the fact his workshop was less a workshop and more a man cave, and I liked being out there with him.

Sure, there were lots of tools and work benches and sawhorses and equipment around.

But there was also a beat-up couch, an even more beat-up recliner, a massive flat screen TV, a game console, and to my hilarity, a lot of posters of scantily clad women on the walls. Not so scantily it was gross Ledger would see them, but the sheer number of them was impressive.

He had a shiny motorcycle, heavy on the chrome, parked in there, and two ATVs.

I had started journalling (admittedly, this was mostly about Riggs), so I did it in there with him, finding copious times to study him while he worked. Enjoying the vibe he gave off, the feel of the creative space he entered, the intensity of his focus, and watching the piece he was working on take shape (an intricate arbor made of iron that was going to be installed outside the local fancy hotel with the award-winning spa, the Pinetop Lodge, so people could get married under it).

Since I couldn't read around him, sometimes I went back to the cabin to do that, and I'd broken the seal on the hammock (which was *heavenly*).

Then there were my daily trips to spend time with Gia (yes, we were making progress, no, we weren't making Hutch's usual progress, yes, he was going to let me have her anyway because he said she moped when I wasn't around, which, of course, meant my baby needed to come to her new home as soon as possible, this being set at Monday).

I also shared more honestly with friends about how things were going, and yes, this included telling Maribeth all about Riggs (she was beside herself with glee I was "moving on" from Trevor, "finally"—she was more excited when I texted her a picture of Riggs).

As for Riggs and me, we gave up my porch loveseat that was temporarily unavailable to us in order to sit in front of his fire in his living room, and I endured his gentle probing about my mom, my grandfather, and some about Maribeth and Susan and other friends. In fact, my entire life in Chicago.

I knew this was all a lead-up so he'd have the history and know the players when I finally laid the big stuff on him. But he made it safe, and I liked talking about my life.

Though, I tried to ignore how he'd sometimes seem to retreat and get broody when I talked about all I had when I was home. And I did that because it indicated to me, he didn't like the idea that I'd be returning.

It might not be that, but it wouldn't be easing into anything at this early juncture in our relationship if I demanded, even carefully, to know his thoughts about that, so I let it be.

When or if he was ready to do that, or I was, we'd discuss it.

We also caught a few more episodes of *Only Murders in the Building* because it all couldn't be weighty all the time.

I went to sleep every night in Riggs's bed, but before I fell asleep, I was elated he spent a great deal of time in me.

And Riggs and I woke up in plenty of time I could do my thing, hustle back to the guest room, change clothes, and he and I could deal with Ledger in the mornings.

He resolutely did school runs, concerned that Angelica might take that opportunity to show and take potshots at me. Also, because it gave him more time with his son.

But tonight, Abigail was over, and we were cooking dinner, and Riggs had decided (and I agreed) that tonight was the night we were going to tell his son and his mother we were a thing.

"Nadia."

I turned from putting a knife on one of the placemats I bought Riggs to see she was standing by the stairwell column, closed off on the dining room side, but still wood paneled so the part of it that extended into the round room was a feature.

"Call down to the boys, would you?" she asked. "Give them a heads-up dinner will be ready in twenty minutes."

"Will do," I said.

She disappeared.

I finished setting the table and headed to the window.

Riggs and Ledger were on the pier, had the tarp pulled back on an edge of the fishing boat and were doing something.

The windows were open to let in the fresh air, so I called through the screen, "Guys! Dinner in twenty!"

Ledger turned and waved.

Riggs, who was crouched by the boat, twisted his neck to look up at me, and still, in that position, managed to jut his chin out at me.

God, he was totally and completely such *a man*.

But I liked it.

Trevor had been *a man* too (not as much as Riggs, but he had). And I definitely liked him.

I was about to move away from the window when something caught my eye. A flash in the woods some ways down from my cabin, close to the southern end of the lake.

I didn't see it directly, but it seemed like the sun struck something and caused a reflection.

I kept my eyes aimed that way, but it didn't happen again.

In normal circumstances, I wouldn't think about it.

In these circumstances, I made a note to tell Riggs. It was probably nothing, but it might be hunters or someone on his land who shouldn't be, and he should know.

I rejoined Abigail in the kitchen. We were making her menu of roast rosemary chicken, mashed potatoes with roasted garlic, gravy, green beans and dinner rolls. Not to be outdone by my stout cake both Riggs boys kept raving about, she'd brought over a homemade carrot cake that looked dreamy.

I didn't have a competitive bone in my body.

But a cake competition I could get into.

"The potatoes ready to whip up?" I asked.

She stopped testing them with the tip of a knife and turned to me.

"I'm going to apologize in advance to you. Some of my friends say I can be too direct. But I'm afraid it's something I can't rein in when it comes to one of my children."

Here we go.

She didn't delay.

"I thought you were returning home after Doc completed his work on your house," she noted.

"I was. But he's not comfortable with me going back until I get Gia. And Hutch says I can bring her home on Monday."

"Gia?"

"The guard-dog-slash-pet I'm getting. She's a trained guard dog. But she's also very cute and slobbery and cuddly, so I sometimes forget that, thus, I'm kind of a bad influence on her."

Abigail's lips quirked.

"You should know," I started. "My name is Nadia Williams, but I'm an Antonov, as in an Antonov Vodka Antonov. My grandfather sold the company, but he did it for a lot of money."

"I see," she said softly.

"Which means I'm loaded, and that means Riggs is worried about me being alone in that cabin, especially after the break-in. Even though we're assured as much as we can be that they got what they came for, Riggs is a lot less assured than me."

"You use the word 'we' a lot with regard to my son."

Well, one could say I blew *that*.

"Um…"

"Let me guess, Doc wants to get into that at dinner," she deduced.

"Got it in one," I mumbled.

"I hope you don't mind, but I went in and had a few words with Harry," she stated. "And I can assure you, he did his best to guide me to discovering what I wanted him to tell me from the source. Though, I'm the kind of woman who doesn't take no for an answer when something is important. So I knew you're an Antonov."

"Okay," I said slowly.

Her face changed, and I braced against the change.

"I also know what happened recently, and I can't tell you how sorry I am," she said gently.

"Thanks, but no offense, I'm not really good at talking about it," I said in a rush.

"No offense in return, darlin', but you better get good at talking about it, or it'll eat you up."

"Abigail—"

"My friends call me Gail."

That was nice.

"Gail, I'm not good at talking about it because I haven't fully processed it."

"It's a lot to process."

It sure was.

"I will share that Riggs is all in to help me when I'm ready," I admitted.

"That's my son. From a young age, he was so determined to prove to everyone he wasn't his father, he learned to be helpful. Did it so much, and he was so good at it, it became a part of him. It's now just as much of what makes Doc as that brain he has, which works in miraculous ways, and the dark hair on his head."

"Yes," I agreed.

"He's told me he's told you about his father."

I nodded.

"Okay, then we have to get to mashing potatoes to feed our boys."

Our boys?

She carried on. "But the first thing I'd like to say is, if I'd realized the man John was in time to do something about it, and I had the resources to cut him out of my life, I would have done that without a second thought. I further would have done everything in my power to keep him away from them. I would also have made up some fanciful story so my children would think the second half of the whole that created them was an amazing man they could be proud of."

Apparently, Harry had told her quite a bit, and I fleetingly wondered how he knew.

I looked away.

"I see your mother did that," she remarked.

"It was a lie," I told the counter.

"It was a mother's love," she refuted.

A mother's love.

Tears hit my eyes, a whole load of them, instantly.

The front door opened.

Automatically, I looked that way.

Riggs was in first, he took one look at me and lost his mind.

"*What the fuck?*" he exploded.

"Doc—" Abigail began.

"Again, what the fuck?" he demanded, though he hadn't given her the opportunity to answer the first time.

"I'm fine," I assured.

"You're fucking crying," he retorted.

"Are you okay, Nadia?" Ledger asked, staring with worry at me.

I sniffed and got it together. "I am, sweetheart."

Riggs was now in the kitchen. He hooked me at the waist and dragged me into his side, his eyes on his mother.

"*Explain,*" he barked.

"Actually, it'd be nice if you and Ledger would go wash your hands so Nadia and I could finish our discussion. I'll call you when we're done," she replied.

Though I admired how ballsy she was, that wasn't the right thing to say, I could tell right away.

Quickly, I put my hand to Riggs's throat and his head angled down.

"We were talking about my mom, baby," I said quietly.

He relaxed.

"And I'm okay. Honestly," I continued. "But can you take Ledger somewhere and explain it to him?"

"Right," he muttered, gave me a squeeze, let me go and turned to his boy. "Let's go, kid. We'll clean up in my bathroom."

"'Kay, Dad," Ledger mumbled, walking away, his gaze on me.

When we lost sight of them, I turned back to Abigail. "Sorry about that."

"Some kid in high school called Kate a fat ass within Doc's hearing, and my son was suspended for a week. It took some fancy dancing for me to convince his family not to press charges."

"Whoa," I whispered, though I wasn't really surprised.

That was pure Riggs.

"Sadly, my Kate smoked. Fortunately, it wasn't for very long. However, when she did, she was out at a bar with her brother, and some man tried to bum a smoke from her. She refused, so he called her stupid bitch, and luckily my son was older and wiser, so that time, he just chased him out of the bar. That said, it's probably good he didn't catch him."

I pressed my lips together and spread them out.

"I can see you're not ready to talk about your mom, darlin', so I'll lay off," she shared.

"Thanks," I replied.

"But I hope I've also shared I'm there if you need me."

"Thanks for that too," I repeated more heartily.

"And the other thing I wanted to get into was that I've waited a really long time for my son's remarkable intelligence to catch up to, and then surpass, the damage of his father's abuse."

I braced again.

It was good I did. She wasn't done.

"He saw things and experienced things I will go to my grave regretting I allowed him to see and feel."

"I'm sure you—"

She held up a hand.

I shut up.

She dropped her hand.

"You can try to absolve me. My kids have tried to absolve me. It's a mother's burden. Even if it wasn't that extreme, anything that hurts them, we take accountability for it. It's our job, Nadia. I think from the emotion I just saw around losing your mom, you know that."

I remembered, as stark as if it happened yesterday, seeing the depths of my pain plain on my mom's face when I walked out of Trevor's hospice room after we lost him.

And one of the things that plagued me was knowing she not

only died fighting for her life, but she did it knowing I'd not only lose her, but I'd find out about my father, and know he did that to her. I knew her through to my soul, so I knew those were her last thoughts.

And I hated that with a power my mind couldn't contain, so I refrained from thinking about it at all.

So yes.

Oh yes.

I knew that.

I nodded.

"Therefore, I cannot tell you how happy I am, when he finally extricated his head from his ass, it was with a woman like you."

Oh Lord.

"I see you see how things are now," I noted. "But I feel I have to tell you, we're very new, and we're easing into it, and we don't even know what this is yet."

"Did you experience the same thing I just experienced when my son walked in this house?"

I did.

Don't hope, Nadia, don't hope!

I nodded again.

"He's never, not once, even as a teenager, had a relationship with a woman that lasted more than a couple of weeks, and I don't count that woman who bore his child."

Oh my God.

He hadn't?

Abigail kept going.

"He's terrified of becoming his father in every way, and he loves me very, very much. And the thought he has that in him, what his father did to me, his sister, eats at him. But I see the progression. How he is with Ledger. How much his son is devoted to him. How he's not making the same mistakes his father did. And now, I see he's learned he's able to give himself you."

"I'm not sure, in that way, Gail, he's a man that can be tamed," I cautioned carefully.

She looked to the door Riggs had come through, and she did this pointedly, before she looked at me.

And then she said, "We'll see."

I CAME, and per usual, I did it hard, digging my heels in Riggs's back, arching my spine, fisting my hand in his hair.

He lapped at me through the aftermath of my orgasm, then he gently pulled my legs from his shoulders before he kissed the skin above my pubic hair, then my belly, my midriff, between my breasts, the base of my throat, finally, Riggs, and his stubble, marked my neck, something he had a fondness for doing.

I'd woken up with mild beard burn every day for three days, and it wasn't just around my mouth.

I also wasn't complaining.

He rolled us so he was on his back, I was tucked to his side, and since he'd had his earlier (and I'd also had my first, Riggs was just a man driven to overachieve—again, not complaining), he pulled the covers over us.

I settled in.

"Think that went good," he murmured.

"Yeah," I replied drowsily. "You just ate more pussy leaving a woman satisfied. Fuck you, Bubbles."

His body moved as his chuckle sounded, his arm tightened around me, and he said, "I mean telling Mom and Ledge about you and me."

Oh.

"It did, after you shouted at your mother. Then you jumped the gun and told Ledger about us when you two were up here washing your hands."

"I changed my mind and decided it should be him and me alone when I told him," he began. "It was a good time to do it. We could get into it and give you more time to finish talking…and finish dinner. You hadn't even whipped the potatoes."

God, it was good he was so talented with giving head (among other things), because he wasn't just *a man*, he was *a guy*.

"That wasn't the part that went wonky," I remarked.

"You and I have talked a lot, honey, and I haven't made you cry," he pointed out. "She can be harsh."

"It's called direct."

"When she makes you cry, it's harsh," he stated, and his words were steely.

I jostled him with my arm. "She was actually being gentle. It was just that she explained, succinctly, why my mother lied to me about my dad having died in a plane accident when I was a baby. It's been something that's been screwing with me, now I get it, so you can let it go."

"Right," he grunted.

"Yeah. Right," I confirmed.

The steel came back. "Moving on."

So, Andrew Doc Riggs didn't like to be wrong.

Noted.

I let him have it. When he yelled at his mom, he was being protective of me, which I had no problem with, and his mom not only held no ill-will, she liked that he was, so it was all good.

"That's how your mom explained it to you?" he asked.

"Yes."

"Honey," he whispered gently.

I'd already faced as much of that as I could in one night, so I didn't say anything.

Riggs read I was done on that subject, thankfully.

"Ledger seemed good," he noted.

If him crowing victoriously, "*I knew it!*" when he told his gramme what she already knew (though Riggs didn't know she did at that time, I hadn't had a chance to tell him) was an indication, yes, he did.

"Yes," I agreed "Though I think he thinks *we're* getting a dog."

"*We* are. She's just staying with you at the cabin."

I got up on a forearm and looked down at his shadowed face.

"Oh no you don't," I warned. "You two Riggs boys can't be sweet and charming and affectionate and steal Gia from me."

"From what I saw, it was instant devotion both ways."

"You didn't get close. She didn't get a good whiff of you. She's a girl. She's susceptible."

Amusement was tingeing his voice when he said, "We'll try not to steal your dog from you."

I collapsed into him, because two big orgasms and emotion, and a huge meal (slice of cake number two, I saw upon reflection, was a bad idea) had taken it all out of me, and I mumbled, "Appreciated."

He started twirling my hair.

And his voice was actually tender when he asked, "Are you like your mom?"

Okay, maybe Riggs didn't read me.

I closed my eyes tight.

Then I told him. "No. She was like your mom, times a thousand. She was a ballbuster. I grew up in the cocoon of her love and protection, and my grandfather's, so I got to be…well, *me.*"

"I owe her, huge."

God.

So sweet.

I turned my face and shoved it in his pec.

Riggs cupped my shoulder and squeezed. "We'll stop talking about it."

I drew in breath, put my cheek to his skin, and whispered, "I wish she could meet you. She'd like you. And my *dedulya* would love you. You could take turns pissing in corners and fighting over the remote, and ogling pin-up girl posters, and debating Malinois versus cane corso until the wee hours of the morning and have a competition on who can do the widest manspread. He'd have the time of his life."

More amusement in his tone when he asked, "Manspread?"

"You know, when you sit down and you haven't appropriately contained the family jewels, or you wish to declare to all the other male species in your vicinity your manly endowments are bigger than theirs. I don't know why you guys do it. But it's when you spread your legs really wide, even if you're sitting in the middle seat of an airplane or something."

"You have a lot of experience with someone in the middle seat?"

Not even close. I had the means, so I was first class all the way.

"No," I allowed.

"You own your own plane?"

I didn't answer.

He shook me, and there was vastly more humor in his, "Nadia?"

"*Dedulya* sold it," I mumbled.

He bit back laughter, because we were "out," but we were still keeping our nighttime sleeping arrangements a secret from Ledger.

"Do I do the manspread?" he asked when he got control of his hilarity.

"Not that I've noticed. But we haven't really been out, as it were, like sitting in a booth together or something."

"We'll remedy that tomorrow. Mom knows. Ledge knows. Mom, I know, went right home and called Kate, so Kate knows. The whole of MP might as well know. You ready for that?"

It had only been a few days, so it was crazy, but still, I was ready for a whole lot more.

"Sure," I replied.

"We'll go to the Double D for breakfast or something. Since Ledge has his sleepover at Dustin's tomorrow, we're fucking and sleeping at the cabin, though."

Lord.

A fantasy come to life.

"Good for you?" he asked.

"Totally."

"You make yourself come, thinking of me in that bed?" he asked right out.

That was a big fat *yes*.

"Um…"

"Definitely this bed, thinking of you," he shared. "Also, the shower."

I was getting turned on again.

"Um…"

"Fuckin' cute how you get shy," he murmured, turning toward me so we were face-to-face, tangling our legs, and the cherry on that sundae, gathering me close in his arms.

Yes, I'd learned Riggs was naturally affectionate, and this included a lot of cuddling while watching TV, hanging in front of the fire, definitely post-sex. We might separate in the night and go our own way, but we always fell asleep something like this.

And since he did this, I knew he was ready to go to sleep.

And Lord knew, I was.

It hit me, sleepily, after I was nearly out, that I forgot to tell him something.

"Riggs?" I mumbled.

"Right here, princess."

"You might wanna check the south end of the east side of the lake." I was still mumbling. "I saw a flash in the woods there before dinner. Like the sun hitting a mirror. I think you might have hunters."

Then I was out.

And because I was so drowsy, and then I was asleep, I missed Riggs's body getting tighter and tighter with every word I said.

TWENTY-FIVE

Chaos Theory

Nadia

I was shaken awake by Riggs.

I opened my eyes.

It was already full-on sun, but dawn came early this far north in the summer.

However, I could tell it was earlier than normal, since I was an early riser (if Riggs let me go to sleep at a decent hour (not complaining), which he had last night), and I'd still been dead asleep.

So I blinked at Riggs, sitting fully clothed on the bed beside me.

"Is something up?" I asked.

"We're going into town for breakfast. You can go back to bed, but thought you might want plenty of time to get ready. Though, in a couple of hours, gotta ask you to wake Ledger up so he can get showered and be good to go."

I pushed up to an arm. "Are you going somewhere?"

"Gonna check the south side of the lake."

"What? Now?"

"Honey."

That was all he said, but I didn't like the way he said it.

"What?" I whispered.

"Hunters take care not to have anything reflect off them. Not easy to shoot a deer if you warn them you're coming."

Oh shit.

"Are you…going to take your gun?"

"No, I'm gonna take Harry, who's waiting downstairs for me, and he's got his gun. So I gotta go."

"Oh."

"Kiss me."

I pushed up and kissed him, we both used tongues, but it was Riggs who ended it, and he did this too soon.

"Be back in a while," he promised.

I nodded.

He leaned in, kissed the top of my head, then he was gone.

YOU'D THINK, the amount of time I spent around children, I'd be good at keeping something from just one.

But perhaps it wasn't that I was bad at it, instead, that Ledger clearly took after his father in more than looks, but also in brain capacity (and I was a professional—I could ask him to take tests, but I already knew he was significantly advanced in far more than reading).

As such, I was about to learn that I sucked at keeping stuff from him.

"Was there another break in at the cabin or something?" he asked. "Is that where Dad's at?"

I was drinking coffee.

So he wouldn't feel left out, I made him a mug of cocoa. Thus, we could be two buds sharing a mug at the kitchen bar waiting for his dad to come home and take us to breakfast.

I thought about how Riggs was with his boy in everything but that he and I were sleeping in the same bed and shared, "I saw something yesterday in the woods. He and Harry are checking it out."

"Oh. Okay," Ledger replied blithely, such was the power of his dad to see to all the mysteries and ills of the world, then he took a sip of his cocoa, leaving a cocoa mustache.

Which…honestly?

His reaction made me feel much better, because I was also finding Doc Riggs had the power to see to quite a number of the mysteries and ills of the world.

When Ledger was done swallowing, he announced grandly, "I wanna say something."

"You can say anything to me," I told him.

"Okay. Then I'll start by saying, I don't want to make you cry or anything, I just want you to know how sorry I am that your mom died."

Official.

I was falling in love with this kid.

"Thank you, sweetheart," I replied.

He nodded and went on, "That makes it hard to say what I gotta say next. But I gotta say it. My mom was being a dick to you the other day, so I'm gonna apologize for her."

I wasn't sure where Riggs stood on the word "dick" coming out of his son's mouth in that capacity.

I was sure Ledger and I had now spent quite a bit of time together, but we still weren't in a place I felt I could admonish him, because I thought nine was too young to use the word "dick."

Not to mention, he was being so earnest and sweet, I didn't want to color the moment.

Thus, I let it lie and focused on the sweet part of what he said.

"That's okay," I replied. "But I appreciate your apology."

"Nah, it isn't okay," he returned. "I miss my brother when I'm with Dad, but Stormy's cool about having me over so we can hang, or bringing Viggo over here."

This was news.

"He's only three, but I know he misses me too," Ledger continued. "But I'm gonna ask Dad, when he leaves again, if I can stay with you or Gramme instead of going back to Mom."

Oh shit.

"Why would you ask for that, sweetheart?" I queried carefully.

"Because Dad taught me, everything you do has consequences. It's called the mosquito effect."

"Sorry, Ledge, I think that's the butterfly effect."

"Oh, that makes more sense," he mumbled.

I wasn't sure how, but I wasn't a budding genius.

"Anyway," he kept at it, "it's like, at recess, you tell a girl she's pretty, and her shirt is green, and she feels good you said she was pretty, and for the whole rest of her life, she loves the color green."

I also wasn't sure that was strictly how the butterfly effect worked, but I wasn't a student of chaos theory.

Regardless, I was interested in something else.

"Is there a girl you think is pretty?"

"Yeah. Madeline Yamada," he threw out casually. "But I'm not talking about her. I'm just saying. Mom's gotta learn that she can't just show at Dad's place and be a dick and it not have an effect. You know?"

I did know.

"You're very smart and mature for your age," I said truthfully.

He sat straighter.

"But I think you need to have a long talk with your dad about this."

"It's not a big deal," he told me. "When I'm off in the summer, he doesn't take super long jobs. His crew likes it like that too. They can go kayaking and camping and stuff like that. They work a lot in the winter, but June through August, they're home most of the time. His next job is only gonna last two weeks. And then he's off for six whole weeks."

Hallelujah!

"So she's gotta feel the consequences for only two weeks," he finished as the door opened.

His math didn't exactly add up, because his dad would then be back, so she'd feel the effect for two months.

I didn't correct him since he was looking toward the door.

I turned that way as well.

Riggs came in first, Harry, out of uniform, came in after him.

"Harry!" Ledger shouted, jumped off his stool and ran down then up to get to Harry on the front landing.

No cool kid here, he threw his arms around the man.

The way Harry smiled when he put his hand on Ledger's head, the other on his shoulder (I already liked the guy and had noted he was handsome, but I liked him a ton more), and with that sweet look on his face as he peered down at Ledger, I thought he was borderline beautiful.

He didn't wear a ring, but I hoped he had a special someone, and I further hoped they had kids.

"How much have you grown since I last saw you? Eight feet?" Harry asked.

Ledger popped back. "You saw me last week."

"Question still stands."

Ledger turned to me. "He's a goof."

"He seems pretty awesome to me," I said, right when Riggs made it to me.

"He does?" Riggs asked under his breath.

I looked up at him. "Third place, after the Riggs Boys."

His lips quirked.

"Everything good?" I asked.

"Talk later," he muttered.

Fantastic.

"I gotta head," Harry announced. "Hey and bye, Nadia. Good to see you again."

"You too, Harry. Hope the plainclothes mean you have the day off."

"I never have a day off," he replied like that didn't bother him. "Doc," he bid and looked down. "Ledge. Later." His lips tipped up. "And you got a chocolate mustache."

Ledger's arm went up immediately to rub it off, and he whirled on me.

"Why didn't you tell me?" he demanded after he dropped his arm.

"We were talking chaos theory, I had to concentrate," I semi-lied.

The truth: I hadn't told him because it was cute.

"I'm out," Harry interrupted this.

Ledger swung back to him.

"Later, Harry," he said.

"Thanks for coming out, man," Riggs said.

Harry left and was barely out the door when Riggs called, "Kid, vamoose. Find something to do outside. Nadia and me will be out in a minute, and we'll hit the Double D for breakfast."

"You find something from the trespassers?" Ledger asked.

Riggs glanced down at me, then to his son, he said, "No. I wanna make out with her."

"Barf!" Ledger yelled and scrammed out the door.

Riggs looked down again at me, and this time, he kept doing it.

"Well, that worked," I remarked.

"Yup."

"Are we gonna make out?"

"Yup."

I grinned.

"But in a minute," he said.

I frowned.

That meant he grinned.

Then I explained, "I told him you were checking on something I saw. I thought that was what you'd do. He didn't seem alarmed."

"It's what I'd do."

"He also told me something, and to keep our growing bond thriving, I'm not going to tell you what it is. And it's not bad. Just that you might want to carve out time to have a chat with him."

"It's not bad?"

"No. He listens to you as well as processes what you say in a deep way that's beyond his years. He's processed something and made a decision about it. He'll bring it up to you anyway, just wanted to give you a warning."

"Right. This have something to do with chaos theory?"

"Yes, actually."

He shook his head with amusement.

"Okay, then, now can we make out?" I queried.

He smiled again. "Not yet."

"Ugh. So, does this delay in making out mean you found something?"

"It took some looking, but yeah. We found a multitude of foot-prints. Two people. One's either a guy with a small foot and not a lot of weight on him, or a woman. The other, definitely a guy or a female shot putter who's not afraid of getting caught doping."

I started laughing.

He kept talking.

"They came in around where you said, moved around a lot, went back to an old, now unused access road off the main one where they parked their car. No clue what they were doing, but they weren't hunting or camping."

"Is there another reason for someone to be there?"

"Not that I know. I've had to tell folks who come in to chop down trees for firewood to get off my land. Not often, but it's happened a couple of times. One group of them were out-of-towners who thought they could ignore the signs their footprints passed right by to chop down a Christmas tree."

"Losers," I muttered.

"Agreed. I do get hunters. Trappers too, but that isn't much anymore, 'cause I spring those fuckers, confiscate them and melt them down to use in my work, and some of that shit can be expensive."

"I take it you aren't a hunter."

"My dad was a hunter."

"Ah."

"I grew up here, so I get how it's part of tradition and even a way of life."

"I sense that's not the entirety of your opinion about it," I remarked.

This time he smirked.

It was hot.

"You sense right," he confirmed. "It boils down to the fact that we've managed to discover ways to sensitively raise and slaughter animals for consumption, and I can't wrap my head around stalking a living thing through its natural habitat for the purpose of killing it. I know a number of things that are challenging and prove you've got mettle that don't include taking the life of a living creature. If it poses an immediate threat to you, okay. If you go out for the purpose of ending its life so you can hang its head on your wall, absolutely not."

I very much agreed.

But he wasn't done.

"And I don't buy the argument that I eat meat so I can't be against hunting. I don't work in an abattoir or on a ranch, and neither do the vast majority of hunters. I don't grow my own vegetables either, and I eat those. I don't mix my own shampoo, and I use that shit. Seemed the animals had a way of controlling their own population when humans weren't around. It's humans that invaded their patch who didn't like them killing their chickens or cattle. To keep their investment safe from predators, it'd cost money. People like to keep their money. My take, that's a price you pay for being in that business. Sure, that price would be passed onto the consumer, which might drive them to eating more vegetables, and they can't have that. So it's down to greed. You don't eradicate the wolves and mountain lions so you got so much deer they starve in the winter so you gotta open a hunting season for greed."

"I fear you've missed your calling as an anti-hunting lobbyist."

Another smirk, then, "On the other hand, until the majority of American citizens decide hunting is abhorrent, it's a lawful activity, so even though that's my opinion, and I don't understand why someone hunts, they might not understand why I occasionally enjoy a joint. They keep out of my business, I keep out of theirs, we both carry on in a lawful manner, it's got nothing to do with me. Unless you do it on my land. That's where my law comes in."

"I like your law. Can it be Doc Riggs's law to trap humans who trespass on your land?"

His body moved with laughter, but it wasn't audible, though his one word shook with it.

"No."

"Pity."

He kept laughing a beat before he got serious. "I got a lot of acreage to cover, but neither Harry nor me liked those tracks. We couldn't get a lock on why they were there, though it seemed like they were looking for something. And they definitely made sure their car wasn't visible on the main road, which is suspicious. This means, gotta spend some time doing some wandering and having a look around to see if it's just someone fucking around, or if I got an issue."

"I can walk with you," I offered.

"That'd be good," he said.

"Can we make out now?" I asked.

His smile to that was wide. "Not yet. Got something to tell you that Harry shared with me."

I leaned into him and begged, "Please tell me you buried the lead, and they found the wine burglar."

"No. That's still an open case. And he's talked with Bubbles three times, and the asshole is sticking with the I-took-a-trip-to-Sonoma story when it comes to what he's sharing with Harry. So no movement on that."

"Bluh," I uttered, sitting back.

"Remember I told you he was going to have a look at the Whitaker case file?"

I leaned back into him and made my eyes big.

Another smile and, "He also called the station in Seattle that handled the finding and processing of Lincoln Whitaker's body."

This was unexpected.

"And?"

"And, when Harry got the detective on the line who was called to that scene, and Harry told him why he was calling, the man's first words were, 'Finally, someone is lookin' into this shit.'"

I slapped a hand lightly on his chest. "What?"

He nodded.

"Why?" I asked.

"Because this Seattle cop has always thought something was hinky with that. He's of the mind, to this day, that Lincoln Whitaker was murdered."

Oh.

My.

God.

TWENTY-SIX

Oboe

Nadia

By the time we hit a very crowded Double D, I could sense Riggs's mood had taken a huge hit, mainly because he wasn't hiding it.

This was because we had to park five blocks away, off the main drag, in the residential section of MP that fed back from it.

It was also because we had to wade through a plethora of Charles-Haden Savages, Olivers, Mabels, Cindas, Howards, Bunnys, Tim Konos and tie-dye hoodies to get to the Double D.

I'd never seen so much fake orange fur in my life, and the weather was back in the low seventies.

I felt bad Riggs was in a shitty mood, but I thought it was hysterical.

It didn't get better when we had to fight our way through the residents of the Arconia even to get in the door of the Double D, and within seconds, a passing waitress shared, "Wait's at least half an hour. Probably longer. We got a list going. Write your name on it, and we'll shout it out when we got a table ready. You don't come at first call, we give it to the next name."

She then swung her fully loaded arms to a clipboard sitting on the counter at the curve of the horseshoe bar and scurried away.

"Whose idea was this?" Riggs grumbled.

I wasn't about to remind him it was his.

"Yo, Doc!" we heard shouted.

I looked right just as Ledger yelled, "Jace! Jess!" and raced through the crowded space to the huge, circular corner booth that…*oh my God*…had *Delphine Larue* sitting in it.

I noted she had a very good-looking man of the Riggs variety at her side, except he was older, and had a more Outdoors Guy feel than a Good-Time Guy.

With them were two other men who were clearly of his loins.

And they were identical twins.

Riggs put his hand to the small of my back and began to lead us that way, as I said under my breath, "Is that Delphine Larue?"

"Yup."

"Star of the seminal sitcom *Those Years*?"

"Mm-hmm."

"Author of one of the greatest books of our time, *We Pluck the Cord*?"

There was now humor in his, "Yeah."

"*Oh my God*," I breathed.

"Hey, Doc," the man beside Delphine greeted when we got to their table. "Sit with us. We got room."

And I'll repeat.

Oh my God!

I was going to have breakfast with Delphine Larue!

One of the twins got out so Ledger could sit between them, and all the others scooched in so I was sitting next to Delphine Larue's man, and Riggs slid in beside me.

It was a tight fit, but it worked, and it was a lot better than waiting more than thirty minutes to eat.

I was famished.

"Nadia, this is Cade Bohannan. You know of Delphine. And these are Cade's sons, Jess and Jace," Riggs introduced.

"Pleased to meet you all."

"And you're Nadia," Delphine said with a smile.

"Sorry," I said to her. "I'm gonna warn you, I'm going to be giving off a hefty fangirl vibe. But it'll wear off, I promise. Just love your show, but your book is in my top five favorites." I thought about it. "No, top three."

"Who do I share company with?" she asked.

"*Rebecca* and *A Confederacy of Dunces*," I answered.

"That's lofty company," she replied.

A place her work deserved.

Waters were dropped in front of us, and the waitress, whose nametag said her name was Betty, though I suspected it actually wasn't, looked at Cade and said, "Take it you're gonna wait to order until the newcomers figure it out?"

"Yeah," Cade answered.

"Ugh," she replied then scampered off.

"We didn't just get here," Jess explained. "But shit is going slow."

"Here's a menu," Cade offered me as Riggs leaned forward and pulled out his phone.

I didn't peek as he checked his screen, then turned the phone face down on the table.

I did notice, as we perused menus, sipped water then the coffee that was brought, finally ordering, chatting, getting served and eating, that all four of them were great with Ledger. They liked and respected Riggs a good deal and showed it. All the men were of the hunky, cool, confident variety, and they were all devoted in their own ways to Delphine, and they showed that too. All in all, they were interesting, funny, kind people, and I was glad we happened on them to have breakfast, and not just so I could share a meal with Delphine Larue.

Oh.

And I also noticed that Riggs's phone screen lit up against the table a lot.

This had me considering two things.

The first, my time in Misted Pines might have started solitary and slow, but since Riggs's peace offering, it had been very full of activity and meeting and getting to know good people (Angelica not included).

This was something I needed to journal about because it was definitely something to consider in view of the fact my beloved mother had been beaten to death not five months ago, and I had to admit, even if that gloom never went away and often hit me like an invisible blow at unexpected times, for the most part, I was happy.

No.

For the most part, I was the happiest I'd been since Trevor shared his diagnosis with me.

The second thing I was considering was that someone really wanted to get hold of Riggs, and I was both curious who it was, and really hoping it wasn't Angelica in order to give him more grief.

We were finished, and Riggs, Cade, Jace and Jess were having a four-way Man Discussion about the bill, which I was tuning out at the same chatting with Delphine about how great the spa was at the Pinetop Lodge.

This was when Kimmy, who was not wearing Christmas duds, but instead a normal outfit, if you didn't count her carrying an oboe, showed at our table.

And her attention was directed to me.

Riggs let out a huge sigh, and if I was correct in hearing others over his, so did Cade. Though, Jess and Jace were smiling.

"Hey, Kimmy," Delphine greeted.

"Yeah, yeah," Kimmy replied waving a dismissive hand at her, but her attention was on me. "I don't have a lot of time. I gotta get back. My shop is wall to wall people. I just broke up a Detective Williams who was in a fight with an Uma over my last Elf on a Shelf. But I heard you were here. Any sightings?"

"No," I answered.

She threw up both hands, the oboe spiking in the air.

"What's taking so long?" she demanded. "You've been out there at least three weeks."

"The fact that there's no such thing as ghosts?" Riggs suggested.

"Argh!" she cried, then she dashed off, knocking the backs of two chairs with her oboe as she went.

The people in those chairs didn't even blink.

"I see you've met Kimmy," Delphine noted to me.

"Indeed," I replied.

Her eyes sparkled.

"Do I wanna know about the oboe?" Riggs asked.

I looked to him. "We haven't gotten that far in the show, but this year, she's a Jan."

I knew he lost interest when he muttered, "Whatever."

We waded through the volatile quagmire of four *Men!* sitting at the same table and paying the bill. We were then out on the sidewalk, and I was gabbing with Delphine, watching how adept she was at ignoring the people who stared blatantly at her or took pictures of her on their phone. Jace and Jess were hanging with Ledger. And Cade and Riggs were in a huddle.

They broke, Riggs came and claimed me, but I didn't say my farewells since Riggs called, "We'll be right behind you. See you at your place," to Cade.

After he said that, he turned me down the sidewalk with Ledger jogging off the other way between Jace and Jess.

"Is something up?" I asked.

"We're not gonna have the chill day I wanted us to have," he answered.

"What's going on?"

"Cade has something to share with me. We're going to theirs."

"Something?"

"He's an FBI profiler, or he was. He's retired. Word is, he's one of the best ones they ever had."

"Whoa," I said. Then asked, with a little shock, because if he was the best, this was not much to merit his attention. "Is this about the wine burglars?"

"Nope. It's about the Whitakers."

Interesting!

I suddenly had a pep in my step as we kept walking.

"That's not all," Riggs said.

"What?"

"Storm asked if he can come over, or if I can hit his. He's made a decision, and considering it will affect Ledger, he wants me to know what it is."

"Oh boy."

"Yeah."

"Is that what all the activity was about on your phone?"

"Some of it. Others were buds wanting to know if we can have a get-together at my place tonight. I'll text them later that's not going to be a thing." We kept walking, me under his arm, mine along his waist, thumb hooked in the loop of his belt at his other side, as he looked down at me. "You up for that next Saturday? Mom can take Ledge, and we can blow it out."

On the one hand, I wanted to meet his buds.

On the other hand, I wasn't a partier.

"Maribeth will be here. She's coming on Wednesday and staying the weekend," as a hedge, I reminded him of something I'd already told him.

"All the better," he replied.

In the Maribeth department, it was, seeing as she *was* a partier, even if she was now a married lady with two kids.

"Murphy's also coming out," he shared. "That's another of the texts I got. Looks like Mom also got to him, and he's not gonna waste time checking you out."

I didn't know if this elated or terrified me.

Riggs pulled me tighter to his side. "He'll like you."

If he was like Riggs, and I huddled in a chair, sipping a gin martini, while other women were throwing their bras into the pines, I wasn't sure about that.

"I don't want to change a hair on your head, honey," Riggs remarked. "But I do wanna have a go at teaching you how to let it down. Your girl and my boy in town, that says party."

He was right.

It did.

"Okay. I'm in."

He shot me a big, happy smile.

It was only then I was truly in.

"Well, not a chill day, but an interesting one," I noted.

"I wanted to hang with you and my kid before dropping my boy off at Dustin's at four, then spend the rest of the day in your bed at the cabin. Now, due to the Cade and Stormy parts of this shit, Jace and Jess are gonna take him to do something, so I lost the Ledger part of that."

"We deal, then we get on with it," I reminded him.

He looked down at me. "Yeah, honey. And another reminder, on other important fronts, you're not doing much of that."

Hmm.

It was occurring to me that Riggs thought he was sitting on the emotional ticking time bomb of me.

Truth.

He was.

So he was right.

I had to deal with that.

But first I needed to learn how to party.

TWENTY-SEVEN

Eternity

Nadia

T he Riggs boys owned a lake.

The Bohannans occupied a bona fide compound on a lake.

Their lake was probably ten of Riggs's. It was huge, and they didn't own it.

But they did inhabit some impressive properties at one end of it.

As we drove up, Riggs told me Delphine and Cade occupied the main house. Cade's daughter, Celeste (who was at the first marathon screening of season one of *OMitB*, something that had started at six that morning), lived in a smaller pad close to it. And Jace and Jess occupied cabins across from each other a ways up each side of the lake.

Upon entering, I discovered the interior of Cade and Delphine's house was impressive, and attractive, if not as interesting and eccentric as Riggs's house.

Though their view of that lake was smack-you-back spectacular.

Delphine moved off to make us coffees as Cade led us to his office.

It, too, was impressive. And unlike the rest of the house, which was gorgeous, but gender neutral, this space was entirely masculine.

I'd had the opportunity to do a full-house tour of Riggs's place, and he had an office too.

However, unlike the rest it (I'd learned he'd somehow miraculously and painstakingly renovated it in only three years between jobs, commissions, having Ledger and having a good time), his office was a small, dark, cramped, untidy room at the very back of the level where the kitchen and dining room were.

The level above it angled to the north west and into the slope. It held Ledger's room, which had a three-quarter bath attached to it.

Or, if I'd figured out how Lincoln had crafted it, his daughter's room.

This I guessed because opposite that were two smaller bedrooms that shared a Jack and Jill suite (for Lincoln's boys).

And pushing deeper into the earth of the natural slope, the guest room with en suite that I officially still occupied, but unofficially had only briefly occupied.

The kitchen/dining room level didn't dive as deeply into the slope, but it also included a very large room that held a pool table and a very fancy, full wet bar.

Riggs's bedroom was mostly a level all its own. Though some of it was built over the living room, most of it jutted off over the lakeside of the house.

So, yes.

Eccentric.

We settled in Cade's office, and I figured Cade had shared what he had to say already with Delphine, because he launched right in before she returned with coffee.

He started by putting his hand on an enormous pile of papers and folders resting on his desk that had to be at least ten inches tall before he shared, "Harry gave me copies of everything he could pull on the entire Whitaker mess, including the local and Seattle case files, court documents and depositions. And I've spent the last four days reading through them."

My goodness.

That was a lot of work.

Cade took his hand from the pile. "Now, you can guess I have experience with twins, and because I had my own and do what I do, I researched the various phenomena about them. But that isn't fresh research, and I didn't have time to dive back into it."

"Right," Riggs said when Cade paused.

"Saying that," Cade continued, "got firsthand knowledge of the link they share. They communicate intuitively in ways we don't. They have an uncanny sync. They also feel each other's emotions, and sometimes even physical pain. Last, they have a closeness where, in major life events, for them it doesn't feel like they've fully experienced it unless they either experience it with the other, or until they share with the other that it happened."

Riggs and I nodded.

This was common knowledge with twins, except that last, which I found intriguing.

"That said, they are each their own man with their own thoughts, opinions and personalities," Cade shared. "They are not one person split in two. They're two distinct people who look the same."

More nodding from me, not Riggs.

Cade kept at it.

"From what I could tell, this was the same with Roosevelt and Lincoln. But it was the way in which they were brought up that Roosevelt became the dominant of the two."

"What does that mean?" Riggs asked.

"It means, he was a clear favorite of their parents. It's like the Carpenters' experience."

Now, he'd lost me.

Fortunately, he kept talking.

"The Carpenter family thought Richard was the prodigy. As such, the entirety of that family shifted all their attention to Richard. When it emerged that it was Karen who had the singular talent, they couldn't adjust."

Oh.

He was talking about the Carpenters musical group, fronted by

Karen's extraordinary voice, backed by Richard's not-as-extraordinary, but still skillful talent at a keyboard.

I was again following him.

"This caused some dysfunction with that family, but with Roosevelt and Lincoln, Roosevelt actually was the prodigy. As twins, and this is a guess, Roosevelt couldn't abide being singled out as a favorite because he had the double issue of feeling that awkwardness, at the same time, feeling his brother's pain at not being the same. And just to say, that's vice versa for Lincoln. My further guess is, this was the primary reason Roosevelt left home in Seattle as soon as he could and came to MP to forge his own path. It was also why he looked after his brother in the many ways he did, along with shaping the man he became, solitary, except for the bond with his brother, and not big on attention."

Again, this tracked.

Delphine came in with four coffee mugs hooked precariously in her fingers, and seeing this, Cade got up immediately to help her dole them out.

Once we had our mugs, she sat on the side of his desk next to where he sat in his chair, and he idly wrapped his fingers around her thigh.

Man, they were cute together.

Cade went back to it.

"I'll share this is entirely theoretical, but with the way Roosevelt and Lincoln grew up, and Roosevelt's protectiveness of his brother, I think this formed an unusual bond. Particularly when Sarah came into their lives."

Now we were getting to the good stuff.

Cade kept going.

"In their depositions, the Whitaker parents reported that Roosevelt always had a thing for writing. And they had evidence to that effect. The guy started writing essays and short stories when he was thirteen and had finished his first book by seventeen. This is an explanation why they got published so young. He'd already spent years honing his craft."

I hadn't thought about how young he had to have been to have that many books published by the time he died, but he'd only been forty-three when that happened.

So that was astonishing.

Cade continued, "In depositions taken from the different editors the men had, it was shared, on the first three books, they definitely worked together. Roosevelt plotted and wrote the action-driven narrative. Lincoln was responsible for the snappy dialogue and interpersonal relationships. However, two things happened. One, the series became popular for its action, not its relationships. And two, Roosevelt learned as he went along how to cover the things Lincoln did. Future books were more action focused, and the editors said that Lincoln contributed very little to all of them, except to do a final pass-through after Roosevelt wrote the book, making tweaks. From book four onward, he acted as more of an editor, not a writer."

Riggs and I looked at each other because we'd already heard word of this, though it was fascinating to have it confirmed.

Cade carried on speaking.

"Sarah arrives on the scene, and in her parents' deposition, everything that has anything to do with the brothers and Sarah, they refer to the brothers in plural. She met *them*. She became involved with *them*. The sister reported that Sarah actually met Roosevelt first, but he quickly introduced her to his brother."

"Is that significant?" I asked, thinking that they were twins, so it wouldn't be.

"It is, if my theory is correct, and Sarah and Lincoln had an open marriage, with the third member of that situation being Roosevelt," Cade answered.

"Fuck," Riggs grunted.

"Holy shit," I whispered.

"Oh yeah," Delphine murmured before taking a sip of coffee.

"So you're saying you think Lincoln knew about them?" Riggs queried.

"Knew. And outwardly approved," Cade said.

"Outwardly?" Riggs pressed.

"He built a house where he couldn't see his brother's cabin. This tells me he didn't want to know. That makes sense. It also doesn't. Because, if I'm reading between the lines, it was less an open marriage and more a brother-husbands type of deal. They were all one family. They had joint bank accounts. They built a trust that covered their assets like they were one unit. They frequently spent time together. They shared all holidays together, including with the kids when they came along. And considering publishing contracts from the third set of books, this being book seven and on, no longer included Lincoln's name at all, Roosevelt was providing for what he considered his entire family. Not his brother and his wife. *His family.*"

"This is totally wild, and it also makes total sense," I stated.

Cade aimed a small smile at me.

"Now, there are things that put a wrench in this theory," he allowed. "We'll start with Roosevelt living a quiet life and not being one to toss his money around. Lincoln was the opposite. Roosevelt stayed in MP. Lincoln and Sarah went back and forth. This kind of thing can cause some friction and doesn't relate. But all families have friction. I think it's a stretch, because your brother likes his dose of city living, he takes the woman you share with him, you get fed up with it, get in his face, and he's moved to murder. I think it's even a stretch that it's clear Roosevelt didn't want to sell the rights for motion pictures even for the first three books, because he knew if they took off, the writing was on the wall, and it'd have an effect on his life he wouldn't want, so Lincoln killed him and his wife because he was ticked about that. I think families have these differences and disputes. I think they also get over them or figure out a compromise. But in both instances, if you're pissed at your brother, you kill your brother. You don't also kill your wife."

"Nadia's friend in Chicago read through some of this stuff, and the Whitaker parents say that last part was getting heated," Riggs remarked.

"That's what they say. And yes, it was under oath. But Roosevelt communicated copiously with his parents, at their instigation, because again, he was the favorite. A lot of it was through email, and they have a good deal of evidence to present about the majority of their claims, but nothing to back that particular assertion up. They swore to that testimony, but I think they're lying or reading things in a way that would skew the estate in their favor."

"So Roosevelt and Lincoln both shared Sarah from the beginning, and there's no beef about the books, which means Lincoln has no reason to kill them," Riggs broke it down.

Cade nodded. "Exactly."

"So who killed them?" I asked.

"I don't know," Cade said. "And the answer to that question lies at the end of a variety of thorny paths. Starting with her parents, who are intensely, religiously conservative. If they were aware of this situation, and from what I can tell by the unnecessarily vitriolic way they refer to the brothers, it's a good bet they were, they could have motive. It's thin, but it could be the sister, because the Whitaker men weren't only rich and talented and both known to be good, dependable men, they were good-looking and fit, and it might be a sibling rivalry gig. It could be some unknown, but that wouldn't explain why Lincoln took the fall for them."

He drew in a breath and finished his litany of suspects.

"It could also be one of the kids, for two reasons. One, if they're aware of this situation and aren't the only ones who were, and they got teased or bullied about it in school. Though it's important to note, it's never been brought to light in thousands of pages of reports, motions and filings, it's my theory. Or more likely, two, because not all of them are of Lincoln's seed."

"Holy shit!" I cried.

"Oh yeah," Delphine repeated.

"What's your take on that?" Riggs queried.

"If I was forced to provide a report on this, I'd land on the fact that the oldest son is Roosevelt's, the younger two are Lincoln's, those kids knew that, and the younger two felt some sense of vulnerability or misguided loyalty, because Roosevelt was the breadwinner, and even that Sarah preferred him to Lincoln."

"*Did* Sarah prefer Roosevelt?" Delphine asked, showing that Cade hadn't told her that part.

He looked to her. "My theory has not even been hinted at in a foot-high stack of papers, but from reading between the lines, it seems this is the case. Both younger kids state as often as they were given the opportunity that their mom hung out 'all the time' with their uncle, thus underlining Lincoln's supposed actions. That said, even the older boy doesn't dispute this, but instead, corroborates it."

"That could be a motive for murder," Riggs commented.

"Yeah, it can," Cade agreed. "What supports Lincoln doing it is his wife's supposed preference, and the manner in which your house is situated, or if I'm dead wrong, and they were simply cheating. It could be, though, that he was just giving them privacy, because if his house is like that, the cabin is too. It could have been an agreement. The brothers give each other privacy in their living spaces with Sarah. Where I'm stuck is on the overkill of the fire, specifically the wetting down of the area around it. Something, although there wasn't much to go on in Dern's file, but even so, it seemed skewed."

"Skewed?" I asked.

"From the photos, there was evidence of water everywhere, but specifically, between the stables and the cabin," Cade told me. "That was drenched. Like he really didn't want the cabin to catch fire. And that was Roosevelt's place, so if Lincoln killed Roosevelt in a moment of jealous rage, that doesn't make any sense."

It really didn't.

"But overall," Cade kept at it, "there simply was no reason for the overkill of the fire. There are many incidences of people behaving in all manners when they're in a heightened emotional state, and these states can last a long time, in extreme cases, even days. But if you're in a heightened emotional state, you might set a barn ablaze for indiscriminate reasons. You don't guard against a fire spreading. That takes thought, consideration, an understanding of and follow-through to avoid consequences."

Cade shook his head and carried on.

"From what I read about him, Lincoln had not once in his life acted in what could be considered a blatantly irrational manner. All three of his kids testify they loved him deeply. He was reportedly good-natured and social. He had a lot of friends. He was thought of highly. He was the face of the duo, would go on book tours and speak to thousands of people and sign thousands of books. Yes, I could see him flipping his shit if he caught his wife with his twin brother. And yes, I could see when he came back to himself he'd be filled with remorse and turn himself in. But the fire? That's sketchy."

"Okay, so if it's Lincoln's kids, they were in Seattle and not old enough to make their way to MP on their own," I pointed out.

"One thing I've learned in this business," Cade replied. "If there's a will, there's a way."

"So you think a fifteen and fourteen year old murdered their mother and uncle?" Riggs asked.

"I think it's a possibility. But I think they'd need help, and it wasn't the older boy. It could be the grandparents, but they were estranged from them. It could be the aunt, but if it was her, since she's involved in highly contentious litigation, I would think someone would have turned on somebody by now, or, if I'm correct, at least outed the nature of the marriage. It could be the girl's boyfriend, who was seventeen."

"What happened to the boyfriend?" I asked.

Cade shook his head. "Don't know. He was mentioned in some of Roosevelt's emails to his parents, and Roosevelt liked him. Thought he was a solid guy. And it was noted in the last email he sent to his folks, which was two days before his death, that the boyfriend was going to be with the other kids when the oldest drove them out for the weekend. After that, I have no clue. Though, she's unmarried and there's no mention of her having a current partner, same with the youngest boy. Then again, in this case, they wouldn't factor."

"Harry tell you about what we found this morning?" Riggs asked.

Cade took a sip from his own mug while shaking his head.

"Yesterday evening, someone was at the southeast end of my lake, tramping around. Not camping. Not hunting. Just tramping around a big, but not large, though contained location. We think a man and a woman," Riggs told him.

"The younger brother and sister?" Cade queried.

Whoa!

What?

Why would it be them?

"No clue. But if you're right, it could be," Riggs said. "Whoever it was knew of an access road that's still there, but mostly grown over, and you wouldn't know it was there unless you knew it was there. It's my understanding, Roosevelt used that road when he thought it was time to thin out the forest in that area and get some firewood or whatever other shit he got up to in those woods when he didn't want to hoof it. But it's been unused since his death."

"Looking for something?" Cade inquired.

"Was the shotgun found?" Riggs asked.

"Lincoln had it with him when the first responders arrived," Cade told him.

"Then I don't know," Riggs said.

"Is all the money accounted for?" Delphine asked.

"It's dwindling by the day, because at this juncture, a judge has allowed its use for the children and their schooling, and the oldest boy is now a medical doctor, as well as other living needs, which means they're also using it for attorneys' fees, and as you know, this is contentious in the extreme, and motions are filed regularly. But bottom line, yes," Cade answered.

"So it's not like there's buried treasure," she said.

Cade's lips twitched in a way I thought this was some kind of private joke before he replied, "Not unless Roosevelt was keeping something from the surviving members of the extended family."

Which begged a question I hadn't had the chance to ask yet.

What would someone be out there looking for?

"Did Harry tell you what the Seattle detective said?" Riggs probed.

"Yep," Cade replied.

"Thoughts on that considering your theory?"

"Yep," Cade repeated, then launched in. "It was well known that Lincoln was a man who enjoyed the finer things in life. He indulged himself, his wife and his kids. And we're seeing the results of that last. If I'm correct, and he came home from the fishing trip only to happen onto his two youngest having killed his brother and wife, and he made the split decision to take the fall for them, he had seven very long years to consider that decision. Now, if I'm a kid fucked in the head enough to commit what could only be charged as capital murder against members of my own family, I'd be a little jittery Dad faced the horrors of prison, having time to ruminate on his dead wife and twin brother, doing it with no waterfront view, doing it for me, and knowing what I'd done."

"So you think they killed him," I remarked.

Cade nodded. "I think it's not a coincidence he saw those kids in the days before. And he did not see all his kids together. He visited his oldest son at college, and the younger two together, meeting them wherever they were frittering away his brother's legacy. And I think whatever happened during that visit scared the absolute fuck out of them, and they moved in. That said, they did that shit by forcing a bottle of arsenic down his throat, so I also believe they were prepared for Dad to get out and see which way it swung."

Cade took his hand from Delphine's leg, sat forward and rested his forearms on his desk.

"That cop said he felt Lincoln's hotel room had been straightened after what could have been a struggle. He was found lying serenely on the bed. Death by arsenic poisoning isn't pretty and would include seizures, and yet the bedclothes were unperturbed. Outside that, the detective couldn't put his finger on it, and he had no proof, but in his gut, he thought that room looked wrong. He also noticed bruising around the man's jaw consistent with someone taking a forceful hold and pushing his head back. Last, as pertains to the scene, there was no suicide note."

Interesting.

Cade kept at it.

"They found traces of alcohol and a mild sedative in his system. But there were no suspicious prints or DNA found on the scene, and only his fingerprints on the bottle of arsenic. The coroner had no explanation for the bruising on his jaw, but, except for another minor contusion on his shin, there was nothing else on his body to indicate a struggle. And although they didn't find evidence of him having a sedative in his possession, something he'd take to calm anxiety or the like, it isn't outlandish to think the guy needed some hooch and a pill to deal with what had become of his life. That said, you can get drink at a bar, you can't say the same about sedatives. And the tests show the man was definitively, if not significantly, as in, he'd been given Rohypnol, sedated. So how do you take two or three pills in your hotel room, and not have the pack?"

How indeed.

Lord, this was a tangled web.

"This detective was interested enough to actually investigate," Cade continued, "and all three of the kids, the sister, and all of the parents had alibis. It's just that the two younger kids' alibis were each other. That said, the investigator was under pressure to close a case that seemed not to merit resources, so he did as his superiors requested and closed the case."

God, he was good at this.

A sentiment to be shared.

"You're crazy good at this," I announced.

Another smile from Cade.

"You should have seen how closely he pegged Ray Andrews," Delphine noted.

Cade aimed his current smile Delphine's way before he kept going.

"What's of note is that Lincoln's express wishes while he was in prison, the only word they have from any of the three about how their assets were to be distributed, are why that judge ordered the monies to be used for schooling and living expenses. And the only one of them who went to college was the first one. What's also of note, is that the oldest is being the least contentious of all those vultures. He simply wants an equitable split between the offspring. He's repeatedly said that was what his mom, dad and uncle-maybe-dad would have wanted. But he's not hiding his growing fatigue with these proceedings, to the point that I would be surprised if soon, he didn't withdraw. Further, he hasn't had much to do with his brother and sister since well before his father was released from prison. When he went to college a year after the deaths, he got stuck in his studies, and essentially, if not officially, broke ties with all of them."

"How did Dern's case file look?" Riggs asked.

"It had Lincoln's mugshot, prints, his written confession, a report that's precisely three paragraphs long, a lot of pictures of a burned building, a picture of the shotgun, and a copy of a lot more thorough report from the coroner. And that's it," Cade informed him.

"So they didn't test Lincoln for gunshot residue?" Riggs asked.

"Now why would he do that?" Cade asked sarcastically. "He had a confession, and probably a beer and a game to get back to."

"Does this mean Harry is going to be up to his neck in shit if that gets out?" Riggs pushed.

Cade shook his head. "Harry, being Harry, has already asked Polly to pull the bigger cases Dern worked on to do an audit, so when this gets out, he's not blindsided. It still could be an issue. The thing he has going for him is the guy confessed and went down without a whimper. Dern definitely should have done more. They don't even have notes on an interrogation like they didn't ask the guy that first question. And they certainly didn't interview anyone else. If there's a case that's going to turn over, this would be the one."

Cade took another sip then asked his own question. "You worried about those footprints?"

"Nadia and I are going to start tramping around ourselves."

"I'll help with that, and Jace and Jess aren't on an assignment, so I know they'll be on board to help too. If you don't mind me making suggestions, give us quadrants, but we concentrate around your house, the cabin, the east side of the lake down to where there was evidence of trespassers. If Roosevelt hid something, he was an outdoorsman, I wouldn't put it past him putting it on the more remote side of the lake. But it'd be better to concentrate our efforts, then expand."

"Your help would be appreciated. But, Cade, if someone is actually looking for something, they've had fifteen years to find whatever it is, and it obviously hasn't been found," Riggs noted.

"And Roosevelt Whitaker was a clever thriller writer," Cade returned. "If there's something to be found he didn't want to be found, it's probably going to take eternity to find it."

That meant, whoever was looking had to be found.

And if I understood what Riggs and Cade were talking about, that "whoever" had been looking for fifteen years, they hadn't found it, but they were definitely in to keep looking.

Well.

Damn.

TWENTY-EIGHT

Chartering A Plane

Nadia

"I have a theory," I announced on our way to Storm's house after we left the Bohannans.

"Sock it to me," Riggs invited.

"I sense from what we discussed with Cade, and what you two were talking about, plus what you found this morning, this someone from the Whitaker debacle possibly looking for something, might also be the 'ghosts' who chased people off the property. I mean, if whatever it is, is a big deal, like worth money, whoever owns the property actually now owns whatever that is. And before you bought it, whoever it is might not be someone who's supposed to have whatever it is they're looking for. This means, they couldn't exactly have people around while they were looking for it."

"Sorry, honey, but we already came up with that theory when I talked Harry into opening the file."

"Oh."

No wonder that had been the bent of their conversation.

"Forgot to mention it," he said.

"That's okay."

He kept driving.

I went after something else that was on my mind.

"Does Harry have a partner?"

"The sheriff doesn't normally work with a partner."

"No, I mean in life."

His response was openly guarded. "Why do you ask?"

I looked to him. "Is it a secret? Is he gay or something and there are shitty homophobes around who'd have a problem with it?"

"No. But you said he was awesome earlier, and now you're asking if he has a partner, and last night, and the night before, and so on, you been fucking me, so gotta wonder why the interest in Harry."

Now I was staring at him.

I did that awhile before I said, "Riggs, I'm only not laughing my ass off right now because I don't think you'd appreciate it, considering that's ridiculous."

"He's a good-lookin' guy."

"He's nowhere near as good-looking as you. And I doubt he makes brats as good as you, because, as far as I can tell, no one can. And I don't know if he's a dad, but he'd have fierce competition to be a better one than you. And I wouldn't like being able to make him smile as much I like making you smile, because I don't like making anyone smile as much as I like to do that for you. And I love my very dearly departed husband, and he didn't stink in this department, but he was nowhere near as good in bed as you. Do I need to go on?"

"No," he grunted.

"Is this a macho-man jealousy thing?" I pressed.

He didn't answer.

The things his mother said, not to mention what he said, hit me like a bullet.

"Riggs, you're all that," I said quietly.

"Okay," he said quickly.

"You really are."

Riggs had no comment.

Something else hit me.

So I went after it. "The day after we first did it, I asked if you were for real, and you had an odd reaction to that. What did you think I was asking?"

"What are you talking about?"

"I think you know."

"Did it?" he teased.

It was a cute tease, and I liked him teasing me.

What I didn't like was him dodging me.

"Had sex, copulated, fornicated, whatever you want to call it."

"Princess, that was solid gold fucking."

Now he was being hot and teasing, which, if I didn't nip it in the bud, would work.

"Stop deflecting," I warned.

He blew out a sigh and said, "If memory serves, I didn't know what you were talking about then, and I asked after it."

"It was just that?"

"Honey."

That was all he was going to say.

"Talk to me, Riggs," I demanded.

"Right, I wake up to a woman, I scoot her on her way. I don't tell her to put her toothbrush in my bathroom."

"Okay," I said cautiously.

"And I reckon you know that. Saying that, I'm not a player. But I get myself some. It's just the women I got it from know that's all I'm after."

"I do know that."

"So I wasn't sure how you'd behave knowing I didn't consider us a one-and-done situation, not even close to it."

"You thought I'd think it was?"

"I didn't know. It seemed like a weird question for you to ask."

"I was just surprised you had any motor skills at your command. Even though I did my best, you did most of the work, and I was still shattered."

That made him smile.

"Riggs, I'm into you," I said softly.

"I get that," he said brusquely.

Okay, this was making him uncomfortable. I had to let it go.

That said.

"For your information, there is no way I'd get involved with my neighbor if I wasn't seriously interested. Especially after learning he had a son. And that's not about you having Ledger and me thinking that's baggage I don't want to deal with. It's about another human being in the mix. So the decision I made was considered, and made mostly because, I'll repeat, I'm into you, and I am because I really like you."

He reached out, squeezed my knee, put his hand back to the wheel and muttered, "I really like you too, honey."

"Good."

"And to answer your question, Harry is not gay. Harry was married to a really amazing woman, he was head over heels for her, she felt the same, but a year after they got hitched, her horse threw her. She broke her neck, the kind of break where she lost her life."

"Oh God," I whispered.

"He still has his stables, but he got rid of his horses, and part of him died when she did. I don't think he's had a single date since that happened, and it was years ago."

Poor, handsome, good-with-Ledger, good-friend-to-Riggs Harry.

"I understand that," I said. Though, I got myself some (as he put it) on occasion.

"Bet you do," he muttered.

I didn't want him to think I was that mired in my grief for Trevor, so I shared, "So you know. I, um…saw to certain needs. I dated and such. Just never really got into it."

"Right," he said gently, did the reach-out-and-touch-my-knee thing again before he put his hand back to the wheel. Then he remarked, "Surprised you didn't notice his wedding ring. Don't keep tabs, but do know he still wears it."

"He wasn't wearing it today."

I watched his face. Thus, I witnessed the slow smile that spread across it.

"What?" I asked.

"We had occasion to get in each other's shit recently, and I might not have been subtle when I told him to stop fucking around and get on with his life. Seems he listened."

I hoped he did.

We drove the rest of the way in silence that was comfortable, something I liked, considering we'd had some awkward words, and then Riggs was just over it.

And I'd find that Angelica either had a type or researched her baby daddies in order to push out the kind of children she wished to create, because Storm also lived in a mountain house, even if his wasn't as secluded as Riggs's (there were other houses around, not close, but not near as far as Riggs's was from mine) and there was no lake.

But it was rambling and rustic and appealing.

He was too, if the tall, fit, black-haired man, with the very full, somewhat long beard, wearing a plaid flannel, jeans and boots, ambling out the front door after Riggs parked next to his shiny, silver, big (but not as tall) truck, was Storm.

We got out, strode up his walk, and they firmly shook hands, exchanging low, "Heys" before they broke, and Storm turned his stormy eyes to me (oh yes, that was where he got his nickname—his eyes were an extraordinary moody pewter, unlike any color I'd seen before (but definitely as unique as Riggs's silvery gaze), the effect with his tan skin and coal-black hair was fantastic—though that stormy nickname could also be about him being a man who threw mugs).

"Storm, this is Nadia, my woman. Nadia, this is Storm, Viggo's dad," Riggs introduced.

But he didn't stop there, and by a small miracle after he referred to me as "his woman," I managed to follow what he said next.

"And, man, so you know, she was with me when Lucille spilled. She helped me through it better than I did for you, so I didn't break any mugs, and she and Ledge are getting tight. This means she's gonna be around Viggo. And I'm down with her knowing whatever you're gonna say."

"I could also go sit in the truck and play phone games," I offered.

"Come in," Storm invited. "I don't give a shit who knows this. And I know that sounded short, but I actually just don't."

I nodded.

Riggs took my hand, and he led us inside the house of a man with a three-year old boy. There was an abundance of toys overflowing from a large crate in a corner and a freestanding booster chair an older toddler could crawl up into himself at the kitchen table.

And these were on open display, not tucked away or easily hidden.

In other words, if Storm had visitors of the female variety, they went in knowing he was a proud dad, and if things sparked, he came as a package.

I decided from that, I was going to like the guy.

Other than that, its décor was "Single Mountain Guy Who Has Money." The furniture was comfortable but attractive. The prints on the wall had masculine personality, with a montage of pictures on one wall that shared he liked skiing, camping, white water rafting and had a number of friends who sported tans like he did and smiled a lot, often while they were drinking beer.

"Sit. You guys want a beer? Soda?" he offered.

"I'm good," Riggs said.

"Me too," I put in.

We sat together on the couch.

Storm sat in an armchair off to the side.

"Viggo here?" Riggs asked.

"He's napping," Storm told him.

Bummer.

I would have liked to have met him.

"I'll cut to it so I don't fuck up your Saturday any more than I already have, and appreciate you coming to mine," Storm started.

"We were out, not a problem," Riggs replied.

"Still. Appreciate you," Storm murmured. He then announced, "I've already talked to my attorney. I'm going for full custody of Viggo. And when I told my lawyer what went down, considering what's already gone down, he said we have a good chance at getting it. I gotta confess, I've been thinking on this awhile, so some ground-work has been laid. I've had an investigator follow her, and I got some pretty damning info. It's not like a single mom shouldn't be able to enjoy herself, but she goes to the liquor store often, she goes out and ties one on often, she fucks around a lot, she brings men back to the house when the boys are there, which means she gets a lot of babysitters."

Angelica brought men home when the boys were there?

Riggs didn't react to this like I thought he would, that being blowing his stack.

He simply said, "I hear you." He then turned to me and said quietly, "Sorry, I meant to get into this with you tonight, but we're here, and after what happened with her, I don't think it's gonna surprise you." Back to Storm. "I made the decision I'm gonna promote Easton to foreman. If I don't give him more responsibility, he's gonna bail and find it for himself. I got commissions lined up so far out, the waiting list is eight months, and I'm turning shit down. I can head out to a site and see how the boys are doing, but I'm gonna stay home for the most part. This means I'm taking her back to court to get an order to reflect that change and have shared custody. If she balks, because that will mean support is cut, I'll change that demand to full too."

I stayed silent even if this made me gleeful.

Not that Angelica was going to possibly lose a lot of time with both of her boys.

Because Riggs was going to be home most of the time.

Storm glanced briefly at me, something I translated as him thinking I was a part of Riggs's decision-making, before saying to Riggs, "I hear you."

"Gotta admit, it's more than that," Riggs continued. "Ledge has impressed on me he's getting older, and he needs a man around more often. That man is gonna be me."

"I hear that too," Storm replied. "So, I wanted to give you that heads up. Though, I'll give you this to think about. My attorney says my case will be even stronger if we're co-plaintiffs. Which means yours would too. That'll be up to you. And I'll remind you, she's gonna lose her shit, because she'll lose all support from me, and that was what she was after in the first place. Bottom line in this, it's looking good that Viggo will be with me, so we gotta work something out on the regular so our boys have time together. I don't want Viggo growing up not knowing his brother."

Okay, official.

I liked this guy.

"Same," Riggs said. "If you get full, alternating weekends when we have them?"

Storm nodded. "Sounds good. And regular sleepovers. You put me on Ledger's drop-off, pick-up list. When Viggo is in school, I'll do the same. And maybe we go out to dinner or take them camping or some shit on occasion."

"Works for me," Riggs agreed.

"Then we're sorted," Storm said.

They reached out and shook.

I made a show of pulling out my phone and pretending to stab at the screen.

Silver and pewter eyes came my way.

"Don't mind me. I'm chartering a plane so I can fly you two to DC so you can do a training session on working together with Congress," I quipped.

They both burst out laughing.

"Unless you want a beer and to sit out on the deck and shoot the shit, that's all I got," Storm said after he quit laughing.

"I got one more thing to talk about," Riggs replied.

"Hit me," Storm invited.

"Would it fuck your play if I got on my phone with her and lost my goddamned mind that bitch is bringing men home when our kids are there?"

Annnnnnnnnnnd…

There it was.

Storm seemed surprised. "You didn't know?"

"No fuckin' clue."

"Ledge didn't tell you?"

Oh boy.

Riggs shook his head.

"Protecting her," Storm deduced on a mutter.

"Probably," Riggs agreed.

"Gotta tell you, I've already shared my opinion on that, and she told me to suck her dick." He looked at me. "Sorry about the language, Nadia."

I shrugged and smiled to say I was unoffended.

"So she knows you know, and she knows we talk, so it won't fuck your play I make my feelings clear about that," Riggs stated.

"I don't know, brother," Storm said, visibly chewing on it, before giving it to us verbally. "Maybe being on the record as discussing it with her prior to hauling her ass in court and putting it in front of a judge is a good thing. Maybe not. Every interaction I have with her, I gotta write a whole brief and send it to my attorney so I got it on record. But she's free to live her life the way she wants. She isn't legally bound to either of us."

"How often does this happen?" Riggs asked.

"I've known a couple of the guys, and they're not assholes, but she's got a reputation, considering." He flicked a hand between them to indicate what she did to them both. "So most of them I don't know, and my guess is, they don't know us. But we both get that she's a woman who measures her worth by how many dicks she can suck." Again, to me, "I'll repeat the apology."

"Please, be real. This is important. Don't mind me," I replied.

He jerked up his chin.

Yeah.

Mountain man.

"To end, my issue is not about her getting herself some. And I don't think it's regular the men come to her place, but it happens. My issue is, one strange guy in the house with my kid, or Ledge, gives me the shivers. But also, she's a mom and she needs to be home with her kids, not every second, but she's at a bar nearly every damned night. If she wants to live her life unencumbered, she can give them up so they can have a parent around. I don't want my son, when he isn't with me, raised by a babysitter I also have no hand in picking," Storm finished.

"You want me to give you a heads up if I lay my thoughts on her?"

Storm shook his head. "You do you. If we decide to team up when we take her to court, we'll start sharing more closely."

"That also works for me," Riggs said as he stood. He stuck his hand out again, and Storm rose and took it as Riggs said, "Thanks for the offer of a beer. But I need to go get my boy so he can sort himself out to go to Dustin's."

"Right," Storm replied, following us to the door. "Thanks again for coming."

"Thanks for the heads up."

"Nadia, good to meet you."

I offered him my hand, and he took it, but when he gave it a firm squeeze, he cupped his other on top of it. This was fleeting, but added warmth to the gesture that I thought was nice.

Totally liked this guy.

"Hope to see you again," he said when we broke.

"We're having a get-together at mine next Saturday. You wanna come, you're welcome," Riggs invited.

"Viggo's back with Angelica then, so might come over for a few."

"Great."

"Look forward to it."

"Later."

"Later."

"Bye, Storm," I bid, and Riggs threw his arm around my shoulders and guided me to the truck.

We were in and on our way to wherever Ledger was with Jace and Jess when I asked, "How angry are you about the men coming over?"

"Scale of one being you, cute with your hair a sexy bedhead, getting in my shit about having a loud party, and ten finding out my friend and my baby momma colluded to trap me into being a father, I'm at a two thousand and fifty-three."

"Mm," I hummed.

"You're a woman, and I can't say I knock myself out, but I give a passable try at not being a chauvinist asshole. Are Storm and me off about this?"

"Well, on the one hand, you say she's a good mom and loves her kids, so my hope would be, she also wouldn't bring anyone dangerous to the house. On the other hand, I've only had one inter-action with her, and it wasn't good, something that significantly skews my opinion about her, so I feel ill-equipped to have any opinion on this."

"If you had a kid, what would you do?"

It was my turn not to answer.

"Honey, this is important," he prompted.

Shoot.

"First, I'd like to make it official on behalf of my entire gender that, even though it seemed for Storm this wasn't the issue, I doubt he lives his life like a monk, and I know you don't, I'd take grave affront if either of you went on attack because she enjoys a healthy sex life."

"To confirm and save you that affront, I don't give a shit who she fucks. I give a shit if it affects my son and Viggo."

Good to know.

"Okay then, onward," I continued. "I think with this situation it's important to note, even though you didn't ask about this part, I'm a teacher and I have intimate knowledge that Storm's right. Parents should be home to parent their children. At their ages, they go to bed early, but they should do it, for the most part, feeling safe that Mom's home should they need her."

"Yeah," he grunted.

"Getting back to your question, I would never have a man in my house who I didn't know well, hadn't spent a good deal of time with and felt as safe as I possibly could that he was okay to be around my child. And this would happen only if I was in a relationship with him, and he and I both understood that relationship was going somewhere."

"And you hesitated to say that to me because…?"

"Because one, I'm not Angelica. Two, I don't know Angelica, and you're right. This is important. So I'm uncomfortable judging Angelica for the decisions she makes in her life. And last, I'm sleeping in your bed, and it isn't like we've been seeing each other for a month and have had several, deep, heartfelt conversations about when to introduce the idea of a future of us that included Ledger. Nor did we give Ledger very long to get used to that possibility."

"That had extenuating circumstances."

"Would Angelica see it that way?"

"See your point," he muttered.

"Now, I came over for dinner first. Your mother has been around. And you did make a somewhat big thing of putting him in a safe space when you let Ledger know we were together, so he'd understand I was going to be a part of his life beyond me going back to the cabin and carrying on as your neighbor. And yes, it had extenuating circumstances. And I doubt Angelica is hiding she's sleeping with these men like we are, when it's my opinion, obviously, it's a delicate matter to expose a child his age to the intimacies of two adults sharing a bed at night. Even if he probably doesn't understand what happens there. And it seems clear she's not in relationships with these men. But I'll note, you put me on the pick-up list without informing her."

"Thought about that on my walk that night, and it shits me to admit, she didn't handle how she communicated her concerns about it real well, but I fucked up with that pick-up list thing."

I loved it that he could see that, and admit it, even with the circumstances surrounding it.

"Are you upset Ledger didn't tell you?" I asked.

"It fucks me, but I think this is one of those things where I gotta let him learn to be the man he's going to become. I also gotta trust my kid. If he thought one of these guys was shady, he'd tell me. Of that, I'm sure. And he's got good instincts. Him not telling me is all about him not wanting me to be pissed at his mom."

"Okay."

"Christ, Nadia,"—he blew out a hassled breath—"this is my life."

It was me who reached out and squeezed his leg at that.

But he covered my hand with his when I did.

So I left it there.

TWENTY-NINE

People Like Us

Nadia

I loved being back on the loveseat on my porch at the cabin with Riggs.

And I loved it more that this time we were there making out.

It was late evening, after dinner.

We hadn't spent our time after dropping Ledger at Dustin's house in my bed at the cabin, seeing as Dustin's parents were good friends of Riggs. Particularly Kirk, Dustin's dad, who was a year behind Riggs at school, but they'd known each other since they were kids, and from the stories, ran around together (and made some trouble of the kid sort together) since they met.

They asked us to hang for a drink and some chips and guacamole, and we were both peckish, so we accepted.

We then hit the grocery store, because Riggs wanted to fry up some hamburgers for dinner, and neither of us had ground beef in our houses.

We came back and made dinner together, an activity I enjoyed immensely.

Considering Trevor's job and the hours he had doing it, and

then the state of his health and the urgency of seeing to certain things because of it, not to mention our ages and that we tended to prefer to be out or with friends most of the time, he and I hadn't had the chance to settle into the kind of domestic bliss that included learning how to partner up in the kitchen.

But I found navigating that with Riggs far from sucked.

I'd also had the occasion to think about how it seemed Riggs knew everyone, and everyone knew Riggs.

I'd never lived in a small town, and he'd lived in MP his whole life, so naturally, his knowing a ton of people would be the case.

There was just something I really liked about it.

It was like you were always running into family. You slid into the corner booth with them when there was a crowd at the diner. You ate some guacamole and told stories on the fly. You got invited for a beer and to shoot the shit if you had time.

I wasn't the good girl because my grandfather was bold, my mother was ballsy, and that's the role I had to play to fit in with my family. It was just me. I liked to go out to dinner. Share a drink with friends. Hit a movie. I was social.

But for the most part, I was a homebody, and due to my family's wealth and fame—and now I could see, the man my father was and the lessons my mom learned from that—I'd been taught to exercise extreme caution and be smart when it came to connecting to people.

And in a sense, this made my life somewhat insular.

Riggs didn't live an insular life, and experiencing that phenomenon through him, where I felt safe, as if he'd vetted the people who would touch my life, I liked it.

Enormously.

These were definitely subjects to journal about.

Copiously.

Now, dinner consumed, dishes done (we did those together too), dusk was falling.

And it was time to get busy.

Riggs had that same thought, I knew, when, not stopping kissing me, he pulled me over him to straddle his lap.

He then lifted the skirt of the little knit dress I'd put on to be more comfortable while we made dinner. After which, he dove directly in from the bottom edge of my panties and up to claim both cheeks of my behind in a grip that, if I had any mental acuity at that juncture, would make me pause to ponder if my behind was actually his.

Though, in a physical sense, I processed it, and that processing made me tremble in his hold.

The pads of his fingers dug in as I rubbed against his hard crotch.

Abruptly, his head jerked back to break the kiss.

I wasn't thrilled he did that, or how he did.

"Baby?" I called.

"Car," he said.

That was when I heard a car door slam, followed closely by another one.

Good Lord.

What now?

We both sat there, silent, and didn't move an inch.

My front door was opened, the storm door closed and locked, and the back door the same, except that door wasn't locked.

We heard the loud knock at the front storm door.

Of the same mind without a word to confirm it, we still didn't move.

Another knock.

Riggs caught my eyes. His were beleaguered. I sensed mine were the same.

Yes, it was awesome he knew a ton of people and it all felt like family.

But this was getting ridiculous.

That feeling came out even more when we heard movement and rustling coming down the side of the house.

Riggs sighed, dropping his head to the back of the loveseat and closing his eyes as he took his hands out of my panties and pulled down my skirt, but he didn't move me. He just rested his hands to my bottom, now over my skirt.

Thus, I was straddling him with my arms around his neck and his hands on my ass when we both turned our heads to see Lucille stop dead and cry, "Oh!"

However, she wasn't alone.

She had a man with her who was maybe a couple of inches taller than she was (and she was around my height of five seven) who looked like someone had tried to sculpt him back together (poorly) after they'd run him through a meat grinder.

Bubbles.

My vision got blurry, my blood pressure skyrocketed, and I concentrated on not having a stroke as Riggs drawled, "Someone doesn't answer your knock, they're in the middle of something."

"And workin' hard at it, as usual, or just gettin' hard workin' it," Bubbles quipped on an affable grin, like he still had the right to joke with Riggs.

My entire body turned to stone, a sensation Riggs felt too, considering his expression did the same.

Then I was up in the air and down on my ass in the loveseat, as Riggs put me there before he surged up beside me and turned their way.

"Are you shitting me?" he asked in a quiet, terrifying, low voice as I scrambled to my feet.

The man lifted a casted hand Riggs's way, his head tipped way back from his position on the ground beside the porch, his eyes glued to Riggs.

"Now, Doc—"

"If you're not about to affirm that you're shitting me then get the fuck outta my sight, I got no time to hear what you have to say," he growled as I pressed close to his back.

"Please, hear him out," Lucille begged.

Riggs turned his attention to her. "You're a good woman, Lucille, so it fucks me to point this out, but serious as shit, haven't you done enough damage?"

I felt for her when she cringed and then her face fell.

But Riggs was right.

"I need to explain," Bubbles decreed.

Riggs's regard sliced back to him. "I don't give a fuck what you need."

"Doc, you gotta get where my head was at."

That was when Riggs lost it.

Honestly?

He'd been taking so many hits lately, I was impressed it took this long.

He leaned toward Bubbles and roared, "*Jesus fucking Christ!* Do you not fuckin' *get* I give *zero fucks* where your head was at!"

"It's not like you got a bad end of that deal!" Bubbles shouted back. "You got Ledger!"

"Do not try to pretend you don't get where you landed me back then, Bubbles. I think you want people to think you're stupid, but I know you are not," Riggs returned.

"I came here to explain," Bubbles reported. "I came here to apologize. I came here to tell you that gettin' the shit kicked out of me was a wakeup call, and I'm gonna work on not bein' such a fuckup all the time."

"Congratulations," Riggs fired back. "And now you've done all *you* wanted to do, get the fuck outta here."

This was when Bubbles lost it.

"Christ, brother, don't you fucking get it?" he yelled. "This whole town thinks you're the chosen son. They think more of you than even Cade Bohannan, and that guy stops *killers* from *killing*. And all I got is Lucille, Mom...*and you*."

"Bubbles, I'm not your brother. Not anymore," Riggs declared to Bubbles's head lurching with anguish. "And since that's the case, I'll point out...again...you don't have me anymore. And last, we all got our own damage we gotta navigate. You know mine, and still, you throw that shit in my face. I didn't earn mine, Bubbles. But the same can't be said for you."

Bubbles swung his torso back and threw up his arm to indicate himself. "Look at me, man. I'm a joke. All you gotta do is walk down the street, and every woman who sees you creams their panties."

"I hate to break this to you, but we're not fourteen anymore. I don't think my manhood centers around how many women I can dip my wick in, and you shouldn't either. Grow the fuck up," Riggs replied.

"Of course you don't get it," Bubbles muttered. "You'll never get it."

"Oh yeah, man, I get it," Riggs returned. "I get you haven't heard a fuckin' thing I've said because everything is all about you. But I got that when you showed here, and I knew you went to my place, and you were so determined to get what you needed outta this, you tracked me down at Nadia's and then ignored the fact I didn't come to the goddamned door. I get somehow you absorbed all the shit the mean kids flung at you instead of rising above it, and seeing you weren't the asshole, they were. And the last thing I get is that you did me seriously fuckin' dirty, and you still got your head so far up your ass, you don't understand how totally fuckin' out of line it is for you to be standing right where you are. It doesn't matter I got something great out of what you did to me. What matters between you and me is that you did me dirty in a way you can't walk back. Never, Bubbles. Hear me. You can never walk that back."

Bubbles opened his mouth.

But Riggs wasn't finished.

"Now, last thing I'll do for you is give you the heads up you're probably gonna be subpoenaed, the both of you." He included Lucille in that. "Storm is pissed right the fuck off, and he's gonna take action. I'm not going to the lengths he is, but I'm pissed too. Now, you can lie under oath and risk whatever they nail you with for perjury, or you can make that minimal effort to right a huge fuckin' wrong. That's on you."

"I'll tell a judge what I've done," Bubbles said.

"Terrific," Riggs bit off.

Bubbles didn't move.

Riggs didn't either.

Lucille elbowed Bubbles.

"Shit," he mumbled.

"Serious to Christ," Riggs said with a low rumble of extreme impatience.

It was a warning.

I pressed closer to him.

"And I'm gonna talk to Harry about the wine," Bubbles said like each word was dragged forcibly out of him.

"Like you're doing me a solid when the damage is already done?" Riggs asked. "You assured me that bottle was safe to give to Nadia, when it obviously was not."

"That's going to swing my ass way out there, Doc," Bubbles declared.

"You are missing the fact that I *do not* care," Riggs retorted. "Don't mistake that as a favor for me, Bubbles, you doing the right thing for once. You can't use a friend to shield you from a bullet then retreat to the high ground and throw a rock at the bad guy from behind the walls of a fortress, shouting to your friend, 'I got you.' It doesn't fuckin' work that way."

His metaphor was kind of funny, but no one was laughing.

Bubbles's attention came to me, and he mumbled, "Of course, she's a knockout."

To that, Riggs stopped being subtle and issued an unmistakable warning. "Do not make me call the sheriff to deal with you. Partially due to you and the people you deal with, he's fuckin' busy."

Bubbles looked hard at Riggs.

And then, if I didn't dislike him intensely, I would have felt sorry for him at the expression that came over his face.

"Gonna leave you with this. I love you, man," he said.

"And I'll leave you with this. I used to love you too," Riggs shot back.

I thought for a second Bubbles might cry, if his brutalized face beginning to collapse was any indication.

Maybe he didn't want Riggs to see that, or maybe I was wrong.

But with a minor hitch in his step, he limped, what looked painfully, out of sight.

"We shouldn't have bothered you," Lucille said on a whisper.

Riggs didn't confirm or say words to make her feel better. He was silent.

I was too.

She followed Bubbles.

He turned to me then, and since I was behind him, I hadn't been able to see his face.

But witnessing the ravaged expression on it?

Well…

That was when I lost it.

So I darted past him, jumped off the porch and heard him call, "Nadia!" as I zigzagged through the pine trees on my bare feet.

I caught them before they'd gotten in the car.

Both froze, turning startled eyes to me.

I stopped and ordered Bubbles, "If you truly love him, stay away."

"No offense, woman," Bubbles started cautiously, "but you haven't been around for——"

"Shut up," I interrupted. "You want to figure it out, listen carefully, I'll tell you where to start. If you honestly love him, no matter how much it hurts, no matter what it costs, you *stay away*."

I felt Riggs come up behind me, but knew he was approaching because Bubbles and Lucille looked to him as he did.

Lucille turned back to me. "We won't be bothering either of you anymore, Nadia."

"You," I pushed at Bubbles. "I want to hear it from you."

Riggs slid an arm around my belly from behind and murmured, "Nadia, come back around with me."

"Love is not selfish," I said to Bubbles. "And it certainly isn't causing pain. It can get complicated and twisted and have to be straightened out, but if it's true, it's never selfish. So if you love him, promise right now, unless he calls for you, stay away."

Bubbles looked from me, to Riggs, to me, to Riggs, back to me for a long spell, then to Riggs for a longer one.

And it was to Riggs, he said, "I'll stay away."

"Get in the car, sweetie," Lucille told him gently.

Bubbles didn't move. He stared at Riggs.

I didn't look, but I had a feeling Riggs was staring back.

Finally, with effort, and visible pain, Bubbles folded into the car.

Lucille shot a sad look our way before she got in beside him, started it up, and Riggs and I stood where we were and watched them drive away.

Their taillights were in the distance when suddenly I was up in Riggs's arms.

I slid one of mine around his shoulders automatically as I asked, "What are you doing?"

"You're barefoot."

He carried me to the back porch, and in front of the loveseat, set me down.

He then announced, "I'm making fucking martinis."

That was when it happened, though for the life of me, I didn't know why it happened then. I'd journal about it later and settle on the fact that I knew he could take no more.

I also knew I couldn't be part of anything he had to take, to look after, to worry about.

I further knew, if I had another week with him, or another fifty years, he was a man who'd break his back and sell his soul to look out for me, so I had no real power over saving him from that.

But he was going to get that back from me.

Which was why, with really crappy timing, I asked, "Do you know that the police don't clean up crime scenes?"

I watched his long body still, before he was on me, his hands cupping my jaw, his face in mine.

"Honey."

"Before you meet Maribeth, you should know, she was the one who discovered what bioremediation specialists were. And she's the one who hired them. She's also the one who paid for it, even if I'm loaded, she's loaded too. And last, she was the one who went with me before they came, because I had to see. And I saw, baby. I saw everything."

If his expression had been ravaged before, it was wrecked now.

Totally crappy timing.

He slid his fingers back into my hair, cupping my head, one over the other, and shoved my face in his chest.

My voice was husky and muffled by his tee when I said, "I can't have you taking anymore. Enough is enough. I don't want to be the emotional time bomb you're worried about while you're forced to deal with everything. So I'll tell you, I've been trying to figure out how to begin to tackle it, but I honestly don't know how to process the sheer ugliness of it. I'm landing on the fact she fought like a hellcat. And I'm so damned proud that she did. I know it's not selfish to think this next, it's just my mom. I'm certain she died not wanting to die. Knowing she had so much more life to live. But she also died before she actually died, knowing what her dying would do to me. And that was part of why she fought so hard to stay alive. It was for her, definitely, but it was also for me. And that means everything to me."

He let my head go and wrapped his arms around my shoulders, crushing me to him so powerfully, it squished my face into his chest, and I had to turn my cheek to it in order to breathe.

"I think—" I stopped and started again. "I think I don't need to speak words. To share my pain in order to understand it. I'll never process it, Riggs. I don't know him, I never did, I never will, and I'm glad of that. He not only doesn't bear contemplation, he doesn't deserve it. I know who he was will mess with me occasionally, but in the end, he's a nonentity. He doesn't matter. Mom was right way back then. My real dad died in a plane crash, and what I became was about her and *Dedulya*. That man had no real part in making me."

"Yeah," he grunted.

"And no matter how much I think about it or talk about it, bottom line, I'll never understand how one person can do that to another. Not if they share a child. Not ever. So it'll be a waste of time and effort and emotion to try. I'll never come to terms with how I lost her. Because the bottom line is, she's gone. I've lost her. I'll miss her until I die. So it's just about time, and using it to learn how to live with it."

"Yeah," he grunted again.

"So stop worrying about me. I'm okay."

"Okay, princess," he murmured, his voice gruff.

I tipped my head back to look up at him, and no evasiveness, he looked right at me with red rimming his beautiful, silvery eyes. He wasn't crying, as such, but he was fighting it, probably so he could be strong for me (as well as maintain his macho-man badassness).

And I was in denial if I didn't admit to myself, I was fighting falling in love with him.

That didn't scare me.

I was okay with it, even if what we had lasted just a week.

Because me, and Mom, and Trevor, and Lincoln, Roosevelt and Sarah Whitaker, and people like us, never knew how long we had, and way back when Riggs and I first started to become the us we were now, Riggs was right.

The best way to fuck the ones who fuck you was to get as much out of life as you can, be as happy as you can, and do the things you enjoy as much as you can.

So I was going to do that, now and forever.

Starting with Riggs.

"You said something about martinis?" I prompted.

For a second, he looked blank with surprise.

Then his lips twitched.

After that, he smiled.

THIRTY

Ice Cold

Nadia

I woke when the bed shook mightily.

It took a beat for me to realize it was because Riggs had left it in a hurry.

I knew this because it was really dark since Riggs let the shades down, but even so, his even darker shadow was beside the bed and moving like he was putting on his jeans.

It was only then I heard the scratching on the window.

I sat up, and like he had the vision of a cat, his finger was on my lips as I opened my mouth to speak.

"Hush, princess. And put clothes on," he ordered quietly.

I was naked, considering, mid-martini, we got busy again, and since we had emotion to work out, that busy was *busy*.

Now I started to do what he said, but we both froze when the scratching at the window by the reading nook stopped, but it started almost immediately at the window on the bed side, down by the bathroom.

That was new.

And even creepier.

Were there two of them?

There had to be. No other explanation. No one could make it around the cabin that quickly.

Riggs grabbed my phone off the charger, found my wrist then slapped it in my palm, wrapping my fingers around it. Then he moved away only to come back and sit on the edge of the bed to put his boots on.

I was trying to figure out if I should call the sheriff's office first, or get dressed, when the scratching at the window by the bathroom became the same by the living room.

Oh shit.

Were there three? Or had the first one moved around?

I slid out of bed, feeling for clothes with my toes, and ran into my dress.

I bent and snatched it up.

Riggs let out a low whistle, and I looked his way.

"Call. Whisper," he commanded in his own whisper.

Then I stood, fixed with panic as his shadow moved to the storage closet, he went in it and came out of it incredibly quick.

The panic part came when he headed down the back hall.

He'd reinstalled it, so the door opened without a sound, but still, I knew he was opening it.

Shit!

Frantically, I searched for my clothes, ran into my panties, tugged them on, found my bra on the back of the armchair in the living room (Riggs really wanted rid of that, it seemed, because he'd thrown it a long way). I struggled into it, then I went back to my dress I'd tossed on the bed. I wasted no time pulling it over my head.

After that, I sank to my bottom beside the bed, yanked the quilt over my head (just in case they could see inside somehow, I didn't want them to see my screen light up), and I activated the phone.

I went to favorites, hit the number and put it to my ear.

I jumped when I heard a thud against the outside wall by the kitchen.

"Fret County Sheriff's Office," a man answered.

"Hi. This is Nadia Antonov," I whispered. "Out at the Weaver

Cabin on County Road Thirty. I have trespassers scratching at my windows. I'm with Doc"—another thud, *Lord*—"Riggs, and he's gone out to, I don't know, deal with them."

"Sending a cruiser out to you now. Are you safe?"

"Yes…"—something heavy hit the front porch—"but I think maybe you should hurry."

"Got it. Stay inside. Stay safe."

"Um…okay. I don't think I can talk anymore. He's trying to be stealthy."

Though, I had a feeling he started that way, but now, not so much.

"Fine, but please remain on the line," the man said.

"Okay," I replied just as I heard some scrambling on the front porch.

That sound eventually stopped, thirty seconds slid by, a minute, two, five, an eternity. I was pretty sure I was going to either scream or throw up when the deputy asked, "You there?"

"Yes," I whispered.

"Okay, unit en route. ETA ten minutes."

"Right," I kept whispering.

I heard more noise I couldn't decipher from the front porch, someone talking I thought was Riggs, but it was so low, I couldn't tell. But it was a man.

After that, nothing.

Until I saw lights come on inside from under the quilt.

I pushed it off, jumped to my feet and turned to see Riggs sauntering shirtless from the back hall to where his Clash tee was on the floor by the bed (apparently, I didn't have his toss strength, because I'd really wanted to be rid of that too).

As he tugged it on, I told the deputy in my normal voice, "Riggs is back inside, and he's fine."

"Status of the situation?" he asked.

"I don't know," I replied just as Riggs came to a stop in front of me and held out his hand. "He'll tell you."

I gave him the phone.

He put it to his ear and started moving again, turning on lights and talking. "Who's this?" Then, "Hey, Raul. Got two punks tied up on my front porch. Are you sending a cruiser? We're pressing charges." Pause then, "Right. Thanks."

He beeped off my phone and tossed it so it landed on the couch.

"Tied up?" I asked.

"Nabbed digital cable," he told me, snatching the keys off the hook by the door (he'd given Brenda strict instructions, so unlike his storms, mine could only be opened, inside and outside, with a key).

The cable thing was genius.

He unlocked and opened the front door, unlocked the storm and flipped on the front lights.

He then strode out.

I ran to the back hall, slipped on my Birkenstocks, then raced to the front door.

I looked through the screen and ornate wrought iron scrollwork (Brenda had an eye), and saw two boys, probably around sixteen, one tall and scrawny who still looked more boy than man, but when he caught up, he'd be cute. The other one was much shorter, already built and already cute.

They both sat on their asses, back-to-back, and had white computer cable wrapped firmly and tightly around their wrists that were behind their backs, as well as around their ankles.

I couldn't say I'd paid much attention to Dave and Brenda's Wi-Fi setup, but it was clear they got the ultra-long cords so they'd have locational options, because, yeesh. That was a lot of cable.

"It's okay, honey. These sacks of shit aren't going anywhere," Riggs called.

I stepped out on the porch.

Alas, in the kerfuffle, four of Brenda's pots had turned over, and one had fallen off the porch. There was potting soil and flowers strewn everywhere.

I'd do my best with those tomorrow.

I went to where Riggs stood over the boys. When I arrived, he curved an arm around my waist and pulled me into his side.

"I guess Dave wanted choices as to where he put his router," I noted.

I felt Riggs's regard and looked up at him.

"What?" I asked.

"Princess, I just wired five cameras in your place last week. Left the overage in your storeroom since Dave insisted on paying for it."

"Oh."

He started laughing silently.

"How'd you cut it?" I asked.

"Carry an army knife."

"Oh," I repeated.

He kept laughing, still silently.

Both the boys were staring at their gym shoes looking a mixture of freaked and pissed (though more freaked, then again, there were two of them, one of Riggs, and they were the ones now tied up and facing what came next).

I pulled from Riggs, but he dogged me as I approached the shorter one and crouched carefully, due to my skirt.

"Hi, I'm Nadia."

He kept his gaze averted, but red was creeping up his neck toward his cheeks.

Mm-hmm.

Easy to be a punkass when you're not confronted with who you were punking.

Harder to have her right there.

"I get it might *seem* like fun to go into the woods and scare the crap out of a woman alone who you don't know, but just to say, my mother was murdered five months ago, and I loved her very much."

His gaze darted to me, it was wide, and the color reddened his entire face instantly.

"With age and maturity," I went on, "I hope you'll learn how cruel what you did is just normally. But maybe right now you can learn that you'll never have any idea what someone else is going through in their lives, so being a total dickhead is never okay, no matter how fun it might seem when you're hanging with your boy, thinking life in rural Washington is boring and looking for a thrill."

It took him a second to dig deep past his mortification to find the punk within before he asked bitterly, "You gonna press charges?"

"Absolutely," I replied. "I hear the fines in these parts for trespassing are pretty harsh, and carry jail time, so I hope you didn't have any assignments due on Monday. And I hope your parents aren't too pissed that they'll probably have to dip into savings to deal with your crap."

The red in his face got redder.

Yes, his parents were going to be pissed.

I was done so I stood and turned to Riggs.

"Ice cold," he murmured, his lips tipped up in approval.

I wanted to think my return smile was lethal, but it was probably just normal.

"I'm going to go inside," I shared. "It's chilly out here. Do you want me to bring a throw out for you or something?"

"I'm good," he replied.

"I'm just going to put on some more clothes. I'll be back out in a second."

"You got it, honey."

I rolled up to my toes to brush my lips on his.

Then I walked on my cute Birks inside to change clothes, pleased as punch the ghost of Roosevelt Whitaker (or Sarah) was finally laid to rest.

Thousand-Piece Puzzle

Riggs

It was Tuesday, early evening, and Ledger was out somewhere in the woods, showing Gia the lay of the land.

Riggs and Nadia were in the kitchen, making dinner.

And he hadn't asked her, but he knew they were both riding the wave of three days where no irritating shit went down.

On Sunday, after they fucked, cooked breakfast and ate it, they went out into the cold and threatening wet to start looking around her cabin for evidence of trespassers.

They didn't find anything, and Riggs marked trees so they wouldn't waste time going over old ground.

Considering their convo about Angelica the day before, he and Nadia made a deal, so he alone headed back to his place around the time Kirk was returning Ledger from his sleepover.

So it wouldn't be all Nadia all the time, he took his son out on the boat for some bud time, but they had to go in when it started raining. They hung out in front of the TV, until Riggs got a call mid-afternoon from his mom asking them over for dinner.

He called Nadia and had a chat with her about whether she

should come or not, since his mom invited her, with Riggs pushing for her to come. She'd be moving back to the cabin the next day, and although they had plenty of time during the day while Ledge was at school to connect, he'd lose her beside him in his bed at night, and he wasn't looking forward to that, for more than one reason.

She wasn't sure, but she caved, walked over, and as was his way, Ledger showed how excited he was to see her the second he saw her.

At that, Riggs had raised his brows to her, because she was the one who suggested she back off and give the Riggs men some time. In response, she had rolled her eyes.

And they went to his mom's.

Monday, they met Hutch at the cabin so they could accept delivery of Gia, and Hutch took that opportunity to do some more training.

This meant Riggs got to see how hopeless those two females were with that.

They had "sit," "down," "stay," "close," "here" and "heel" all set.

But they sucked at anything that started with "go," seeing as going meant Gia couldn't be with Nadia, and being highly trained, Riggs figured part of that was because Nadia wasn't committed to the command because she didn't want her dog to go.

So "go inside," "go ahead," and "go out" were all a bust, though the canine did all of them for Hutch no hesitation, even if she was leaving Nadia standing beside Hutch.

In the afternoon, Riggs had to leave her to get Ledger from school, and they'd decided again to give his son a break from all Nadia all the time. This meant they spent last night without her, even if Ledger was dying to meet Gia. Riggs had told him they needed some time alone to get to know each other and for Gia to get the lay of the land.

The next morning, Ledger was done with waiting and asked in a way that was more like a demand to meet "their" new dog when he got home from school.

And Riggs was done with not having Nadia around.

His head wasn't fucked up about it anymore. He didn't have to consider how she was after Lucille spilled. The way she literally and then verbally took his back when Bubbles showed. Her hilarious fake chartering of a plane after Storm and him talked. How good her stout cake was. How good she was with Ledger. How much his mom liked her. How cool-headed and ice-cold she was with the two dumbasses who were screwing with her. How real she was about how she was dealing with her mother's death. How she hooked her thumb in his beltloop when they walked close. How mind-blowingly phenomenal she was in bed.

He was there. She didn't hide she was there.

But they had to have a talk about it, because she had a life to get back to it was clear she enjoyed, and a lot of people she'd leave behind. But he had a life in Misted Pines he couldn't leave because he had a son.

She needed to know where he was at, what he wanted for their future, that being them looking at getting serious about working on having one together, and she had to think on that, because if she was in, she was the one who'd be making the big sacrifices.

He didn't get into it with her that day.

Instead, he'd walked over in the morning, and they'd spent another hour looking for evidence of trespassers before he took her back to the cabin in order to fuck her.

They'd then gone to his workshop where she'd hung with him while he worked, scribbling in her journal, and she'd walked home to meet Hutch for more training about an hour before Riggs had to go get his son from school.

Which brought him to now.

The only thing of note beyond that was, he'd taken the time to draw out the quadrants before he'd sent them to Cade, Jess, and Jace. The latter two didn't fuck around and texted they were heading out within half an hour of getting his text. And Rus had also gotten in touch, saying he heard about the search, and he wanted to help out, so Riggs needed to send him details of his patch, which he did, along with his gratitude for helping out.

Riggs was pissed he had to spend time doing that shit.

But if their theory was correct, and it wasn't just asshole kids over the years getting bright ideas, instead, it was someone looking for something, and maybe that someone was a person who killed two and possibly three people already, he had his son and his woman on that land.

He needed to know what he was dealing with.

He heard the car pull up before Nadia did, but it didn't take much longer for her eyes to go to the front door, then come to him.

He shook his head, moved from where he was cutting potatoes into wedges to the sink to rinse his hands, and he took the kitchen towel with him as he dried them and walked to the front door.

Harry's cruiser was parked out front and Harry himself was headed up the walk.

Riggs pushed out the storm door and called, "Hey, brother."

"Hey, Doc. I'm not interrupting dinner, am I?"

"Nope. We're in the middle of making it."

"You got a few minutes to take a break for a quick brief?"

"Sure. But wanna stay longer and have dinner with us?" Riggs offered. "We got plenty."

Harry looked to the house and back at Riggs. "What are you having?"

"Homemade, pickle-brined fried chicken sandwiches, slaw and fried potato wedges."

No hesitation from Harry before, "I wanna stay."

Riggs grinned, jerked his head to the door and went in, Harry following him.

"Hi, Harry," Nadia called from where she was mixing slaw.

"Hey, Nadia," Harry replied.

"He's staying for dinner," Riggs told her.

"Excellent," she said. Then to Harry, she asked, "Off duty? Want a beer?"

"I'd murder a beer," Harry told her.

Her head twitched, she gave him a look, then she went to the fridge.

After she did, Riggs gave his friend his own look and kept doing it.

"Everything cool?" he asked.

"Actually, yeah, but on the other hand, it never really is," Harry answered.

No truer words spoken.

"Grab a stool," he bid. "Ledger's outside somewhere with Gia, so beware. He cottons on you're here, you could have a nine-year-old kid and ninety-pound dog that could rip off your arm all over you at any time."

The skin around his friend's eyes wrinkled, and he took a stool.

Nadia put an open bottle of beer in front of him.

Riggs tossed the towel aside and resumed cutting potatoes.

Harry took in Nadia wearing her apron, the beer she gave him, the potatoes, Riggs, and opened his mouth.

Riggs got there before him. "Fuck off."

He felt Nadia look at him, but Harry just hid his smile behind a drag off his beer.

"So what's up?" Riggs asked.

"Pertinent to you," Harry began, "Evan Pugh's parents want to know if you and Nadia are good with him coming out here accompanied by them so he can apologize formally for being an asshat."

Pugh was one of the boys who'd fucked with Nadia, the shorter one she landed her brand of ice on.

Riggs looked to Nadia.

She shrugged.

He turned again to Harry. "Not necessary, but if his parents think it is, we can work that out."

"Great. I'll tell them. Next up, Casey Grimes is dedicated to the task of remaining a douchebag. He's pissed I got his son in my cells and I'm not letting him go, and he's ticked about the fine levied. He told me to tell you that if you didn't drop charges against his kid, he's going to sue you in civil court for assault."

Bryce Grimes was the other kid, and the ringleader who, Harry found out after they dragged the kids to the station, did it on his own until he corralled Pugh into getting in on the act Saturday night.

And yeah.

His dad was an asshole. He made serious cake. Had some big job for a medical equipment company in Seattle, something everyone knew since he wouldn't shut up about the device he helped design that did something about heart attacks or angina or some shit. But he worked from home in Misted Pines because he saw himself as a mountain man. And as much as he could, he swung his dick and flashed his cash around MP.

He hunted, just sayin', and it wasn't a family tradition and not even close to a way of life.

"Maybe banged up a bit, but not a mark on either of them, Harry," Riggs reminded them.

"I know. And I impressed upon him visually, showing him the video you sent me, that you got Bryce dead to rights. He was on your patch uninvited, and you'd walk even if you shot him, which I also impressed on him he should be grateful didn't happen, because in these parts, that's a possibility. So it's highly likely he'll not only lose, but a judge will be so pissed he wasted his time, the judge will make him pay court fees and your attorney's fees. Since he's got money to burn, he doesn't care. He says you laid hands on his son, and he's just a kid, and that's not on."

"His kid is six foot, seventeen years old and was out here not knowing I was here, thinking he was fucking with a woman alone at three nineteen in the morning. He's a kid, but not a kid, and old enough to know better," Riggs returned. "Though, with a dad like his who isn't teaching him that lesson, I can figure out why he doesn't."

"I shared that too. He says it's the principle of it. And I think we can both agree that his principles and ours don't align."

Before Riggs could reply, Nadia piped up.

"I have money to burn too, and access to a team of lawyers, Harry. So you might want to share my maiden name with him, and tell him, if he doesn't back down, I'll suddenly have a case of post-traumatic stress, and be suffering flashbacks and mental trauma.

Thus, if he doesn't want to be mired in litigation for the next ten years, whereupon, during that time, I might lay claim to a good deal more than the fine Fret County levies on trespassers, he might give significant consideration to fucking right off."

Harry's brows went up at Nadia, in her girlie fifties apron, delivering her words, before he busted out laughing.

But Riggs had turned his head to stare at her, because it was in that moment, unusually slow on the uptake, he realized the reason he wanted to work at building a future with her was because he was falling for her.

Jesus.

He thought if that shit ever happened, it would scare the fuck out of him.

But it didn't.

It felt great.

She caught his eyes. "Too much?"

"No, honey, you're never too much," he said quietly.

Her brows drew down at his tone, but to get them out of this moment, which unfortunately wasn't theirs alone, and still make it a moment, he bent to her and kissed her softly.

He returned his attention to Harry. "What she said."

Harry was looking at Riggs with such a satisfied expression on his face, Riggs's first instinct was to lean into one of the few things his father taught him, and like all the rest, it was no good. This was to say something in asshole to wipe that look off his friend's face and share he had a dick, don't mistake him for having feelings and being weak enough to show them.

Instead, he just held Harry's gaze steady, because he wasn't an asshole, he had feelings for Nadia and he was proud she returned them, and bonus, if Harry remembered how good Riggs had it, maybe Harry might find his way back to that too.

"Done with those two assclowns?" Riggs asked.

Harry shook it off and nodded.

Then he said, "Other piece of news. Bubbles came into the station yesterday. He suddenly remembered he didn't buy that wine in Sonoma, but instead he was given it by someone who told him to sell it as house red in order to get rid of it. He did the research on it, found how much it was worth, and didn't do as he was told, since he was hoping to sell it and make a lot more than seven bucks a glass on it. Somehow, word got back to who gave it to him, and they weren't thrilled he didn't do as he promised."

Riggs let out a slow breath.

Jesus.

Bubbles.

"This is where his shit gets hardcore, and arguably hilarious," Harry said.

Riggs felt his shoulders tense.

"What?" he asked.

"Apparently, there's some wise guy snitch the US Marshalls placed in WITSEC in Wenatchee. Obviously, he's supposed to keep his nose clean. Instead, he got bored, rounded up a local crew and started hitting decent-sized scores in two counties. One of them was the house of a county judge, which was supposed to be just shits and giggles for this guy. So as to be certain they didn't have anything lead back to them, they essentially dumped everything they took from him, including a case of wine that was clearly a big deal. My guess is, Bubbles has his suspicions of who he told he sold that wine to you, in other words, who ratted him out to a supposed-to-be-retired mafia guy. But there was only so far Bubbles was prepared to go, because he didn't tell me who that was. In the end, it was the big man himself with a couple of his crew who came to deliver the message he wasn't thrilled Bubbles didn't follow through with his orders."

Riggs had stopped moving while he listened to this, and he felt Nadia had done the same thing at his side.

Which was why Harry said, "I know. Only Bubbles could get messed up with an ex-mafioso in witness protection."

Yeah.

Only Bubbles.

But…

Mafia?

Harry kept going.

"So last night, the Chelan County Sheriff, along with the marshals, and a few **FBI** guys thrown in for fun, rounded up this crew, including the mafia witness, who's already testified. So now he's on his way back to Vegas, seeing as he broke the terms of his immunity agreement. Not to mention, he fucked with a judge, and they take that shit super fucking seriously."

"Mafia?" Riggs finally asked, feeling something strange in his throat.

Nadia shifted closer.

"If you're worried about Bubbles, brother, don't," Harry advised. "This guy has a lot of things he's gotta worry about, the least of which is figuring out who swung him out there. Primarily, staying alive now that he's back in a zone where they know where he is and can find ways to get to him. He survives that, he's gotta answer to the charges they scuttled to get him to testify, since he doesn't have immunity on them anymore *and* he has to deal with the shit he pulled up here, including fucking with a judge. He's gonna see prison time, so then he has to survive prison as a snitch, and a snitch who snitched on the mafia, and his odds are not good on that."

When Riggs said nothing after Harry quit talking, he started again.

"No one knows Bubbles talked, Doc. One thing Bubbles has a good reputation for is not being a rat, even if he just became one. Even so, they delivered a pretty unmistakable message to him, so they probably won't consider him the prime suspect of who leaked. The brainiac who trusted Bubbles with that wine, one of the names Bubbles did give us, was the weak link in that crew, and we know that because he dropped the dime on every member of his team practically before we could say boo to the guy."

Riggs knew Harry saw he remained unconvinced, because Harry kept going.

"This **WITSEC** guy doesn't have a lot of friends anymore, Doc, seeing as he squealed on them and is probably going to be doing time alongside them, if he makes it that far. And if they knew it was

Bubbles who put him there, they'd probably send him another case of that wine."

"You sure?" Riggs pushed.

"I'm never sure about how people who live those lives are gonna behave. But I'd pull in every marker I had to get Bubbles safe if I thought there was a credible threat," Harry replied. "The man makes a lot of bad choices I wish he wouldn't, but I don't want him at the bottom of one of our lakes."

"And you're sure you got that entire crew?" Riggs pressed.

"If it'll help you feel better, I'll let you watch the interrogation tape. Just to say, we had a clean pair of jail underwear available because it was dicey there for a while. This team was slick, but one of the members was this guy's brother, and he convinced the mastermind to take a chance on his baby bro. And the man even dropped the dime on his brother."

Riggs relaxed, because that shit was stone-cold wuss.

"Any word on other shit that's pending?" he asked as Harry took another pull of beer.

Harry's eyes flicked to Nadia, and he said, "Doesn't leave this room."

"Promise," Nadia replied immediately.

Riggs smiled, because serious as fuck, she was into this shit.

"Won't breathe a word," he told Harry something he already knew when it came to Riggs.

Harry nodded. "So, Wade had the great idea, since we're doing a quiet audit, not to make it quiet seeing as it's well-known Dern was shit at his job. And instead, let it out in a subtle way that we're just making sure all the I's are dotted and T's crossed because the new sheriff is thorough that way."

At that, Riggs grinned and shoved the potatoes in the waiting colander.

Harry kept going.

"Using that as cover, we can go over old ground with the Whitaker situation, which folks will think is safe, considering he confessed. So we've interviewed some of Roosevelt's old friends, and his assistant. Cade told you his theory?"

"Yes," Nadia said, again immediately.

Seriously into it.

Riggs chuckled and replied, "Yeah."

"Well, we can just say, not everyone in town will think we're just doing due diligence after a spell of incompetent law enforcement supervision."

Having finished the slaw, Nadia shoved the flour coating she was mixing aside, leaned into her forearms to get closer to Harry, and she asked, "Really?"

"Yeah," Harry answered. "No one said anything outright, but some were uncomfortable, others were cagey as fuck, though with all of them, it seemed they had something they wanted to say, they just didn't. The general consensus Rus and I have is that they don't think Lincoln did it. And there's a reason why, and not the normal one where your average person wouldn't blow holes in two people he loves then burn them to dust."

"So the brother-husbands theory holds weight," Nadia pushed.

"Didn't say that, but there's something they're not saying. It's something big, and everyone is dead that was involved. I don't think any of them know who did it. I do know, there's no reason not to talk about anything regarding that family now, so there aren't many reasons why you wouldn't. But one of them is loyalty, and in this matter, loyalty could take the form of not saying shit people might think is whacked and hurting the only thing those three got left, specifically the two brothers, considering their celebrity. That being their reputations."

"That makes sense," Nadia said.

"Any way you can press that?" Riggs asked.

Harry shook his head but said, "Rus and I both left the assistant wishing we didn't have to, in order to keep the cover of this being administrative bullshit. We're trying to figure out another way to come at her. She knows something more than the others. I can feel it."

"Like what someone might be looking for on my land?" Riggs pushed.

"Maybe, brother, I don't know," Harry replied. "She worked for

Roosevelt for five years. Both Rus and I sensed she had feelings for him that went unreciprocated, but they're still there. She invited us inside, and to start, she's never been married, so the torch she holds might be lasting. She also has pictures of the two of them together, more than one, but not enough to make it skeevy. Still, my last boss was Dern, so obviously I don't have photos of the two of us decorating my living room. But I don't think that's the norm."

"I'd call my entire crew buds, and I don't think they have pictures of me either," Riggs said.

One side of Harry's mouth went up before he noted, "One thing that might free our hand is that detective in Seattle. Now that he knows we're sniffing around, he's after the powers that be to reopen the case. He does that, it'd give us an opening, which is good. The downside is, I made him promise if he gets the all-clear, he tells me. Not only so we can rip the lid off, but if whoever did this thinks they didn't get away with it, they may make some desperate moves. Especially if we're right and they're the ones who've been coming back to this land. They might go into overdrive to find whatever they're looking for."

Fantastic.

"You got my word, Doc, you'll know so you can take measures, and I can too, to make sure you're good," Harry promised.

Riggs jerked up his chin.

Harry huffed out a sudden laugh and kept going.

"And, brother, you gotta know, you've made Rus's year. Not like he isn't settling into the quiet life, seeing as he's got Cin and Maddy to go home to. But he's all over this case. In his element. I think Cin has had to call Delphine three times in the last week to send his ass home, and the woman works late at the club. And can't say Cade isn't a dog with a bone either."

"Saw the stack of papers he got through in four days," Riggs noted.

Harry lifted his chin and the corners of his mouth. "They're like kids with a thousand-piece puzzle. They're not gonna get up from the table until the last piece of that fucker is set in place."

"Don't pretend you wouldn't be right there if you didn't have shit like Pugh, Grimes and Bubbles to deal with," Riggs scoffed.

"I'm not," Harry returned. "Which means, I'm glad the Haunting of Weaver Cabin and the Mystery of the Missing Fancy Grape Juice is solved so I can get stuck in."

All three of them laughed at that.

While they were doing it, they heard Ledger come in the back, shouting, "When's dinner? I'm dying here!" He stopped when he came out of the back hall, then shouted, "Yo, Harry!"

The second mother and child reunion Riggs had witnessed earlier as pertains to Gia—this time with Ledger being the child—asserted itself right then, when she headed him off on his dash to Harry to the point, she nearly knocked Riggs's son over.

She then took position in front of him, barked ferociously three times at Harry and settled into a scary-as-all-fuck growl aimed his way.

"I think she works," Harry joked.

"Gia! Friend!" Nadia commanded in a voice she didn't use at all when Hutch was working with them.

Gia immediately relaxed her stance, whined, then, her tail wagging her body, she went to Harry, sniffed the hand he bent on his stool to keep low for her before she licked it.

Harry petted her head.

Ledger dropped on his knees beside her, declared, "She's so awesome," and hugged her full around her middle.

This confused Gia because she couldn't get Harry's scratches and lick her boy's face at the same time.

She didn't take much time to decide.

She twisted her neck and slobbered all over her boy's face.

THIRTY-TWO

Bluetooth

Riggs

Riggs sat slouched on the pads sitting in the furniture he built out of logs for his outside seating area, his feet up on the low table he'd also made, staring through the trees toward the lake and making a decision, because Nadia was right.

He didn't have enough outdoor area, and none of it gave the best perspective to enjoy the view.

So that summer, in between commissions, he was going to build a deck.

He planned to set it a few steps down, so it wouldn't mess up the view from the windows, doing this from a hole he was going to carve into the outside wall of dead space at the landing, which afforded the kitchen a view and separated the living room from the dining room. He was then going to install French doors that led out to a huge-ass deck with a walkway down to the pier.

Next year, he was going to build a balcony off his bedroom, and maybe another smaller deck off the guest room.

When that was done, his pad would be perfect.

It was Friday, early evening.

Maribeth had flown in on Wednesday, and Nadia had driven to Seattle to pick her up.

Riggs and Ledger didn't meet Nadia's friend until Thursday night, due to girl time and spa appointments.

He and his son had walked over for dinner, and Riggs had learned that Maribeth was just like Nadia, except petite, slim, Black, and unlike Nadia, who was making a pass at dressing like a nature girl instead of an heiress (and she sometimes failed), Maribeth obviously had money, and although she wasn't in your face about it, she didn't hide it.

She was also outgoing, smart as fuck, funny as hell, cool with him in a way he sensed also held some gratitude, and great with Ledger.

Though she was more of the outgoing part than Nadia, and Riggs reckoned it was only because Nadia had sustained the recent blows she'd been dealt. He'd caught glimpses of the brightness inside that had dimmed because of that shit.

Once she settled into a life without her mom in the world, she'd come back to herself.

He'd see to that.

They'd had a nice dinner, Riggs had expended the effort of tearing Ledge away from Gia, and they'd gone home.

That day, Murphy had shown, and Nadia and Maribeth left the men to it to have guy time. The women were coming over soon for drinks and dinner.

Riggs thought about Gia, and how she was with Harry, and how that gave him peace of mind.

Also how he knew Nadia thought she was going to get an invoice from Hutch, but she wasn't, since Riggs had already paid for the dog and the training.

When she figured it out, it was going to be fun.

On this thought, he smiled before he lifted his bottle of beer to his mouth and took a sip.

He heard ice rustle and looked to the side to see Murphy pulling a fresh one out of the cooler that sat between them, but his eyes were on Riggs.

"I gotta talk Emma into moving back," Murph declared. "The shit you piled on me when I met her and got lost in her, I can't return if I'm in Cali. This woman I'm about to meet owns your dick, brother, and I gotta get mine back."

"I was being an asshole back then, so have at it. I deserve it," Riggs invited.

"Took everything I had to stop Em from coming with me so she could lay eyes on this Wonder Woman who tamed the Untamable Doc Riggs," Murphy ribbed.

"She's welcome any time," Riggs returned before another pull on his beer.

"Yeah, I feel that, Riggs," Murphy replied. "I remember not giving a fuck you razzed me unrelentingly. I knew I was going back to Emma, so what did I care?"

"I now see why it was so fucking frustrating I couldn't get under your skin," Riggs remarked.

"That's why I'm gonna let you off the hook," Murph announced. "Because, if I approve of this woman once I meet her, I can just be happy, after you had to put up with that bitch who fucked you over so goddamned bad, that you finally have a good one in your life and get it."

Suffice it to say, he and Murph caught up.

Murphy not only knew all about Nadia, he also knew about Angelica, Bubbles, the Haunting of Weaver Cabin, the Mystery of the Missing Fancy Grape Juice, and all that was going down, or they were theorizing, about the Whitaker Family.

Riggs offered the neck of his beer to his friend, and Murphy clinked as Ledger raced to them from doing whatever kids did when they were outside and not hanging with the adults.

It'd be good when Viggo got a few more years in. Ledger would always be a lot older than his brother, but at least he'd have someone who could string a sentence together to hang out with when Viggo was at Riggs's.

Ledge stopped close to Murphy's chair and leaned into it, so Murphy casually wrapped an arm around his son.

Riggs liked to see it. They were close. And he'd had to feel it when his bud moved away, but also feel it that Ledger wasn't a fan of that happening either.

"Nadia and Maribeth are coming up the trail. And *Gia!*" Ledger announced elatedly.

"A gentleman escorts the ladies to the party," Murphy noted.

Ledger didn't need more coaxing. He broke free of Murphy's light hold and took off toward the trail.

Eyes to the trail, Murphy asked, "Is that about the dog or the woman?"

"Right now, the dog. But he and Nadia are getting tight. He's just known her longer."

"Hmm," Murphy hummed.

Both men took their feet when the party came into view, Nadia holding Gia's lead, Gia sticking close to her side, but the dog's attention went right to Murphy.

"Fucking hell, she's a bruiser," Murphy muttered.

She could be, she'd made that clear.

But if Nadia claimed you, she was a musclebound love bomb.

Hutch hadn't gone the way of clipping Gia's ears or docking her tail because, even if both could be vulnerabilities to her if she was in a situation, Hutch didn't do what he did only to make a living. He was an animal lover and found those practices barbaric. On top of that, he had explained to Riggs that dogs communicate with their ears and tail, both to humans and other dogs. Since he trained his animals to work in sync with each other, and communication with their owners was key, it fucked with their ability to do their jobs.

When they got close, Nadia, who had discovered the tone that worked and kept using it (so Hutch said he'd be back a couple more times to check that things were cool, but Nadia had continued with her training, even though Maribeth was there, and had texted Riggs that day to tell him they'd essentially "graduated"), thus Nadia went through the "friend" command again.

Introductions were made, with Riggs getting the addition of Nadia getting in his space, putting her hand on his abs and rolling up to give him a soft kiss.

Riggs nabbed the opened but corked bottle of rose from the

cooler and the two glasses he'd brought out, and he poured the women a glass of wine while Nadia let Gia off the leash, commanded, "Go," this to Ledger calling her and slapping his hand on his leg.

Gia loped to his son, and they took off. The women settled into the two chairs angled opposite the men at the table, and Riggs decided to carve out time to make a matching loveseat for the set that summer.

"Is Murphy up to date?" Nadia asked him.

"Yup," Riggs answered.

She launched right in. "So, Maribeth thinks the assistant did it."

Maribeth leaned forward, her pretty face animated, and Riggs saw that, yeah, these two were peas in a pod.

"Two words. Woman scorned," she declared.

And yeah.

They could both be cute.

"Sorry, Maribeth. Doesn't explain why Lincoln would go to the lengths he did to cover for her," Riggs noted.

"Well, obviously because she'd been around awhile," Maribeth returned. "She probably knew all about the whole brother-husbands thing, and when that Roosevelt guy didn't initiate her as a sister-wife, she got ticked. It was her who showed and found them in the hayloft, and she'd had enough of yearning from not very afar, so she took care of business. Lincoln happened onto this, and she told him if she went down, she'd share their secret. So, to protect his brother, his wife, and maybe their franchise, because, yes, most people would think the arrangement sordid, but people get off on sordid, so that's going to sell books, as is people thinking he murdered his wife and brother. But in the end, either way you cut it, their legacy is screwed. So he decided to take the fall."

On that, stating her case, Maribeth sat back and took a sip of wine.

"Then why'd she kill Lincoln in Seattle?" Riggs asked.

"Because Lincoln had enough time to consider he'd paid dearly for something he didn't do," Maribeth answered. "I've no idea, but the idea of prison, as bad as that idea might be, is a lot better than actually *being* in prison. By then, he didn't care if she spilled, and maybe he wanted to clear his name, say, his kids thought he did it too, and he didn't want them to think that. So he had chats with them all and then calls this woman and tells her to brace," Maribeth answered.

"It makes sense, Riggs," Nadia chimed in. "Because those kids were all very young. Kids can do crazy things too, but that's super crazy. And none of those kids came back here after, right? The estate tried to rent these properties, so they couldn't have. But she's lived in Misted Pines the whole time. She'd have access to do the 'hauntings.'"

"Okay, say that happened, then why didn't the kids say anything about Lincoln being innocent after he died?" Murphy asked.

"Because she killed all their parents," Maribeth told him. "I might keep my mouth shut if I thought I, or one of my siblings, was next."

"If that's the case, what's she looking for out here?" Riggs asked.

"They didn't have bodies to check to see how long they were dead, seeing as Lincoln, or maybe the assistant, burned them," Maribeth said. "He took the time to hose down the area, maybe he had the time to hide some evidence that proved he didn't do it."

"He had the shotgun with him," Riggs pointed out.

"But they didn't test for GSR," Maribeth retorted. "Can't do it now, but they didn't do it then either, so they also can't prove Lincoln had it on him."

GSR.

Gunshot residue.

He knew what these women had been up to that day, or maybe since Maribeth arrived.

"She could have written Roosevelt letters," Nadia said. "Or made some threats to Sarah in a way they could keep them. If Lincoln shared with the police that he and his brother were both, in a way, married to Sarah, and he was okay with that, his motive melts away. But if he can prove this woman had a thing for his brother, or she made threats, hers takes shape."

"This theory holds merit," Murphy remarked.

It did.

There were holes in it, but Harry had said he had a gut feeling about her.

He'd let Harry know and see what he thought.

Riggs took a sip of his beer.

"Are we gonna eat?" Ledger shouted from down the slope. "Or are you gonna starve your son?"

"We're ordering Luigi's because Murph needs his fix!" Riggs shouted back. "What do you want?"

"Duh! Pepperoni and sausage calzone!" Ledge yelled. "And don't forget the bomboloni. I want one filled with pastry cream!"

Riggs leaned forward to dig out his phone, suggesting, "Pull up the menu on your cells, ladies, so I can get our order in before my kid expires."

"I don't have to look. I know what I want. Six of those bomboloni with pastry cream," Maribeth declared.

Nadia looked at her.

"What?" Maribeth asked Nadia. "This is the first long weekend I've had away since I endured eighteen hours of labor to bring Caleb into the world." She looked to Murphy. "That's my first. He's five. I have two. Layla's three." She went back to Nadia. "And Carter survived one single day doing what I mostly do at the same time I have a full-time job just like he does, before he called his mother to move in for the time I'm away. I'm not only letting loose because I'm on vacation, I'm celebrating, because Carter finally gets it. Yes, his getting it will last precisely two weeks, then he'll call me to pick Caleb up from kindergarten because he's vomiting all over the crayons because he's got the flu. But that two weeks he chips in will be bliss. I can return to the drudgery of avoiding carbs when I get back home."

Nadia listened to this then looked right to Riggs. "Please order her a calzone too, baby. Pepperoni and black olives. And some salad, because town is far away, and I don't have laxatives at my cabin."

He was laughing when he said, "Got it."

"Don't have to say, the works for me, brother," Murphy put his order in.

Riggs got Nadia's order, made the call, got a delivery time (another reason to order from Luigi's, it wasn't only awesome, they were one of the few places who delivered all the way out here), then put his phone in his pocket, his beer to his lips, and he killed it.

He opened another and settled his eyes on Nadia, who was curled into her chair, turned to Maribeth, and smiling at something she said.

His chest expanded.

Feeling his friend's eyes on him, he turned his head.

Murph had a look on his face Riggs had never seen, but seeing it then, his chest expanded even more.

Then Murph tipped the bottom of his beer Riggs's way, and looked to the women, saying to Maribeth, "Trade you pics of our kids."

They both pulled their phones out.

"We could use music, baby," Nadia said softly to Riggs.

To which, Riggs shouted "Son! Go get the Bluetooth!"

"On it, Dad!" Ledger shouted in return.

Riggs settled back.

And life was good.

THIRTY-THREE

She Shed

Riggs

The next day, Murphy was in town, visiting some of his other friends, and Riggs was in his workshop, getting some work done, when Nadia showed.

He looked at her through his mask, killed the blowtorch, set it aside, tossed off his gloves and pulled off the mask, and then dropped it to the workbench before he headed her way.

"All good?" he asked.

"Murphy in town?"

He stopped in front of her. "Yeah."

"Ledger fishing with Kirk and Dustin?"

"Left first thing this morning."

"Maribeth is in the shower."

Riggs grew still.

They hadn't fucked since Tuesday.

"She takes long showers," Nadia told him.

Riggs jumped her.

They kissed and groped as he backed her to the couch.

He stopped them at the arm, she flicked off her ridiculous Birks, and he took care of her jeans and panties.

Then he leaned into her, and they both went over the arm of the couch.

He pushed her tee up, tugged the cup of her bra down and sucked hard at a nipple.

She sifted her fingers in his hair and whimpered his name.

He moved up to take her mouth again, dove a hand between her legs and encountered her sweet, hot wet.

She went after the buttons on his jeans.

She'd pulled him out and was stroking, tight and hard, at the same time he was finger fucking her, when it hit him.

He broke their kiss.

"Fuck, honey, my wallet is in the house."

"You clean?" she breathed.

"Totally."

"You sure?" Her voice was still wispy because he was still finger fucking her, and she was still jacking him.

"I'm active, Nadia, so I take precautions and get tested. So yeah, I'm sure."

"I am too. Had my annual with my gyno before I left Chicago. And I have an implant."

Fucking fantastic.

"Ungloved?" he asked.

She slid her hand down his dick, holding him tight at the base, and...*fuck*. That felt good.

"That's up to you," she whispered.

He stared into her blue eyes.

She stared into his.

Then he slid his finger out and jerked his jeans over his ass.

"Legs," he grunted.

She let his cock go and rounded him with her legs.

He used his hand to guide him, caught, and slipped inside, for the first time feeling her wet as her usual heat and tight closed around him.

Christ.

Gorgeous.

He dropped his forehead to hers and saw the tears in her eyes.

She felt it too. All of it. How important this was. The trust he just gave her after what happened to him. What this meant for them both.

Then he slanted his head, kissed her and fucked her.

After he took care of them both, they didn't have time to keep at it or do much aftermath making out and feeling each other up. She had to get back to her friend.

She slid out from under him.

He rolled to his ass and stayed seated as he yanked up his jeans and did the buttons, his eyes tracking Nadia while she extricated her panties from her jeans and pulled them up.

She'd been hungry for him.

She probably had fifteen, twenty minutes, and she'd hightailed her ass down the trail to spend it with him.

It was time.

"I'm falling for you, princess," he declared.

Her head snapped his way one second, the next, she was astride his lap, doing her best to stick her tongue down his throat.

He cupped her ass in both hands and kissed her back, but she ended it when she realized he was doing that while laughing.

"I hope that's happy laughter," she warned.

"What else would it be? Since you used your tongue to communicate direct with my larynx you feel the same," he replied.

She slapped his arm and ordered, "Stop it, Riggs."

He gave her ass cheeks a squeeze and belatedly answered, "Yes, it's happy laughter."

"Good," she murmured, her eyes moving all over his face like she was drinking him in.

"Can't express how thrilled I am you're there with me, Nadia, but it isn't lost on me this is complicated," he warned.

"The most foolish thing a woman can do is uproot her life for a man," she replied.

His whole body got tight.

"But most women don't have an occupation where they can find a job practically anywhere, and a massive bank account to fall back on should things go awry," she continued, and put a hand to his cheek. "It's too soon to make this decision, but I want you to know, I'm falling for you too. I've already fallen for Ledger. Gia won't like my apartment as much as she likes this lake, and Ledger may never forgive me for taking her away from him. And I like Misted Pines, although I'm uncertain about Kimmy, but she seems harmless. So you should know, I was already considering it."

That landed her on her back in the couch so he could kiss her and feel her up.

When they broke for air, she whispered, "I hate it, but I have to get back. I left a note for Maribeth telling her where I was going, and I suspect she knows why I came here, but she flew across the country to be with me, not hang out alone while I got busy with my boyfriend."

"Yeah," he grunted.

She gave him a quick kiss and slid out from under him again.

She had her jeans and Birks back on, and was halfway to the door after another quick kiss, before she turned back and asked, "Do you think Dave and Brenda would consider an offer on the cabin if I made it worth their while? It'd be a nice guest house, and when we don't have guests, a fabulous she shed."

Only Nadia would consider the option of a thousand square foot cabin for a she shed.

"I think it's mostly been a hassle and a money drain for them since they bought it, so yeah. But I can't say that for certain."

She shot him a sunny smile. "I bet I can talk them around."

He'd bet the same.

"See you tonight," she bid. "We'll be over early to help set up for the party."

Set up was opening bags of chips, tubs of dips, filling coolers and tossing some hotdogs on a grill. All of this taking him and Murphy maybe half an hour.

He didn't tell her that because he wanted her to come over early.

He said, "Later, honey."

Another bright smile, and Riggs watched her slip through the big barn doors.

Yeah, when she got used to a world without her mother, she'd come fully back to herself.

Because he was going to make it that way.

On that thought, he got back to work.

THIRTY-FOUR

Family

Riggs

That night, Riggs was lounging on a blanket on the ground with his back to the blanket-covered log next to the fire he and Murphy had built, Nadia draped up his chest through his bent legs.

He'd spent an hour making a playlist, and it set the mood.

So right now, "Year of the Cat" was playing loud enough to be heard, but low enough people didn't have to shout at each other, and Riggs had noted earlier that none of his friends gave that first shit his music was setting the night to chill. They were just as good with mellowing out with some chips, dogs, beer, tequila shooters and pot as they were with loud and rowdy accompanied by chips, dogs, beer, tequila shooters and pot.

In fact, maybe more so, considering Easton was making out hot and heavy with Courtney across the fire from him and Nadia. His bud Jaeger was sitting close and deep in conversation with Ashley on the blanket to the west side of the fire. And Riggs had enough experience doing the same thing, he saw Storm, successfully on the make, sitting next to Lynne on a log.

By his estimation, those two would be leaving soon.

Harry, he knew, was behind him on his furniture, talking with Rus, something he could do every day at work, but also Murphy, something he couldn't.

He'd prefer Harry talking to Lynne, who was a fine woman Riggs sensed was looking for more than a good time, one reason why he and Lynne had always only been friends. But Storm was a good and decent man, so maybe that would take, and Viggo would have a fine woman in his life like Ledger now did.

But it was a minor victory Harry was there at all.

Step one, he'd taken off his wedding ring.

Step two, showing at Riggs's for a party.

And Riggs hoped step three would lead to good things.

Maribeth was standing off to his left with a huddle of his work crew, doubled over laughing, so he suspected they were entertaining her with stories of how he could be a detail-oriented hardass when they were on a job.

He'd called Hutch to ask how Gia would respond to this situation, and Hutch felt it was too soon to introduce her to thirty people and a party at Riggs's lake. So she was confined to the cabin.

Another reason to keep the noise down. If she heard it, she might not like it, and considering Nadia wasn't with her, they didn't know how she'd respond to that either.

"Brother, share," he heard from above him.

He looked up, and Murphy was standing there holding out his hand, the tip of his forefinger pressed to his thumb.

Riggs drew off the joint pinched in his fingers then handed it to his bud.

He held that smoke deep.

"Always been a weed hog," Murphy grumbled and strolled off.

Nadia giggled.

Riggs exhaled.

He hadn't put the pressure on, but he'd offered it, and she didn't hesitate taking it. He'd asked, and she told him that wasn't her first time smoking weed, and it wasn't Maribeth's either.

Riggs had noted there was one difference between the two outside the color of their skin.

Maribeth got high.

But Nadia got chill.

"Year of the Cat" slid into "Steal Away" as Riggs dragged her up his chest and kissed her.

When he ended it, she whispered, "Murphy just stole your marijuana."

"He's like that. He says I hog it, but he uses it as his excuse to be a mooch."

She giggled again.

"Having fun?" he asked softly.

She gave him a little shake with her arms around him. "You have good friends."

"Yeah."

"I really like Murphy," she said.

He grinned. "Me too."

"And he really loves you."

His grin died, but not for bad reasons, for the best ones.

"Yeah."

"Not to mess with the mood, but you should know, another reason, outside you and Ledger, why I was considering Misted Pines is that you have a big family. They're everywhere you turn."

He heard her, and he got it.

She'd lost the last of hers five months ago.

He slid his finger from her temple to behind her ear to slide her hair away from her face, then he tangled his fingers in it. "Maribeth is good family too."

She nodded and turned her head into his touch. "She totally is. But Chicago is big. You're always a bit alone in a big city. You can get lost in it. And after what happened, I knew it wasn't healthy to be lost. I think maybe I didn't realize it while I was doing it, but I picked somewhere like Misted Pines so I wouldn't be lost. But I got here, and I didn't know how to get found." She gave him another shake. "Until you found me."

"Princess," he murmured, curling his fingers around her head and feeling what she said heat his chest in a way he liked a fuckuva lot.

"Thank you, Riggs."

He pulled her to him again and kissed her.

They were straight up making out when "Steal Away" slid into, "Make It with You."

He'd been waiting for that song to come on, and he was glad it happened when they were right there, just as they were.

He slid his cheek against hers and said in her ear, "Picked this one just for you."

She stilled, listening to the song.

He tugged her head back so he could watch her face in the firelight while she did it, and he ran his thumb along her cheekbone and lips as the lyrics hit her, and they did this hard.

But that wasn't in a bad way either.

No, thank Christ, he could see it was really fucking good.

The song moved into, "You Make Lovin' Fun," when she said, "I wish they hadn't stolen that wine."

"Why?" he asked.

"Because I think there might be reason I'd want to keep that bottle forever."

That made heat light up his chest too, and he was about to reply, but he heard a sharp, "Doc. *Hup*," coming from his right.

He looked that way to see Jaeger's eyes on him, and the man was taking his feet.

In fact, everyone was.

And they all had attention aimed in the same direction, at something happening behind his back.

He lifted up, taking Nadia with him, and turned to look over his shoulder.

And he saw Angelica bearing down on them, openly raring to go.

He hadn't heard a car pull up, not that there was much room with the vehicles in his drive and lining the lane, but they weren't so far back he wouldn't hear another one approaching. And other than the lights that illuminated the pier, only a few scattered camp lanterns and the fire were giving the space light, so he hadn't seen her headlights either.

Which probably meant she parked on the road and hoofed it so she could do this.

Take them unaware.

He pushed up to standing, again bringing Nadia with him, but he then moved her to his back as he watched Murphy try to head Angelica off.

She purposefully slammed her shoulder into him as she walked by him, snapping, "Fuck off, Murphy." She stopped a few feet in front of Riggs, her gaze shot from him, to Nadia, to Storm, back to Riggs, then she announced, "You two, fathers of the year, so fuckin' high and mighty. Where's my kid at, Doc, while you get high and laid?"

Storm came up to his side. "Where's mine, Angelica?"

"Kiss my ass," she sniped at Storm.

"Thanks, no," Storm retorted. "Still have no clue why I went back three times. The first was tolerable, at best."

No warning, nails bared, she launched herself at him.

Riggs moved to intervene, but Harry got there first, catching her at the waist and pulling her away.

That was when Rus slid in at Harry's back.

"Let me go, Harry!" she shouted, fighting his hold.

"You either calm down right now, or you do it at the station," Harry warned, not letting her go.

She stopped fighting and aimed her glare at Storm, then moved it to Riggs. "Bubbles is a piece of shit liar. Everyone knows that."

"This isn't happening here, and it sure as fuck isn't happening now. Go home, Angelica," Riggs returned.

"Was minding my own business, having a drink at the Halfway —" she began.

"Which takes me back to my question," Storm cut in. "Where's my son, Angelica?"

She ignored him and kept at it, eyes to Riggs.

"—and Kimmy comes up to me. She fakes tearing something in half and setting it on fire, and she says, 'That was your membership card to the sister club.' And walks away. I don't need that bullshit in my face when I'm kicking back, Doc."

Seemed word was getting around.

No surprise.

It was the way in MP.

And seriously, Storm had been ticked.

"Your bed," was all Riggs said.

"Was at Aromacobana the other day, and people were actually pointing at me," she bit out.

She was getting heated…again.

"Not sure why you're here telling me this crap," Riggs returned.

She leaned into him and shouted, "Because I'm your son's *mother!*"

Riggs sighed, too mellow from weed and Nadia and firelight to bite, and he repeated, "Go home, Angelica."

"You're not invited, means you're trespassing," Murphy put in.

Harry let her go, but moved to put himself between Angelica, Storm and Riggs.

Murphy moved up to his side, Easton to his other, and Jaeger was approaching.

"He's right. You need to be smart, Angie," Harry suggested calmly.

Arm straight, she pointed Riggs and Storm's way, and yelled, "They get off, there's consequences,"—she jerked her thumb to herself—"and *I'm* the bad guy?"

"Didn't happen exactly that way, woman," Easton growled. "And you fuckin' know that shit." He left his killshot for last. "You should change your name to Audrey."

Oh yeah.

Word had gotten around.

At raising the name of a woman who was well-known in those parts as having been single-minded in her determination to find a man, no matter the costs (and the costs turned out to be extreme), Angelica's mouth dropped open in offense.

She closed it, but immediately reopened it to say something, but someone behind him, a woman, he thought it was Lynne, hissed, "*Sss.*"

"*Sss,*" one of the other women joined in.

"*Sss,*" more joined.

And they were moving, still hissing, closing in on Angelica.

Easton stepped back to give them room, Murphy did too, but Harry stood his ground. Rus shifted to his side, shielding Riggs and Storm even as Angelica started shuffling backward.

Harry finally pushed through the women, approached her, and they stopped hissing when he offered, "I'll walk you to the car."

"I can walk to my own fuckin' car, Harry."

"It's late, it's dark, and I can walk you to it, or I can follow you and make sure you get to it safely," Harry returned. "Half a dozen and six to me."

Angelica glowered at him, aimed this at Riggs and Storm, then she turned and stormed off.

Harry cocked his head side to side before he followed her.

Christ, Riggs didn't know how he faced it, day in and day out. Couldn't even kick back on a Saturday night with his buds without having to take care of business. His friend had the worst job in the world.

Rus moved to shadow Harry.

"Don't let her break the mood, man," Easton called to Riggs. "It's a good night. Let's just get back to it."

Riggs nodded to him but looked at Storm.

"Your lawyer contact her?" he asked.

"Yup," Storm answered. "I told him not to mess around. Probably should have given you that heads-up. Sorry about that."

"We gotta share every time she fucks with us, or forces us to fuck with her, I'd have to let you and Viggo move in so I don't have to bother hitting your name on my screen every five minutes."

"That's the fuckin' way of it," Storm said on a heavy breath.

Lynne approached and grabbed his hand. "C'mon, Stormy. Let's get another beer."

Storm and Riggs exchanged harassed glances before Storm threw his arm around Lynne's shoulders and led her to a cooler.

Riggs turned to Nadia.

"I'm not uncertain about Kimmy anymore," she declared.

He busted out laughing.

When he was done, she whispered, "Family," then got deep into his space and wrapped her arms around him.

He bent his head and put his face in her hair, smelled the beauty of it and instantly felt better.

Murphy was there.

"Hand me your stash, I'll roll another one. Because, as always with that woman…*damn*."

Again, Riggs took Nadia with him as he bent to the side and swiped the tin box he kept his weed and papers in off the blanket.

He handed it to Murphy.

Murphy wandered back to his chair with it.

"Did he just use Angelica being a bitch to steal *all* of your marijuana?" Nadia asked, her eyes aimed beyond him to Murphy.

"It's likely."

She collapsed in giggles against his chest.

"Jeez, Riggs." Maribeth was now there. "Nadia was right. More happens in Misted Pines in a day than an entire week in the Windy City."

This wasn't true, but he smiled at her anyway.

She smirked in return and explained it, saying, "'Make It with You.' *Smooth*."

That was when Riggs started laughing again.

Nadia and Maribeth did it with him, but Nadia did it better, because she was squeezing him with her arms.

"Yo! MB! Got a fresh one!" Murphy called.

"Laterzzzzzzz," Maribeth said to them and took off toward Murphy.

Yeah.

Family.

THIRTY-FIVE

Our Land

Riggs

The next night, Riggs woke in the middle of it, knowing something wasn't right.

His body got solid when he opened his eyes and saw the flashing police lights coming through the windows of his room.

Yeah.

Something wasn't right.

Fuck.

He threw the covers back and bolted off the bed, grabbing a pair of jeans from his chair and tugged them up on the move.

He also buttoned them on the way, his heart in his throat, his feet moving fast.

He got to the front door, yanked it open, and saw Wade Dickerson out on his deck, in uniform, his head bent to his phone, probably to call Riggs so he didn't ring the doorbell and wake, therefore alarm, Ledger.

Wade's head jerked up when he opened the door, and he said, "Hey, man. Everything's okay. She's all right."

She.

His gut dropped.

Riggs unlocked the screen door and pushed it open.

Wade came inside, and when he stopped with Riggs on the landing, Riggs demanded, "Talk to me."

"Someone's fucking with Nadia again, and they're escalating that shit."

Goddammit.

"Why didn't she call me?" Riggs muttered a question he assumed Wade didn't have an answer to, about to make a move back to his stairs to finish getting dressed.

But Wade did have an answer.

"She told Harry she didn't want you disturbed. Said she'd tell you tomorrow. Murphy left today, and she knew you were here with Ledger, and you couldn't leave him, you couldn't bring him with you. But Harry knows you'd lose your shit if he didn't tell you, so he sent me here to stay with Ledge so you could head over there."

That was when Riggs moved, and he did it saying, "You know how to make coffee, bud. Make some if you want, anything else you want is yours."

His stairs weren't designed to take two at a time, but by damn, he took them that way.

He hit his room, pulled on a tee, tugged on his running shoes, then he jogged back out.

Wade was sitting on a stool at his kitchen bar, doing something on his phone, and Riggs bid, "Owe you one. Later," and raced out the door.

By the time he got in his truck, started it up and made his way to the cabin, he could run there, so that was what he did.

Riggs sprinted down the trail, only memory and moonlight to lead his way, until her cabin came into view.

And it was all lit up, shining like a beacon. Every light inside and out seemed to have been turned on.

When he got close, he saw the back door was open, so he made his way there.

The loose hold he had on his shit got weaker when he saw the state of Nadia's back porch.

There were two rocks on the porch, big, around the size of a couple of softballs, one in the seat of one of the wicker chairs, and two of Brenda's pots had been smashed by two more rocks, dirt and flowers all over the place.

Two women inside, middle of the night, those big stones hitting the porch, they had to be terrified.

His head hazy with anger, he hit the back security door, went through and knew how edgy the vibe was because of three things.

One, Gia growled at him before she realized who he was. Only then did she whimper and make her approach.

Two, Maribeth looked freaked right the fuck out.

And three, Harry looked pissed, but Riggs knew him well enough to know this was hiding concern.

Riggs took a moment to get a hold on it, because the two women were still in their pajamas—Nadia had pulled on her robe, and Maribeth had tugged on a sweater, but they were alive and unharmed.

So he bent to give Gia a rubdown, thinking, Maribeth didn't leave until tomorrow. They'd had a long enough spell of good times, good friends and other really good shit, that Riggs thought he'd wake up tomorrow morning knowing Nadia and Maribeth were going to head to Aromacobana at around nine to grab coffees before they hit the road to get Maribeth to the airport in Seattle for her flight.

Which meant Riggs's afternoon plans were meeting Nadia around two at the cabin, which would be plenty of time for a quickie. Not to mention, time for him to inform her that he was going to give it another week before he sat Ledger down and asked him if he was cool with Nadia spending the night a few times a week (Riggs was going to go for five, maybe six), doing this in his dad's bed.

Murphy had walked Maribeth back to the cabin last night, while Nadia stayed with Riggs, since Ledge was at his gramme's.

But he'd been alone again tonight, and he was done with this sleeping alone shit, and that wasn't because of the state of play right then.

This schedule would leave Nadia zero time to rebut his plans to talk with his son before he had to kiss her and go get his boy from school.

Now, their good stretch was shot to shit.

But his plans weren't because that six nights a week at his house was going to be seven if this crap didn't stop.

Nadia came right to him.

"I told Harry not to tell you," she said when she made it to him and had her hands on his chest. "I'm fine. It's good. I was going to give you a call tomorrow."

He was in no mood to field that right now.

"What happened?" he asked through his teeth, and he didn't ask Nadia.

He asked Harry.

But Nadia answered. "Riggs, it's okay. It's just kids being jerks again."

He looked down at her. "You set Gia on them?"

She shook her head. "No. Because it's *just kids*. She might have hurt them."

"Riggs, a word," Harry said tightly.

He was already walking Riggs's way.

He passed him without Riggs responding, but stopped, looked back, and aimed a hard stare at Nadia. "Please do not follow us."

"Come here, sis," Maribeth called. "I'm going to mix us a cocktail."

He felt Nadia's attention on him as he followed Harry out the back door.

Harry moved off the porch into the cleared back area and off to the south side.

Riggs followed him there too and stopped where his friend stopped, well out of hearing of the cabin.

"What's the deal?" Riggs asked, watching his friend carefully.

"I'll show you the deal in a second, but first, have a word with your woman. She has an exceptionally trained guard dog. If she's got people on her patch who should not be on her patch, I don't give a fuck it's Greta Thunberg scouting a location for a protest, she…lets…that animal…*out*."

"Okay. I got a loose hold, Harry, and you're not helping."

"Gia started barking well before they started throwing rocks, the barking waking those women," Harry explained. "Nadia said it's been happening since she got her because Gia isn't used to her new space and all the critters who are moving around in the night, and that makes sense. Except for the fact Hutch lives more secluded than you, and that dog has grown from puppy to now, every night, hearing animals moving around all day and all fucking night."

Jesus Christ.

Nadia, babying her baby.

Fuck.

Harry kept at it.

"Maribeth says Gia eventually started losing it. What she didn't say out loud in front of Nadia was, the dog was giving a clear warning shit was going down, and it wasn't going to get better, and Nadia still didn't let her out. They apparently had words, because Maribeth wanted her to let Gia do her job, but Nadia was dead set against it. In the end, Nadia called my station, but she didn't let Gia loose."

"You think Bryce wants payback?" Riggs asked.

"No," Harry forced out. "Now, I'm gonna tell you, they took out three of your cameras physically. Southside, back, and the one trained this way."

"God fucking dammit," Riggs bit out.

"But we checked the feeds, and Maribeth reported timings on what we viewed, and about ten minutes before Gia started barking, the feeds all went to static."

Riggs chin went into his neck. "Jammed?"

"Yeah," Harry confirmed. "So we got no visual this time."

"Grimes saw that video of last time," Riggs reminded him. "He knows there are cameras. Why don't you think it's him?"

"Rus and Karen are here. Wade saw the tracks, and they've spent the last half hour following them."

"Where do they lead?"

Harry locked eyes with him. "To the access road."

"Fucking shit," Riggs snarled.

"Brace, brother, and come with me," Harry said.

Then he moved in the direction of where the stables used to be, and Riggs didn't like that, but he followed.

He stopped in what Riggs figured was the middle of where those stables were, switched on his Maglite and held it high but aimed to the ground.

Riggs looked that way and felt a chill enter his bloodstream.

Stones were arranged on the ground to make words.

GET OFF
OUR LAND

"Use of an unused access road," Harry began. "Tracks are the same we saw, male and female. Access to resources, the Wi-Fi jammer. And the word 'our.' There are only three people alive who would refer to this land as 'our,' and they're all suspects in three homicides."

Fuck.

"I've never asked, because I thought it was all horseshit, but what kind of crap went down to chase other people off this property?" Riggs queried. "I know about the scratching, anything else?"

"Heard word of whispering outside the windows, as well as scratching on them. What sounded like rocks being smacked together unnaturally. Loud noises of movement in the night in this area, where we are now, that was not the movement of animals. The sound of horses whinnying when there shouldn't be horses anywhere near. And this isn't the first message written in stone either."

Damn.

Harry wasn't done.

"I know of at least one small, contained fire that was lit in this same area that the people in this cabin didn't light, but they woke up when the light of it was coming in their windows. Porch furniture moved around during the night. Messages written on windshields in soap, a lot like this one, though 'our land' is new. It was more 'go away,' 'leave,' and 'you're not welcome.' One incident that was reported to Dern we just uncovered in the audit was a shit ton of blood spilled all over the back porch steps. It turned out to be pig's blood, but it understandably scared the fuck out of the tenants, and they broke their lease the day after they walked out to see that on their porch. And a couple of times that I know of, a woman's scream, then shotgun blasts."

Damn.

Thank fuck they hadn't pulled that kind of shit on Nadia.

Harry still wasn't done.

"Both those times, not one, but two fires of the gun. Which I'm sure you can imagine a scream and a couple shotgun blasts in the middle of the night would scare the shit out of about anyone, including me. And that's just what's gone down at the cabin. The litany of shit that's gone down at your house before you took possession is just as long. Straight up, when you moved in, I had reservations because this crap has been so relentless. Though, as you know, they've left you alone since that time, they haven't done the same with the renters Brenda and Dave have tried to put in this cabin."

Fuck.

He should have asked his question sooner.

That wasn't just kids messing around.

That was someone who was pretty damned determined to scare people off this land.

Nadia had told him about the rock noises, and that didn't happen in the middle of the night. It happened when she was awake, alone and couldn't miss it. But it stopped when he approached the cabin.

So that wasn't Bryce.

That was these fucks, whoever they were.

"I want all the footage on your cloud," Harry went on. "If they knew there were cameras they had to deal with, that means they've cased the place sometime recently. Maybe one of the cameras caught them while they were doing that."

"I haven't noticed any indication anyone's been around who

shouldn't be, except what we found, and Nadia and I searched all around this cabin. Cade, Jace, Jess and Rus have been looking too. They've all finished their patches. Nothing. Jace and Jess were going to head to the other side of the lake tomorrow."

"They might have had warning we're suspicious, if Sharon Swindell gave them a heads up. Now they're covering their tracks. Taking more care."

"Who the fuck is Sharon Swindell?"

"Roosevelt's assistant. You told me last night of Maribeth's new theory, and I don't know if it holds water, but I sure as fuck am not gonna discount it."

Riggs pulled a calming breath through his nose.

It didn't calm him.

Then he asked, "That Seattle cop nosing around? Is that what tweaked them to escalate things?"

"He didn't warn me, but he's my first call in the morning. Then again, if Swindell is involved, Rus and my visit to her would be enough to tweak them."

"So, we got all this shit, and the fact that Gia's been barking and maybe warning Nadia that someone is out here, and she's been doing that for days," Riggs broke it down.

"That's what we got," Harry confirmed.

Riggs pulled in another calming breath.

It again failed to calm him.

"Nadia know about this message?" Riggs asked, jerking his head to indicate the ground.

"No. Sorry. I gotta take 'em where I can get 'em, so that's gonna be your job."

Great.

"That all you got for me?" he asked Harry.

"For now. Get me those feeds. First thing."

Riggs nodded then turned and jogged back to the cabin.

When he hit the main room, he ordered the women, who were both sitting at the kitchen island sipping at martini glasses, "Pack up. You're spending the rest of the night at mine."

Maribeth looked relieved and immediately put down her drink and moved to the closet.

"What did Harry say?" Nadia asked Riggs.

"He's pissed you didn't use the resource I paid fifteen large for in order to protect your ass."

He heard Maribeth's gasp from the closet.

"You paid already?" Nadia demanded.

"Nadia," he said slowly, then thumped his fist twice on his chest. "You're right there, honey. But, Jesus, fuck, I'm in no mood right now."

Maribeth stuck her head out of the closet. "You tell her, brother."

Her head disappeared.

"Thanks for the help!" Nadia shouted toward the closet.

Nope.

He was in no mood.

And with this situation, she needed to be in the same mood as him.

"There's a message for you outside in the dirt," Riggs told her.

She looked back at him. "What's it say?"

"Get off our land."

The color drained from her face.

"Yeah, princess. Now…*pack.*"

She dashed to the closet.

Gia sat her ass beside him.

He looked down at the dog.

She looked up at him, panting, but she closed her mouth to swallow before she opened it to lick his hand.

He scratched her head for a while then, not long later, he adjusted the driver's seat of Nadia's Range Rover to accommodate his longer legs and cracked a window in the back for Gia to sniff at when he drove all three females to his house.

More Happy

Riggs

Riggs didn't want to do it.

But he had to do it.

So, while his son was wolfing down breakfast the next morning (both women were upstairs getting ready to hit the road), he leaned into his forearms on the counter across from his boy.

"I told you when I woke you up, Nadia had another situation at her cabin last night," Riggs reminded him.

"I know," Ledge said, shoveling scrambled eggs into his mouth. He chewed maybe twice, swallowed, then looked to his dad "That's why MB is in the guest room and Nadia is up with you. And Gia is here."

His kid aimed his eyes to the floor where Gia was lying at the foot of the stool by her boy.

Ledger then resumed eating.

"Well, got some things to cover with all that," Riggs told him.

"All right. And no shade, Dad, but Nadia's eggs are better than yours. She puts cheese in them."

He felt his lips quirk. "I'll take that note. Now I gotta tell you,

I'm gonna call your mom and ask her to take you until Harry can figure out what's going on with that cabin."

Ledger lifted both shoulders. "It's just people goofing around and being dorks."

Damn it.

"Ledge, we don't think it is. We think it's something more, and it might be dangerous."

Ledger's eyes slashed to his.

Seeing his son's face like that, he hoped Harry caught these assholes, at the same time he didn't because he wanted to be the first one to get his hands on them.

"So I want you to stay with your mom," Riggs finished.

"No," Ledger replied, not bratty, calmly but firmly.

Riggs pushed up from his forearms and said low, "Ledge."

"You promised you'd listen to me when I thought something was important. This is important."

Shit.

It was.

Riggs crossed his arms and nodded for him to go on.

"If stuff is going down, I don't want to be at Mom's, worrying about stuff going down. I want to be with you, so I know you're okay."

"Yeah, well, I'll be worried about you if you're with me."

"No, you won't. Because you know you won't let anything happen to me. Nadia or me. You and Gia won't let anything happen to us."

"Ledge—"

"Please don't make me go, Dad," Ledger whispered.

Feeling something uneasy slither up the back of his neck, he narrowed his eyes on his son. "Is there something to that I don't know about?"

Ledger looked to the side.

"We're talking about something important, and, buddy, you need to share when there's something I need to know," Riggs reminded him.

Ledger looked back to his dad.

"I'm not safer at Mom's."

That didn't make anything slither.

Riggs felt his neck instantly get tight.

It took a good deal out of him, but he kept his voice modulated when he asked, "Why?"

"Because she's never there, and Cami, our babysitter, is, like… seventeen years old."

His son had been doing his best to protect his mom, be a big boy and take it, and he did good, but apparently, there was only so much a kid could take.

So…

Right.

Decision made.

Easy.

He was going for full custody, and he was going to be co-plaintiff with Storm.

"Then I want you staying at your gramme's," he amended.

"When you said you'd listen to me if something is important, you also said you were going to try not to stand in the way of me becoming a man," Ledger returned.

"This is one of those times I gotta make a decision with you still being a kid."

"Would you let anything hurt me?"

"Never. But—"

"How would you feel, even at my age, if someone sent you away from Gramme?"

Goddammit.

He tried to find an argument for that.

He couldn't find an argument for that.

"Shit goes down, you do what I say, no backtalk," Riggs gave in.

Ledger smiled. It wasn't victorious. It was grateful.

"Thanks, Dad."

Fuck.

"Right, now. Second topic," Riggs began. "If I can do better at talking Nadia into doing what I think is right for her, unlike how this just went down with you, Nadia's going to be staying with us again."

Ledger went back to his eggs, muttering, "Cool with me."

"Ledger, it's gonna be different this time." Shit, this was tougher than he thought it would be. "See, she and me are together this time. We care about each other. And we like spending time together. And when a man and woman are like that, they sleep in the same bed."

Ledger began studiously eating his eggs.

"I know your mom has men staying over," he said quietly.

Ledger took a massive bite of toast so his mouth would be full so he didn't have to respond immediately.

God, he loved his kid.

"I'm gonna let it slide, you didn't tell me," Riggs shared. "Part of that not standing in the way of you becoming a man. But Nadia and me being together isn't like that. This is going to be now, while this stuff gets sorted out, and after that happens, it's going to be regularly. And if it works out with her and me, and we take the next step, it'll be all the time."

"I like her," Ledger said.

"I know. But you and me need—"

"Dad, thanks for talking to me about it, but I like her. I like you having her because you seem, I don't know, different. Happier, or something. Whatever. So, yeah, she's around more, and you're more happy, and I like her, and I'm more happy, and we get Gia at our house more, so I'm okay with it."

"All right, kid," he muttered.

And thank fuck that was done.

Ledger munched toast.

Riggs warmed up his coffee.

And when it was time to take his son to school, he shouted up the stairs, "Don't drag that suitcase down! I'll do it when I get back!"

"Can I take you back to Chicago with me so you can teach Carter how mountain men do it?" Maribeth shouted back.

"Carter carries your suitcase!" Nadia started shouting with them.

"Yeah, but he expects payback, knowwhatImean?" That was Maribeth.

"I do too. Just sayin'!" Riggs finished it.

"Riggs!" Nadia yelled. "Stop it!"

He was chuckling as he walked to where his son was hanging, waiting for him at the door, and when he got to his kid, Ledger said, "See? You say things are weird with what's going on at Nadia's, but still, you're laughing. More happy."

He wasn't wrong.

Riggs grinned at him. "Get in the truck, genius."

Ledger raced out the door.

THIRTY-SEVEN

Family Activity

Riggs

Early that afternoon, in his workshop, Riggs stepped away from the arbor he was building to clean up because Nadia would be back soon.

But he stopped to take a beat and give his work a critical eye.

He'd thought it'd skew dark, considering all the shit that was hitting him while he made it. And dark wouldn't work for the prominent feature of a wedding venue.

It hadn't gone dark.

Not even close.

It had become something he made while Nadia was hanging on the couch in his workshop with him, and while Nadia and he were finding their ways to each other.

So.

"Damn," he muttered and moved to a workbench to open up his sketch pad and start drafting different arches, because he wasn't going to sell that one.

No fucking way.

He was going to install it at the trailhead that led to Nadia's cabin.

This meant he was way off schedule for the arbor for Pinetop, and he was going to have to bust his ass to make the date he gave them for installation.

A new design idea was coming to him when Gia got up off her belly, took a stance, and barked twice at the barn doors.

Riggs put his pencil down and watched her turn, lock eyes with him, circle back around and resume her stance, attention to the doors.

No wonder Maribeth knew she was giving clear warning, because that was precisely what she was doing.

He moved to within reaching distance of a crowbar just as Jess walked into the door.

Jess took one look at Gia, who was now growling, and stopped dead.

"Gia. Friend," Riggs commanded. Gia relaxed her stance, circled around to look at him again, and Riggs said, "Go."

She approached Jess.

Jess bent to offer his hand, and Riggs took a second to try to understand how he could tell the two brothers apart.

It boiled down to Jess having a cocky vibe, and Jace having a confident one.

Other than that, if you couldn't sense that nuance, you couldn't tell them apart.

Even so, those vibes were so strong, if you knew the men, you couldn't miss it.

This meant, if Roosevelt, Lincoln and Sarah were actually a thing, Riggs could see how it worked.

Kind of.

Rubbing Gia down, Jess noted, "Totally calling Hutch this afternoon. Gotta get me one of these babies."

"Highly recommend," Riggs replied.

After Jess gave Gia her rubdown, he asked, "Got a second to come with me? We found something and want to show you."

Riggs didn't know if this was good or bad.

Jess sensed that and went on. "Nothing big. But we got a take on it and want you to see it while we explain it to you. I'll drive you and bring you back."

"You good with Gia coming with?" Riggs asked.

Jess gave her another rubdown and answered, "Absolutely."

They left his workshop and piled in Jess's truck. Jess opened the back window for Gia, and she stuck her whole head out to feel the breeze. In that manner, he drove them to the access road and down to the end of it, which was right by the edge of the lake.

They got out and hiked into the woods at the north end about three hundred yards before they stopped.

Jace was in the distance. He had several small, orange flags on wire stands sticking out his back pocket. When he saw them, he pulled one out, planted it where he was and jogged their way.

Jesus, these two guys had it down.

Riggs gave the command to Gia so she wouldn't flip Jace out, and Jess showed him what they found.

It was a hole dug in the ground. Not deep, but it looked like an animal did it with their front paws, the soil flung back several feet from the hole. It also wasn't fresh, but who, or whatever dug that hole did it relatively recently.

Beside the hole was a rusted metal can, like one beans came in. No label.

He turned his attention to the twins. "They're using metal detectors."

The twins exchanged a glance and looked back to him.

Jace nodded. "You snapped to that quickly. And it was our take. People do metal detecting as a hobby. But they don't claw like a dog at what they found."

Riggs turned his attention to Gia.

She'd come to sit by his side and didn't seem to have any interest in the hole or the can.

She was trained to stick by her person, but he hadn't given her that command, so she was free to roam.

And if there was any residue of food left in that can—though, considering the state of it and its apparent age, that'd be impossible

—he would suspect she'd have some interest. Even the hole, if it had the scent of an animal, might interest her. Enough she'd at least eye it.

She was squinting into the breeze and panting.

Because no animal had interest in metal.

And no animal clawed up that hole.

Jess piped up. "Called Harry. He's sending Sean out to take pictures and grab the can for evidence and printing. There's a lot of rust, not likely they'll get a hit, but they might. And anything they got could help them paint a picture."

"Right, thanks," Riggs replied.

"You came to the same conclusion we did right off, sorry I pulled you from work to look at this," Jess said.

"I'd wanna see it, so I'm not sorry. Glad you did and grateful you men are helping out," Riggs returned.

"Not a problem," Jace said, then on a nod, he took off with his flags.

Jess turned to him, but Riggs said, "Me and Gia will walk back. We can use the exercise."

Jess nodded too, and he turned to head toward Jace.

Riggs and Gia found the lake trail, and that was something else he needed to turn his attention to. His running was not going to keep it clear. And he'd wanted to edge the entirety of it with stone because it would look good. It'd also be an indication to people who weren't supposed to be there that someone maintained, thus owned that property, so if they missed the signs, they should take a hike.

He was momentarily indecisive about whether to take the east side, which had been crawled over in the last week by six people, or the west.

He chose west and kept his eyes peeled, but he didn't see anything.

He'd washed up and was in the kitchen, making himself a sandwich, when Nadia came in the door.

"Hey, honey," he called. "MB get off okay?"

"Yes," she replied, giving Gia her greeting before coming to the bar, tossing her purse on the end of it, then moving to him and tipping her head back.

He took the invitation and brushed his lips against hers.

She looked to the counter and requested, "Can I have one of those?"

In answer, Riggs reached for the bread.

She rounded the bar, hefted her ass on a stool and got right down to it.

"Okay, before you say anything, Maribeth lectured me halfway to Seattle. She's right, Harry's right, you're right, and I'll add, Gia was also right. That's why we got her. I need to let her do what she told me she needed to do. But I honestly did think it was just kids, especially since that one kid's dad is the kind of dad that isn't good with pointing out how life can teach you lessons, and you should learn them. I also got worried that I couldn't control her. Hutch said we may have graduated, but I need to keep up her training, at least an hour a day, so she stays sharp, and I can come to trust I have command of her."

She gave him that, Riggs didn't make a deal of it.

Instead, he said, "When I bring Ledge back from school, after his snack, I think we should all work with her."

For a beat, she seemed startled about that suggestion, then it hit her how important it would be, especially as things were now, that Gia was used to adhering to commands from all of them, and she nodded.

"I had a conversation with him this morning," Riggs began.

"I know. I'm back so I'm horning in on Riggs boy time again," she replied.

He took that to mean she knew she was staying, and he was pleased he didn't have to tangle with her about that.

"He doesn't think you're horning in, honey. He likes you. He likes me with you. He says I seem happier."

That alleviated her listless mood after taking her friend to the airport and having to deal with what she dealt with last night.

She smiled.

"I told him you're going to be here until all this shit is sorted, sleeping in my bed," Riggs shared. "And you'll be spending the night regularly, also in my bed, after it is."

Her expression shifted to concern. "That's fast, Riggs."

"He doesn't care, Nadia. He likes me happier, and you give that to me, so he's all in."

Her face got soft.

With that look on it, Riggs wished she was close enough to kiss, but she wasn't, so he kept assembling sandwiches and talking.

"I wanted him to go back to his mom's until this was all done, and he shared he doesn't feel safe with his mom for the sole reason that she leaves them with a seventeen-year-old babysitter all the time. He backed me into a corner about staying with us and not going to his gramme's instead, which I'm too humiliated he bested me to go into detail about."

That got him a wide grin.

He returned it and kept sharing.

"But it led me to the decision to be co-plaintiff with Storm and go for full custody. I already called him and my attorney. That's happening."

He probably shouldn't be surprised at how relieved she looked, but he was, and he realized how much she was holding back about her opinion of Angelica when she gave him that.

Riggs was happy she agreed, but he still asked, "Where does that reaction come from?" He put down the spreader he was using to add mayo to their sandwiches and lifted a hand her way at the careful expression that came over her face. "And don't give me all the stipulations about you not being in a position to judge. You're in this now, Nadia. You get to have an opinion."

It took her a second, but then she asked, "Have you and Ledger talked about chaos theory yet?"

"No."

"Have you told him that you're not going out of town for jobs for long periods of time anymore and that you're going for half custody?"

"Yeah."

She nodded and replied, "Okay, I'm still going to let him talk to you about what he told me, if that's in the cards for him. But with this latest from him, I think he's been trying to figure out how to be only with you for a while, without putting his mom in it."

When she told him that, Riggs decided he'd press her on this chaos theory business if Ledger didn't give it to him, because obviously, he needed to know what that shit was about.

But now, he was going to let it go.

Nadia kept talking.

"And from what you say, and what I've seen, she might love and care about her children, but she has no interest in being a mother. And although you and Storm are probably going to be facing life-long issues with that with your children, because it hurts to have a parent who doesn't have any interest in being a parent—"

Shit.

What was the matter with him?

He led her right to that place.

"Honey," he whispered.

She shook her head. "It's not about me, baby. I didn't live my whole life thinking my dad didn't have an interest in being a dad. This is about Ledger and Viggo, so even though you both are going to have to keep an eye on that, it's my opinion they're better off with one parent who loves them deeply, wants the best for them and offers guidance and support, than having to spend time with the other who keeps them fed, and clothed, and maybe loves on them some, but leaves them to do her own thing, which is more important to her than her children."

A vision assailed Riggs of a baby girl with blonde hair and blue eyes his son could watch over and Riggs could spoil the fuck out of.

"You really need to reconsider the having-kids thing, princess," he said gently.

"I really already am, baby," she replied in the same tone.

That had him grinning wide.

"A little girl," she said.

So they were on the same track.

"Dark hair and silver eyes," she continued.

Right.

They weren't on the same track.

And...*silver?*

His eyes were gray.

Riggs let that go too, in order to get into something more important.

"Blonde and blue-eyed," he retorted.

"That's not dominant," she reminded him.

"You think the Russian won't out?" he asked.

She started laughing, and through it said, "If you put it that way."

Riggs finished their sandwiches.

After they ate them, it sucked, but they didn't have time to fit in a quickie before he had to go pick up Ledger.

But after they got back, and his kid had a snack, they did their first organized family activity, and worked with Gia.

Making sure the ones he cared about could use the resource he'd bought to keep them safe might not been the activity he would have chosen.

But it was awesome all the same.

THIRTY-EIGHT

Podcast

Riggs

It was that night, Ledger was in bed, and Riggs and Nadia were hanging in front of the TV watching *Only Murders in the Building*, when his phone rang.

He pulled it out, saw it was from Harry and took the call.

"Yo, brother," he answered.

"Hey, Doc. Nothing to be alarmed about, and sorry it's late, but I need you to trust me and come to the access road."

He felt Nadia's fingers curl around his thigh, so he knew she felt his vibe, and he looked at her.

"Trust you about what?" he asked suspiciously.

Her brows shot up.

"You'll see when you get here," Harry replied.

Shit.

"Be there in a few," he said.

"Right, see you then," Harry returned then disconnected.

"Harry wants me to come to the access road," he told Nadia.

"Oh boy," she replied. "Do you need to take Gia?"

"I don't think so. He didn't sound alarmed. But he sounded evasive, and I'm curious, so I'm gonna go."

"Okay."

He touched her lips with his, bent and nabbed the boots he'd taken off earlier, put them on, then he hauled his ass out of the couch, grabbed his keys and went out the door.

When he got to the access road, he honestly didn't know how anyone could find it in the dark. It had seen some activity recently, but the entrance and the road were so overgrown, there were only two thin patches of worn dirt to guide the way, and no indication it was there from the street.

He turned in and drove all the way down, stopping only when he pulled up behind Harry's cruiser.

And beyond that was Bubbles's truck.

Topping that, Bubbles was sitting outside his truck in a camp chair, a cooler beside him, a Bluetooth speaker and a lit camp lantern on top of it, another camp lantern on the ground beside the cooler. A folding camp table was on his other side, with a pizza box from Luigi's on top of it.

Oh yeah…

And Bubbles had his shotgun resting across his thighs.

Slowly, Riggs got out and walked to Harry, who was leaning against the side of the cruiser, arms and ankles crossed.

"What the fuck?" Riggs asked.

"We got this road on radar, doing random stop ins," Harry explained. "Raul stopped in, found this, called me, I drove out, had a chat with him, he won't leave."

"I know you're talking about me!" Bubbles yelled.

Dammit.

Riggs moved to him.

"You can stay away," Bubbles said, and Riggs stopped. "And technically, I'm stayin' away. Tell your woman that. But heard someone is fuckin' with you and your woman, and they're usin' this road. So they can fuck right the fuck off or face the wrong end of my shotgun."

Holy shit.

"Bubs—" Riggs started.

"This is not a marker," Bubbles interrupted him. "Not me paying one, not me expecting one from you. Friends don't hold markers. And I know you're not my friend anymore, but I'm yours, and no one is messing with you on my watch."

Riggs dropped his head and looked to his boots.

He lifted his head when Bubbles continued.

"Got my pizza. Got my podcast. Got a six-pack. I'm set. You can go home."

Bubbles had done the unforgiveable, but pure Bubbles, he was so intent on doing what he could to make friends, it made it impossible not to like the guy.

Riggs had to think on this and talk to Nadia about it, so all he said was, "Be careful."

Bubbles lifted up his beer can to Riggs.

Riggs went back to Harry, and Harry pushed away from his cruiser to walk Riggs to his truck.

They stopped and faced each other when they hit the driver's side door.

"Update," Harry began. "The powers that be in Seattle have no interest in opening a closed case. Especially not a high profile one. That detective also hasn't done anything on his own time. So either they went after Nadia last night in their fifteen-year commitment to keep people off this land, or Rus and me tweaked Sharon."

"Right," Riggs said.

"And Sean, Raul and Karen are all considering resigning because they've spent hours today going through your feeds, but it was worth it."

Riggs's attention spiked. "Yeah?"

"Shadowy figure. It was night. They were wearing dark clothing, including a hoodie with the hood pulled up. Kept their head down. Maybe noted Nadia's Range Rover wasn't there, and they had a flashlight, which fucked us, because they caught a string of luck and shined it right into the camera when they looked at the house. Obscured the view, didn't see a face. The light went away, they were running from the house. Sharon Swindell is attractive, tall, slender, but built tough like any mountain woman should be, and fifty-four years old. I wouldn't swear the person wasn't her, but whoever it was, was taller than her and moved more like a man, and definitely someone younger."

"Bryce or Evan?" Riggs asked.

Harry shook his head. "Not Evan. He's five ten. This person was more around your and my height. But again, it was shadowy. And they weren't built, so it wasn't Evan, but could have been Bryce. We're pulling him in tomorrow after school to have a talk."

"Casey's gonna love that," Riggs muttered.

"Casey can leave my town and go somewhere where they pamper their kids to the point they grow up thinking the world revolves around them. Because I know you agree that it is a thousand shades of fucked up to do that to any woman anywhere, but one who's in my town to find a peaceful place to grieve the violent death of her mother is unconscionable. He might not have known that at the time, but he knows it now, and bottom line, it doesn't matter. What he did was fucked up."

Seemed Harry was getting more impatient with all this shit than Riggs, and Riggs had zero patience for it.

Then again, Harry was right there at nine thirty at night, dealing with this shit, and not at home, shaking it off.

His friend needed to get home and do whatever he did to decompress from his day so he could face the next one.

"Thanks for the callout, brother," Riggs said, clapping him on the arm.

"What are you gonna do about Bubbles?" Harry asked curiously.

Riggs sighed.

Then he said, "He's right. I got Ledger out of his shit. But I also just dropped fifteen thousand dollars on a dog, and I'm facing attorney's fees because Storm and I are suing for full custody. Onward from that, probably occasionally having to eat shit for a lifetime and watching my son do it, because Angelica is Angelica. But they've said I was smart since the second grade, and I still can't figure out why, no matter the crap he pulls, Bubbles is so fucking likeable."

"That was what I was chewing on the entire time it took you to get here."

"Gotta say," Riggs muttered, "I feel safer, him sitting out here."

"Yeah," Harry replied quietly.

"Get home, man," Riggs urged.

Harry nodded and headed to his cruiser.

You could hear the faint drone of a podcast in the distance, so Riggs looked that way to see Bubbles munching a slice of pizza.

Christ.

Bubbles.

He got in his truck, reversed to a safe spot he could do a three-point turn, then headed home.

THIRTY-NINE

One Of Theirs

Riggs

It was Thursday night, and they'd hit another zone where life was just good.

Riggs had time to get stuck into the new arbor, and so he could hit it early and keep at it until later, Nadia took his boy to school and picked him up.

Before starting dinner, they worked with Gia as a unit, and individually, with Hutch sending him directions on how to do that. He also offered to let him borrow Hannibal, one of Hutch's personal dogs, an older one who'd worked with Gia on synchronized guarding.

"Two, in any situation, is better than one," Hutch said.

But Riggs didn't need his son and woman falling in love with another animal, and considering he was still concerned that Nadia would be tentative to act with worry she couldn't control the dogs, he didn't need her worrying about that with two of them, so he declined.

Bubbles was still at the end of the access road every night, and Nadia, who he was learning could hold a mean grudge, offered her usual stipulations that she didn't know Bubbles or Riggs's history with Bubbles enough to provide an informed opinion, so she only allowed, "It's a nice thing to do, but not that nice."

His mom was over for dinner that night, and they were kicked back at the dining room table, shooting the shit over the crumbs of a banana cake that Nadia had made, when the call came in.

He pulled out his phone, looked at the screen, and, sliding his gaze through Nadia's where she sat beside him, he got up with a muttered apology and walked to the kitchen.

"Hey," he answered.

"You want him, you got him. You and Storm should start fucking each other, you're so good at fucking other people right up the ass."

And with that dulcet declaration, Angelica hung up.

Riggs walked down into the living room, up to the landing and out the front door.

He didn't call Storm until he was in the seating area.

"So you got the call too," Storm said as greeting.

"You did as well?" Riggs asked.

"She just hung up on me five seconds before you called."

"You hear anything from your attorney?" Riggs queried.

"No. I'm calling him at eight on the dot tomorrow, though. She's in this mood, I want her to sign her name to it as soon as possible."

"I'll give my attorney the heads-up as well."

"You think it's gonna be this easy?" Storm asked.

He hoped so, for him and Storm. He hoped not, for Ledger and Viggo.

"We'll see," he replied.

"Right. Tell Ledge and Nadia I said hi."

"You still hanging with Lynne?" Riggs asked, because he was interested, for Storm, and for Ledger and Viggo.

"Lynne?" Storm asked back, like he didn't know who she was.

Riggs started chuckling.

Storm did it back, but assured, "She's just a friend, man. Good woman, but I've been burned, you hear me? I'm gonna wait for someone like Nadia. Sweet and easy to look at, but more, funny as all hell."

Lynne was a fine woman, but she was no Nadia.

"I hear you."

"Later, Doc."

"Later, Stormy."

He turned and was mildly surprised it wasn't Nadia standing on the front deck, waiting for him.

It was his mom.

He walked to her.

"They're doing the dishes," she informed him when he hit the deck in front of her.

"Going in to help," he replied.

She didn't move out of his way.

"What takes you away from your family?" she asked.

He talked to his mother. He didn't go into detail, especially about all that had been going down. But she lived in Misted Pines, so what he left out, she could ferret out, and she was a mom, so she always did.

"Either Angelica is in a snit, or she just called to tell me she's not fighting my petition for full custody. She doubled down with the same thing for Storm. So we're getting our lawyers on that before she changes her mind."

His mom's shoulders slumped with relief.

He wasn't certain he should do what he was going to do this early.

But he did it.

"Gonna make at least one blonde baby girl with Nadia, and she won't carry this baggage."

His mom's eyes lit, she pulled him into a tight, but brief hug, slapped him on the back once, then let him go and went inside.

So yeah.

It was good he did it.

Riggs followed her in.

. . .

"DAD."

Riggs opened his eyes to a moonlit room and his woman tucked in front of him in a spoon.

His shoulder moved and his son called in an urgent, but quiet, "Dad!"

He shot to sitting and turned to see Ledger by the side of the bed, reaching toward him.

Gia, who slept in Ledger's room at their order and her preference, was standing at attention beside him.

"Outside," Ledger said.

"What, buddy?"

"Come."

"Riggs?" Nadia asked sleepily.

He was out of bed, pleased when he had not been earlier when one of her stipulations to staying with them, especially considering shit was going down in the middle of the night, was, after they fucked, they put pajamas on just in case something happened.

Something like whatever this was.

He followed Ledger to the window, Gia dogging their heels, and he pointed to the west side of the lake.

"Look," Ledger said.

It took him a beat to see it, but he saw it.

A soft glow in the trees. And there was another light, bobbing, like someone was holding a flashlight and walking.

He moved immediately to the chair, turning his back to his kid to pull off his pajama bottoms, and he grabbed his jeans, ordering Nadia, "Call the station."

After he had his pants up, he turned back to see she was standing at the window with Ledger.

But her eyes were on him.

"Are you going out?" she asked.

He was buttoning his jeans. "Fuck yes, I'm going out."

"Riggs."

"Call the station, honey," he repeated, pulling on a shirt.

"Take Gia," she demanded, dashing to her nightstand for her phone.

"She stays with you two."

"Take Gia," she reiterated.

He sat on the bundle of clothes on his chair to put on his running shoes.

"Dad, take Gia," Ledger urged.

Fuck.

He should have borrowed Hannibal.

"Yes, hi. Sorry. This is Nadia Williams out at Doc Riggs's house on Coun—" Pause then, "Yes, hi, Karen."

Fuck, his woman hadn't been there a month and she knew every deputy in the department by their first names.

So, oh fuck to the yeah.

He was going out.

He went to his boy, wrapped his hand around his head and kissed the top of it. Went to Nadia, did the same but kissed her forehead. Went to his side of the bed and snatched up his phone and army knife. Then he raced out, calling, "Gia! Here!"

She took off with him.

He found his Maglite in the kitchen junk drawer, tested it, went to the laundry room and grabbed his stash of digital cable, drawing the ring of it up his arm to hang from his shoulder. He then clipped on Gia's leash.

And they headed out.

He found the trail and didn't use his Maglite because he didn't want them to see him coming. He used the moonlight as he tore down it, Gia running at his side.

When he suspected he was getting closer, he slowed, she did the same the instant he did, and when he saw the lights in the distance, he whispered, "Gia, quiet. Heel."

She crept beside him as he moved as carefully as he could, but without light to show him where he was walking, and with a dog, it'd be impossible not to step on a branch. He'd be lucky he didn't stumble over a fallen log.

But by some miracle, they managed to make the high ground without them noticing he and Gia were there, and he stopped to look down at them.

Two of them, a man he'd peg at about Jess and Jace's ages, that being around thirty, and an attractive woman in her fifties.

They had a few camp lanterns lighting what looked to be a makeshift center of operations, which consisted of a shovel, two thermoses and a backpack. And both of them had flashlights and metal detectors and were sweeping the ground several yards from the lanterns.

Since Riggs was looking, and not at the ground, he caught something—movement, or a reflection off a balding head—and he saw Bubbles lurking behind a tree, down from him and at least thirty yards away.

Bubbles had seen Riggs and was doing action movie hand gestures, that if Riggs read him right, said he was on the man, Riggs was on the woman.

Riggs shook his head.

Bubbles did the gestures more sternly.

Goddammit.

He shook his head again, and before Bubbles fucked this, he shoved his flashlight in his back waistband, shifted his hand to the clip on Gia's lead and moved out from cover, making an intentional racket.

Both the man and woman swung his way and froze.

He pointed at the man, and shouted, "Gia! Attack! Bite!" unclicked her leash, and she went flying through the woods.

The man started running.

The woman did too.

Riggs went after her.

He caught her easily, hauled her up, turned her, and slammed her down to her stomach, not giving that first shit she was a female, even when he heard her pained, "*Oof!*"

While she was winded, he pulled the digital cable down his arm, his knife out, slit the plastic fastener on the cable, and wasted no time hog-tying the bitch.

He heard the snarling, and the screams, over which Bubbles yelled, "Doc! I'm on him. Call this beast off!"

He ran that way, and only when he was close enough to inter-vene, did he shout, "Gia! Stop! Sit!"

She instantly let go of mauling his leg, sat and started panting.

Christ, Hutch could train a freaking dog.

Bubbles fell into a knee on the guy's belly.

Riggs moved in.

They worked together to turn him, and since he wasn't going to get anywhere on that leg for a while, Riggs just bound his hands behind his back.

Bubbles got off him, and Riggs didn't care about his cries of pain when he dragged him to the woman.

He pulled out and clicked on his Maglite, and ordered Bubbles, "Put the lanterns down by the lake."

Bubbles moved to do that.

He looked down at the two, aiming his light at them, first checking the damage to the guy's leg to make sure he didn't need to fashion a tourniquet or something.

Gia did a number on him, but it wasn't that bad.

He moved his light to take them both in.

She, still on her stomach, turned her face away.

The man was more concerned about the pain in his mangled leg, so he was on his back, giving all of his attention to groaning and wincing.

But Riggs had occasion in his life living in Misted Pines, with all the lore, to remember with clarity the times he saw Roosevelt, Lincoln and Sarah Whitaker.

And there was no mistaking this asshole was one of theirs.

FORTY

Emphasis On The Criminal Mind

Riggs

He was standing in the observation room with Cade, Jess and Jace watching Sharon Swindell in an interview room clam up after what the men had reported to him when he'd shown, and what he'd seen himself for the last half hour.

Not saying much for the two hours they had her in there, outside pointing fingers at anyone but herself.

She'd just lawyered up on Harry and Rus, when suddenly, everyone in the interview room turned their heads at a knock on the door.

Harry called out at the knock, Wade swung his torso in and said, "You'll want to go speak to who's waiting in Conference Room A, sir."

"Give her her phone call, then book her for criminal trespass, criminal menacing, stalking, attempted burglary and accessory to murder. We'll start with that, until I can prove whether or not she's the one who pulled the trigger, twice, then forced arsenic down a man's throat," Harry said to Wade as he and Rus got out of their seats and left the room.

357

Riggs smiled massively at the expression they'd left on Sharon Swindell's face, because they'd been pressing her hard about what she was doing on Riggs's land, what she was looking for, if she was involved in a fifteen-year conspiracy to scare people away from his lake, and if that was true, why.

But they hadn't mentioned murder.

Wade went in the room, and Riggs, Cade, Jace and Jess turned to each other.

"Harry sure knows how to have the last word," Jace muttered.

That was when they all smiled at each other.

The door to the observation room opened and Harry was there.

"Cade, Doc, with me," he said.

Then he disappeared.

They all looked at each other again, before Cade and Riggs walked out.

Harry was following Polly, his assistant and overall mom to the department (and half the town) down the hall, and they followed him.

They hit the main bullpen and headed through it to one of two conference rooms at the back, both of them having one wall of windows, the one that faced the bullpen.

And in one of them stood a tall, straight, handsome man with sandy-brown hair and the unmistakable look of a Whitaker.

A man Riggs had seen in town years before, when he was still a boy.

Rus was already in with him.

Harry didn't look back, but Cade and Riggs exchanged glances before they hit the room.

Rus closed the door behind them and dropped the blinds.

"Dr. Truman Whitaker?" Harry asked.

The man jerked up his chin and cast his intelligent hazel eyes through the rest of them.

"I'm Sheriff Harry Moran. You've met Lieutenant Zachariah Lazarus, my chief deputy. This is Cade Bohannan, former FBI. And Andrew Riggs, who lives in your old house and is one of the victims in this scenario. You can ask for him to leave, but considering all that's happened to him and his family, and that he had to get out of his bed at three in the morning to chase your brother and your uncle's old assistant through his woods tonight, it's unorthodox, but I believe he's earned the right to stay."

Truman Whitaker gave Riggs a once-over before he looked him dead in the eye and surprisingly said, "I agree."

"Let's have a seat, then. Coffee. Water?" Harry offered.

"I had coffee at the hospital," Truman told him, pulling out a chair and folding into it.

"How's Jefferson?" Harry asked, doing the same, as did everyone else, with Rus on Truman's side, the other three men across from them.

"He'll live," Truman answered, like he didn't care either way.

And there might be something behind that indifference coming from the good doctor, seeing as Jefferson was the youngest Whitaker child, and he'd been arrested, then taken to the hospital after Gia did a number on his leg.

"I'd like to video this conversation if you don't mind," Harry put in.

Without hesitation, another surprise, Truman jerked up his chin.

Harry reached out and hit a button in a console in the middle of the conference table and a red light came on. Riggs looked to the corner to see the camera there had a red light illuminated.

"Record to reflect, Dr. Whitaker agreed to be videoed for this interview," Harry announced to the room, and to Truman, "Right, Dr. Whitaker, please tell us why you're here."

"You can all me Tru. I don't even let the nurses call me Dr. Whitaker, not even in front of patients. Dad taught me no man or woman is above another, to the point he felt it was at the root of society's ills. Even over money, though it's usually having money that makes people think they're better than others. I understand my patients need to feel I have the respect of the staff, but they also need to feel comfortable sharing candidly with me. In that scenario, the latter is preferrable."

Cade shifted in his chair, his interest even more piqued, and yeah.

Tru hadn't said much, but what he said was seriously telling.

"All right, Tru," Harry replied. "And you're here because…?"

"I'm here because Kennedy is a mess. She's hysterical. She had to be sedated. She was in no place to make a considered decision about what I'm about to do, but I think her screeching at me, 'Enough with the secrets, Tru!' fifty times, I get the gist. However, I agree with her. Because Dad deserves it. So does Mom. But mostly…Lincoln."

It was Riggs shifting at that, Harry, Rus nor Cade gave away that Cade had called it about their family situation.

"Dad" was Roosevelt to Truman Whitaker, the eldest Whitaker child. And Lincoln was "Lincoln."

"Do you know what happened that night outside your father's cabin?" Harry asked.

"I know what Lincoln told me. I think part of it he figured out. Part of it, Jeff told him. And the last of it, he knew, because he was there," Tru replied.

"And what did your uncle tell you?" Harry asked.

"Do you know that from what I said? That Lincoln was my uncle. Or do you know it because Sharon told you?" Tru asked back.

"It was our working theory that your parents had an open marriage of sorts, from Cade Bohannan, who was an FBI profiler," Harry told him.

Tru looked to Cade. "That's always fascinated me. I was going to get into psychiatry with an emphasis on the criminal mind. After what happened, I changed course and went into emergency medicine."

There was something off about this guy, Riggs just couldn't put his finger on it. He didn't know if the man was emotionless, or keeping a lock on it so he wouldn't fly apart or give anything away.

Tru returned to Harry. "Your working theory?"

"With the persistent issues that have been happening at the lake, we've reopened the case on your mother's and father's murders. We'd just begun reinvestigating, but I'll share, we had some concerns with the veracity of your uncle's confession," Harry informed him.

"Seems you're a lot sharper tack than the imbecile who used to have your job," Tru remarked.

Harry just dipped his head at the understatement.

"You probably want to know from the start," Tru announced.

"If it'll fill in the whole picture," Harry replied. "Yes. Please."

And that was when Tru put the puzzle pieces in place for all of them.

"As you now know, my dad was Roosevelt. He was also my sister's, Kennedy."

So Cade got one thing wrong.

No one was perfect.

Tru kept going.

"Jeff was Lincoln's. They were…" He shook his head. "There really isn't anything in normal society to explain what my parents were. Dad loved Mom, and they were committed to each other. Lincoln loved Mom, and they were legally married, but also committed to each other. Obviously, I've thought about it over the years, especially recently, since I've asked a woman to be my wife, and did it knowing I'd lose my mind if another man touched her, or she touched another man."

Regardless he had little affect, at hearing that, Riggs was leaning toward liking this guy.

"Maybe it was because they were twins," Tru kept on. "But they were two very different men. I just know, there was never any issue with both of them being with Mom." He shrugged. "That isn't to say there weren't arguments, disagreements. They each had their own partnership with Mom. I'm engaged. I've had other relation-ships. That happens with a partner. It happens between siblings. But it was never anything big. As much as no one will get it, and we were all very aware no one would get it, primarily Mom's parents taught us that, thus we kept it a secret, but it worked. We were a happy family."

"So your maternal grandparents knew of this situation?" Harry queried.

Tru shook his head. "No. But they guessed. They called Dad and Lincoln *unnatural*. Said they'd made Mom the same. Sinful. Filthy. I'm sure there are pious people who are quiet about their faith who are good people. The ones who are the loudest, though, usually are not."

Riggs couldn't disagree.

"They had an arrangement," Tru shared. "Lincoln had Mom in Seattle. She was with Dad when we were here. Lincoln had to come with her most of the time so it wouldn't seem weird, so no one would notice. But he gave them their privacy when they were here. Even when us kids were. He had that in Seattle. Dad had it at the lake."

And there was the explanation of why he'd built his house as he did, not to mention why Lincoln and Sarah spent six months a year in Seattle.

"The reason why your brother and sister contend she liked to spend more time with Roosevelt," Harry remarked.

Tru nodded. "They were doing what Lincoln told them to do, though. So was I. Giving him motive."

And there it was.

Lincoln didn't pull the trigger.

Rus glanced at Riggs.

Riggs cocked his head to the side.

"So Lincoln was okay that your mom was with your dad when he was at your house on that lake?" Harry asked.

"Yes," Tru answered. "It's how it was. It's how they worked it. It's how they shared. Mom was all about making sure neither of them, nor any of us kids, felt like she had favorites. She knocked herself out to do that. She was the one who asked Lincoln to figure out how to make our dining room have a circular table in the big house, because we always had dinner together when we were at the lake, and she didn't want Dad or Lincoln to have to give up the head of the table."

That explained his dining room.

And maybe, if Lincoln thought like Riggs did, when he sometimes used movement in design to communicate emotion, that explained the circling back on itself of the winding staircases.

Sarah wound her way to and from each of them in a continuous cycle, always circling back to one after returning from the other.

Tru carried on sharing.

"She even wanted to have another baby, because Dad had two, and Linc only had one. She got pregnant after Jeff, twice. Miscarried both, the second baby deep into her second trimester. Losing him so late, it destroyed her. Her going through that, it wrecked Dad and Linc. She was so into making sure it was all equal between all of us, she wouldn't hear of not trying again. So Dad and Linc both got vasectomies."

A ghost of a fond, sad smile hit his lips, the first indication of any emotion from the guy.

"When she found out they did, it wasn't an argument or a disagreement. That caused a fight. But it was two against one. She was outnumbered," he said quietly.

Okay, it seemed both men really did love the same woman, and they were all right with that.

And the kids, at least this one, were okay with it too.

When no one spoke, Tru continued.

"Like I said, it all worked. Really well. I know a bunch of crap came up in all the infighting. But Lincoln held up his side of the family, even after he quit writing with Dad. He managed the money, the accounts, the investments, paid the bills, the taxes. He went on the book tours, did all the interviews, because Dad hated that. When they negotiated Dad's third contract, he fired his agent, and Linc negotiated everything after that. Yes, Lincoln wanted to sell more movie rights and Dad didn't, but money is money. They owned a lake, for God's sake, managed three houses, and had three kids to put through school and pay for weddings, not to mention, they had three retirements to cover. Mom liked to travel. She liked to shop too. Linc and Dad both would have spent all their time at the lake if Mom didn't like having her time in the city to hang with her girlfriends and go to Nordstrom."

Tru put his hand to the table, seemed to be about to rub the surface with his forefinger, then he put his hand back in his lap.

And when he kept talking, they'd find that movement was because he felt guilt that they might have construed he'd just talked shit about his mother.

"That isn't to say Mom was greedy or flighty or all about money," he stated.

"We weren't thinking that," Harry assured.

Tru nodded.

And kept going.

"Linc also managed their website, responded to fan mail. He did all of Dad's research. Dad liked crafting stories. He wanted to have the time to branch out to a new series. He didn't want to be bogged down in doing all of that. Linc loved doing it. He also contributed more than anyone said to the books. Dad sucked at dialogue. It drove him crazy because he loved writing, but that never came easy to him. Linc didn't just do pass-throughs. He did a lot less than the first three books, but Dad counted on him to give them more depth. Bottom line, Linc knocked himself out not only for our family, but so Dad could be free to do the thing he loved to do."

When he stopped speaking, Harry inquired, "I'm afraid I don't understand why your sister was aligned with your brother in all the, as you referred to it, infighting. It's understood you spent a lot of time with your dad. Were all three of you kids not okay with the manner in which your parents formed your family?"

One side of the guy's lips hitched up and he said, "Kennedy was a mini-Mom. She's just like her today. She loved our dad. She was just not about fishing and hiking and stuff like that. She was about doing her makeup and getting coffees with her friends and talking about boys and gossiping with Mom."

His gaze on Harry suddenly intensified.

He then asserted, "We honestly were happy, sheriff. No one knew, but close friends, and when they saw us together, they got it. We loved each other. Linc was more of another dad to Kennedy and me than he was our uncle. We had more than most people do, and that wasn't about money."

"Then what happened?" Harry asked.

"Sharon happened," Tru stated.

That made all the men shift in their seats.

Because here they were.

"Take us through that," Harry prompted.

"She had a crush on Dad. *That* caused a disagreement. Not with Mom. Mom got having a crush on Dad, obviously. And she knew Dad was all about her. With Linc. Linc got a bad feeling off Sharon. Called her Annie Wilkes."

Well, shit.

"Linc wanted Dad to fire her," Tru continued. "But she was devoted, and Dad could get distracted. You didn't bother him when he was writing, for one thing. He was all about the book. Wouldn't shower for weeks, another reason why Mom and Linc were good with being in Seattle and away from him. He needed his space when he wrote. But when he was out of a book, he was all in. He wasn't really sociable, a complete introvert. But he had good friends. And he was all about his family."

"And he didn't let Sharon Swindell go, like Lincoln asked," Harry noted.

Tru shook his head. "No. And I can't speak for her. I have no idea why she would do what she did. I thought she was okay. She could be a bit skeevy around Dad if Mom or Linc weren't around. But most of the time, she was just a normal person. An employee. Mom was nicer to her than Linc or even Dad was. But whatever reason she did it, she did it."

"What did she do?"

"She instigated a psychological campaign to turn Jeff against his family, one she succeeded in, I'm sure you've figured out by now, spectacularly."

Well…

Shit.

"And what came of that?" Harry pressed.

"In the end, she lost it. Why? You'd have to ask her."

"Lost it?" Harry kept at it.

"Jeff was here, sheriff. In Misted Pines. He was here when it happened. We had a long weekend off at school. I was going to drive Kennedy and her boyfriend to the lake for the weekend, because we had a party to go to in Seattle, but Mom and Jeff came out the day before."

"No one mentioned that," Harry noted.

"That would be because Lincoln forbade us to because Jeff shot my mom and dad and set fire to the stables."

Harry sat back.

Everyone remained silent.

"Linc didn't *catch them*," Tru said the last two words with such deep sarcasm, it was like a physical thing in the room. "He was at the big house. He saw the fire and ran to the cabin, terrified out of his mind. When he got there, Sharon was there. And so was Jeff, holding the shotgun, covered with blood. First thing Linc did, though, was ask after Dad and Mom. Jeff said they were in the stable, so he tried to go in and get them, but the fire was raging. Then he tried to stop the fire. Jeff was bloody, but Dad didn't know what that meant. If they were dead or not. He grabbed the hose, went after it. But there was no stopping it, not with a garden hose, so he just made sure it wouldn't spread, especially to the cabin. Dad loved that place. We all had happy memories in that place."

Cade gave Riggs a look, which Riggs returned.

And yeah.

Nadia was right.

Cade was good at this shit because he'd called into question the drenching of the area on the cabin side.

Tru sucked in a big breath, let it out and kept talking.

"Once he accomplished that, he had to deal with Sharon and Jeff. Dad never trusted her, but even if he didn't figure it out right then, he had a great deal of time with not much else to occupy his mind to figure it out later. So he talked to Jeff about it, and Jeff confirmed what Linc figured out."

"And what did Lincoln figure out?" Harry queried.

"That she'd been messing with Jeff's head about Dad, me and Kennedy being Mom's favorites, Dad being the man with the money and all the power, and how she knew, because Dad told her, when he did *not*, that Dad was done sharing Mom and his family with Lincoln. So he was cutting them off. Including Jeff. Especially Jeff, because he abhorred even looking at the child his brother made with the woman he considered his wife. That they were going to be cast out. No Mom. No brother and sister. No Seattle house. No home by the lake."

Jesus.

What a fucking cunt.

Some bitterness crept in when Tru said, "What gets me about that is, not only did Dad love Jeff like Linc loved me and Kennedy, but also how hard Mom worked at making us all know that wasn't the case. He was only fourteen when it happened, but he wasn't thick. And it wasn't like he was eight. By fourteen, you should be forming a moral compass. You should be able to rationalize things, especially when everything around you is screaming the exact opposite of what a woman your own father openly distrusts is spewing at you. They gave me that. They gave Kennedy that. The only way I can make it work in my head is that we all pampered him so much, somehow, it was underdeveloped in him. He shot Mom to death, and still, that seems the worse betrayal."

Riggs could see that.

Tru kept at it.

"At the scene, Sharon told Linc that she'd tell everyone about their 'sordid' life, and how fucked up Jeff was. That he'd be tried as an adult, and even if he wasn't, his life would be destroyed forever because he murdered his mother and uncle, and everyone would know it and guess why. She really did a number on Lincoln, who had just, it shouldn't be forgotten, lost the love of his life and his twin brother, and his son committed the murders. She knew that, I'm sure, so she went in for yet another kill. So he told Jeff to take off his clothes, which he threw on the fire, and ordered him to go home and take a shower and not to say a word or leave the house. Then he called the cops."

"Are you sure of this story?" Harry asked.

"I'm not sure of anything. I wasn't there," Tru answered. "I know what Linc told me, because it was up to me to make sure everyone kept their mouths shut so Jeff didn't get into trouble. At the time, he just said there had been a terrible accident, Jeff was at fault, things were going to be out of his control, and we all had to do what we could to protect Jeff. Imagine my surprise when I found out that 'accident' was my fourteen-year-old brother shooting my mom and dad to death then burning their bodies. At least they let the horses out."

Riggs didn't want to imagine it.

But yeah.

At least they let the horses out.

"I know when Linc got out of prison," Tru carried on, "he came to me and shared how he was concerned that Jeff and Sharon were still close. Something I had no clue was happening. I hadn't seen her since before we lost Mom and Dad. Though, Lincoln didn't share about Sharon's psychological manipulation, I know he had deep concerns about her. Before he was sentenced, and after he went to prison, he'd warned me multiple times to be certain she had nothing to do with Kennedy or Jeff. He was also upset that I'd become estranged from them."

"And Kennedy in all of this?" Harry pressed.

Tru blew out a sigh before he said, "Jeff was our baby brother, sheriff. You don't know it's stupid to spoil him and let him get his way and do everything for him when you're doing it. He's cute and your little brother. You just do it. Though, Kennedy learned how stupid that was tonight. Hence her being hysterical. But we got the full story at the hospital, which is why I'm here."

"And what was that?" Harry asked.

"Sharon was messing with Jeff's head. And for her to get at the money, probably in another effort to screw over Linc, and posthumously, Mom and Dad, she used Jeff to mess with Kennedy's head. Though, I'll say, that might be jaded when it comes to Sharon, since Jeff is after the money himself. My sister and I aren't estranged. Medical school is no joke, and residency sucks all your time and energy. So there's that. We also just don't see eye to eye on some important things, the unending lawsuits being the biggest one of them. Though, she's more about keeping Mom's folks from getting the money. However, we were all flabbergasted Dad's folks and Aunt Mary got in on the act. Greed, I've learned, makes people do shitty things. They saw the money was possibly up for grabs, and they pounced."

Greed sure did that to people.

Riggs was living that nightmare in his own way with Angelica.

Tru continued, "But Kennedy's always been the worst, along with Mom, in spoiling Jeff and seeing to his every need. Now *Jeff*," he nearly spat the name, the emotion coming out of him now, "he and I were estranged. But this had a lot to do with him killing my mother and father in an 'accident' and ruining a man I loved very much, who busted his hump and gave, essentially his life to cover for him."

"It's my understanding, in the lawsuit, Kennedy asserted that you didn't get along with Lincoln and your mom," Harry commented.

"No, *Jeff* asserted that," Tru contradicted. "They filed those papers, and Kennedy didn't read them before she signed them. She lost her mind. Called me and apologized. Told me she read Jeff the riot act. But I don't blame her. Honestly, there's so much paperwork with that crap, it's a wonder I got through my residency with all the stuff I had to wade through. I could see just signing your name and being done with it."

"Right, so with all of that, I'm wondering why all of you kept this secret even after Lincoln died," Harry noted.

"Because he told us to from the very beginning. Because he didn't want everyone all over the globe talking shit about Mom and Dad. The books have been translated into over thirty languages, sheriff. It'd be everywhere. Also because he knew Jeff was a fuckup, and he wanted him to get help, not be sent to juvenile detention, but he wasn't in a position, considering he was in prison, serving Jeff's time, to get it for him. And if Lincoln was going to put himself that far out to protect their secret, and his son, I loved him too much to go against it."

Couldn't fault the guy for that.

Tru still had more.

"And I have to say, things didn't get better after it all happened, because we went to live with Dad's parents, and they were devoted to Dad more than Linc, in a way that, I loved them before they got in on the legal action, but even I thought it was weird. I think they sensed, too, that things were not as they seemed, even if they weren't in on the secret. As such, they sensed Kennedy and I were their precious son's children, and Jeff was their less precious son's. Don't ask me how. All I know is, they treated him differently, *not* spoiled and nurtured and cosseted. And I think that got under his skin, the reality he murdered two people who adored him got under his skin, and since Sharon somehow managed to stay close to him, she worked that angle too, because it corroborated all the shit she was filling his head with."

"Did Jeff tell you this?" Harry queried.

Tru shook his head.

"Not back then, though Linc knew it, because Jeff told him. Even Kennedy didn't know it, until about an hour ago at the hospital, when Jeff told us. I knew bits and pieces. Nothing about Sharon, except Lincoln's concerns about her. I only knew that Mom and Dad were dead. For some reason Jeff shot them. Linc was going to go down for it. And we all had to look after Jeff because he was fourteen, he got his head mixed up, so he was *troubled*." Again, he nearly spat his last word. "The rest of this is brand-new to me."

And now they had the explanation behind his detached demeanor and the slow leaking in of emotion.

He was just finding this crap out.

Christ.

He had to feel like he'd been hit by a train.

Harry asked Riggs's question when he said, "Why do you think Lincoln didn't tell you about Sharon?"

"At first, because I was only seventeen," Tru answered readily. "Then, I was in college, grad school, residency. Frankly, sheriff, Linc loved me, and his son took my mom and dad. Jeff had already fucked up my life. It was a lot, and all of this is a whole lot more, specifically, Jeff being weak enough to fall for her crap. So I don't think he wanted dealing with Jeff fucking up my entire future."

Lincoln Whitaker was clearly a solid guy.

Tru was still talking.

"Now, Jeff's freaked that he's finally going to have to face up to what he did to our family, and he's freaked Sharon is going to throw him under the bus. And mark my words, she will. So, now, he lays this quagmire on Kennedy and me, asking us to help him out. Consequently, Kennedy is also freaked. Though, I don't think she's too broken up about Jeff. She's pissed as hell he's *still* been hanging with Sharon, when, after we lost Lincoln, he promised her he'd ceased all communication with her."

"Why didn't your uncle deal with his estate appropriately?" Harry asked another question Riggs wanted to know.

"Honestly?" Tru asked in return.

Harry nodded.

"I don't know," Tru said. "It's been a total headache. I'm done with it. When he came to visit me after getting out of prison, he was all about us getting back to the lake. Pulling together the pieces of our family. Seeing to Jeff. Helping him heal. Like I had a lot of interest in doing that, which I didn't. But I had interest in helping Lincoln pick up the threads of his life, and I was all in to do *that*. And if part of it was dealing with Jeff, okay. Linc was the only parent I had left, so I loved him enough, if that was what he needed, I was there. So when I got the call the day after he left me, telling me that he'd committed suicide, I was heartsore, sick with it, but also, I was utterly staggered."

Harry didn't give anything to that, like the fact that there was a reason to be surprised, seeing as his uncle might have been killed.

But at least that was an explanation of why the estate was a mess.

As far as Lincoln was concerned, he'd given instructions as to how to use the money on the kids while he was in prison.

Then, he was out, and since he was alive, and fresh from doing time for a crime he didn't commit, he was intent on dealing with other things. Not seeing immediately to his estate, when he was only fifty years old, he thought he had a lot of life left to live.

Harry moved them in a different direction.

"Do you know what they were looking for at the lake?"

For the first time, straight out, the guy showed his feelings.

He smiled, huge, and said, "Yeah. That was something Lincoln did tell me."

"And it is?" Harry prompted.

"Lincoln didn't write the books after the first three, but he worked closely with Dad, and bottom line, he was still a thriller writer. And I know this was to get back at Sharon. So, when she visited him in jail, he told her he printed out Dad's last manuscript after she'd left, deleted the digital files, took the pages and some contracts he told her he'd persuaded Dad to sign, which sold the movie rights to the next six books in Dad's flagship series, put them in a lockbox and buried them somewhere by the lake before he called the cops."

"Why would he bury those things?" Harry inquired.

"He didn't," Tru declared. "There wasn't a last manuscript, and there wasn't a contract. Lincoln had given up on talking Dad into selling more, because the attention made Dad uncomfortable, and Lincoln felt that, *literally*. But Sharon came to Dad first as a huge fan. The main character of the books has an identical twin, no surprise, and I think in her twisted head, she thought Dad was Lucas Washington. And if there's a missing Roosevelt Lincoln book, it'd be worth a lot of money. And if there was a contract for film rights, that'd be worth a lot more. And those were what I figure Jeff was after. And for his part, he couldn't have any of the rest of us knowing until he figured out how to cut everyone else out and get a lock on my father's estate."

Fucking pissant.

"But Sharon would *kill* to read that manuscript," Tru went on. "Which makes it even more insane she machinated the author's death. Because she could have had a lot more. But Lincoln knew that it would drive her even crazier than she already was, the idea there was a Lucas Washington story she hadn't read yet. And if there were more movies, she'd have even more Lucas Washington."

At least Lincoln got a little of his back, sending her on a fifteen-year quest to find nothing.

"However, saying that," Tru carried on, "I can't imagine he had any idea that she'd spend fifteen years doing what she did. I know in my soul, he did it just to fuck with her. In the end, she had a hand in taking precious things from him, and as a father who loved his son, a husband who adored his wife, and a devoted brother, he had no choice but to do what he did. That was his only way to take something precious from her."

Tru turned to Riggs.

"And he'd be gutted to think anyone shattered the peace on that lake where we were all so happy. The only place we could be a family as we truly were. Absolutely gutted that the people who came after us weren't as happy as we were."

"We're happy, Tru. Sharon and your brother were just occasional pains in our asses," Riggs assured him.

That urged another smile to the surface from Tru.

"I'm going to have to speak to your brother about the murders, Tru," Harry warned.

Tru turned back to Harry.

"Not that I have a say, but I'm good with that. Lincoln's name needs to be cleared. I know what you videotaping me means, and I'm fine to go on the record with all of this. I shouldn't speak for her, but my guess at this juncture, Kennedy will be too," Tru told him.

"This will mean your family will have deeper scrutiny," Harry warned.

"Sheriff, I've spent the entire thirty-three years of my life hiding the fact I'm Roosevelt Whitaker's child. My father was a good man. He was a good dad. He loved me deeply, and he didn't hide it. He taught me to be all the good things I am. I owe him everything. I miss him every day. People with small minds who do not know my family will think whatever they like. I can *finally* claim my dad. So bring it on."

Right, then.

There it was.

Riggs liked this guy.

FORTY-ONE

Something The Cat Dragged In

Riggs

A little after eight in the morning, Riggs turned into his lane.

Last night, he'd had about fifteen minutes to bring Gia back to the house and show Nadia and Ledger he was all right before he needed to head to the station to give his statement.

But while he was gone, Nadia had texted him to suggest he allow Ledger to stay home from school that day, and he agreed. So he'd called the school and texted Angelica to let her know everything was all right, and that Ledger was taking the day off. If she needed to know why, he'd call and explain later.

Which meant, as he came to a stop in the drive, the door immediately opened and Gia galloped out toward his truck, with Ledger following right after.

He'd jumped down from his truck, slammed the door, got a hand on Gia, but then had to brace as Ledger hit him like a rocket.

Riggs gave his son a hug, and Ledger tipped his head back.

"Told you, you and Gia would never let anything happen to us," he declared.

Christ, he loved his kid.

Riggs kept him held tight to his side as he walked to the front deck where Nadia was standing.

Ledger and Gia squeezed around her, but Riggs took her in his arms, gave her a tight hug, got one in return, and he kissed the side of her head.

After that, they went in.

"Hungry?" she asked.

He was…and beat. He needed sleep.

"Yeah," he told her.

"Eggs or pancakes, or something else?" she inquired.

"Whatever, honey," he muttered, taking a stool at the kitchen.

Ledger climbed up on the one beside him.

Gia slid onto her belly at his feet.

"Eggs, they're fastest," Nadia mumbled.

She set a cup of coffee in front of him before she got to work.

He took a sip, then aimed his eyes to his boy.

Ledger knew exactly what he was asking without verbally asking.

"Okay, Dad, so you were right. All the stuff going down, I was worried."

Nadia's hands stilled in putting the egg carton on the counter, but she got back to it when Riggs urged, "Hit me."

Ledger gave it to him.

"Since you said it might be dangerous, I haven't been able to sleep real good," he admitted.

Riggs took another sip of coffee before he prompted, "Go on."

"And remember when we were camping last summer, the day before we were going to go horseback riding, and I was all jazzed?" Ledger didn't give him time to answer, he kept talking, "And we were sleeping outside. And I couldn't get to sleep. You told me to count the stars, and it'd make me sleepy. So I did, and I fell right asleep."

Riggs nodded. "I remember."

"So when I couldn't sleep, and reading wasn't making me sleepy, I got out of bed to look at the stars, start counting them, and I'd get sleepy and then go back to bed. That worked the first few nights.

But last night, before I even looked at the stars, I saw the lights by the lake, so I went to get you."

It made sense.

And it seemed Ledger understood why Riggs had been worried that same thing would happen if he stayed with them.

But Ledge seeing those lights meant they caught those fuckers, so it sucked his boy had to feel that for a few days, but it was all good in the end.

Therefore, he didn't say another word.

"You look tired, Dad," Ledger noted, studying him closely.

"I'm wiped," Riggs muttered his admission, and Nadia's hands stilled in beating the eggs, then got back to it, double time.

His lips twitched.

"You should take a nap," Ledger advised.

"You sleep after I took off?" Riggs asked.

Ledge shook his head.

Riggs turned his attention to Nadia.

She shook her head too.

"We should all take naps," Riggs decreed.

"No way!" Ledger cried. "I have a full day off school. I'm not gonna sleep it away."

Riggs sighed.

"Ledger and I can find something to do," Nadia said from where she was now, across the kitchen, dropping bread into the toaster. "You eat breakfast and hit the sack."

He'd rather sleep with her, but Riggs nodded.

He was halfway through his eggs and toast when there was a knock on the door, right before it opened.

His mom came in.

"Polly?" Riggs guessed at who told her, this being why she wasn't at work, but right there.

"I don't divulge my sources," his mother replied.

It was Polly.

She came in, set aside her purse, kissed his cheek and then gave his son a hug where he sat and kissed the top of his head.

"Coffee, Gail?" Nadia offered.

"Love a cup, darlin'," his mom accepted.

Riggs ate.

When he was done, his mother noted, "You look like something the cat dragged in."

"Thanks, I was goin' for that," Riggs joked.

"Go to bed," his mother ordered, and swept Nadia in that with a swing of her gaze, smart enough not to tell a woman she looked the same way Riggs did, which Nadia did. Exhausted. His mom then looked down to Ledger. "We're taking the boat out."

"All right!" Ledger cried, throwing his hands up.

Riggs needed no more encouragement.

He shot his mom a grateful smile, got up, hooked Nadia around the waist, then hustled her to the stairs, and up two flights of them.

His bed was made, something Nadia did every day when she was with him.

He hit it with a knee, taking her along for the ride, then hit the pillows, pulling her seriously belatedly back into their spoon.

"You're gonna have to tell me everything," she warned.

He heard the motor on his boat fire up outside.

"I will," he muttered, tucked her closer…

And then he was out.

THAT NIGHT, Riggs walked down the stairs after putting Ledger to bed. His boy had fallen asleep between them while they were watching TV, and he'd done this two hours before his bedtime.

Riggs had started to carry him up, but like a determined sleepwalker, Ledge had kinda woken and demanded to be put down. Still in hilarious sleepwalking mode, he'd gone through the motions of getting his pajamas on and making a pass at cleaning his teeth before he fell dead into bed.

Riggs pulled the covers up and tucked him in. Gia settled with a groan at the side of the bed, Riggs gave her a pat on her head, turned out the lights, and now he and Nadia could properly celebrate it was over.

But when he got downstairs, he saw the show they were

watching was paused, she was stretched out on the couch, had her phone to her ear, and she was saying, "You were almost totally right, Maribeth. It was the assistant!"

After they woke from their naps, he'd filled her in.

Considering they were clearly going to celebrate later, Riggs changed trajectories to go get a beer.

He was uncapping it when his phone rang.

He pulled it out and looked at the screen.

He took the call, "Hey, Harry," then sucked back some beer.

"FYI, brother. Got word. Considering recent developments, Seattle PD is reopening the file on Lincoln Whitaker's supposed suicide."

Standing in his kitchen, hearing that, Doc Riggs smiled a very slow smile.

FORTY-TWO

Aftershocks

Nadia

The cracking of the Mystery of the Hauntings by the Lake didn't end with a whimper.

It exploded in a variety of bangs.

THE PEOPLE of Misted Pines were now dab hands at the media descending when a high-profile case sprung up in their illusory, quiet and charming (but still quaint) small town.

Though, Kimmy told me, even with me being who I was and a minor player in all of this, it didn't garner near as much as the Ray Andrews and Crystal Killer cases. Maybe because Delphine Larue was a bigger name than mine (she'd been involved in the Ray Andrews nightmare). Maybe because people were experiencing Misted Pines fatigue. Maybe because, even if the outing of Roosevelt, Lincoln and Sarah Whitaker's unconventional way of life could be salacious, in the end, the cases were old, the population was growing more and more cynical with decades of the constant barrage of a news cycle…

And fortunately, much bigger celebrities were embroiled in a bitter, ugly divorce that was hogging the national limelight and lighting TikTok up with a salvo of new content.

Even so, what happened that night at the stables wasn't going to fade easy in a starry, mountain night.

Not even close.

It, and what happened after it, was going to cause loads more drama, and trauma, and get *way* more interesting.

IT BEGINS HERE...

UNSURPRISINGLY, Jefferson Whitaker immediately started pointing a finger right at Sharon Swindell.

At first, she didn't speak a word.

But Jeff had a lot to say.

The first twist was, he claimed he did not shoot his uncle and mother.

No.

He shared in the statement he made to the police that they weren't shot at all.

Instead, Sharon had drugged them (something which would be easy for her to do, since she stocked Roosevelt's larder, doing this also when Sarah was around), then she dragged them to the stables, and it was she who lit the fire in order for them to expire in it.

She'd then covered Jefferson in blood and gave him the shotgun, knowing the fire would bring Lincoln running.

Jeff admitted to being there and doing what she ordered, saying this was both because she'd convinced him of terrible things about his family and he was terrified of her.

What she ordered was for him to let the horses out and make sure they ran away.

Other than that, he had nothing to do with it.

Sadly, the investigation of the situation was woefully mishandled. They had no traces of the blood she allegedly drenched him with to test. The scene had not been properly examined. And although the bodies had been examined, they were burned so badly, the coroner couldn't report if they'd sustained gunshot wounds or had been drugged or had died prior to being burned to ash.

More metal detectors had been dispatched, and the area was swept, but they found no evidence of spent shells or shot.

That said, fifteen years had transpired, so this could have been washed away by rain or melting snow or scattered by animals.

Or Jeff had had plenty of time, not to mention he'd revisited the area frequently—and he'd put no small amount of effort into successfully keeping it vacant of anyone who could see him doing it —in order to pick up after himself.

A jury would have to decide.

THE NEXT TWIST WAS, even if they didn't have this evidence, they did have the shotgun.

And when Harry pulled it from the evidence locker, he found almost immediately that Lincoln had turned over a weapon with the double barrel fully loaded.

This definitely gave credence to Jefferson's claims that the gun had never been fired, and Sharon had made a mistake in first, not firing it, or second, at least not unloading it before she handed it to Jeff. Because who would reload a weapon after they used it, supposedly successfully, and before they turned it over to the police as the apparent murder weapon?

And it showed even more how shoddy the policework had been around the case, because all you had to do was cock the barrel open to see this, and then a lot of questions would, and should have been asked and answered.

Maybe saving a man's life.

SHARON REMAINED SILENT, and in the end, Harry was forced to charge Jeff solely with criminal trespass and criminal malice.

Jeff pled guilty to these, admitting that yes, he and Sharon had spent years doing a number of things to keep people away from that lake and looking for the "lost manuscript" (the fake existence of it something Jeff's father had shared with Tru, but not with Jeff, though perhaps it was understandable he hadn't because he thought Jeff was fragile about Sharon).

Though, Jefferson agreed to this in a deal he'd made where he would also testify against Sharon.

SHARON TOOK IT TO TRIAL, and Maribeth (obviously) had to take time off work to come to MP so she could go with me every day to watch it unfold.

And this was something my bestie did.

AT FIRST, Sharon, who was rather attractive in a tough-nut sort of way, seemed calm and docile.

I could see that.

The case was old. They had a confession from a man who was now dead, so he couldn't speak. Without a murmur of dissent, someone had served seven years of his life for the crime. And the investigation had been bungled, so they didn't even have circumstantial evidence against her, barring the shotgun (though, that was pretty damning).

On top of that, she could ride the wave of a jury who might find the way of life of the Whitakers distasteful.

However, she wasn't counting on the Whitaker family having very good friends, quite a number of them, all of them very keen to speak on behalf of the dearly departed—in fact, they'd been waiting years to have the opportunity—and at least two children who loved their parents unconditionally.

As testimony unfolded about what a happy family they were, how deeply the parents loved their children, and yes, each other, along with how creepy folks thought Sharon was, not to mention Lincoln being clear in his concerns about Sharon—and not in a hearsay way, some of them had text messages they'd saved all these years for this eventuality—things took a dramatic turn.

That turn was cataclysmic for Sharon after Truman and Kennedy took the stand.

Truman was forthright, believable, and when his emotion came, it was openly genuine and utterly gutting.

Kennedy, on the other hand, was a mess. But that wasn't surprising. It too was clearly genuine, and you'd have to be dead for your heart not to go out to her at the family she loved being torn apart in that manner.

Jefferson was supposed to be the prosecution's ace in the hole. However, it wouldn't turn out that way.

Sure, he painted a picture of emotional terrorism that was diabolical and chilling. He testified as well to their happy family life, and even shared guilt that he let the things she said penetrate.

But he gave off the vibe of a thirty-year-old punk-ass kid who looked back at appalling actions that were the work of psychological control with more of an air of being pissed he had to deal with this situation, than taking any responsibility for his part in it.

The only reason this didn't work in Sharon's favor was that she was seeing where this was all leading. And instead of keeping a brave face, or entering into plea negotiations with the prosecution, she suddenly started acting out in what could only be an attempt to set up an appeal on the basis of mental incapacity.

And she did this, terribly unwisely, starting with Truman and Kennedy, both sympathetic witnesses.

She interrupted them, shouting things like, "You know your father loved me!" She would dissolve into loud wails. And once, she melted off her chair in a dead faint.

The judge cautioned her several times, and when she banged repeatedly on the defense table and chanted, "Liar, liar, liar," at one point during Jefferson's testimony, the judge paused proceedings for the afternoon to get her attorney to calm her down. He did this warning, if it happened again, she'd be charged with contempt of court.

No more outbursts happened after that, but she made faces,

made a show of scribbling on a legal pad obsessively, and often whispered loudly in her (very beleaguered, I should say) lawyer's ear.

The defense called both Sarah's parents and sister to the stand, as well as Lincoln and Roosevelt's parents.

Finally, the defense had the opportunity to put to the jury how bizarre and "despicable" the Whitaker's way of life was and give the jury something to think on regarding Lincoln's alleged jealousy.

It was a fatal mistake.

First, the jury had already heard about how this was untrue from plenty of others, all of whom were much more earnest and credible witnesses who knew and loved the family.

Second, the prosecution managed to get the litigation about the estate entered into evidence, and as such, when he had his shot at them, he made mincemeat of all five of them (particularly Sarah's parents, who eventually came off as nothing short of religious zealots).

Sharon was the final one to take the stand in her own defense, and it was another mistake because her lawyer couldn't hide how dead set he was against it, not to mention she was again histrionic. She tried to convince them she wasn't there that night. Instead, a fourteen-year-old boy, with no motive to do so, killed his mom and uncle, and talked his father into confessing to the crime.

This last sounded absurd, and the way she related it made it seem even more so.

And why she deviated from the Lincoln Did It Theory, which was firmly established by Lincoln himself, and instead went after Jeff, was anyone's guess. Although it did make her look like she had it out for Jeff, which was precisely what she should have avoided.

While she was testifying, it was openly apparent no one in that courtroom believed a word she said, not the spectators, and worse for her, not the jury.

Jefferson had been a punk-ass, but he didn't seem like it was that bad he'd kill two members of his family, especially when he had zero motive to do so. And the only times there seemed honest remorse and discomfort were when he had to directly discuss anything about the murders or his dad.

Upon copious discussion, and Riggs supplying us with cocktails during it, Maribeth and I decided the true Sharon came out in her behavior and testimony, but she wasn't crazy. You couldn't be if you did the things you did in a calculated manner.

The prosecution summed up shrewdly, painting a horrific picture, shying away from the obsessive fan stuff and the part Sharon crafted that Jefferson played, and leaning into a woman spurned who then took her revenge on an, albeit alternative, but exceptionally happy family.

The defense, going in with all the cards, in the end, was forced to try to guide the jury into believing the word of a single woman, the defendant, who had acted bizarrely in the extreme during the trial, when she simply said she wasn't there. But she had no alibi for the time it happened, though she did have multiple people who testified she had means, access and motive.

Sharon might be able to lean on her behavior in court in future appeals, but it backfired in the present.

The jury was out for two and a half hours, and Maribeth and I thought that length of time mostly had to do with Jefferson being an obviously spoiled brat.

They came back with a guilty verdict.

She was given two life sentences, to be served concurrently, with the possibility of parole.

This meant she could be out in twenty years.

And Maribeth and I figured the apparent leniency of that sentence was because of Jeff too.

AS AN ASIDE, Maribeth told me it was the best vacation she'd ever had in her life.

THINGS WENT FAR WORSE for Sharon Swindell in Seattle, however.

I didn't attend that hearing, except for one day, when Riggs was forced to go with me. But Harry did, and he gave Riggs and me the full skinny of what we missed.

THIS DETECTIVE, uneasy for years about this case (and on top of that being a big thriller reader, and Roosevelt Lincoln was one of his many faves), went after it like a mad dog.

Therefore, he uncovered a bartender at Lincoln's hotel who had witnessed Lincoln and Sharon arguing at the bar the evening Lincoln supposedly committed suicide. The bartender remembered it because he recognized Lincoln after the big brouhaha of his arrest and confession, and because they were having said argument, which he described as extremely heated on Sharon's part, but Lincoln appeared quite calm.

Though, he had to admit he didn't see Sharon slip anything in Lincoln's drink. However, he hadn't been watching them the whole time because he was at work and had a job to do.

Further damning was the investigator tracked down a hotel employee who saw Sharon come out of the elevator later that night. She remembered this because Sharon seemed mildly disheveled, which was odd, because it was a very nice hotel, so it caught her attention.

It kept her attention when, halfway across the lobby, Sharon started laughing rather maniacally—at nothing—and that stuck in the employee's brain, because she thought it was super weird.

The hotel had no record of Sharon being a guest, ever. And Sharon could not produce evidence that she was there to visit someone she knew. So she had no reason to use the elevators at all, as the bar was on the lobby level.

She just said she wasn't there, but was in Misted Pines, home alone with her dogs, which wasn't a stellar alibi, especially when two people who didn't know her, and had no motive to lie, pointed her out in the courtroom with no hesitation.

But the smoking gun was that a friend of Sharon's had come forward to admit she'd procured a bottle of arsenic at Sharon's request. Sharon had told her she'd been having issues with mice and rats getting in her house, and she needed it to poison them.

This, even though rat poison, which was not arsenic, was easy to find.

This friend further admitted that she wondered for years, not only because Sharon could have gotten her hands on what she needed herself, but especially after Lincoln died in that manner, and she knew Sharon had "a serious thing against Lincoln."

She just couldn't believe her friend would do something like that. And Sharon, at the time, had been significantly distressed and was behaving in an agitated manner, because Lincoln had been released. Therefore, her friend felt Sharon might not have the wherewithal to follow through with an easy errand. Not to mention, she'd been complaining about having trouble with rodents for weeks.

Though, what she could do was identify from pictures the bottle discovered at the scene as being the one she procured.

Truman, Kennedy and Jefferson all testified at that trial as well, reiterating their alibis and the nature of their visits with Lincoln prior to his death. Jefferson adding that his dad had taken him aside and shared that he was going to work with him to help him deal psychologically with what had happened at the lake.

They explained Lincoln seemed sad, and tired, but not morose, and he definitely had plans for his and their family's future.

And they were all firm in relating that he did not seem to be a man who was about to take his own life, and that they had all retained open communication with him and visited him as often as they could in prison. Though all of this, he'd never given indication this was at hand.

At this juncture, it was almost cruel how deep a pile Sharon was under (though, not cruel to her, because she was a snake), when the prosecution produced Kennedy's ex-boyfriend, who Kennedy was living with at the time.

He testified that he'd been home the night of Lincoln's demise, when Jefferson had arrived to have dinner with his sister, because they were going to talk about Lincoln's visit and the possibility of returning to the lake with him. The boyfriend had eaten dinner with them, hearing this discussion, and testifying that both of them intended to make arrangements to go back to the lake to spend time reconnecting with Lincoln. He left to have drinks with his buddies, because one of them had been promoted, but when he got back a little over an hour later, Jefferson was still there.

And where they lived, neither Kennedy nor Jefferson could have gotten to the hotel, forced arsenic down Lincoln's throat, and gotten home in time.

Adding insult to injury for Sharon, the prosecutors then called on a woman from Misted Pines who shared she'd not only been retained by Lincoln, but she had also gone to both the big house and the cabin to clean them, as well as stock the big house with food. And the day of his death, Lincoln had arranged payment for her efforts.

He requested this of her because, Lincoln told her, he intended to arrive the next day, and he'd shared, due to his big grocery order, the children would be coming that very weekend.

Not incidentally, she, too, had made it clear she'd been astounded to learn he'd committed suicide. So astounded, she reported her concerns to the local sheriff, but when nothing came of it, she just figured she was wrong.

Information and photographs from the hotel and the autopsy were presented, showing that the bruising around Lincoln's jaw was consistent with not only the size of the pads of Sharon's fingers, but the spread of her hand and where those pads would rest on a man's jaw (this was rebutted, rather well, because it was weak, but the damage had been done).

And an expert testified to what arsenic poisoning would do to a body, and the peaceful manner in which Lincoln had been arranged was not at all indicative of how a body would be found after dying from taking that poison (this was rebutted, poorly, and possibly hurt an already crumbling defense).

And to the vehement objections of said defense, the prosecution was able to enter into evidence Sharon's activities at the lake when Riggs caught her.

This evidence was provided by Riggs and Bubbles, and even Bubbles, who for some reason dressed all in black—black suit, shirt and tie—and thus it made him look like a member of the mob or an unimaginatively dressed bouncer, delivered damning testimony. Because by that time, Sharon would have no reason ever to be at that lake, definitely not swinging around a metal detector at three in the morning.

Truman surmised in his testimony, and the prosecution bore down on it in their summation, that Sharon had arrived at the hotel to demand to know the whereabouts of the last manuscript, and Lincoln may have taunted her with it, but he didn't give that information to her even after she drugged him, so she killed him out of obsessive-fan fury.

Sharon had different attorneys during this trial, and she'd either learned to keep her mouth shut and her dramatics under wraps, or her attorney had her on a tight leash, because she sat stoic throughout the proceedings.

It didn't matter.

This time, it took only thirty minutes of deliberation for the jury to reach their guilty verdict.

For the murder of Lincoln Whitaker, Sharon Swindell was sentenced to life, without the possibility of parole.

I HAD TO ADMIT, I had my doubts about Jefferson.

I believed he was manipulated by Sharon, but it was hard to wrap my head around the idea that Lincoln would be so distraught, he wouldn't question Sharon's narrative that night. Of course, the situation was heartbreaking, and on the surface, dire. But to serve seven years in prison when Jefferson hadn't even shot them? And Jefferson not only not telling his father that, but waiting a further eight years and some change to tell anyone he didn't do such a thing?

I didn't know.

And I'd never really know.

But the next twist pushed me to lean the other way.

. . .

THIS WAS THAT, from prison, Sharon wrote an identical letter to Dave and Brenda, and Riggs, begging, if we found that manuscript, we'd let her read it.

And by now, it had been testified about frequently in her presence that such a thing didn't exist.

So, frankly, that was totally unhinged.

Riggs, Dave and Brenda gave the letters to Harry.

And I decided it was likely Jefferson Whitaker was a spoiled brat, but he was also controlled by, and perhaps even terrified of, Sharon Swindell.

At least he'd been when he was fourteen.

And Roosevelt, Sarah and Lincoln paid the price.

But in the end, for Jeff, it was all about getting his hands on that contract and the manuscript.

Which truly was a great "fuck you" to Sharon that lasted a long time, was still messing with her head in a way that it seemed it would for the rest of her life, and eventually, it brought her to justice.

But it also ultimately led, through no fault of his own, to Lincoln's demise.

THIS COULD MEAN that there was a possibility that Roosevelt and Sarah had been alive when they'd been taken to the stables that night and had died in the fire.

To that, all I would allow myself to think was that they had to be completely unconscious and didn't know what was happening to them.

The alternative didn't bear contemplating.

But at least, in the end, they were together.

There was a crucial link missing, and he'd go through hell and have to live seven years without either of them.

But he lived those years doing his utmost to take care of the thing they all held most dear.

Their family.

THE THREE WHITAKER children banded together after all of this and beat back their challengers on all the claims on the estate.

A judge awarded what was left of it to the children, as well as anything that came from it in future royalties, not to mention, they now held the rights to sell for television or movies.

The estate was distributed equally between all three.

The Whitakers tried to make amends to their grandchildren after that, as did their Aunt Mary.

Word reached us, they were having none of it.

Word also reached us, they'd been approached for the rights by several producers.

It was said, the youngest two now looked to Truman to guide the way, and his guidance was that their family had had enough.

So far, they'd declined all offers.

I heard Sarah's folks were interviewed on some religious channel about what to do if your child was taken into the devil's thrall.

I never saw it.

And I had no interest in ever seeing it.

THE PROPERTIES BEING in Sarah's names alone, properties that, regardless that he'd supposedly killed her, Lincoln inherited on her death (and no one, not even Sarah's parents, had contested that in seven years, for unknown reasons), obviously, were bundled in the estate.

This was one of the outstanding questions no one had answered, and I had to know.

Therefore, Riggs mentioned the change to the trust to Harry, Harry had asked Tru about it, and seeing as he'd only been around fifteen at the time, he told Harry he had no idea why his parents did that.

So that would remain a mystery.

. . .

SADLY, the bungling of the Whitaker murders turned the spotlight on Harry and the sheriff's office.

Fortunately, Harry already knew this would happen, and at a town council meeting that was growing contentious, Megan, the president of the council (a ballbuster, no-nonsense blonde who was a good friend of Delphine's, and would become one of mine too) let Harry have her microphone.

With only Rus standing behind him, Harry explained how the department was already deep into an audit, they'd identified five cases that bore more scrutiny, and was continuing its search.

No, he would not say which cases they were at this juncture.

But yes, if it was discovered they required further investigation, an announcement would be made, but, Harry warned, they couldn't comment much on active investigations.

After a lot of gavel pounding from Megan, this announcement eventually calmed the citizenry and left them with new mysteries to chew on.

Which, I'd noted, was exactly as Misted Pines liked it.

Only Murders in the Building, indeed.

IN THE MEANTIME, Evan Pugh and his parents came to visit Riggs and me.

My heart went out to the guy. He clearly felt terrible about what he'd done at the cabin.

Riggs had the same reaction, I knew, when he asked them to stay for a slice of his mom's leftover lemon cake.

They accepted.

ON THE OTHER HAND, and in another twist, we were all at the Double D for dinner one night when I met Casey Grimes.

Bryce was with him.

Casey immediately got in Riggs's face with his threats about a civil suit.

I could see Riggs wasn't taking this well, didn't like his woman's and son's dinners interrupted with this guy's shit, and he was about to slide out of the booth, and I was trying to figure out how to handle that, when Bryce approached his dad, tugged hard on his sleeve and snapped, "God, Dad, why do you always have to be such *a jerk?*"

I feared Casey's head would explode when this came from his son, and I didn't want it in my onion-less patty melt.

But before it could, Bryce looked at me.

"I was a dick. It was uncool. Everyone at school thinks I'm a jackoff. But that's not the only reason I'm sorry." He then mumbled, "Sucks you lost your mom."

With that, he shuffled out of the diner, leaving his father fuming.

He didn't fume in our presence for long.

He took off after his son.

So that was that.

And no case was pending.

ON THE MONDAY after all our troubles were over, Angelica signed over custody of Ledger and Viggo to Riggs and Storm.

She then carried through with her every-other-weekend visits with them for precisely a month before she moved to Spokane.

This might have to do with the fact she'd become a pariah in Misted Pines. But call me cynical, I thought it had more to do with her being outed, so there wasn't a man in the entire county who would touch her.

She called Ledger on occasion and came to MP a few times to see him and his brother, but mostly, she was as she had been when she was around.

Absent.

Ledger honestly didn't seem to mind. He seemed relieved. And since Riggs and Storm made sure the brothers had time together (and Viggo was *a doll*, a total Storm-mini-me, like Ledger was with his dad, including his stormy-colored eyes), it seemed all good for Ledger.

But we were keeping an eye.

. . .

MY THEORY about Angelica proved true when, not four months in Spokane, she phoned Ledger and gave him the "happy" news he was going to have a little baby brother or sister.

Not only that, she was getting married to a real estate agent future daddy who was apparently a big deal in that city.

So, I guessed, the third time was a charm for Angelica.

HAVING BROKEN THE SEAL, I spent a lot of time with my journals, either on the front or back porches of the cabin, on the pier, in the hammock, in the cabin, or out in the workshop with Riggs.

There was a lot to put down about him and Ledger, Angelica, Storm and Viggo, the Whitaker tragedy, my life in Misted Pines.

But eventually, I got around to pouring into it my thoughts and emotions about what happened to Mom, as well as how I felt about her.

And the man who sired me.

This wasn't easy.

Sometimes, I'd have to put my journal aside and race down the trail to find Riggs, throw myself in his arms, and burst into tears, whereupon he'd hold me and murmur to me and be there until I was all right.

Sometimes, I'd just have to put it aside and cross the workshop to him.

So, yes.

Misted Pines, in the end, gave me the space to face all of that, and even though I'd never come to terms with it, it also gave me Riggs, Ledger, Gail and a big, wide family.

So I could live with it.

If not peacefully, the life I was living that it was a part of was happy.

. . .

RIGGS GOT his commission done just under the wire, working at it sometimes until dinner, then going back to it after.

My heart melted when he told me why he was going to install the first arbor on his property.

He did that at the trailhead to the cabin from the house.

He then called Harry and asked him to contact Truman and Kennedy in order to ascertain what their mom's favorite color rose was.

They told him it was peach.

So he planted two rose bushes of that color at the base of each side of the arbor, where they would grow and intertwine with the beauty Riggs had crafted out of iron.

It was perfect to denote the beginning of the path Sarah would take to lead her to Roosevelt, and the end of it when she went to Lincoln.

And the route Riggs had taken to guide him to me.

IT WAS NOT LOST on me that much (though not all) of Riggs's genius was tied up in his art.

Simply put, what he crafted in that workshop was extraordinary.

He was far from stupid, obviously, so he knew that too.

He probably also knew that it could be shown in galleries and might earn him something more than money.

But he was like Roosevelt. He loved creating it, but beyond that, he had little interest.

Though, he was also like Lincoln, because he made sure, with everything he made, he got paid.

AS FOR RIGGS, Ledger, Gia and me, I put my foot down about things steadying, so now we had the time to take, in order to ease Ledger into his dad's new relationship.

Throughout the summer, and into early autumn, Gia and I spent three to four nights a week at the cabin, giving Riggs and his boy father-and-son time.

This ended the night we threw a big party to celebrate his crew getting back from a job (Riggs held true to his word, promoted Easton, and during the first job, drove the two hours to oversee things four times, but the ones after, how often he would check in could be as little as once), as well as Riggs finishing the massive deck he'd built on the lakeside of the house.

The deck was pure Riggs, dark wood and logs with some stout branches and interesting wrought iron. It fit the house perfectly, and it had an amazing view.

You could also see the cabin from it.

He'd managed to do that and everything else because Harry, Cade, Jess, Jace, Rus, Jaeger, Easton and Storm often came out to help.

And yes, Bubbles.

That man tried hard with me, I just wasn't there yet.

It didn't stop him trying.

And it was annoying, because just that fact alone made him a loveable guy.

Maybe I'd get there one day, but Riggs was already moving on, so I wasn't a complete bitch to Bubbles (though, Riggs thought it was hilarious how I held on to a grudge, and I supposed that was good, considering other men would find that terrifying).

This party was louder and far rowdier than the first I attended, but I knew nearly everyone, so even though it really wasn't my scene, and I much preferred the quieter variety, I had fun.

I definitely got tipsy, and Riggs had more than a few, so we left everyone else outside so we could hit his bed and get busy.

We got so busy, the ruckus outside had grown quiet by the time I was fucked out, but before I passed out, Riggs slid something on my left ring finger.

He said not a word when he did it.

I pried open my eyes and stared at the humongous simple solitaire diamond protruding obnoxiously (not complaining...*at all*) from a slim platinum band.

I then looked at him and asked, "Seriously?"

He grinned.

I kissed him as an unspoken answer to his unspoken question. And passed out mid-kiss.

AFTER A CHAT WITH LEDGER, I moved into the big house the next day.

OBVIOUSLY, Misted Pines was my future.

And when the word hit the ears of Trevor's parents, they called me out of the blue and asked if they could come for a visit. I knew it would hurt them, but I also knew it might help them do what I was trying to do after I lost mom.

Learn to live with a terrible loss, and see that life carried on.

They came and met Riggs, who they obviously liked, and Ledger, who cut them to the quick, but they loved.

Then they left.

And after that, I never got more than birthday or Christmas cards from them.

That hurt.

But I loved them, and I got it.

So I gave it to them.

A MONTH after I moved in officially with Riggs and Ledger, we closed on buying the cabin.

Dave drove a hard bargain, and we paid four times what he bought it for four years previously.

I didn't care.

I had my she shed.

And my family owned our whole lake.

Epilogue

FALLING PETALS

Nadia

After I watered the pots of flowers all around, I wound the garden hose around its holder on the side of the cabin, then walked in my now not-as-velvety-gorgeous Birks to the trail.

I wasn't even close to the big house when I saw all the activity.

The white chairs being set out in rows. The thick swags made of deep red and orange roses being hung from the railings of our deck. More being draped around the large white tent that had been erected on the other side of the drive.

I was glad I didn't have to do all that work.

And I was thrilled the weather was going to cooperate.

I walked under the arbor, which, with Brenda's assistance, since they were planted last year, I had managed to coax the peach roses to grow, and we trained them around Rigg's delicate scrollwork, so now they were nearly up to the curves of the arch.

And they were blooming profusely.

I was inside, had flipped off my Birks, and was at the kitchen sink washing my hands when Riggs walked in.

I dried my hands and called, "Hey, baby."

He didn't respond, unless coming to me, fitting himself to my back and shuffling me out of the kitchen, murmuring in my ear, "Time to get ready," could be considered a response to a greeting.

It actually wasn't time. It was early.

But today was a day of romance.

So I allowed my man to take me to our bed. I also allowed him to take off my sundress and panties. And I watched as he lifted both arms to put his hands between his shoulder blades to tug off his tee.

But I helped him with his jeans.

We had time, so we took our time going over old ground that somehow always seemed new.

Riggs had a thing for getting his mouth between my legs (truth told, I had a thing for it too, and mine was a bigger one than his, I was sure).

I also had a thing for getting him in my mouth (ditto with me suspecting that was bigger for him than me).

And when we were ready, Riggs covered me, our mouths connected, our hands exploring, my legs curving around his thighs, and he slid inside me.

It was unhurried, and gentle, until Riggs slipped a hand between us, I put a hand against our headboard to hold myself steady, and it was not.

We didn't come simultaneously, but I wasn't fully down from mine before Riggs found his.

It was perfect, as ever.

And it was perfect for this day especially.

I WAS at the vanity in our massive bathroom, getting ready, and it had occurred to me before.

But that day, of all days, it hit me.

Hard.

Riggs had shared, like the rest of the house, he'd updated that bathroom, but he hadn't deviated much from the layout. He had no need for a rather dramatic vanity area where a woman could sit, do her hair and makeup, and have everything, even her jewelry, at hand (yes, it had this much storage, and the jewelry drawers had locks, so Mom's jewelry was safe).

Considering he never thought he'd find a woman to call his own, he'd shared he'd done it the way he had for resale value.

But I was thrilled he had, seeing as I could use it.

Though, it wasn't lost on me that Sarah had sat there, in a bathroom Lincoln had designed, able to pamper herself in the way both her husbands wanted her to have.

Lavishly.

Riggs walked in looking delectable in exceptionally cut, midnight-blue dress trousers and a beautifully tailored shirt that was one shade lighter, his hair drying, but still wet and curling around his ears and neck.

His eyes seemed to sparkle white gold in that shirt.

Seriously.

"Ready to be dazzled?" he asked.

I already was.

"Always."

"Strut your stuff, kid," he called.

And in came Ledger, followed by Gia and our cat, Sheba (Ledger named her, and picked her, but Gia claimed her, so Ledger had taught our dog to cart our cat around with all four of her paws dangling from the sides of Gia's thick neck, which is how Gia carted her into where we made camp when we went camping two weekends ago—my first time, also, my last (outside-bathroom-going was *not* my thing, in future that could be Riggs Boys' Time)).

Ledger then struck a variety of poses in his mini-me suit that was midnight blue, like his dad's, with a one-shade-lighter dress shirt, but he was wearing the jacket.

I slapped my hand on my chest over my robe and cried, "Be still my heart!"

"Such a goof," Ledger replied, but he was grinning ear to ear.

I stopped messing around and gave the suit a critical eye. "Fits perfectly."

"I look hot," Ledger pronounced. "But this monkey suit is *un*comfortable."

"You can take off the jacket after the ceremony," Riggs told him.

"Cool," Ledger replied.

"Now, vamoose. Nadia has to finish getting ready. She's running late." Riggs turned to me. "The guests are arriving."

"Shoot!" I exclaimed and whirled back to the vanity.

Both Riggs boys left, but one of them came to me to give me a kiss on the side of my neck before he did (just in case there were questions, it was the taller one).

I finished with my makeup and hair, then I went into the walk-in (an extraordinary room that Riggs did up big also "for resale," but Lincoln had given Sarah, even before it was the "it" thing in houses) and went to my dress.

It was a lot. Too much for an outdoors gig in the mountains.

But I was me. A city girl. And I'd learned in the past year it was amazing living in the woods by a lake, but I had to be me.

I put on my dress, my heels, then went back to my vanity to add my jewelry.

And that day, I brought Mom with me.

After that, I went down to greet the guests.

RIGGS and I were sitting beside each other on our white chairs, Ledger on my other side (Harry on his other side), when Riggs leaned into my ear and murmured, "Good I fucked you and shot a heavy load before I saw you in that dress, or we wouldn't be sitting here right now."

I turned to him, slapped his arm, and hissed under my breath, "Stop it, Riggs."

He grinned, wide, white and unrepentantly at me.

He then slung an arm, now encased in his suit jacket, around my shoulders.

I'd gone for a family matching look, so my dress was a sheer chiffon (with a matching underlay) in midnight blue, with big, yellow and red flowers and green leaves emblazoned on it. It had a long, tiered skirt that dusted the ground. It had sleeves that were straight, but from a seam around the elbows, blossomed out fuller and were gathered at the wrists. It had tiny, fabric-covered buttons from where the vee neckline plunged to my midriff down to the first tier of the skirt. But the collar had a long, wide scarf attached that I wound round and around, and tied in a big jaunty bow at the side of my neck.

I wore my hair up in a complicated twist full of curls, because… *obviously*.

The dirt and gravel weren't easy to navigate in my strappy, green, high-heeled sandals, but once I hit the floor put down in the tent, I'd be good.

Regardless of Riggs being such *a man*, I was pleased.

It looked like we three belonged together.

Because we did.

"I hope they have **PBR** in that fancy-assed tent, 'cause I don't do sissy beer."

This came at us from behind, and Riggs and I turned to look over our shoulders as Bubbles leaned toward us.

I aimed my gaze at Lucille beside him.

She rolled her eyes, appearing as she was.

Longsuffering.

"I got some in the workshop so you won't go wanting," Riggs assured him.

Bubbles adjusted his tie like he wanted to tear it off, grunted, "You da man," (yes, he actually said *you da man*) and sat back.

I shook my head at Bubbles.

He tossed his arm around Lucille and winked at me.

The congregation seemed to be stirring, so we paid attention and watched a line of men come from the back of the house and down the stairs at the side of the deck to stand in line to one side of the outside-of-the-roses-no-other-décor arbor.

The wedding procession started not long after, the women coming from the front door of the house.

Kennedy did great, until she was walking down the white sheet laid down the center aisle, and she turned and saw Harry, Ledger, Riggs and me.

It was then, she started silently crying, and when she made it to the front, her brother's concerned eyes stayed glued to her, and they were red-rimmed.

Her other brother was not there. We'd been told he'd been doing some soul-searching, and he wanted to be there, he just wasn't ready to come back to the lake (and we didn't share this, but Riggs and I weren't ready to have him there, either).

They'd been taught by their parents to love and forgive, and definitely move on, so this was understood by the other two siblings, and it had been shared with us, there were no hard feelings.

Things went on the upswing when the gorgeous bride showed her face, radiant and happy, and showed off her gown, which was amazing.

We stood as she walked to her very soon-to-be husband, her face shining, her smile bright as the sun.

Then we sat and watched Truman Whitaker marry the woman he loved surrounded by peach roses, woods and a tranquil lake.

And another happy memory was created to soak into the soil and feed the pine trees, which I could swear, rustled joyfully, stirred by a peaceful breeze, as a beaming Tru and his luminous bride hustled back up the aisle through a jubilant cheer and under a hail of gently falling peach rose petals.

The End

There will be more mysteries from Misted Pines...

Discussion/Reflection Questions

1. There are elements in all of the Misted Pines books that have a supernatural vibe, including *The Woman by the Lake*. Do you believe in the supernatural or paranormal (such as ghosts) or do you think all the strange happenings that make the hairs on the back of your neck lift can be explained away by science and nature? Or possibly a healthy imagination?

2. What are your thoughts on the lore of why Nadia's cottage had sat empty for so long? Would you have stayed after learning the story, especially after what Nadia experienced on night one?

3. What were your feelings about Roosevelt, Lincoln and Sarah's relationship? Did those feelings change after Tru explained his family dynamic?

4. As with most Kristen Ashley books, music plays a role in *The Woman by the Lake*. What does the soundtrack of your life sound like?

5. Did you figure out what was going on at the cabin and in the past before all was revealed?

THE WOMEN LEFT BEHIND

There are two dead bodies in Idaho, and the gun used to kill them has been traced back to a sixteen-year-old robbery in Misted Pines.

Sheriff Harry Moran has a broken heart and a stack of case files on his desk that the corrupt sheriff who came before him might have bungled.

Or he may have framed innocent people.

The first case Harry dives into, the woman left behind lives just a block away from his office.

When Lillian Rainier opens the door to the sheriff, Harry, who's been a dead man walking since his wife died, comes back to life.

As for Lillian, she's had a crush on Harry for forever, Harry showing at her door, and how he is when he does only makes her fall deeper.

As Harry and his team dive into these suspicious cases, Harry and Lillian have to figure out what to do with all they feel for each other, how hard it hits them, and how deep it goes.

But as a voice from the past becomes a witness in the present, and Harry and his crew dig deeper, they sense something sinister happened years ago.

As they weave together the threads of a cold case, they realize how messy it is.

Worse, the man behind the mess is desperately cleaning it up …

And no one in Misted Pines is safe.

Prologue

GUT

Harry

S hitty police work was one of the ugliest stains on society.

This was the thought Sheriff Harry Moran had as he sat in his ergonomic chair behind his desk at the sheriff's department.

He was staring at the two files in front of him trying to ignore the email that was up on the monitor of his computer.

Those files were two of fifteen stacked on his desk.

Each of those files had one thing in common: the shoddy, lazy or corrupt investigation overseen by Fret County's last sheriff, Leland Dern.

Dern was the man who came before Harry.

Which meant Harry was the man who had to clean up Dern's mess.

Due to recent circumstances—the latest being a double murder that wasn't properly investigated and an innocent man served prison time—a full and exhaustive, time-consuming and resource-heavy audit of every investigation under Dern's tenure had been done.

There were shambolic cases they'd had no choice but to file away. The police work hadn't been up to Harry's expectations of his department, but there was nothing that pointed to an injustice being done.

Now, he and his team had to go back over those fifteen cases and hope what Harry expected—Dern playing favorites, taking bribes, looking the other way or preferring to go hunting rather than working—wouldn't land them in lawsuits.

He was starting with these two.

He glanced at his monitor and felt his neck muscles tighten, which meant he again looked to the files and refocused.

They were the two cases that intrigued Harry the most, because the woman who had connections with both lived a block away from his department, only a five-minute walk from where he sat right there at his desk.

Lillian Rainier.

He'd lived in the town of Misted Pines his entire life, and because of his job, he knew or knew of a great many people in all of Fret County, and he'd never heard of her.

But Dern suspected, and investigated, her parents of a robbery sixteen years ago.

The investigation stalled, because Sonny and Avery Rainier had disappeared. And then, the case had simply died. Nothing else had been done. Not an interview, not a single follow-up of a lead.

A year later, Lillian married Willie Zowkower, a man Harry *did* know well.

Willie was a low-level gentleman dealer and a high-level charming asshole who currently had three outstanding arrest warrants in Fret County.

Recently, Willie had also disappeared.

And Lillian hadn't reported her parents, or her husband, missing.

Harry's gut was telling him something was up with Lillian Rainier.

And what was on Harry's computer monitor was telling him whatever that was, it was something bad.

So, no. His gut wasn't telling him anything. It was practically screaming at him to get off his ass, walk to her house and have a word.

Since Harry wasn't lazy, and he thought of law enforcement not as a job but as a calling, he got off his ass in order to walk to her house and have a word.

IT WOULD BE a good bet Harry had passed Lillian Rainier's house thousands of times in his life, and he never noticed it.

Standing outside it now, he wondered why.

A small cracker box painted a pale yellow with white trim, sporting a green roof and a shocking-red door, there were profuse plantings of bronze, butterscotch and yellow button mums in appealing but mismatched terracotta pots dotted up the front steps and all over porch. An attractive fall wreath of leaves, berries and pinecones was on the door. A white picket fence rounded the property, and he could see the numerous rose bushes that likely ornamented that fence in the summer had been cut back in preparation for winter.

There were two Adirondack chairs on the porch. They were painted white and had yellow, brown and green plaid lumbar pillows upstanding against the back of the seats, a wooden table with a lantern resting on top between them.

No kitschy SWEATER WEATHER! Or HAPPY FALL Y'ALL or FALL IN LOVE! signs marred the neat, well-kept property.

As he opened the gate on the fence and stepped foot on her front walk, that feeling in Harry's gut intensified.

Something was up.

Something was about to happen.

Something big.

He walked up the steps to that bright-red door.

He knocked.

He stood in his uniform and looked through the box of six square-paned windows at the top of the door, when he sensed movement inside.

And then there she was.

She opened the door.

The instant she did, the moment his eyes caught hers, Harry's chest caved in, and his stomach curled up.

Yeah.

Something was about to happen.

Something big.

And he wasn't ready for it.

About the Author

Kristen Ashley is the *New York Times* bestselling author of over eighty romance novels including the *Rock Chick, Colorado Mountain, Dream Man, Chaos, Unfinished Heroes, The 'Burg, Magdalene, Fantasyland, The Three, Ghost and Reincarnation, The Rising, Dream Team, Moonlight and Motor Oil, River Rain, Wild West MC, Misted Pines* and *Honey* series along with several standalone novels. She's a hybrid author, publishing titles both independently and traditionally, her books have been translated in fourteen languages and she's sold over five million books.

Kristen's novel, *Law Man*, won the *RT Book Reviews* Reviewer's Choice Award for best Romantic Suspense, her independently published title *Hold On* was nominated for *RT Book Reviews* best Independent Contemporary Romance and her traditionally published title *Breathe* was nominated for best Contemporary Romance. Kristen's titles *Motorcycle Man, The Will,* and *Ride Steady* (which won the Reader's Choice award from *Romance Reviews*) all made the final rounds for Goodreads Choice Awards in the Romance category.

Kristen, born in Gary and raised in Brownsburg, Indiana, is a fourth-generation graduate of Purdue University. Since, she's lived in Denver, the West Country of England, and she now resides in Phoenix. She worked as a charity executive for eighteen years prior to beginning her independent publishing career. She now writes full-time.

Although romance is her genre, the prevailing themes running through all of Kristen's novels are friendship, family and a strong sisterhood. To this end, and as a way to thank her readers for their support, Kristen has created the Rock Chick Nation, a series of programs that are designed to give back to her readers and promote a strong female community.

The mission of the Rock Chick Nation is to live your best life, be true to your true self, recognize your beauty, and take your sister's back whether they're at your side as friends and family or if they're thousands of miles away and you don't know who they are.

The programs of the RC Nation include Rock Chick Rendezvous, weekends Kristen organizes full of parties and get-togethers to bring the sisterhood together, Rock Chick Recharges, evenings Kristen arranges for women who have been nominated to receive a special night, and Rock Chick Rewards, an ongoing program that raises funds for nonprofit women's organizations Kristen's readers nominate. Kristen's Rock Chick Rewards have donated hundreds of thousands of dollars to charity and this number continues to rise.

You can read more about Kristen, her titles and the Rock Chick Nation at KristenAshley.net.

facebook.com/kristenashleybooks

instagram.com/kristenashleybooks

pinterest.com/KristenAshleyBooks

goodreads.com/kristenashleybooks

bookbub.com/authors/kristen-ashley

tiktok.com/@kristenashleybooks

Also by Kristen Ashley

The Colorado Mountain Series:
The Gamble
Sweet Dreams
Lady Luck
Breathe
Jagged
Kaleidoscope
Bounty

Dream Man Series:
Mystery Man
Wild Man
Law Man
Motorcycle Man
Quiet Man

Dream Team Series:
Dream Maker
Dream Chaser
Dream Bites Cookbook
Dream Spinner
Dream Keeper

The Fantasyland Series:
Wildest Dreams
The Golden Dynasty
Fantastical
Broken Dove
Midnight Soul
Gossamer in the Darkness

Ghosts and Reincarnation Series:
Sommersgate House
Lacybourne Manor
Penmort Castle
Fairytale Come Alive
Lucky Stars

The Honey Series:
The Deep End
The Farthest Edge
The Greatest Risk

Also by Kristen Ashley

The Magdalene Series:
The Will
Soaring
The Time in Between

Mathilda, SuperWitch:
Mathilda's Book of Shadows
Mathilda The Rise of the Dark Lord

Misted Pines Series
The Girl in the Mist
The Girl in the Woods
The Woman by the Lake

Moonlight and Motor Oil Series:
The Hookup
The Slow Burn

The Rising Series:
The Beginning of Everything
The Plan Commences
The Dawn of the End
The Rising

The River Rain Series:
After the Climb
After the Climb Special Edition
Chasing Serenity
Taking the Leap
Making the Match
Fighting the Pull
Sharing the Miracle
Embracing the Change

The Three Series:
Until the Sun Falls from the Sky
With Everything I Am
Wild and Free

The Unfinished Hero Series:
Knight
Creed
Raid
Deacon
Sebring

Wild West MC Series:
Still Standing
Smoke and Steel
Smooth Sailing

Other Titles by Kristen Ashley:
Heaven and Hell
Play It Safe
Three Wishes
Complicated
Loose Ends
Fast Lane
Perfect Together
Too Good To Be True